# RELUCTANT QUEEN

The story of Gabrielle d'Estrées is one of love, betrayal, intrigue and tragedy. All she wanted was to marry for love, and enjoy the respectability of a happy marriage. But in the court of sixteenth century France this was almost impossible to achieve. She was sold by her own mother to three different lovers before catching the eye of a king. Is the love of a king enough to secure Gabrielle the happiness and respectability she craves, and a crown for her son as the next dauphin of France?

# RELUCTANT QUEEN

*by*

Freda Lightfoot

**Magna Large Print Books**
Long Preston, North Yorkshire,
BD23 4ND, England.

British Library Cataloguing in Publication Data.

Lightfoot, Freda
    Reluctant queen.

    A catalogue record of this book is
    available from the British Library

    ISBN   978-0-7505-3508-3


First published in Great Britain 2010 by
Severn House Publishers Ltd.

Copyright © 2010 by Freda Lightfoot

Cover illustration © Jill Battaglia by arrangement with
Arcangel Images

The moral right of the author has been asserted

Published in Large Print 2012 by arrangement with
Severn House Publishers Ltd.

Magna Large Print is an imprint of Library Magna Books Ltd.

Printed and bound in Great Britain by
T.J. (International) Ltd., Cornwall, PL28 8RW

# Part One

# MARGOT

## 1578

'My sweet one, I love you more than I can say. I do understand your concern, but no other woman is prettier or more charming than you. I cherish the day Madame de Tignonville, your dear mother, was chosen as companion and governess for my sister when she returned recently from Paris. Otherwise I might never have met you.'

Jeanne cast a sideways glance up at him from beneath her lashes, carefully studying his expression for evidence of his sincerity. This was the King of Navarre she was refusing, after all, not some young courtier with no manners or money to his name. Was that wise? Her caution lay not simply with regard to her virtue, virgin though she undoubtedly was, but with the sad fact that the King was not free as he possessed a wife already. But then Queen Margot remained in Paris, held captive by her brother Henri III and her mother Catherine de Medici. Even as Jeanne heeded her own mother's wise advice not to yield too easily, she felt giddy with the possibilities of what heights she might reach by capturing the King's heart. 'Sire, I must guard my reputation. I am an innocent.'

'Your innocence enchants me. I adore you.'

'But how can you say that when you hardly know me?'

'Your modesty does you great credit, but you

7

are not so innocent as to fail to see how the very sight of you sets my pulses racing. I must have you. I need you by my side, day and night.'

Jeanne was instantly alarmed, a flush of pink flooding her soft cheeks. 'Sire, you speak wild. I am a maiden. My mother would never consent.'

'I am not asking your mother. Besides, how could she deny a King?' he teased. 'Ah, but I see I am rushing you, my little one. Will you grant me a kiss at least?'

Henry gazed into her blue eyes, entranced. He was all too aware that falling in love was as natural to him as eating the pigeon pie he loved so much, or drinking his favourite Gascon wine. He was quite unable to resist a beautiful woman, particularly one as young and delightful as this one. Her dark hair was so soft that he ached to stroke it, her childlike form so delicate his fingers itched to caress her budding young breasts. He had been pursuing the girl for some weeks now, ever since his sister Catherine had come home, yet she resisted him still.

Capturing her in his arms he attempted to steal a kiss, but at the last moment Jeanne averted her face. 'What is it my lovely, do I repulse you?'

'Of course not, Your Grace.' She looked appalled by the very idea, which soothed his bruised ego somewhat. Nevertheless, Henry very reluctantly let her go.

'Why then do you deny me? I am not an unkind man, a most generous one in fact, known for my good humour and equable temper. Nor would I ever force myself upon a woman. Ah, could it be that you have never been kissed before?'

8

The flush deepened and Henry laughed out loud. 'That is the way of it, eh? An innocent indeed.' The prospect of teaching this delightful child all about love making excited him more than he could express. What a diligent teacher he would be! 'Perhaps, as our friendship develops, and if I am very good, you will permit me a little licence?'

Soft lips pouted as she considered the matter, blue eyes bright with wounded pride. Jeanne felt confused and untutored in these matters, uncertain how to protect herself and yet not lose his interest completely. 'I do not see how a maid of honour could dare to refuse a king anything, so I beg of you, Sire, not to presume upon me by asking.' So saying, she sank into a curtsey and begged leave to depart. Chuckling with delight Henry granted her wish. Oh, but he would enjoy wooing this little one, and one way or another, he would win her.

Catherine had hated the years she'd spent at the French Court, as had Henry. She had accompanied him there in 1572 for his wedding to Princess Marguerite, an event swiftly followed by the horrors of the St Bartholomew massacre. Henry had been fortunate, or sufficiently daring, to make a dash for freedom after three years largely held under house arrest at the Louvre simply for being the wrong religion. Catherine wished she could have escaped with him for she had never fitted in to the glittering, hedonistic lifestyle of the court. She'd spent her time largely on the fringes, knowing she was considered dull and far too Puritan, although, like her brother, she too had been forced to abandon her religion and agree to take the Mass.

Now she was immensely relieved to finally be allowed to join her brother and be back home in Nérac with the people she loved. At the banquet held to celebrate her homecoming, Henry, his face uncharacteristically solemn, had asked if she had forgotten what it was to be a Huguenot.

'Indeed not,' Catherine had hastened to reassure him. 'I have ever remained a Huguenot in my heart.'

He'd kissed her fondly on the cheek. 'I am glad to hear it. Aubigné too will be mightily relieved. You know how very seriously my chamberlain views these matters.'

'He need have no fear. I remain true to our mother's faith.'

Now, as she walked through the gardens that her mother Jeanne d'Albret had created by the River Baïse, Catherine mused on how they had ever been close and were great friends. She had no quarrel with her brother, not on religion, nor any other matter.

But she was no longer an obedient young girl striving to please. She was twenty years old and it might well be a different matter when it came to affairs of the heart. Catherine had yet to confess to Henry that she was in love with her cousin Charles, the Comte de Soissons, and he with her. She had no reason to suppose he would disapprove, yet for some reason she hesitated to broach the subject.

This morning Catherine hurried to meet her beloved in the gardens, just as they met in secret most days. The pair dreamed of marriage and she could not begin to imagine how she would feel if Henry set his mind against the match. Such a prospect was unthinkable. Charles was a fine soldier, if a touch hot-headed, brother to Prince de Condé, and a Bourbon like herself.

She caught a glimpse of his beloved figure emerging from behind a tree, a broad smile on his handsome face. Feeling her heart lift with anticipation, Catherine quickened her pace and ran to meet her lover.

'I do not understand what it is you ask of me.'

'It is perfectly simple, I wish you to persuade Mademoiselle Jeanne de Tignonville to change her mind and accept me as her lover.'

An angry flush appeared on the old man's sallow cheeks. 'It is not my task to procure your mistresses for you, Sire. I shudder to think you should even make such a request.'

'Ah, but I do make it. It is your role in life is it not, Aubigné, to perform whatever task is necessary to please me? The girl is devout, too much so. Convince her that her soul is not at risk for loving a king.'

'Sire, I beg you to have a care for your own soul. The constant seeking of pleasure, even for a king, is a dangerous pursuit.'

Henry frowned. Were his nature less affable he might take exception to a servant, even a pastor, daring to issue such a lecture. But he knew Aubigné for a narrow-minded Calvinist, dedicated to his God and his religion, and that he was equally devoted to his king. 'I will let that com-

11

ment pass, since I think your tongue runs away with you. Nevertheless, it was your idea to award the post of governess to her mother. Therefore you are responsible for bringing the girl to my notice. Now I am dying for love of her. I must have her.'

'I did not allow her mother to bring the child to court in order for her to be deflowered.'

Henry was growing bored with the argument, irritated by his chamberlain's stubbornness. He believed he loved the girl as he had loved no other, and, tolerant though he may be, he refused to be spurned by her. Such a thing was unheard of. He really didn't understand what all the fuss was about.

'I do not see a problem. She will be well rewarded. Make the girl appreciate that it is perfectly seemly to surrender her virginity to a king. See to it, Aubigné. I will not be bested in this matter.' Whereupon he strode from the room, leaving his chamberlain wringing his hands in silent despair.

Aubigné did not speak to the girl, despite his monarch's firm instructions to do so. He refused absolutely to involve himself in what he considered to be personal affairs, particularly of the romantic sort. Although he was aware that kings lived by a different set of rules to common folk. Henry's own father, Antoine de Bourbon, had also kept many mistresses, but procuring a woman for the King was not a part of his duties.

When it became clear that his chamberlain was to take no action, Henry grew uncharacteristically cool and distant towards him, no longer clapping him on the back in a friendly fashion, or laughing and joking with him. Aubigné quickly realized that he would suffer for his obstinacy, and his comfortable life began to fray at the edges. He found that his pay was delayed or withheld, and as a consequence he fell into debt. Personal items would disappear from his chamber: the sermon he'd taken such trouble over, a book he was reading, his comfy slippers. Nor was he allowed to choose his favourite dishes. Food would be set before him at dinner that the King knew he disliked, yet Henry would oblige him to eat it and smile at his dismay.

'Is not a little suffering good for the soul? Is that not what you are at pains to teach me?'

So many tricks were played on him that Aubigné grew increasingly miserable, feeling himself the butt of ridicule in the court. He came to loathe *la petite* Tignonville, as the King insisted on calling the chit, for causing him to lose favour. Yet he did not back down.

Nor did Jeanne. Months went by and still she kept the king dangling, enchanting him with her ready smiles and beguiling glances, but managing to maintain a firm hold upon her chastity. The court watched the courtship progress, and the King's desperation increase, with high amusement and avid interest.

Jeanne was in a sulk. The king purported to love her yet she knew he courted other women. His *amourettes* seemed too numerous to count. No maid of honour was safe from his lewd glances and wandering hands. And yet he was always sweetly complimentary towards herself, making it abundantly clear that she was the one he truly loved and wanted.

'These other women are but trifles to amuse me,' he told her. 'For you, my little Tignonville, I would give my heart and soul were you but to agree to love me a little. A kiss would suffice.'

Jeanne rewarded him with a teasing smile. 'I think you want a great deal more than that.'

Henry laughed. 'I think you are right. What would you take for a kiss? A pretty new gown, a ribbon for your glorious dark hair? What can I do to win you?'

'I want for nothing.'

'Your bright blue eyes tell me different. Will you sit on my knee and let me fondle you? There, what is so wrong in that? Are you not comfortable and happy to be so cherished?'

Jeanne leaned back in his arms and allowed him to kiss her neck and the curve of her throat, unable to deny that it was indeed most pleasant to be loved and petted by a king. Navarre, as she still liked to call him, was not unhandsome. His hair was black, thick and wavy, if slightly greying at the temples, carelessly brushed back from a broad high brow. He had a long face tapered to a firm chin, which indicated a stubborn determination to have his way. But the King's most notable feature was his eyes, which were deep-set, large and luminous, the kind which could sparkle and flash with humour, soften with gentleness or ignite with passion. The fact that few women could resist him did not surprise Jeanne in the slightest. And he was a gentleman, of that there was no doubt. But when he dipped his head lower to kiss the soft mound of her breast she slapped him gently away.

'You are too bold, Sire. Where might this lead? Nowhere, I think.'

His merry eyes looked at her askance. 'I thought it might lead to my bedchamber.'

'How can it when you are not free?' Jeanne retorted, struggling unsuccessfully to free herself from his grasp. 'You have a wife already in Queen Margot. How can I risk my honour and spiritual well-being when you are already taken?'

'You need not be jealous of my wife, she would not be of you.' He was scattering kisses on her mouth, her eyes, the shell-like curl of an ear. 'Margot is in Paris and has lovers of her own.'

'And you are certainly not short of mistresses.'

Henry clicked his tongue in gentle admonition. Oh, how he loved it when jealousy sparkled in those bewitching blue eyes. 'As I have already told you, all other women are but trifles by comparison with your beauty. But I think you protest too much, *ma petite* Tignonville. This little flare-up of jealousy tells me that, secretly, you are indeed enamoured of me. And I can sense it in your breathless excitement.'

Jeanne allowed him one last kiss before slipping adroitly from his lap. 'I am breathless from battling with you, Sire. You must remember that I am but a simple girl. What if I were to fall *enceinte?*'

'I would take care that you did not, my sweet.'

'Even if I didn't, who would marry me once I had given away the prize of my virginity? I would be spoiled goods. The castoff of a king.'

'Why would I cast you off when I love you so?'

'I think you tease me too much!' Exasperated,

15

she dipped a hasty curtsey and walked away without even asking his leave. Henry chuckled to himself for the game wasn't over yet. Tomorrow, he might strike lucky.

But the game was obliged to be put on hold, for next day a courier came galloping into Nérac with the astonishing news that Queen Margot, accomanied by her mother Catherine de Medici, was travelling south to rejoin her husband. She had already reached Sarlat and would be with him in a matter of days.

A hazy summer heat hung over the French countryside as the cavalcade set forth on its long journey south. It was as extravagant and glorious as any of Catherine de Medici's undertakings, meant to impress the local populous and prove the power and magnificence of the House of Valois. Following close behind the Queen Mother's coach came her daughter's splendid litter. With its carnation velvet lining, and gold embroidery decorated with designs of the sun, it was a glittering testament to her status as Queen of Navarre.

After two long years of separation, Margot was at last to be allowed to join her husband.

She was accompanied on her journey by her chancellor, Pibrac, her secretary, treasurer, doctor, clerks, saddlers, bakers, grooms, chaplain, confessor, apothecaries, maids of honour, masters of the royal wardrobe, all manner of people who were loyal to and dependent upon her. She was loved and adored by many, not least Madame de Curton, her faithful old governess and servant, now first lady of the bedchamber, who had been more of a mother to her than her own had ever been.

'We will make a good life in Béarn,' Madame constantly reassured her.

'I know it,' Margot agreed. 'How can I fail with you by my side?'

Overjoyed as she was to be free, and to escape the confines of the Louvre where the Queen her mother, and her brother King Henri Trois, had kept her prisoner for so long, Margot headed south with conflicting emotions of nervousness and excited anticipation.

Henry of Navarre had never been her choice of husband. Margot had known him since childhood as they were also third cousins, but she'd always thought him a country bumpkin, a clumsy oaf with grubby feet, garlic-tainted breath and a fickle heart. Yet he was undoubtedly good-natured and easy-going, amiable and friendly, a man with intelligence and wit. He was also a man who had cheated death by playing the fool. Margot herself had saved his life more than once, and had ultimately assisted in his escape from the Louvre, where he too had been held under house arrest for four long years; ever since their marriage in that never-to-be-forgotten summer of 1572.

As Henry was a Huguenot and Margot a Catholic, their marriage had been entirely political and intended to bring peace to the realm. Yet within days of what had become known as the Blood Red Wedding, the massacre of St Bartholomew had taken place, and thousands of innocent souls had been murdered. It was a legacy to blight any marriage.

On his return to Béarn, Henry had written

17

frequent letters to the Queen Mother, requesting his wife be allowed to join him. But would he still welcome her? Would he even want her?

In spite of the difficulties between them, Margot was a natural optimist, and loved nothing more than a new adventure. She had great hopes for her future in Béarn, and saw no reason why she couldn't win over the people of her husband's court, even if they were sober Calvinists.

Everywhere they stopped along the way, the people were enchanted by the beauty of the young Queen, and by her eloquence and wit when she addressed them. Margot was twenty-five and fully aware that she was at the peak of her beauty, with flawless white skin, firm bosom and a slender, swanlike neck for which she designed beautiful *décolleté* gowns. She never failed to enchant, dressing in silver brocade or her favourite orange-gold. The peasants would gaze at her as her litter passed by, as if they looked upon a goddess.

And if she had not yet won her husband's heart, quite against all the odds they had formed a certain bond, a friendship which had remained reasonably solid through some testing times. Distance had softened his most annoying habits, and there would surely be the opportunity now to develop that friendship further, once they were reunited.

Of course, he was not the most faithful of husbands, and they had quite early on reached an agreement upon the nature of their marriage. Margot herself had taken lovers, out of pride and retaliation, at least at first. First, there had been La Molle who had met with a tragic end, and

18

then Bussy d'Amboise, a most impudent, mischievous knave who had amused her greatly.

Shortly after their departure from Paris, a message had reached Margot informing her that he had been killed. She'd wept copious tears for her one-time lover, the man who had helped her plot and plan her brother Alençon's escape from the Louvre. And he had brought such pleasure into what would otherwise have been a dull life without his audacious wit to make her laugh, and his sexual romps to excite her.

Sadly, he'd been caught by a cuckolded husband in the wife's bedchamber, attacked by a dozen of his men and thrown out of the window to his death. Poor, foolish Bussy.

But Margot's true affections lay not with her husband or either of these entertaining lovers, but with Henri de Guise. He had been the love of her life for as long as she could remember, and, as the coach rumbled on, she turned her thoughts back to their last meeting.

They had lain together in their favourite trysting place in a quiet part of the Louvre, making love for one last time. Margot had been distressed that in future the space in her bed would be occupied by another, even if that man were her own husband. Would he not feel like a stranger, an intruder?

Guise had lifted the heavy curtain of her dark hair to kiss her slender neck and asked how she could bear to leave him for a Huguenot Prince?

'Because he is my husband, and I would be a true wife to him,' had been her very right and proper reply, which had amused him greatly.

'Ha, an impossibility! The fellow drives you to

19

distraction with his many amours. Am I not a better man than he?'

Margot had explained how she had no choice but to go. 'I can stay no longer in this hothouse of intrigue and danger. I need to be free to live and breathe and not be constantly checking my own shadow.'

They'd talked for some time, and made love with a desperate, burning passion. Then he'd captured her face between his two hands and sworn his undying love for her. 'I too would feel happier if you were safe. But not a day will go by when I will not yearn for you.'

Despite its softness, his last kiss had been filled with both passion and love. When it was done, he'd gazed deep into her eyes. 'Go in peace, my Queen of Hearts, and remember my promise to you. Should you ever be in need of my help, I am yours.'

This was a fresh beginning for Margot, a new dawn, and although she could call on her lover if the need arose, she most of all must depend upon herself.

The Queen Mother was feeling old. She was travelling with her daughter not out of love or even affection, but to see her safely restored to her husband and take up her rightful role as Queen of Navarre. She had a second, more important mission, to bring peace to France, and Catherine kept up her spirits as best she may while secretly dreading the many months of travel and hardship she faced.

She was fifty-nine, a large woman, her girth

increasing with age, and bore the characteristic long Valois nose, double chin, slightly bulging eyes and a full mouth. She suffered from gout and rheumatism, although her energy was as boundless as ever; and was sometimes so stiff from travelling in her coach that she would take to riding a mule, so long as one could be found strong enough to bear her weight.

'How my son the King would laugh to see me,' she would chortle, still able to laugh at herself.

Dressed in her customary black, she was today wearing a gown with wide wing sleeves, a bodice pointed at the front and rounded at the back, and a white ruff encircled by a high black collar. It was much adorned with beadwork and jewels, and a black mantle hung from her shoulders. A peaked widow's hood covered most of her hair which had once been black and was now largely grey, although she sometimes wore a peruke. Unlike the English Queen Elizabeth I, she did not pluck her eyebrows, nor widen her brow, but she did like a touch of rouge on her cheeks to brighten skin kept fashionably pale with a white lead paste.

Catherine was never less than elegant, even magnificent in her dress, but she was just a little envious of Margot's youth and beauty.

'My daughter, you look splendid,' she acidly commented as Margot prinked and preened herself for the dinner to be held that evening by some local lord, who would no doubt near bankrupt himself in his attempt to impress.

'Madame, I am wearing only the dresses and ornaments I brought with me from court, for when I return there I shall not take them back with me, but shall simply arrive with scissors and materials, which I shall have made up in the current fashion.'

Catherine gave her loud booming laugh. 'Why do you say that, for it's you who sets and invents the fashions, and wherever you are, the court will copy them from you, not you from the court.'

But the Queen Mother was more concerned with winning over the south, a haven for Huguenots, than worrying about finery Her entourage largely replicated those of her daughter's, plus a small cabinet, her old friend the Duchess d'Uzès, and the Cardinal of Bourbon, as Catherine never stopped working or wasted a moment. The long hours in the coach were filled by reading State papers and signing documents.

She'd taken something of a risk by accompanying her daughter on this journey, but hoped that Navarre would not refuse to talk with her. He surely wouldn't wish to risk offending the King of France, and he did seem surprisingly anxious to have his wife returned to him. Catherine hoped that Margot would bring her husband back to the rightful church, which might then help to solve all their problems.

If Margot failed in this mission, she'd brought along Charlotte de Sauves, who had once entranced Navarre and could likely do so again. The Queen Mother never travelled anywhere without her bevy of beautiful women from her flying squadron, her *Escadron Volant*. Under Catherine's careful instructions de Sauves had seduced both Margot's husband and her brother, the Duke of Alençon, in an attempt to set one against the other, as well as cause friction between man and wife. There'd been a certain amount of conflict created yet the ruse had sadly failed to effectively divide this dangerous triumvirate.

Shrewd and clever as she was where politics were concerned, human nature had ever been a mystery to Catherine de Medici.

But if Henry had tired of de Sauves then Catherine had others in her squadron, including a young Cyprian beauty, Victoria de Ayala, known as Dayelle, who would be sure to enchant him. Of Greek birth, she had escaped from Cyprus in 1570 when the island had been taken by the Turks. Catherine's late son Charles IX had saved the girl and her brother by paying for them to come to France; the boy entering the service of the Duke d'Alençon, and the girl joining Catherine's *Escadron Volant*. One or other of these delectable ladies would help her to persuade her son-in-law to sign the peace agreement she so badly needed.

Catherine de Medici was a woman used to getting her own way, and with her own particular methods of ensuring that she got it. It amused her that rumours were bruited abroad that she had even disposed of her son-in-law's own mother, Jeanne d'Albret, with the aid of a pair of poisoned gloves. True or not, those who had dared to seriously challenge her, such as Coligny the Huguenot leader, Lignerolles, who had done much harm to her favourite son's health with his ascetic practices, and others, had not lived to tell the tale.

Henry of Navarre was secretly most eager to see his wife again. Despite their squabbles and their differences, Margot held a fascination for him which he found hard to resist. Not simply because of her beauty but also for her fire, her spirit, her sense of adventure and her *joie de vivre*. He could not deny that she was warm and spontaneous, generous and loving. There was some magnetism about her, some indefinable charisma. It did not surprise him that she was the darling of the court, and it was perhaps a pity that he could not seem to love her as a husband should. Nevertheless, such sentiment was not essential in a royal marriage, and he still found her extremely attractive and was more than ready to welcome her back to his bed.

He suspected the people of Béarn, however, may have a different view of their new queen, certainly the more narrow-minded Puritans amongst them. Some already spoke of Margot as the Papist Temptress, or the Whore of Babylon.

But then they were not any more trusting of him, their king, since he had been obliged to turn Catholic in order to save his own skin. He'd reiterated his devotion to the Protestant faith of his upbringing on his return, in order to regain his kingdom, yet the people lacked confidence in his loyalty. It perhaps did not help that at his own court here in Béarn he employed adherents to both faiths among his staff. He saw that as enlightened. What was so wrong in tolerating the religious beliefs of others, of allowing people to worship God in whatever way they chose? Others, sadly, took a different view.

In reality neither side trusted him. The Catholics were his enemies, and the Huguenots lived in constant fear of a new massacre. Thankfully, he still had the support of Condé, who was in the north, Turenne, always by his side, and Damville, whose skills as a soldier were beyond question.

Catherine had asked him to meet them at Bordeaux, but he had wisely declined. Henry of Navarre refused to venture far from his own lands, where he felt safe, and many Catholic towns naturally refused to grant him leave to enter. His Queen, and his mother-in-law, would instead be met by the Maréchal de Biron, the King's General at Guyenne: a fierce, uncompromising soldier who liked to pretend he was a Protestant but remained Catholic at heart.

Navarre realized that Catherine de Medici was coming to talk peace, and although he did not have the money to conduct a war, not for a second would he let her know that. He meant to wring from her every possible concession he could, and not be bullied by her, expert though she undoubtedly was in the art.

He did at least possess subtlety, which the Queen Mother lacked, and believed he was as skilled at delaying tactics as she was herself. Not that she appreciated these skills, seeing him still as an empty-headed fool.

Yet this dolt-head, this country bumpkin, might one day be King of France when her two remaining sickly sons died. Henry of Navarre smiled. He must keep that fact to the forefront of his mind throughout his dealings with his two-faced, serpentine mother-in-law.

The King of Navarre met with the Queen Mother

at La Réolle, and was instantly disappointed to find that Margot was not with her. He at once enquired where she was.

'My daughter was feeling indisposed and has remained at Sarlat to rest a little.'

'You look well, Your Majesty, although I fear the journey may have taxed your strength somewhat.'

'Do you accuse me of growing old, son-in-law?' Catherine snapped, and with a merry twinkle in his eye Navarre swiftly refuted the accusation.

'How could that be possible in such a queen as yourself, Madame?'

'Indeed, son-in-law. I am immortal as well as all-powerful, did the gods not tell you?'

'I am not privileged to converse with the gods, as are you, Madame. I must depend upon my own wit, which I do not often find lacking.' And they smiled at each other, a silent acknowledgement that while they trod the path of diplomacy, and enjoyed a gentle jest or two, he trusted her no more than she trusted him.

'I hope you will enjoy your stay in our little kingdom, humble though it may be by comparison with your own.'

'The countryside is certainly very pretty,' Catherine acknowledged.

'And no doubt as we walk in it, that will give us ample time to talk,' he challenged, giving her a sideways glance while itching to be on his horse and away, rid of the need for this diplomatic cross-talk.

'I came with no specific purpose in mind, my son.'

'Did you not?' Disbelief was ripe in the teasing

26

tone of his voice, while his eyes smiled at her in all innocence.

'I came merely to chaperone my daughter and to admire your beautiful scenery,' Catherine lied.

'Forgive me then if I leave you to admire it alone for a while. If you will excuse me, I must ride to see my wife the Queen.' Without waiting for, or expecting, the Queen Mother's permission, the King of Navarre unceremoniously left her, mounted his horse and rode away. He had waited long enough to see his queen, and though it would take several hours of hard riding to reach her, he could wait no more.

'I did not think to find you playing the feeble woman, Margot. Do you hide from your own husband?'

Margot was having serious second thoughts, wondering what on earth had possessed her to imagine that a reunion with the oaf she'd been married to against her will would be a good thing. After the weeks of travelling she was already wishing herself back in the relative comfort of the French Court, despite its dangers, and she was missing Guise badly. She'd feigned sickness to allow herself a little more time to prepare, to choose what to wear and how to present herself.

Now here he was, standing before her in all his robust reality, smelling strongly of the horse he'd just ridden to reach her.

If Margot expected her husband to politely bow in the time-honoured fashion of the French Court, or to kiss her hand in greeting, then she was to be disappointed. Instead, he caught her up in a great bear hug, lifting her off her feet and swinging her about before kissing her soundly full on the mouth.

Gasping for breath she pushed him away, her hands at once flying to tidy her hair, straighten her bodice, smooth down her skirts. 'I see you have lost all sense of the etiquette and propriety I took such pains to teach you.'

'Can a husband not demonstrate his pleasure in seeing his wife again? It *has* been two years.'

Margot looked at him askance. 'Do not pretend you have spent them alone, nor treat me as a fool, Henry.'

'Oh, my love,' he said, pulling a sad face. 'Henry indeed. Why so formal? See, I am still your beloved *Enric.*' He held out his arms as if to demonstrate, then patted his chest. 'Your own nose should tell you. Can you not smell the horse sweat on me, the leather, and the scent of fresh mown hay. I am as I am, still the country bumpkin.'

She looked up into his dark Gascon eyes and suddenly burst out laughing. 'You are incorrigible.'

Henry beamed at her. 'That's better. I cannot abide sulks, almost as distressing as tears.' He grasped her hand and began to pull her towards him again. 'Come wife, let us to bed.'

'What?' Snatching her hand away she stared at him, outraged. 'You have barely been in my company five minutes.'

'But I have waited *two long years!* We may not be the world's most devoted pair, you and I, but you are my wife, my queen, and we've never been lax in the business of the bedchamber, not that I

28

recall.' So saying, he once more swept her up into his arms but this time carried her to the bed, scattering maids and ladies-in-waiting out of the room and kicking shut the door.

It took Henry very little time at all to reclaim his bride. He did not trouble to disrobe, or even take off his boots. He rode her with the same energy and gusto he might use on his finest horse, and she made surprisingly little protest, save to dryly remark that his love making was as equally lacking in finesse as his manners.

'You can spend the next several months, years if necessary, addressing these failings in me, dearest wife.'

Once she was allowed to catch her breath, Margot adjusted her clothing and ordered refreshments for him. Henry sat happily propped against the big square pillows gnawing on a chicken leg and drinking good Jurançon wine, telling her all that had gone on since last they'd been together. Strangely, they had ever been able to talk.

'I am not finding it easy to win the trust of my people, thanks to the measures I was obliged to take to keep my head attached to my neck.'

'I am sure they will come to love you, given time.'

He grinned at her. 'Will you? No, don't answer that. It is not a requirement as my wife and queen, but we can remain on good terms, can we not?'

Smiling, Margot settled back on the pillows, and agreed that they could.

'I remember well how your brother the King did his utmost to come between us. I could hardly believe the tricks he played to foment mischief,

29

keeping us hostage, spying on us, spreading scandalous lies.'

'It was my mother's idea, not Henri's, to set de Sauves to seduce both you and Alençon.'

'Ah, dear Charlotte, what a woman. Yet, still we hung together, he and I, at least at first. But the lies Henri told, the malice and the mischief, were beyond reason. He accused you of licentious behaviour as if he were a saint, and not the most profligate, debauched king that has ever sat on the French throne.'

Margot sighed. 'He has not changed in that respect, if anything his hypocrisy has worsened with the able assistance of his two new favourites, Epernon and Joyeuse. And in gratitude for their loyal service, he showers them with titles, money, and gifts France cannot afford. I could take no more of it.'

'And so you came to me. Very wise.'

She looked at him sadly, and said in all seriousness, 'I have been trying to come to you, *Enric*, for all of these last two years, but neither the King nor the Queen my mother would allow it. Now, it seems, I am of no further use to them at court and they have at last relented.'

Henry frowned as he picked at his teeth, chasing an errant piece of chicken. 'No doubt the Queen Mother has some reason other than your personal happiness?'

'I am sure of it,' Margot dryly commented.

She looked away in despair as he sucked on his fingers, then almost spilled her wine as his hand suddenly slipped beneath her bodice and fastened itself on to her breast. He began most earnestly to knead it, and she gasped, surprised by the sharp ache that suddenly manifested itself lower down. How very different a lover he was from her beloved Guise. Far more – what was the word – lusty?

Henry took the goblet of wine from her hand and set it aside, then he was fumbling with the ribbons of her gown, seeking the hooks of her bodice. So eager had he been to bed her, he'd made no effort thus far to remove her clothes. Now he proceeded to do so, slowly and languorously, stroking and kissing each portion of bare flesh as it became exposed, which Margot found really quite erotic. She pretended not to notice, even as her breathing quickened and that familiar, delightful lethargy crept over her.

'I know the Queen Mother is anxious to reconcile you with Biron,' she murmured. Her eyelids were feeling so heavy she was having trouble keeping them open. 'He is the King's general in Guyenne,' Margot explained, as if Henry did not know that already. 'My mother wishes me to beg you to meet with him, and... *Enric*, what are you doing?'

Henry had slipped off the last of her petticoats and, parting her legs, slid his hands between them, making her squeal. 'No more talk of politics, dearest wife, we have more important business needing attention.'

The new Queen of Navarre made a triumphal entry into Agen, a city restored to her by her brother Henri Trois as part of her dowry. Meanwhile, the Queen Mother continued in talks with her son-in-law as she made the final preparations

31

for her coming tour, in which Catherine hoped to implement the Treaty of Bergerac. Navarre lost his temper with her when she attempted to persuade him to meet Biron, but he was finally persuaded by Margot, and the pair met on 8 October, although nothing was achieved. They may well have come to blows had not Margot intervened, using her considerable charm to placate them.

'See how useful you are to me already? We will make a good team, you and I. You are my soul mate.'

Margot laughed out loud at such a notion. Navarre and his men were in no hurry for the Queen Mother to leave as they were happily enjoying the delightful presence of all the pretty ladies in her flying squadron. These *dames galantes* were also working hard, in their own way, to maintain the peace. Love affairs were rife.

Charlotte de Sauves was one of the party, as Guise had suggested she would be, and Margot noticed how she watched Navarre, a small smile of anticipation playing about her lips. But Henry showed surprisingly little interest in her, much to that lady's disappointment, and Margot's relief.

When Charlotte approached him one day he looked right past her to smile at the delectable Dayelle, with whom he'd quickly become enamoured. Since *la petite* Tignonville was proving so stubborn, Henry felt obliged to seek comfort elsewhere. Now he was entranced by the little Cypriot.

The Queen Mother looked on with delight, and called the girl to her presence. 'I see that you have caught the eye of the King.'

Like everyone else, Dayelle was terrified of the great Catherine de Medici and she trembled as she answered. 'It would seem so, Your Majesty.' She was almost as afraid of Henry himself. At twenty-five, he was much older than herself, and though a fine-looking man she found the prospect of being bedded by a King somewhat over-whelming.

'He spends time with you?'

'He does.'

'And you let him kiss and fondle you?'

The young girl blushed. 'He is a hard man to refuse.'

Catherine gave her throaty chortle. 'I dare say he is. Your task, child, is to make yourself in-dispensable to him. You must persuade the King of Navarre to return to Paris with us.'

Dayelle was appalled by this demand, which seemed well nigh impossible. 'But how am I to do that, Your Majesty?'

Catherine pinched the girl's cheek, making her wince with pain. 'By doing what comes naturally. You have considerable charms, use them. He must become utterly besotted, so that when you tell him that you will be returning to Paris with me, he cannot bear to be parted from you.'

Dayelle found this hard to imagine but was cer-tainly not going to argue with the Queen Mother, and naturally agreed she would do all she could to ensnare the King of Navarre.

Henry's passion for the beautiful young Cypriot did not detract him in any way from the attention he continued to give to his wife. Margot had no reason to complain of his neglect, or the friendship and honour he paid to her, but, as always, her pride was piqued by his blatant infidelity. Why could she not be enough for him?

She noticed too that since escaping from the Louvre he had again fallen into his old, coarse, Bèarnese ways. His determination not to bathe was a great irritation to her.

'Why would I?' he protested, when she challenged him on the subject one evening when he came to her room. 'I'm not some mincing fop like your brother, who smells of violet powder, or one of his curled and perfumed *mignons*. I am a man, and men sweat from doing men's business.' Lounging in a chair, he poured himself a goblet of wine.

'But if you sleep in my bed, Sire, on my sheets, I would prefer at least your feet to be clean,' she haughtily informed him. 'See, I have had my maid bring a bowl of warm water and soap. Allow her to bathe them for you.'

'What?' Navarre stared at the bowl as it was set before him, and at the maid who cowered beside it. 'Do you expect me to take off my boots?'

'You cannot sleep in your boots, and yes, I would prefer you to take them off when we make love, not leave them on as you did on our first encounter.'

The young maid stifled a giggle and Margot silenced her with a glare. 'Let me help you, Sire. I will unlace them for you.'

Navarre stood up and kicked the bowl away, sending water cascading all over the tiled floor. 'I think not, Madame. Get out of here,' he ordered the maid, who hastily scampered away as fast as

34

her feet could carry her.

'How dare you!' Margot stood before him in a fury, hands on hips. 'That is no way to treat a servant. The girl has done no harm to you. Nor is this any way to treat a wife, one you say you have waited two long years to see again. All I ask is that you wash your feet.'

'Do you imagine you can make me?'

'I swear you will not get into my bed, lest you do!'

'There are other beds, more welcoming.'

'I dare say there are,' she snapped. 'But if you want an heir you must needs visit mine occasionally, and I will only allow that if your feet are clean.'

Navarre folded his arms across his chest, and they stood facing each other in a fine temper, both too stubborn to back down.

After a long moment, Margot whirled about, picked up the bowl and refilled it from a flagon of water that stood on the commode table.

'Well, are you willing to allow *me* to wash your feet for you?'

For a moment it looked as if he might fling the bowl over her this time, but then he looked into her defiant, lovely face and suddenly put back his head and roared with laughter.

'What a woman you are, my Marguerite. Wash my damned feet then, if you must.' And dropping back into the chair he allowed her to kneel before him, unlace his boots, and with her nose wrinkling against the smell, wash his dusty, sweaty feet. Only then did she allow him into her bed.

But when he had left her in the early hours, she

called her maid and had the sheets changed, and the room sprayed with perfume. She would be his wife and queen, but dear God there was a limit to even her tolerance.

It had finally been decided that the peace talks should take place in Nérac, being a Huguenot stronghold, which were finally achieved in February 1579.And taking almost a month to persuade the Puritan pastors to come to any sort of agreement. They bitterly contested every offer Catherine made, always demanding more. She likened them to birds of prey in their sober black garb, calling them *les oiseaux nuisantes*, the nighthawks.

She aped their speech, practising it with her ladies at her *coucher* to gales of laughter, trying out these newly learnt biblical phrases on the Protestants, although with little appreciation.

They in turn marvelled at her energy as she was always the first to reach the council table, following an early Mass, and spent every spare moment writing letters to her son, Henri Trois, and to her dear friend Madame d'Uzès, who by now had returned to the French Court. Catherine was frequently heard to complain of missing her son who rarely responded to her letters. She would beg the Duchess to give her all the gossip from court, and tell her what her beloved Henri was doing.

Spring had come and the air was filled with the scent of almond and cherry blossom, and the Queen Mother was anxious to be on her way. Having done all she could in Nérac and the South, and, despite all the problems and difficulties of her constant journeying back and forth, Catherine

36

believed she had managed to establish some sort of peace in Languedoc, Guyenne, Provence and the Dauphiné. Now she wished only to say her farewells and return to Paris.

The King and Queen of Navarre offered to accompany her to Castelnaudary, and once again she called little Dayelle to her.

'What progress have you made, child, is the King besotted?'

'I – I know not, Your Majesty. He seems very fond.'

Catherine grabbed the terrified girl by the arm and gave her a little shake. 'But is he fond enough? Have you told him that the time draws near for you to depart? That he will lose you if he does not accompany us to Paris?'

The young Cypriot was utterly tongue-tied. She dare not explain to this great queen how the King her lover had laughed when she'd suggested such a thing.

'I almost left my head behind the last time I was foolish enough to visit the capital. Much as I love you, my dear Dayelle, I love my head more.'

'I will speak to him again,' she promised the Queen Mother, and sent up a silent prayer that when yet again she failed, Catherine would not seek retribution against her.

The farewells were duly made, the Queen Mother's entourage departed, and Dayelle went with it. Henry of Navarre and his queen, who was no more anxious to return to Paris than he, stayed safely behind in Béarn, and much as he missed the charming Cypriot, Henry soon sought consolation elsewhere.

37

After parting from Catherine at Castelnaudary, Navarre and Margot travelled on to Pau. At first she was enchanted, thinking the Palace there quite beautiful and with breathtaking views of the Pyrenees. Henry showed her the bedchamber of his mother, Jeanne d'Albret, where he had been born; the *tortue de mer*, the turtle shell which had apparently served him as a cradle, and all around the room were the portraits and artefacts of his ancestors the Kings of Navarre. There were beautiful gardens too, and Margot thought she might be happy here.

But she had reckoned without the bigotry of the Calvinists.

Navarre's tolerance in religious matters meant that he was perfectly willing to allow his wife, and a few of her closest friends, to hear Mass in the Palace chapel. It was quite small, only able to accommodate little more than a dozen people.

The Palace drawbridge was always pulled up beforehand, but somehow the people of the town came to realize what was happening and on Whit Sunday a group of them managed to get inside. They crowded into the tiny chapel as best they may, begging the Queen to allow them to hear Mass as they had been deprived of it for so long.

Margot took pity on them and without hesitation agreed they could stay, although it was a dreadful squash.

One of her ladies, a Mademoiselle de Rebours, was fiercely ambitious and nursed a fancy to replace the recently departed Dayelle. To capture the attentions of a king, even if his heart was not

38

engaged, would be immensely exciting and surely lead to an increase in her own power and standing at court. In order to achieve this, Rebours felt it important to distance Henry a little from his queen, upon whom he was showering great affection.

When she heard what was happening in the chapel, Mademoiselle de Rebours saw her opportunity and ran to tell him of this scandalous behaviour. But halfway to the King's apartment it occurred to her that perhaps she shouldn't be the one seen to meddle. She decided this news might be better coming from another source, and went instead to his secretary, Jacques Lallier, Sieur du Pin. The man was a bigoted Huguenot and had no time at all for this Catholic Queen.

'There are *Catholics* in the Palace chapel,' Rebours burst out in shocked tones the moment she was admitted to his private cabinet. 'Brought there by the Queen.'

Pin was outraged, and, calling his men, marched them down to the courtyard. He did not stand on ceremony, did not even pause to knock but barged right into the tiny chapel, dragged the peasants out, and had them flogged right there in the courtyard.

Horrified, Margot cried out in protest. 'Stop that at once!'

'Madame, step back. This is none of your concern.'

'Indeed it is! I demand that you let these people be.'

Pin brushed her aside and had the Catholics arrested and thrown into a cell.

Margot caught up her skirts and ran. Bursting into her husband's apartment she breathlessly told him what had just occurred. 'I insist that they be released immediately.'

Navarre was startled, deeply disturbed by this unfortunate incident, which at first glance seemed of no consequence, and yet had clearly made his wife angry. 'I cannot do that. You ask too much, Margot. Be grateful that I at least permit you and your people to hear the Mass. I cannot allow half the populace of Pau to partake of it too. This is Huguenot territory. You are being unreasonable.'

'*I* am being unreasonable? What of that bully of a secretary of yours? He has no right to imprison innocent people simply for their beliefs. I would have thought that you, of all people, would see that. The insolence I suffered at the hands of that little man was unspeakable. The fellow should be dismissed at once.'

Henri would dearly like to have released the Catholics, but dare not, knowing this would only enrage the more bigoted Puritans, and stir up hatred even more. He also had not the least wish to part with his secretary, and said as much. 'I will speak to the councillors of the Pau parliament and see what can be done for these people. Pin was doing only what he thought to be right. He's an excellent man, and good at his job.'

Margot was having none of it, and, stiffening her spine, stood tall before him in all her royal dignity. 'Pin is well known for being high-handed. Even your own people accuse him of such. The man is insolent. You must choose, Henry, between your secretary or your wife. I swear if you choose that odious little man, then I will return at once to Paris and tell my brother the King what you have done.'

It was a bluff, of course. Margot had no wish to do anything of the sort, but she was in tears for the poor souls who had been beaten and thrown in to prison, simply for wanting to take part in the Mass. She was also furious with this allegedly excellent secretary for having breached her orders to let them alone.

Pin had to go, and the prisoners were released. Navarre could see no way of avoiding it, for he certainly had no wish to annoy the King of France, and Margot, in her present temper, was capable of cutting off her own nose to spite her face and carrying out the threat.

Perhaps he would be able to forgive the man later and quietly return him to his former status. But the incident put Henry in a bad mood and he did not visit the Queen for some days after that. How he longed, at this moment, for his dear little Dayelle.

Mademoiselle de Rebours thought the King might ultimately learn that it was she who had betrayed the Queen, and decided it best to break this news to him herself. She went to him in tears begging his forgiveness. 'Did Monsieur Pin tell Your Majesty that it was I who brought him word of the Catholics attending Mass?'

'Ah, was it indeed?' Henry was intrigued. 'No, he said nothing about his source.'

She glanced up at him with frightened eyes, damp with false tears. 'Oh, dear! Have I then condemned myself? I did it for the best. I was thinking only that it seemed a dangerous thing for the Queen to do. I was but mindful of her safety. You will not tell her it was I? You will protect me, Sire?'

Navarre narrowed his eyes and considered the woman with interest. She was pale and rather thin, not at all the voluptuous beauty which normally attracted him, although not unhandsome, and there was a fragility about her which reminded him a little of Dayelle. But this woman was no innocent. He knew that Mademoiselle de Rebours had enjoyed two previous admirers, the Comte de Frontenac and his old friend and general, Damville. But he so hated to see a lady in distress.

Besides, it would surely be highly appropriate to find consolation with a lady from his wife's suite, since he was vexed with her.

He put an arm about the woman's shoulders and drew her close to press a kiss upon her brow. 'Fear not, your secret is safe with me. Come, why don't we walk a little in the gardens.'

And so it began.

Margot was no fool, and soon discovered that the secretary Pin had learned of the presence of the people in the chapel from one of her own ladies, and how that woman was now occupying her husband's bed. Furious at being doubly betrayed she called Xaintes, another of her maids of honour, a woman who was both voluptuous and experienced, and particularly attractive to men.

'I dare say you have heard the gossip.'

Xaintes lowered her gaze. 'It is rife, Madame.'

'Indeed! Rebours is a malicious girl who has

42

done me a great disservice. She spies on everything I do and I would have you do the same with her. Report to me everything she does, everywhere she goes.'

Xaintes willingly complied, but the result was that she too caught Navarre's eye. Margot was highly amused and gave the King every encouragement. Rebours was furious, believing, quite rightly, that Margot had deliberately planted this rival for the King's affections in order to make her jealous, and had succeeded.

Margot had been barred by her gender from ruling France, although she felt quite certain she could have done far better than any of her brothers: François II who had died at just sixteen, Charles IX whom she had loved dearly but the poor boy had carried a fatal flaw of madness, and now Henri Trois who surrounded himself with pretty boys, lapdogs, monkeys and a doll-like, obedient queen. Margot had made the decision long since to devote herself to Alençon, her younger brother, instead, although he too had his flaws, being somewhat deceitful and cowardly. The relationship had created much jealousy and soured relations with Henri still further.

But now she was done with all of that and hoped instead to support her husband. She wanted to be his helpmeet, be indispensable to him, even if fidelity was not part of the deal. One day, perhaps, she might be Queen of France at his side.

For that reason, if no other, Margot told herself she should stifle her bruised pride and stop caring who her husband took to his bed. She should banish any hope of finding love in this marriage and be satisfied with friendship. It surely mattered only that these women didn't cause trouble for her.

Unfortunately, Xaintes created as many problems as did Rebours, constantly spreading gossip; some of which she acquired by spying on the correspondence Margot received from Guise and the French Court. This would not do at all. Above all things, Margot loathed having people about her that she could not trust.

She began to wonder if perhaps she could find a girl as young and pretty and innocent as Dayelle to amuse the King; one who would also be compliant and obedient to his Queen. Having some control over whom he took for a mistress might be no bad thing. A great deal of mischief could be manufactured in the bedchamber.

With all pleasure in Pau now gone, Margot dubbing it her Little Geneva as it was at least as Puritan, she suggested they leave and return to Nérac. Navarre agreed, and, more fortunate still, so far as Margot was concerned, Rebours was taken ill and obliged to stay behind until she was fully recovered.

Henry no sooner lost sight of the woman than he forgot her entirely, largely because Margot had cleverly found a most suitable substitute.

The girl was young, barely thirteen, beautiful, bright, cheerful and obligingly willing to do whatever Margot asked of her. She would sit on the King's knee while he laughingly fed her sweetmeats and comfits, tease and play with her as he might a kitten. He would give her pretty gifts of earrings and ribbons, spoiling her as a father would his own daughter, except that Henry did

44

not feel in the least paternal towards this girl. He had other things in mind for her, once she was old enough.

'Does it not concern you that they might grow too friendly?' Madame de Curton asked, ever fearful for her mistress.

Margot laughed, hugging the old lady whom she still kept by her side out of love, although her duties had been reduced with respect for her great age. 'Why should I, and what would it signify if they did? She is but a child, and knows her place. She keeps the King from dallying with other, less biddable ladies.'

Pretty little Françoise de Montmorency, affectionately known as Fosseuse, seemed to be no threat at all.

They reached a little town called Eause where, in the night, the King suddenly fell ill with a high fever and violent pains in his head. Margot was alarmed and for more than two weeks she nursed him, partly out of wifely duty and affection, but also because she was terrified of what would happen to herself should he die. Death was never far away in these dangerous times. Sickness, disease, poisonings, murder; with Catherine de Medici for a mother and Henri III for a brother, Margot had reason to fear. She certainly had no wish to return to Paris and be once more at the mercy of a brother she loathed.

Margot never left her husband's side, only allowing herself to snatch a few quiet moments of sleep in the chair by his bed. She never went to her own bed, nor even took off her clothes, guarding his bedchamber day and night from all-comers, save for the maid. Thankfully, he made a good recovery, and was deeply touched by her tenderness.

'You protected and nursed me. I am most grateful.'

'I did only what a good wife should,' she said, as she urged him to sip some beef broth. 'Who else would have done it? Not that silly girl Fosseuse, although I dare say she has other uses.'

He laughed. 'Were ever a husband and wife better suited?' Their friendship, it seemed, had been strengthened as a result.

Margot had visited Nérac only once as a young girl on her way back from Bayonne. She'd been thirteen at the time and fearful of being married off to Don Carlos, the mad son of King Philip II of Spain. She'd been vastly relieved when the match had come to nothing. But as she'd sparred with a young Navarre, not for a moment had she imagined herself married to this country bumpkin, or becoming queen of this realm. Now Henry made a point of ensuring her that she was welcomed back with a fine feast of pigeon pie, sausage, ham, chicken and good Gascon wine.

Margot had forgotten how very pretty the small town was with its cluster of honey stone houses topped by red tiled roofs. Above the wide river that ran through its heart stood the Palace, small by comparison with the Louvre, but pleasant enough. It was built on four sides of a courtyard, with delightful gardens stretching down to the River Baïse where she could bathe on hot days,

46

should she choose, changing in a bathhouse built for the purpose. Not only that, the weather was a great improvement on Paris, and the rolling landscape, with its many forests, perfect for riding.

Each morning, Navarre and his sister Catherine would go to *Prêches*, while Margot and her retinue attended Mass in the little chapel in the park.

After that, she felt free to walk through the narrow streets with her ladies without fear of being molested, although the people looked at her as if she were a being from another universe. She liked to visit the *boulangerie* and watch the baker make his famous baguettes with their twisted, pointed ends. She might order a delicious pastry made from goose fat, soaked in Armagnac, and filled with prunes as big as plums, or one of apples called a *Croustarde de pomme*. She'd persuade him to make café, and he would smile and bow and enjoy the kudos of serving a beautiful Princess of France in his shop.

In the afternoons, Margot would amuse herself with tilting at the ring, plying her crossbow, or taking a stroll through the beautiful gardens, along the avenues of laurel and cypress that grew by the river bank. She gave instructions for further work to be done on these gardens, which stern Jeanne d'Albret, the woman she'd dreaded having for a mother-in-law, had begun. She called it the walk of the three thousand paces. Later, there would be dinner and a ball, poetry readings and lively discussions.

This was to be no sober Puritan household, but a court as joyous and fashionable as the one she had left behind in France. Margot gathered about her poets and artists, writers and philosophers, with whom she could debate the works of Plato. She possessed a French adaptation of *Banquet*, which she kept by her bed for night-time reading.

'Should not physical beauty reflect the spiritual beauty of the mind?' she would ask.

'Such perfection is surely impossible to attain, my lady,' they would argue.

'Plato thinks it possible, and is not platonic love the most ideal of all love?'

Coming from a woman who could claim to having enjoyed many lovers, this seemed unanswerable. They might also discuss the value of practising modesty in all things, of not seeking novelty and unusual experiences simply for the sake of it; but no one expected this queen, with her passion for devising new ideas and fashions, who believed in equality between the sexes and refused to accept the mundane, to follow such dictums. Her new friends applauded her intelligence and wit, wrote sonnets to her beauty, even as the Calvinists reviled it.

Beguiled as they may be by their new queen's beauty, her glorious gowns, her majesty and *joie de vivre*, the pastors were nevertheless outraged by her behaviour. The elders disapproved of her style of dress which so exposed her bosom, her fondness for wearing make-up, and they were horrified by the moral laxity of her court.

In return, Margot saw them as crabbed, peevish, sanctimonious old men, wearied by long years of civil war. She paid them little heed and every day set out to dazzle them, dressed in white satin sparkling with sequins, azure blue, the colour of the southern skies, or else a robe of Spanish carnation velvet. Her plumed caps, the glittering pendants and diamonds she wore in her ears were all meant to impress and show off her brilliant beauty. Nothing pleased her vanity more than to see their faded old eyes light up when they saw her pass by, or smile when she danced the pavan. They might even tap their feet as she sang a love ballad while strumming a tune on her lute.

The dancing became so popular that even the Baron de Rosny, who as a rising star in Navarre's council was generally thought of as being one of its more austere members, was soon taking lessons from the King's sister, the Princess Catherine. Rosny had accompanied Navarre to Paris as a boy, studied at the College of Bourgogne, and was reputed to have escaped the St Bartholomew massacre by cleverly carrying a Catholic Book of Hours under his arm. Margot admired both his style and his spirit.

She set about improving the Palace with great enthusiasm, ordered fine furniture and tapestries to be made, pictures to be painted to grace the stark walls which her late mother-in-law had favoured.

Her sternest critic was Agrippa Aubigné, the King's chamberlain. He openly criticized Margot's extravagance and the pair took an instant dislike to each other. Margot thought that his mean spirit was written all too plain in his thin face, with its beady black eyes and sharp nose. She made a few enquiries and discovered that despite the airs and graces he gave himself, as if he were of noble birth, he came from humble Huguenot stock. He'd evidently devised for himself an impressive family tree which was entirely fictitious, and his resentment against all genuine nobility, particularly those of the Catholic faith, was strong.

Margot's frankness with regard to the many love affairs that now flourished in the once Puritan court, shocked him. Even the King's sister imagined herself in love when, as a royal princess, she would be expected to make a good dynastic marriage. She would certainly not be allowed to follow her heart, a most unreliable vessel and of far less importance than the immortal soul, in Aubigné's opinion. The chamberlain believed there were far more important tasks requiring a gentleman's attention than love, such as spreading the word of the New Religion, and defending the realm.

And he knew who to blame for this dissolute behaviour.

'The woman takes the rust from men's minds and casts it upon their swords.'

Margot thought differently.

'A *chevalier* has no soul if he is not in love,' she would say to her husband, and Henry would laugh and all too willingly agree. How could he not? He fell in and out of love all the time.

The King was, however, losing patience and growing weary of the game with *la petite* Tignonville. Fosseuse was little more than a child, too young yet for love, but surely he had waited long enough for sweet Mademoiselle Tignonville? She was most certainly old enough, virgin or no. They were sitting together on a grassy bank by the river and, reaching over, he tickled her cheek

50

with a goose feather.

'Smile at me, little one. Grant me one more kiss. Come to my bed. Can you not see how I grow faint for want of love for you?'

Jeanne widened her eyes in all innocence and claimed not to understand. 'Have I not told you, Sire, that I can never be yours – at least...' She paused and Henry breathlessly waited for her to continue. Would she succumb? Was this the moment he had waited for so long?

Picking at an embroidered rosebud on her gown, Jeanne pouted prettily. 'Do you truly love me?'

'Of course!'

'More than Fosseuse?'

'I swear it. You have no need to feel jealous.'

'I don't.'

Henry hid a smile, knowing she lied.

Jeanne let out a dramatic sigh. Her jealousy stemmed more from the loss of the King's favour and all that might achieve, rather than pining for his love. She certainly had no wish to be ousted by another before she'd taken full advantage of her favour with the King. 'It would be a different matter were I a married lady. There would be no fear then were I to fall *enceinte*, or of being soiled goods from losing my virginity, even to a king, if I already had a husband.'

Henry looked at her in astonishment. 'Is that the answer then? Is this what you have wished for all along? A husband. Why did you not say?'

In truth, Jeanne had only recently reached this decision, prompted by her mother. Perhaps she'd secretly hoped that Henry would make her his queen, but now that Queen Margot was actually here, so beautiful and so regal, she'd come to see the impossibility of this dream.

'He must be a man of distinction and wealth, a fine man.' She dare not say handsome, in case the King took exception. 'I feel I deserve some respectability.'

Henry was on his feet in a second, almost as if he meant to dash away and find a candidate that instant. 'It shall be done. You must have all your heart desires. If you wish for a husband, I will find you one.'

The man chosen was Francois Leon Charles, Baron de Pardaillan and Count de Pangeas. Henry made him a councillor of state, a royal chamberlain, a knight of the King's orders, a captain of fifty men-at-arms of the royal companies, commander of the regiment of Guienne and governor of Armagnac.

'Is that respectable enough for you, little one?'

Jeanne was shocked when first she saw her future husband, for he was fat and old with a grizzled beard, not at all what she had expected or hoped for. He was so big and ponderous that Princess Catherine nicknamed him the big buffalo.

Fortunately, he was not expected to share her bed or behave as a husband to her, a task which was to be left entirely to the King. And *la petite* Tignonville proved to be far more accommodating now that she had become Countess de Pangeas, and slipped readily enough now into the King's bed, where she let him do as he willed with her.

Nor did her husband complain, for the new count appreciated that he was indebted to his wife for his rise in station. And the King would surely tire of her eventually. Pangeas was a patient man and willing to wait.

Perhaps that day would come sooner than he'd hoped, as Henry felt just a little disappointed. Sad to say, once he'd tasted this much-longed-for prize, *la petite* Tignonville seemed no different from any other woman. There was nothing Henry wanted more than what he couldn't have, and in a very short time his visits to Jeanne's bedchamber became less and less frequent, and his attention once more turned towards Fosseuse.

The elders never dared to criticize their King for his affairs, accepting his infidelities as a natural weakness in a man. Even Aubigné remained passionately loyal to his sovereign. He said not a word as Navarre paid court to his many ladies – to Dayelle in Pau, to *la petite* Tignonville, and to Fosseuse – as he was well accustomed to the many amours he'd enjoyed in the past.

He was less indulgent of the Queen of Navarre, who refused to adopt the patient fortitude expected in a wife, as the stoic Jeanne d'Albret had shown when faced with the same dilemma. He strongly disapproved of the fact that the new queen played her husband at his own game. The fact that she too acquired a lover was anathema to the Puritan elders of Nérac.

Navarre himself had introduced Henri de La Tour, Viscount de Turenne to Margot, and it was obvious from their first meeting that there was an instant attraction between the two. His eyes sparkled with a familiar challenge and Margot was instantly fascinated.

'Have I not seen you about court when you were in France, Monsieur?' she asked, glancing up at him from beneath her lashes, noting how his gaze swept over her with very evident admiration.

'Indeed, I am flattered you should remember.'

'You were a comrade of my younger brother, Alençon, were you not?'

'We were with the *Politiques* together for a time, that is true. I remember you at the evening balls, Your Majesty. You always showed great skill on the dance floor.'

Margot laughed. 'As you do with your compliments.'

She noticed that he seemed almost to be blushing, yet he was a true gentleman: chivalrous, charming and handsome. 'I feel sure, monsieur, that you and I will be great friends.'

They became very much more than that. Soon it was the handsome Turenne occupying her bed, and he showed far more grace in it than did her own husband. The Court of Nérac was awash with gossip concerning the respective love affairs of both the King and Queen. The tittle-tattle did not trouble Margot in the slightest, only served to amuse her, and she paid no attention to the narrow-minded bigots.

What amazed everyone the most was the complete lack of jealousy or discord between the couple, as they each enjoyed their respective dalliances without let or hinder. Navarre with Fosseuse, who, because of her lack of experience in court etiquette was assisted by Margot's maid Xaintes, herself a former mistress of the King; and Margot with Turenne, all of them great friends

54

together. A right royal tangle!

Only *la petite* Tignonville showed any sign of jealousy, poor child, stuck with a fat old husband and now out of favour with the King.

To Margot, the situation was perfectly straightforward. If her husband felt free to take lovers, why should not the same rules apply to her? She would enjoy her liaison with Turenne for a time, as his charm, good looks, and devotion to her were really most diverting. She would be completely faithful to him, as she was to all her lovers, for as long as the affair lasted. Not that she could ever love him truly, of course. Her heart would ever belong to Guise.

In Paris, at the salon of the Duchesse de Montpensier, Guise's sister, the most eloquent, wealthy and powerful men of the day were made welcome. These included Nevers, Cheverny, Mayenne, and others involved in attempting to overthrow the dynasty of the Valois. She would recline upon her couch, due to a slight lameness, and applaud their daring, her contempt for the King all too evident. Madame de Montpensier's husband had been one of Admiral Coligny's sworn enemies. She too was a zealot, fiercely Catholic, known as the Fury of the League, and had no good word to say for Henri Trois as she denounced the debauchery and dissipation of his court.

Her brother, standing close by, could only agree. 'We cannot allow this situation to go on indefinitely, or the nation will be bankrupt, if not by his profligacy, then by war.'

An impressive figure with his fair, curled hair,

his beard neatly trimmed, and eyes bright with passion and ambition, those present never failed to listen with respect to every word Guise spoke. Even the scar he now carried, like his father before him, seemed to mark him as a man to follow and revere, and he now bore the same name, *Le Balafré*.

'*Vive Guise!*' were words called out to him whenever he went about in the city.

'The people would rise up and follow you, brother. They are weary of being exploited, their hard earned money used merely to feather the fancy nests of Henri's *mignons*. He is giving away bishoprics now to Epernon and Joyeuse, and they are selling them for a fortune. He's even talking of procuring a rich bride for each of these favourites. I dread to think what the cost of such a wedding would be.'

Guise winced, giving a growl of anger deep in his throat. 'Yet the King gives no thought to the needs of the realm, to the steady progress being made by the Huguenots. He may parade through the streets as a penitent, but it's all smoke and mirrors with no substance to his beliefs. For all he claims to be a good Catholic, he thinks only of his own dissolute fops, his lapdogs and his extravagant gowns. Dear God, what an affliction the Valois have been upon France. There hasn't been one good male in the entire bunch that Catherine de Medici produced.'

'Have you heard anything lately from her daughter, the Queen of Navarre?' the Duchess asked, remembering her brother's fondness for Margot.

Guise relaxed as he pressed his hand against

the reassuring crackle of her latest letter, several pages long, and in Margot's own inimitable style, safely tucked within his doublet. 'She is well, and enjoying spending her brother the King's money, as well as her husband's, as she creates a new court in Nérac to rival that of France.'

Madame de Montpensier chuckled. 'A woman of great independence and spirit, frustrated by the power of men, yet I swear she'll beat them all in the end.'

He laughed with her as he refilled his sister's wine glass and brought her wafers. 'You may well speak true.'

Glancing about her, to check they were not overheard, the Duchess continued more quietly, 'I have heard a disturbing tale today. I am reliably informed that Henri Trois is ranting over a letter he has received from Queen Marguerite's court. It comes from one of the Huguenots, Agrippa somebody-or-other. Do you know of it?'

Guise shook his head. 'Do you wish me to look into the matter and see what I can discover?'

'No need, it seems the writer is accusing Margot of blatantly embarking upon an affair with a certain Turenne. He begs the King to step in and control his sister's licentious behaviour. The letter goes on to assert that she is driven by hatred of her brother and jealousy of her husband, who is not faithful to her, and wishes to take revenge by inciting a new war between the two kingdoms. Do you think this can be true?'

Guise sighed. 'Anything is possible with my dear, reckless Margot. Say what you will about her exemplary courage and delightful beauty;

discretion is not one of her strengths. Yet I cannot think that even Margot would deliberately engineer a war for the sake of a little jealousy. I know that the King is certainly jealous of her tranquillity and evident happiness in Nérac. He is incensed that his sister should prefer life in a rural backwater to that in the Louvre with him.'

The Duchess clicked her tongue with impatience. 'Do you wonder at it?' She gently tapped the pouch in his doublet wherein reposed Margot's letter. 'I believe Henri also has this house watched. If so, then he will know of the couriers that pass to and fro. Take care, my brother.'

Guise laughed. 'I always take the utmost care, but let us not get too paranoid.'

'And the letter of which I speak, that the King received? It apparently claims that Margot hopes to destroy the peace which the Queen Mother so carefully procured. Would that be to our benefit, think you, in view of that other matter of which we were speaking earlier?' prompted the Duchess.

Guise rubbed his chin and the crisp sharpness of his beard. 'I will communicate with Philip of Spain – secretly, of course,' he quickly added, smiling at his sister. 'We will see if he is willing to offer practical support to further our cause. It is as much in his interest as ours that France steers her course with the Mother Church, and what better way to achieve that than with the House of Guise at the helm.'

When a letter came from the King of France informing Navarre that his wife was making a cuckold of him, he laughed out loud, and took it straight to Margot's apartment. She was propped up in bed enjoying breakfast, a plate of fresh fruit on her lap, fortunately alone for once as Turenne was not present.

She was surprised to see him, quickly dabbed at a trickle of peach juice on her chin. 'My lord, this is an early call.'

Navarre considered his lovely wife with an amused smile. The famous black satin sheets and pillows she used for visiting lovers serving only to enhance her pale, translucent beauty, as no doubt intended. 'I see that your sainted brother is reaching out his grubby fingers to stir up yet more trouble,' he said, tossing the letter to her.

'What? How dare he spy on me!' Margot cried, as she quickly scanned the letter, hardly able to believe the words before her own eyes. 'Why is he so determined to interfere in my life, to still try to control me, even from this distance? I do not deny the charge of infidelity; but...'

Giving a bark of laughter Navarre took a cherry from her plate, chewed upon it then flicked the stone on to the floor. 'How could you, my love, when all the court knows of it, including myself.'

'But this charge of my wishing to start another war is entirely false,' she concluded, ignoring his interruption. 'Why would I do such a thing? This is scandalous, nothing but pernicious lies. Neither Turenne nor I have any wish to bring about a new conflict.'

Henry reached for another cherry, sucked upon it with a thoughtful frown. He was untroubled by his wife's so-called licentious behaviour, but, like her, extremely concerned about the possibility of another war.

'Make haste and dress, my love, we must speak to the elders.'

In an effort to prevent the seemingly inevitable conflict, Navarre allowed Margot to regularly attend council meetings in the weeks following, and to address the religious leaders. She received letters from her mother the Queen, urging her to do everything in her power to help retain the peace, yet Margot failed utterly to convince them that they had little to gain from another war. Led by Aubigné, they scarcely listened to her arguments. Why would they? She was not only a woman, but a Catholic.

In November, without any warning or discussions with Navarre, his one-time comrade at arms, Condé captured La Fère in Picardy. The two were now very much at odds. The Prince de Condé had grown increasingly pious, and was critical of his cousin's fickleness with regard to both his love life and his religion.

The King of Navarre felt obliged to apologize to the King of France, but the hostilities continued to gather momentum and soon he was again writing to Henri, this time castigating Maréchal Biron for threatening to destroy the Huguenots.

And despite all Margot's efforts, the Huguenots declared war in April 1580.

It became known as *La Guerre des Amoureux*, the Lovers' War, caustically dubbed as such by Aubigné. More likely it was a result of the inadequacy of the agreement Catherine had devised. The Peace of Nérac had conceded a period of only six months for the Huguenots to enjoy the strongholds to which they laid claim. When that time had elapsed, unsurprisingly, they decided to hold on to them, rather than meekly hand them back.

Margot's newfound happiness was suddenly under threat. She felt as if she was between the devil and the deep blue sea. If she aligned herself with Navarre she would be betraying her own faith, which was of great importance to her. She also risked offending her brother the King and the Queen Mother, which would be reckless in the extreme. Margot still largely depended upon them financially, despite their many promises to return her the properties and monies that were due to her on marriage.

Yet if the Catholics won, Navarre and her new life here in Nérac, which until now had been happy, would be in real danger. Besides all of this, she very much wished to remain on good terms with her husband. How else would she get to wear a crown of France?

Margot's own liaison with Turenne ended soon after war was declared. She'd grown bored with him, and one night asked him to leave.

'Are you tired, my love? Shall I return on the morrow?'

'No,' she replied, stifling a yawn. 'I think not. It has been most delightful but all good things must come to an end.' Turenne had never meant much to her emotionally, Margot viewing him only as an amusement. Her lover, however, claimed to be far more deeply attached and was devastated at losing her.

'You cannot mean it. I shall hang myself if you

abandon me. How can I live without you?'

'I'm sure you will find consolation elsewhere,' she said, smiling up at him.

'How could that be possible when you are the queen of my heart?'

'Leave. Now. I can certainly live without you.'

Turenne did not take his dismissal well and requested the command of troops in Upper Languedoc, by way of compensation. Fortunately, he did not carry out his threat, which rather amused Henry who thereafter called him 'the great unhanged'.

Navarre himself went to war, something he now relished almost as much as making love. The first Margot knew of it was when she received a letter from her husband in which he addressed her with great affection, apologizing for the decision he'd been obliged to make, and in leaving without even telling her.

'Do not grieve,' he urged her. 'It is enough that one of us should be unhappy. I kiss your hands a million times.'

Navarre captured Cahors on 31 May 1580, proving himself yet again to be an able and resilient soldier. Henri Trois was predictably furious, both with his brother-in-law, and his recalcitrant sister whom he blamed entirely for this situation. Cahors, like Agen, was part of Margot's marriage portion, therefore the King felt that she had betrayed him by allowing it to be taken by a Huguenot, even if he was her own husband. Henri called his procurator-general and cancelled all her rights to the town.

By early summer, Biron was drawing dangerously near to Gascony, and, in alarm, Margot wrote to her brother the King and the Queen Mother, begging them to declare Nérac neutral.

'I pray you do not make war within three miles of it, and I will persuade my husband to agree to the same on behalf of the party of the new religion.'

Henri Trois agreed to this so long as Navarre did not use the town as a hiding place.

Yet how could Henry resist coming often to his home town, not only to see his wife and sister, but also because he remained deeply enamoured of Fosseuse and could hardly bear to be parted from her for long. He was utterly besotted and must see his *petite fille* as often as possible. Relations with Margot remained good, if more like brother and sister than man and wife, but he still ached to possess Fosseuse.

Having disposed of Turenne, Margot was considering other possibilities, although the court was filled with only ladies since all the handsome men had gone off to war, but she always welcomed her husband's visits to Nérac.

When he heard of these, Biron believed that Navarre had broken the pact, and prepared his arquebusiers to attack. Henry stoutly defended his stronghold by leading his army out to face the troops, holding his ground well. Annoyed, and in a show of bravado, the Marshal fired seven or eight shots upon the town, one of which struck the Palace.

Unfortunately, Margot and her ladies had gone out upon the ramparts to watch the battle, and were almost hit.

'Dear God, he means to kill us,' the Queen cried, as all her ladies ran screaming back into the Palace.

Having made his point, the Marshal dispatched a messenger to the Queen of Navarre with his humble apologies, explaining that he would never have fired upon the town, under the terms of neutrality, were he not duty-bound to attack the King her husband wherever he should find him.

'Have no more to do with the fellow,' Navarre warned her.

'I have had no quarrel with him in the past, and we are of the same religion. Biron has always showed me the greatest respect, and appeared to be very much my friend. During the war my letters have frequently fallen into his hands, which he always forwards to me unopened. And whenever my people have been taken prisoner by his army, they were well treated as soon as they mentioned to whom they belonged.'

Margot nevertheless wrote a scalding response, complaining of the attack upon her frightened ladies, and for spoiling three precious days with her husband.

Much to Margot's delight, her brother Alençon returned from England later that summer, where he'd again failed to win the hand of Queen Elizabeth, who liked to call him her little frog. To cover his disappointment, he threw himself into supporting the efforts of his sister and brother-in-law for peace. After many months of negotiations, the Treaty of Fleix was finally signed, so named because that was where the principal parties were staying at the time. Biron was deprived of his command, and six months of unnecessary war was brought to an end in September.

Henri III was not happy, and continued to blame Margot for having started the war in the first place, now accusing her of deliberately provoking the conflict so that his younger brother could share in the glory of ending it and bringing peace.

'It is always the same old story,' Margot complained. 'Jealousy and envy forever sour him and twist his mind.'

Not that Margot cared what Henri thought, for in these last weeks while in the Dordogne helping to negotiate the peace, she had enjoyed having her younger brother with her. What was even more exciting, she had fallen in love.

Jacques de Harlay, Marquis of Champvallon did not possess Guise's confident swagger, nor was he the fine swordsman that Bussy had been, or have quite the *je ne sais quoi* of Turenne. Yet he possessed stunning good looks. It was generally accepted that not only was he the most romantic man at court, but also the most beautiful: a Greek god in very truth.

Margot had always admired perfect beauty and, two or three years younger than herself, he became her *coup de foudre*. She was utterly smitten, calling him her Narcissus. No one but Guise had ever captured her heart, but here was the grand passion she had so longed for. If she was indiscreet before, now Margot abandoned all self-restraint and gave herself to him utterly.

His family was not rich but neither was it humble, his father being the squire of Césy, and his mother related to the Scottish royal family of Stuarts. He was brave and had distinguished himself by serving the King before joining Alençon's entourage as his master of horse.

Champvallon was also intelligent, and the two lovers would sit in an arbour or stroll through the gardens conversing ardently together, discussing their shared passion for poetry or literature. Something of a poet himself, he would write verses to stir her heart.

After leaving Fleix, the royal party spent some months in the Gironde. As spring approached, Navarre returned to Béarn but Alençon and Margot moved on to Bordeaux for a couple of months, where she devoted much of her time riding and walking with Champvallon, enjoying secret trysts, making love in dappled glades. Romance was very much in the air.

Eventually a message came from her husband suggesting that it was time she return to Nérac, which Margot agreed to quite willingly, seeing no reason why this blissful happiness should not continue.

Margot happily returned to Nérac, accompanied by Alençon and Champvallon. The elders, courtiers and ladies at her husband's court did not immediately warm to the brother of their Queen. He was shorter and less handsome than they'd expected. They did not care for his pockmarked face, or his small, hard eyes that constantly cast darting glances about him, as if anticipating mischief, or perhaps seeking an opportunity to create it.

Wanting to make her young brother feel welcome, Margot threw a fine ball in his honour, making herself look especially magnificent in blue velvet with her favourite diamonds at her throat and in her ears.

Navarre too welcomed him, clapping him on the shoulders in brotherly fashion. There had been little time to speak of personal matters while at Fleix, now they did so, laughing together as they remembered past times and old rivalries; how they had almost come to blows over them both paying court to Madame de Sauves at the same time.

'And how is dear Charlotte?' Alençon teasingly enquired.

Navarre laughed. 'She returned with Queen Catherine to Paris, since she did not care to have her nose pushed out of joint by newer rivals.'

'Then you do not pine for her?'

'Why would I, when I have my beautiful Fosseuse?' Henry drew the young girl to his side to introduce her to Alençon, and saw at once his mistake. The Duke's eyes lit up as they beheld the young beauty, and it soon became clear that he had fallen head over heels in love with Fosseuse at first sight.

Much to Navarre's fury, his brother-in-law spent the rest of the evening complimenting her with all the skills and impeccable manners he had acquired at the French Court. Alençon kept on asking Fosseuse to dance and she kept accepting, clearly flattered by his attention, and so it continued in the days following. Henry began to worry that his *petite fille* was being easily seduced by his brother-in-law's charm because she was feeling homesick for the sophisticated life she had left behind in Paris.

The girl was still young, and Henry had been careful not to be too impatient or seem to rush her. She had not yet succumbed, always drawing back whenever their love making became too intimate. It was little Tignonville all over again, only the prize was surely greater. Now he grew fearful that, pockmarked dwarf though he may be, Alençon might win her first.

'You must speak to your brother,' he barked at Margot when he visited her bedchamber a day or two later.

Margot paused in brushing her long dark hair to look at him with that haughty expression on her lovely face which so infuriated him. 'On any particular matter?'

'You know of what I speak. Alençon is monopolising Fosseuse. He's paying court, panting for her.'

Margot set down the brush and applied a little rouge to her cheeks and lips. 'It is your own fault for sharing the same taste in women. He was ever your rival.'

'Fosseuse is different from de Sauves. She is young and vulnerable. I will not have her spoiled,' Henry declared, pacing back and forth in an agitated manner.

Margot raised mildly questioning brows. 'Not until you have spoiled her yourself first, eh?'

Navarre ignored the jibe. 'You will speak to him? He always did listen to you. I swear he is doing this only to vex me, but I am not amused.

Tell Alençon he may have any woman in the court, but not mine.'

'I will consider the matter.' She cast him a teasing look. 'Now, do please go. I am expecting a visitor of my own this evening, and I'm sure you have no wish to perform your marital duties if your thoughts are so caught up with your *petite fille.*' And dropping her *robe de chambre* to the floor, Margot walked naked to the bed, aware of his eyes upon her.

Navarre could feel himself hardening just watching her. This wife of his was the very devil of a woman. He marched out, slamming the door behind him. Margot lay back on her black satin sheets, laughing. Oh, how she was enjoying her freedom.

The last few years in Nérac had been such happy ones that Margot saw no danger in admitting to her infatuation for Champvallon, nor consider for a moment that her husband would ever object, let alone send her back to her hated brother. How could he criticize her for infidelity when he was guilty of the very same offence? A moment later her lover arrived, and Margot instantly forgot about the problem of Alençon and Fosseuse; too caught up in her own love affair to care.

The court was highly entertained by this new rival for Fosseuse's affections and while the ladies gossiped in corners, the gentlemen laid surreptitious bets on who might win the prize of the girl's virginity; the King or the Duke, even though gambling was strictly forbidden in this Puritan court.

Mademoiselle Rebours was also paying particular attention to this tangle of royal love affairs. She deeply resented the fact that Margot had deliberately brought Fosseuse to the King's attention in order to foil her own ambitions in that direction. The girl was young and healthy, could no doubt easily bear him children, while her own health had never entirely recovered from that illness in Pau. She blamed the Queen for this too, Margot having most casually abandoned her there.

Now she saw her opportunity for revenge.

Rebours put on her most modest attire and went to see Aubigné. With artful cunning she was careful not to attack the King, but instead pleaded for the chamberlain's advice.

'I know not how best to proceed. The King is clearly desirous of an heir, and yet Her Majesty spends most nights with her new lover, Champvallon. Not only that, but she seems to be encouraging her brother to steal the affections of the King's beloved Fosseuse from him. I really do not see how I can stop her from behaving so recklessly. I feel I should do something to help His Majesty, but cannot think what.' At which point she burst into floods of dramatic tears.

Aubigné was unmoved by her weeping, made no attempt to comfort her, yet white-hot rage flooded through him. How dare that Jezebel, that Whore of Babylon so betray his sovereign lord? No wonder the King was obliged to seek comfort elsewhere when his own wife refused to do her duty by him.

'Say nothing, woman. Do nothing. You can safely leave this matter in my hands.'

Rebours slipped quietly away, dark eyes gleaming with triumph.

Aubigné knew better than to seek an audience with the King.

Henry's attitude towards love had ever been cavalier, to say the least. He went straight to the Queen, insisting upon an immediate audience.

Margot dutifully granted him admission. The wily pastor could tell by her *déshabille*, and the sickly sweet scent of the room overlaid by the smell of something far more erotic, that her lover must have only recently vacated her apartment, perhaps seconds before.

'Your Majesty, I would speak with you on a most urgent and delicate matter.'

'Indeed?'

'You will appreciate how vital it is that our lord King produce an heir, and yet sadly you have both been disappointed in this respect thus far.'

Colour flooded into Margot's cheeks. This was a worry she buried deep inside, and really had no wish to examine too closely. 'How dare you raise such a topic with me!'

'I would be failing in my duty to God and the kingdom, if I did not do so. It is clear that you and the King do not often enough...' Aubigné paused to cough politely and clear his throat. 'How can I put it? It is the will of God that marriage is for the purpose of procreation, yet you and the King do not often enough avail yourself of the opportunity to bring about this most happy result.'

Margot was furious. She glared into the man's mean little eyes above his jutting nose and fat, bearded chin. 'How dare you speak to me in this manner! Pray leave my presence at once.'

Aubigné remained firmly rooted to the spot. 'I am aware of the King's indiscretions, and how difficult it must be to achieve any intimacy between you as a result. Nevertheless, it would perhaps be wise if you were to refrain from following his lead quite so ardently, and concentrate instead on doing your duty as queen of this realm, even if...' The unspoken end to this sentence seemed to hang in the air between them ... even if you have no morals.

Margot stared at him, too stunned by the man's effrontery to think of a suitable response.

'The danger is that you may find there are other ladies – younger, and mayhap more fecund, who would not hesitate to take your place in this respect.'

'Is that meant to be some sort of threat?' The prospect of divorce suddenly reared its ugly head in Margot's startled mind. With divorce came disgrace, loss of status, penury perhaps, and even, God help her, a nunnery.

'It is but a timely warning I recommend you heed. I would suggest that Your Majesty give this matter most careful thought.' Having had his say, he sketched a bow and departed. Margot stamped her foot, let out a scream of fury, and, calling at once for her ladies, started to tear off her bedgown.

Henry considered his wife with weary trepidation. 'What is it now, Margot? I have no time for tantrums this morning, I have papers to attend to.'

'I want that man dismissed.'

He let out a heavy sigh. 'And which of my councillors have offended you today?'

'Aubigné. The man is offensive, insubordinate and downright rude. He has no right to lecture *me*, a queen, upon my duties. I will not tolerate his insolence.' She told Navarre, most succinctly, of how Aubigné had dared to criticize her behaviour, though carefully making no mention of the chamberlain's concern over the lack of an heir. That would have come far too close to an uncomfortable truth. 'I insist that he is dismissed.'

'I cannot do that, Margot. We have been here before, I recall, and you really must not keep dismissing members of my council simply because they have fallen foul of your temper. I will not have it.'

Margot lifted her chin. '*You* will not have it? Yet you would have *me* warn my brother off your *petite fille*.'

There was a short, startled silence. Endeavouring to keep his exasperation under control, Henry finally found his voice. 'What are you saying?'

Margot took a steadying breath. 'I will come to an agreement with you, my dear *Enric*. If you dismiss your insolent chamberlain, I will make sure that Alençon no longer impedes your attentions to the little Fosseuse.'

'Margot, you are impossible.'

She laughed out loud, all temper gone. 'Then we are agreed?'

Navarre thought of the ripe beauty of his darling Fosseuse, like a rare peach ready for the picking, and simply could not find it in himself to say no.

Later that day he faced his loyal servant with pity in his face. 'I am sorry, Aubigné, but I can do no other than to agree with my wife's demands. You have greatly offended the Queen, which of course I cannot condone.'

The chamberlain was shocked. This was not at all the reaction he had planned. 'But Your Majesty, do you choose to play the cuckold? You will be the laughing stock of the court, of the kingdom. Think of your duty to God, and to your people. We need an heir.'

Henry frowned, not quite caring for the fellow's Puritan bluntness. Yet he adored his darling Fosseuse, and must have her, no matter what the cost. The prospect of losing that most coveted prize to his ugly brother-in-law did not bear contemplating.

He went to put an arm about his chamberlain's shoulders. 'Your banishment will be but temporary. In any case, so long as the Queen does not become aware of it, you could continue to visit me in private to conduct our business, at least until her temper has properly cooled and the matter has blown over.'

Margot's discussion with her brother went even more smoothly. Alençon was always agreeable to doing anything his beloved sister asked of him. 'I adore little Fosseuse, but if it is your wish, Margot, then I shall not go near the girl again, nor even speak with her.'

He proved to be as good as his word and not long after that, Navarre took his *petite fille* to his privy chamber one evening to wine and dine, and hopefully bed her. 'Why is it, my precious, that you still resist me? Am I not attractive to you?'

'Of course! Does Your Majesty not realize how much I adore you?'

Her eyes were so trusting, so adoring as they gazed up at him, that he could not fail to believe it. His excitement quickened. This could be the night that he won her at last. 'Then what is it that holds you back, my sweet one? Why so coy? Surely you are not still shy with me now that you are no longer the young child you once were.'

Fosseuse was indeed no longer a child. She had grown sufficiently to understand the extent of her power, and learned through this little intrigue how very important she was to the King. She pouted delightfully at him.

'But what if I were to become *enceinte?* How could I have your child when we are not married? I have no husband to protect me.'

Henry was all too familiar with this concern. It was Tignonville all over again. He smiled, caressing her softly rounded buttocks as he led her gently towards the bed. 'Is that all that troubles you? But such a situation can easily be remedied. You need have no worries on that score. I would always protect you, my sweet one.'

'But you could never acknowledge such a child. He, were it a boy, would be a bastard,' she said, artlessly reminding him of what she could offer.

He was peeling off her gown, his eyes upon the firm ripeness of her breasts, so full and yet so pert, her waist no more than two hand spans, her hips curved but slender, legs long and shapely.

75

She was so innocent, so pure, and tonight she was his for the taking. He was hot for her, impatient as he pulled her down on the bed. 'I would most certainly acknowledge him,' Henry groaned, feeling that familiar, delicious ache in his loins.

'Oh, Your Majesty!'

'You can trust me implicitly, my darling, I would not see you dishonoured.'

He saw at once, by the stars in her lovely eyes as she gazed entrancingly up at him, by the breathless rapture of her response, that she had misunderstood him completely. Navarre was accustomed to finding convenient husbands for his mistresses, or acknowledging a bastard child as his own, which was all he had meant by the remark. But he might have phrased the words carelessly, for this innocent child believed that he had proposed. He paused a moment to consider. Would that be an answer, to divorce Margot and marry little Fosseuse, assuming she were able to give him children?

But she was kissing him with a delicious fervour now, allowing him to ravage her little pink tongue with his own, and he was impatient to thrust into her in other ways. Beyond thought now, he was insensible of everything but the peachy quality of her skin, the soft firmness of her young breasts. Henry moaned with desire, hurting so badly he could barely hold himself in check to prepare this pretty virgin for the moment that he'd waited for so eagerly. No matter what the consequences, he would have her.

From that day on Fosseuse began to change. In

every way she was a loving and devoted mistress, but no longer quite so undemanding. She began to require constant evidence of the King's devotion. 'I have worn that gown three times this month already, and I have barely a piece of jewellery to my name.'

'But I gave you those emeralds only at Christmas, my sweet.'

'You cannot wear emeralds with a rose-red gown, and it is the only one I feel fit to be seen in, even though I have owned it forever. The Queen has diamonds by the score, but I have nothing.'

The King of Navarre bought his love some diamonds, and a new gown to go with them.

Nor was she quite so obedient to the Queen. Fosseuse began to avoid Margot and her duties as lady-in-waiting, even though she was supposedly still a part of the Queen's retinue. She became rather secretive, giggling with her friends and then falling silent and looking all prim and innocent whenever the Queen drew near.

Furthermore, she began creating ill feeling between husband and wife by telling tales about Margot to Henry. These stories were wildly exaggerated, highly embroidered versions of what might pass for the truth, and sometimes downright lies. They nevertheless inflamed his ire, and Henry rarely castigated her or challenged their veracity. Relations between husband and wife cooled as a result.

Margot began to complain to her ladies. 'What is going on? What has happened to the girl?'

'Ignore her, my lady. She is simply behaving like a spoiled miss.'

'But she was once so biddable, and now is becoming a little minx.'

'Pay her no attention. She represents no threat to Your Majesty.'

Margot wasn't so sure. She had many ladies she could rely on in her entourage: Princess Catherine de Bourbon, her husband's sister, Madelaine de la Tour, who had been deprived of an eligible suitor by Henri Trois, and Mademoiselle de Thorigny, who was once threatened with drowning in the Seine by her brother's brutal troops. They were all devoted to her, but Margot was beginning to feel very slightly vulnerable. It was obvious that her husband had by now taken the girl's virginity. But what if this healthy young girl became *enceinte*, where would that leave her?

How she longed for her old governess to advise her, but the old lady had finally passed away last winter. Margot's eyes filled with a rush of tears at the memory of her adored Madame de Curton. She missed her faithful servant and beloved companion dearly. The Duchess of Nevers and other dear friends were still in Paris with their husbands, and at times Margot felt a worrying sense of isolation. She had even quarrelled with her Chancellor, Pibrac, since she suffered from the typical Valois flaw of extravagance of which he disapproved.

Worse, Alençon had now left Gascony to return to Paris, taking his master of horse, her darling Champvallon, with him. Margot was desolate. How could she live without her Narcissus? She felt so low that she took to wearing black like a widow in mourning, and would sit for hours in her apartment writing long, heartrending letters to him.

And all the while Fosseuse continued to strut about court like the proverbial cat who had swallowed the cream.

Henry came to Margot one day to inform her that he was planning a visit to Pau. 'Fosseuse is suffering from a slight colic, so I have promised her a visit to Aigues-Caudes to take the waters, and then on to the chateau at Pau for a change of scene. I would naturally have you accompany us.'

'I think not,' Margot snapped. 'You know how I have disliked that place of penitence ever since the incident over the Mass. They lack any tolerance for my religion. It is like a little Geneva, far too Puritan for me. I have no quarrel with your taking Fosseuse, but leave me out of your plans.'

Navarre was annoyed. 'You know full well that I cannot travel alone with my mistress, it would only give rise to unnecessary scandal.'

Margot laughed. 'It is no secret that you bed her.'

Henry winced. 'Pray show some restraint, Margot, at least in your language if not your behaviour.'

'Do not *you* start preaching at me, I will not tolerate it. Rebours, your former mistress, could act as chaperone. The woman will welcome taking the waters for the headaches which constantly beset her. And I would be rid of the pleasure of her company for a little while.' Having settled the matter to her satisfaction, Margot marched away in a huff.

But it hurt her that they were becoming so

79

estranged. They had used to be such good friends, and now they were forever bickering.

Mademoiselle de Rebours, together with several other maids of honour and gentlemen of the court, duly accompanied the small party to take the waters. She wrote regularly to Margot, keeping her mistress informed of the spiteful comments which Fosseuse was saying about her, and how disrespectful the girl was.

Margot took little notice, knowing that Rebours herself was furiously jealous of Fosseuse, having lost her own place in the King's affections. She did not trust the woman, who was two-faced enough to be likewise slandering her mistress to Fosseuse.

Mademoiselle de Rebours was indeed bitter over the treatment she had received at Margot's hand, and had continued to keep a close eye on her rival. Now, being in the girl's company every day as they took the waters, her suspicions deepened, and she rather thought she understood why Fosseuse had changed.

One wet afternoon, when Fosseuse deigned to join the other ladies for needlework, Rebours watched with interest as she reached down to pick up a skein of silk that she'd dropped. Her movements were awkward, the girl instinctively resting a protective hand upon her belly, and even though she was still as slender as a reed, Rebours knew, in that moment, that the King's mistress was pregnant. A great surge of envy shot through her. It should have been herself in that condition, not this silly child. And it would have been so, had not

Queen Margot ejected her from the King's bed out of revenge for that incident over Mass in Pau.

But Margot herself would surely suffer more, were these suspicions proved to be true. Rebours smiled, for she would take great pleasure in seeing the Queen brought low and humiliated by such a scandal.

She made it her business to engage empty-headed little Fosseuse in conversation as they plied their needles, bathed in the warm waters, or sipped the foul-tasting beverage that was supposedly good for their health. She pretended to be her friend, and, as the ladies were changing for dinner one evening, offered to lend Fosseuse a pretty cap which matched her new gown.

'You are so enchantingly beautiful I am not surprised the King is besotted. Allow me to fix the cap for you and pin up your lovely hair. It will suit you much better than it does me.'

Fosseuse was vain enough to accept these compliments in good faith. 'How very generous you are.'

'It is nothing. I too was loved by the King once, but confess I was secretly relieved when the liaison ended. I suffer badly with my health, as you know, headaches and the like, which are most trying. You can be assured that I feel no jealousy at having lost him to you, for you deserve to be loved by a king.'

Fosseuse looked at the older woman, wide-eyed and innocent, believing every false word. 'You are most kind.'

'And you are so young and healthy.' Rebours smiled, stepping back to admire the result of her labours. 'There, you look utterly radiant, as if lit by a glow from within. I might almost suspect that you were … but dear me, no, it is none of my business. Forgive me, I should not have spoken.'

Fosseuse blushed enchantingly, and again instinctively rested a hand on her stomach as she gave a light laugh of delight. 'Oh dear, you have guessed. Is it so obvious? I thought I had disguised my condition so cleverly by loosening my skirts.'

Rebours smiled through gritted teeth, almost faint with the heat of her rage. There was nothing clever about this silly chit. 'Then it is true? You are indeed *enceinte?*'

Fosseuse nodded, looking suddenly shy and afraid. 'It was meant to be a secret.'

'Do not worry, no one but myself has guessed. Does the King know?'

'Oh yes, I could not keep it from Henry. He has promised…'

Rebours was instantly alert. 'What? It is all right, child, your secret is quite safe with me. What has the King promised?'

Fosseuse's lips curled into a complacent smile, preening herself slightly as she smoothed a hand over the tiny mound of her belly.

'It is still a secret, although it will be known soon enough, I dare say, for he has promised to stand by me.'

'My goodness, what can you mean? You surely aren't suggesting that he means to divorce the Queen and marry you?' The fury that roared through Rebours's veins at this news was almost unbearable. This was too much. A bastard child was one thing, being offered a crown quite another entirely. And it could so easily have been herself.

Fosseuse pouted. 'Why should he not? The Queen has not done her duty by him, chooses instead to cavort with her lovers.' The foolish creature did not seem to recognize the irony of this remark. 'Although, I confess I am terrified of telling her. The King refuses to do so, saying it is my responsibility; since I am officially still in her suite.'

Rebours saw her chance and snatched it. 'We return home soon, would you like me to break the news to Her Majesty for you, my dear? She might take it better from one who has been with her longer.'

Tears welled in the young girl's eyes. 'Oh, I should like that above all things. Thank you so much. What a dear friend you are,' and as they embraced, Rebours allowed herself a secret smile of satisfaction. This was the moment she had dreamed of ever since Pau. This was her opportunity for the sweetest revenge.

Margot listened to her lady-in-waiting's tale with sinking heart. She had never liked Rebours, who was a born liar, and it was plain the woman could scarcely hide the delight she felt in informing her of that chit's condition. Margot, however, being the queen she was, held fast to her dignity.

'So, it is true that Mademoiselle Fosseuse is *enceinte*. It does not surprise me. If you take your vessel to the well it will come back full.' There was a small silence, for that had not been true in her own case. Margot saw by the smirk on Rebours's face that she too had recognized the slip.

Margot felt utterly humiliated, filled with resentment that this girl could so easily fall pregnant, while she had tried so long for a child. She could also see that the thoughts of her lady-in-waiting mirrored her own exactly.

*Where then did this leave the Queen of Navarre?*

Rebours continued the tale, her face solemn, while inside she could barely contain her glee. 'Fosseuse has openly boasted to me that the King means to stand by her.'

'Stand by her? In what way?' Dear God, would Henry demand a divorce and actually marry the silly creature? Surely even he could not be so reckless?

'Apparently, she imagines he might marry her.'

This confirmation of her worst fear fell upon Margot's ear like a stone.

'You think my husband might choose a silly young girl over a Daughter of France?'

'It is not my place to surmise what the King means or might choose to do. I repeat only what the *girl* believes. Mayhap she has misunderstood his promises.'

'Or you are misrepresenting them to me. Send her to me at once, Rebours, and remind her to loosen her skirts well to disguise it. We must at all costs avoid a scandal.'

'Your Majesty.' Rebours dipped a curtsey and hurried away, for once content to do the Queen's bidding.

Fosseuse showed no sign of contrition. She stood before Margot, Queen of this small kingdom and wife of the man whose child she carried, smiling with a radiant beauty as she sank into a deep curtsey. For once in her life Margot was consumed with envy. Why had she never quickened with a child? In all these years, and despite several lovers, there had been no sign. Was she barren? Would Henry ultimately put her to one side for that very reason?

'Do you have something to tell me, child?'

'I know not what you mean, Your Majesty'

Margot was finding great difficulty holding on to her patience, even as she smiled kindly upon the girl. 'You have for some time estranged yourself from me, and, I am told, done me many ill offices with the King my husband. Yet the regard I once had for you, and the esteem which I still entertain for your family, makes me wish to help, for I know you are in trouble. I beg you, therefore, not to conceal the truth. It is in both our interests that you are open and honest with me. You are still under my protection, and I would help you as if I were your mother. Is it true that you carry the King's child?'

Fosseuse gave a careless shrug of her pretty shoulders. 'It is true.'

'You are sure?'

'I am certain.'

Margot rose, wishing to avoid the girl's insolent gaze, and walked over to the window. 'Then we must decide what is best to be done.'

'Is that not up to the King?'

Margot would very much like to have slapped her. 'The King will need my support in this, as will you, my dear, if we are to avoid a scandal.'

Suddenly brisk and businesslike Margot returned to her seat, clasping her hands loosely in her lap, rather as her mother the Queen would do when faced with a difficult interview.

'What I propose is this: that I take a brief sojourn from court, ostensibly to avoid the contagious disorder that has broken out in the town. I will go to Mas d'Agenois, a house belonging to the King my husband that is situated in a quiet spot, and you must come with me. We will stay there until you are safely delivered of the child. Meanwhile, the King will go off hunting in some other part of the country. In this way we can put a stop to the scandalous reports which are already rampant about court.'

Fosseuse had been listening to all of this with increasing alarm. The prospect of being confined in a strange house in a remote region with this queen, the wife of her lover, and daughter of Catherine de Medici, filled her with terror. She had heard of the Italian methods, and she had no wish to find herself, and no doubt her child, poisoned and done away with.

'No, no, I will not go! You cannot make me.'

'Would you risk scandal? Do you intend to have your bastard in full sight of the entire court, as if he were a royal child, a future king?'

Fosseuse started, her face a picture of guilt, revealing all too clearly that was exactly what she intended. 'The King will stand by me. He has sworn it. I will not go with you!' And turning on her heel she ran from the room.

Margot remained where she was, in shock for some long minutes. It seemed that on this occasion Rebours had spoken nothing but the truth. The question of marriage must indeed have been discussed between them, and her own future was now in jeopardy.

The court was soon alight with the scandal. Fosseuse begged the King not to send her away, swearing that the Queen had threatened her very life. Seeing her fears, Navarre could not find it in his heart to do so. Besides, how could he live without her? He went instead to his wife.

Never had Margot seen her husband so angry.

'Fosseuse claims you threatened to kill her. How could you be so cruel?'

'What nonsense! The girl is hysterical and exaggerates. I suggested only that she and I spend a little time away from court, somewhere quiet until after the child is born. How else are we to avert scandal?'

'You must have put it badly and frightened her. You can be far too brusque and insensitive at times, Margot, and she is but a sweet, innocent girl.'

'Not quite so innocent,' Margot bitterly remarked.

Henry's face darkened. 'If anyone claims otherwise, or that she is even with child, I will brand them as liars.'

Margot laughed in disbelief. 'You cannot seriously expect to hush this matter up? It is the talk of the court already.'

'I *will* have my way in this matter. I *will not* have it talked about. Do you understand what I am saying, Margot?'

The subject was never again mentioned. In the long months that followed, Navarre blithely went about his business at court as if his mistress's belly was not growing more rotund by the day. Her condition was plain for all to see, yet everyone looked the other way and pretended not to notice.

The pains began just before dawn. The physician brought the news to the King, ordered to do so by Fosseuse herself as she was in a state of terror. Henry, greatly embarrassed, was at a loss to know what to do for the best. He slept in the same room as his wife, although they occupied separate beds, and he could not think how to own up to the reality of something he had so long denied. How had he ever imagined he could get away with this? Henry still nursed a dread of discovery and scandal. On the other hand, without proper assistance there was a very real danger of losing the child, or worse, the mother, whom he adored.

There seemed no help for it but to admit to the truth at last.

Henry drew back the curtains of his wife's bed, and gently woke her.

Margot sat up, rubbing the sleep from her eyes. 'What is it? What has happened?'

'My dear, I have concealed a matter from you which I must now confess. I beg you to forgive me, not to chastise me for never having agreed to discuss it

Fully awake now, Margot sighed. 'Dear, foolish *Enric*. You are referring to Fosseuse's pregnancy, I assume? I cannot think why you have been so coy and obstinate about this matter when the girl's condition was plain to see. But what has occurred now? Has she had the baby?'

'She is in labour at this very moment. Will you

oblige me so far as to rise and go to her? She is very ill. You know how dearly I do love her, and I beg you to comply with my request.'

Humiliating and exasperating though the situation undoubtedly was, Margot did not hesitate. Nor did she rail or upbraid her husband for his foolishness. He was but a man, and therefore always shrank from emotion. Reaching for her *robe de chambre*, she slipped out of bed.

'Out of respect for you, *mon Enric*, I will go to her at once. I will care for her as if she were my own daughter, for your sake. But if you would avoid any further tittle-tattle, get you gone on a hunt, and take all your people with you.'

'Bless you, my love,' he said, kissing his wife on the cheek. And this time he did listen to her wisdom and quickly left the court.

Margot dismissed the chattering maids of honour who were in a flurry of panic and indecision, and moved Fosseuse to a chamber in a quiet part of the palace. She saw that the girl was provided for, with everything necessary for her comfort and the child's safe delivery, including a doctor, the assistance of a good nurse and two ladies-in-waiting to tend her.

The birth seemed to take hours, and all the while Margot paced back and forth, hovering anxiously close by. The screams and cries of Fosseuse were an agony to her, as if she suffered each one herself. She wished the girl no ill. Yet if it were to be a boy... What then? Would she find herself set aside so that her husband could marry this silly chit? The King of Navarre needed a son, an heir to follow him, something which she had failed to provide. Margot strained her ears for any sound of a baby's cry; knowing that this night would seal her fate.

The doctor came to her at last with the news. 'It pleased God that the child should be stillborn. She brought forth a daughter, but she was dead.'

Margot murmured some appropriate remark, which she could never afterwards recall, while relief flooded through her. She was safe. There'd be no divorce. She would not be cast off or sent to a nunnery. They could go on exactly as before.

Margot found Fosseuse in great distress, her lovely face haggard with grief. The girl clung to her, crying, and begging for her help. It was all terribly tragic, and yet the irony of the situation, that she, the spurned wife, should be the one to whom Henry's mistress turned for support, rather appealed to Margot's wicked sense of humour. But this wasn't a moment for triumph, there was still much to be done if scandal and further humiliation was to be averted.

Once her ladies had washed and dressed Fosseuse in a fresh nightgown, Margot saw to it that she was taken back to her own chamber. It was imperative that it appear as if nothing untoward had taken place. Sadly, this proved impossible. News of the night's business was soon circulating around the palace. When the King returned later that afternoon from his hunting expedition, he went at once to his *petite fille*, as always, and found her in floods of tears.

'They are all talking about me. Everyone knows,'

she wailed.

Poor Fosseuse had seen her dreams crumble. With no live son to offer him, her hopes of catching a king were as dust. She also realized that her entire reputation and hopes for marriage of any sort could be equally destroyed if the tittle-tattle were not stopped before it spread too far.

'Everyone is saying that I have borne you a child and something terrible has happened to it. You must stop them from gossiping, Henry. I cannot bear it.'

Never able to deal with a woman in tears, Navarre was distraught and said the first thing that came into his head. 'My love, do not upset yourself. It will be a nine day wonder, and we can try for another baby.'

But Fosseuse was beside herself with agony, almost in hysterics. 'You must demand that the Queen pay me a visit, as she does when any of her maids of honour are ill. Beg her to come to see me, Henry, or my reputation will be in ruins.'

Having been up since before dawn dealing with the night's traumas, Margot was fast asleep in her bed when the King came to her. He was not pleased to see her there. Navarre grieved for the loss of the child, and for the pain Fosseuse had suffered, and took out his disappointment on his wife. He shook her awake with a rough hand.

'What is this? Why are you lying about sleeping when my sweet Fosseuse, one of your own maids of honour if you haven't quite forgotten, is in dire need of your support and favour. I beg you to go to her at once.'

Margot blinked up at him in surprise. 'Go to

91

her? Why? What more can I do for the poor girl? I have done all that you asked.'

'You could spare her from the scandal that is rampaging within the walls of this palace.'

Margot made a little scoffing sound. 'I do not believe you can blame me for the cause of this scandal. That is entirely your own doing. In any case, Henry, to visit her now would only make matters worse. They would point the finger at me, and I too would become the subject of their gossip, as the wronged wife who has failed in her duty to provide an heir for her King. Why would I put myself through such a torture? You ask too much.' There were tears in her eyes but Henry was too angry to notice.

'I asked you to guard her well, instead you stood by while she lost our child.'

'That is a wicked lie. I did all that could be done, provided the girl with the best possible care.'

'It would seem that it was inadequate. My *petite fille* does not deserve to be treated thus.'

'Nor do I. I am your *wife*, your *Queen*. Have I not suffered enough embarrassment from your mistress, at least for one night?'

'Damn you, Margot, you are the most vexing of women. I will never forgive you for this slight.'

From that moment relations between the King and Queen of Navarre reached a new low. They became so cool and distant they were barely speaking to each other.

Night after night Margot lay back on her pillows and quietly wept. She had never objected to her husband taking a mistress, so long as they

92

created no problems for her and she was allowed a similar freedom. Now she felt deeply wounded by his anger. He had showed not the slightest gratitude for her efforts on his behalf, and for that silly creature he so adored. Margot was also missing Champvallon, her own lover, feeling sorely aggrieved and very bored.

In her despair Margot took to re-reading some of her mother's letters. They seemed uncharacteristically affectionate, but then Catherine de Medici had always been better at expressing herself on paper. They were filled with the assurance of a welcome, should her daughter ever choose to pay the French Court a visit. Margot had always resisted, being far too experienced in Catherine's wiles to be taken in by these soft words. And it was, of course, Navarre whom the Queen Mother really wished to lure to the capital so that she could again persuade him to change his religion. She would be forever disappointed in that ambition.

Now it occurred to Margot that there was no reason why she herself should not go for a few months. Her heart stirred at the prospect of seeing Champvallon again. He was with Alençon in Flanders, but would surely return when the battle was won. She reached for her lover's latest letter, read the familiar words for the hundredth time, and came to a swift decision. She would indeed return to the French Court for a short visit. The break would do her good, allow her to see her friends and enjoy the sophistication which was so sadly lacking here in Béarn.

The next day she put her request to her husband, and at first Navarre saw no reason to object. 'So long as you don't expect me to accompany you.'

'I would not ask it. My mother the Queen has often said that she would meet me part way, perhaps at Xaintonge, if you would escort me there. She has even sent me fifteen thousand *écus* for the journey.'

'I dare say that could be arranged.' Henry thought he would secretly welcome some time apart from his over-critical wife.

Margot hid a small smile. 'You realize, of course, that I would take Fosseuse with me.'

'What?'

'She is one of my ladies, after all.'

Navarre was incensed. 'This is all a ploy to take her from me. Go to Paris if you must, but Fosseuse stays here. I insist upon it.'

Margot was gentle now in her triumph, putting a comforting hand on his arm. 'Don't be foolish, Henry. You are not thinking clearly. How could I rightly leave her here with you, creating yet more scandal?'

In the days following, Henry used every possible persuasion to make his wife change her mind. He did all he could to prevent her from leaving, treating her with more kindness than of late in an effort to win her round, reminding her how they used to be such good friends. But Margot resisted all his ploys.

'It is too late to change my plans, *Enric*.' She always used his pet name when she felt sorry for him, and he seemed a pitiful creature now. Yet she knew that within a few weeks of their departure, the memory of his *petite fille* would quickly fade and he'd be attempting to lure some other woman into his bed. Margot had every intention of making it her business to marry the silly chit off to some suitable gentleman, one who considered it an honour to take a king's former mistress. 'I have written to the Queen my mother, who has no doubt already set out on the journey with her customary energy.'

Navarre was obliged to admit defeat. All arrangements were in place, Margot's litter and baggage carts were even now being prepared.

And if Margot should hesitate for even a second over the decision to return to her brother's court, that hotbed of intrigue and malice, one glance at the sullen face of Fosseuse who had taken a fancy to wearing a crown, quickly strengthened her resolve. She was almost thirty years old, and refused to be ousted from her rightful place by some spoiled child.

So it was that in February 1582, the King of Navarre set out to escort his queen to meet her mother, Catherine de Medici, for a visit to Paris, and prepared to bid farewell to his beloved mistress.

## Paris 1582

Margot arrived in Paris in March 1582 and by April she had banished Fosseuse from court. Navarre wrote to her, furiously objecting, but it was the Queen Mother who answered his letter, scolding her son-in-law for treating his wife so ill for the sake of a 'public prostitute'. Margot simply ignored him, too full of excitement and anticipation, as always, when embarking upon a new adventure.

Her heart turned over at first sight of Guise. He seemed thinner, grown a little older since last they met. Had she? She would defy anyone to say so. Yet he was as handsome as ever despite the scar he now bore, his hair as crisp and curled, his shoulders as broad and the power of the man as impressive as ever. He welcomed her with the usual three kisses, light and courteous. The familiar touch of his lips upon her cheeks brought a rush of sweet memories. What fun they'd enjoyed together. What passion! And how he had used to tease her. He smiled into her eyes now in that wonderful way he had, still able to make her feel special.

'So you could not bear to be away from me any longer?'

'Not another minute,' she laughed.

'I do not wonder at it since I am so irresistible.'

For an instant Margot wondered if she should attempt to reignite their affair? Perhaps not, until she was certain of his other interests. Guise may well still be enamoured of de Sauves. Besides, Margot was longing to see Champvallon who, much to her disappointment, was still in Flanders with Alençon. She'd written him scores of heart-rending letters begging him to take care, terrified he might be killed.

She bought a house in Rue Culture Sainte Catherine but stayed at the Louvre while work was being done on it. To her relief the welcome she received from her brother Henri was friendly, at least superficially, although Margot was aware there was a reason behind his kindness. He and the Queen Mother were disappointed that Navarre had not come with her, and wished Margot to write to her husband and persuade him to join her. She elected not to do so, knowing he would not come.

Margot understood Navarre's fears but thought they may well be groundless. The Queen Mother was showing her age and seemed less interested in stirring intrigue than previously, almost mellow by comparison with her younger self. Margot remembered feeling flattered as a young girl when her mother had first allowed her to take part in the Queen's *lever*. She'd been terrified of doing or saying the wrong thing, of displeasing this all-powerful, all-seeing woman who was in equal parts feared and respected throughout the land.

This morning they talked easily together as Catherine drank her coffee and Margot fastened the ribbons of her mother's petticoat about her waist, scenting again that nauseous mix of stale sweat and perfume. The Queen Mother's rheumatism had grown worse and she sighed with relief as she sank on to a stool for a maid to tie on her stockings.

Margot solicitously enquired after her health, but since Catherine de Medici had no patience with ailments, even her own, she was instead regaled with political and family concerns.

'You know that Alençon is not at all well. My hopes for a secure future for France, for seeing the work of a lifetime fulfilled seem to be rapidly fading before my eyes. One son ailing, a daughter apparently barren. There is no sign of a child yet, is there?'

'Dearest Alençon should spend less time on campaigns and more resting at court,' Margot said, preferring not to respond to the more personal part of the question. But her mother was not done yet.

'Even my beloved Henri has turned against me.'

'How so?' Henri was Catherine's favourite, although he had not always responded well to his mother's adoration.

'Come, let us take the air,' the Queen Mother said, leading her daughter out of the royal chambers, where they could talk more freely away from wagging ears. 'Henri relies too much upon his *mignons*, and he too is still without an heir, and likely to remain so. The people mock him and hate him, saying he has bled them dry and left them near to starvation. He has ruined his own health and that of the kingdom by debauchery. Can they not see that he suffers the flaws that beset all my sons?'

All the Valois brothers had suffered from consumption, and some from other afflictions passed down from the sins of their fathers, but Henri had developed many more of his own. Margot gravely nodded, not wishing to remind her mother of the painful losses she had borne, even as she admired her valiant strength.

'If Alençon does not survive,' Catherine was saying as they stepped out into the spring sunshine, flunkies opening doors for them as they passed by, 'I see no alternative but for the succession to pass to Navarre. That would be a political disaster, unless he agrees to take the Mass. I take it my son-in-law is still firm in his beliefs and remains a Huguenot?'

'Let us not speak of such things today,' Margot said, anxious to avoid conflict. Although it was true enough. Navarre would indeed inherit following the demise of her two remaining brothers. And after him came his cousin, Prince de Condé, a widower with one daughter: a man of fierce Huguenot zeal, unpredictable temper, soured by his grievances against the Valois, and the loss of his beloved wife.

'At least with Navarre, assuming I can persuade him to change his religion, it would mean that you, daughter, would be Queen of France. That is something, I dare say.' Queen Catherine almost smiled. 'You would probably make a better job of it than all your brothers.'

'I doubt it will ever happen,' Margot said, thinking of Fosseuse and how the girl would almost certainly have gained herself a crown, had she shown herself capable of producing a son.

'Can we not trust Navarre? I confess I have never entirely understood how his agile brain works.'

Margot burst out laughing. 'Neither do I. He is an enigma, a law unto himself. Full of affable wit and yet...'

'As wily as a fox, playing the fool while he decides which way to wear his coat,' Catherine finished for her. 'Did he not very cleverly escape by first persuading us to think him too stupid to even contemplate it?' Catherine cackled with laughter, always ready to see the funny side. 'Guise is far less

99

complicated. Mayhap I should have let you have him after all.'

'Don't, it is too late now.' There had been a time when Catherine had offered Margot the opportunity for divorce, but to accept would have put her husband's life at risk. Margot did not dislike Henry enough to do that to him. Though Navarre had his faults, she trusted her mother less.

'You do know, do you not, Margot, that your old amour plots against us with Philip of Spain?'

'I cannot think Guise would do such a thing.' Margot diplomatically responded.

'And against you.'

Margot considered this surprising remark but made no reply, not wishing to believe it. They were by now walking in the Tuileries Gardens, a favourite place of the Queen Mother's for private conversation. She led her daughter along a green alley, seeing no irony in the fact it was the very same one where she had plotted the St Bartholomew's Day massacre.

'Henri of Guise is still bristling with resentment over the House of Lorraine being held responsible for the events of that terrible night.' Even Catherine balked at using the word that best described it. 'Consequently, he feels no compunction in stirring rebellion against us.'

She went on to briefly explain how her spies had discovered correspondence between Guise and Philip of Spain, and even the King of Navarre. 'Philip was so impressed with your husband's gallant capture of Cahors, that he has proposed Navarre join the Catholic League. In return he will provide him with an army to overthrow the

House of Valois, otherwise the King of Spain would see to it that Navarre was excluded from the succession on account of his faith.'

Margot listened until she could keep quiet no longer. 'My husband would not be so foolish as to attempt such a reckless venture. He will see that if the Guises are not loyal to their anointed King, nor would they be to him, whether or not he changes his faith, which I very much doubt he would do.'

Unperturbed, Catherine quietly continued, 'Philip has also offered your husband one of his own daughters, were he to divorce you.'

Margot sucked in her breath, attempting to stifle a startled gasp.

'Nor would Guise choose you to share his crown, were he to win the succession in place of Navarre, as the offer would then revert to him.'

Stunned by this news, and afraid suddenly for her own vulnerability if this plot were ever to reach fruition, Margot held her silence. Later, she took her mother's advice and wrote to her husband, warning him that she was aware of his duplicity; and urging him to come to Paris and prove his good faith. Navarre politely declined.

Once it became clear that Navarre wasn't going to obey the royal summons, Henri's peevish jealousy came once more to the fore, fostered by his *mignons*.

He had collected yet more pretty boys to join his nefarious crew, and in place of those killed in a notorious brawl were two new favourites. These became known as Epernon and Joyeuse, once

Henri had bestowed titles upon them. They were less effeminate than the rest, and even more ruthless, jealous and petty than their predecessors. As always, Henri showered them with gifts and benefices. He married Joyeuse off to Queen Louise's sister, and Epernon was granted several bishoprics and made Governor of Guyenne. Even the Queen Mother feared to offend him.

The duc d'Epernon was reckless and bold, with a fondness for practical jokes, and much the favoured courtier. Joyeuse never quite achieved the same power over the King, for all he was more aristocratic, which resulted in a bitter jealousy between the two. They were jealous too of Margot, knowing how Henri had always adored his sister and wished to control her. They saw her as a new rival.

When, in his bid for a crown, Alençon made an attempt to capture the city of Antwerp, the two favourites convinced Henri that Margot was responsible by supporting her younger brother in this latest bid for power. She denied involvement, but was not believed. Alençon's men became trapped and were mercilessly butchered, resulting in yet another disastrous campaign in what became known as the Folly of Antwerp. Guise offered to go to his assistance but the King refused to give his consent. His bitter jealousy over her preference for their younger brother still grated.

Early in 1583, Margot moved into Rue Culture Sainte Catherine and began to keep open house for poets and artists. She held parties, soirees, dancing and feasting, very much as she did at Nérac. Most exciting of all, so far as Margot was concerned, she was again thoroughly involved in a scandalous affair with Champvallon. She was determined to live life in her own way and if she was aware of the risks she took, she gave no sign of it.

She had few friends around her: no Bussy who had once supported her in her ventures, no husband or brother at her side. Alençon was still in Flanders, and failing. Not even Madame de Curton, her dear Lottie, to guide her. Even Guise could no longer be entirely trusted since he pursued his own ambitions for the crown, something she'd always been aware of but was now too dangerous to ignore.

And her anger with Navarre urged Margot to be reckless. She could not forgive him for the Fosseuse incident where he had blamed her for the death of the infant. And now he seemed willing to plot with Philip of Spain in a bid to divorce her. What would happen to her then she dare not even consider. Margot had never been one for discretion but the growing dangers gathering around her made her, if anything, even more rash. She laughed them all off. Life was for living, after all.

Rumours flew about court, instigated and spread by the *mignons*, that she had smuggled her lover into her room in a trunk. True or not, she did permit her beloved Champvallon to visit her regularly, and to lodge at the house with her from time to time. She had been heartbroken a few months earlier when he'd declared his intention of marrying a high-born widow, even if it were only in order to pay his debts. But she forgave him in the end. A marriage was for financial or political reasons, an *affaire* was personal. Theirs continued as normal, in spite of his new wife.

Paris was highly entertained by the goings-on of their royal family.

Such gossip didn't trouble Margot in the slightest, for she was enjoying herself far too much. Perhaps life was too good in the French Court, or she held a few too many parties and sumptuous dinners, for she began to put on a little weight, which led to the inevitable rumour that she was pregnant by her lover.

Margot's old feud with her brother the King now took a far more serious turn. Henri chose an evening when the entire court was present, so that everyone might witness the scene, to accuse her of this transgression.

'I see that you have brought your immoral ways with you,' as if the French Court were a picture of chastity and rectitude.

'I think you must be judging me by your own standards, brother,' Margot sharply rejoined. 'Or else listening to mischief promulgated by my enemies.' She glared at Epernon and Joyeuse, but then wondered if Aubigné was still in correspondence with Henri. It would not be beyond that gentleman to stir up fresh intrigue against her.

'I am reliably informed that you have borne Champvallon a child. You lead a shameful, adulterous life, sister, and the result apparently is an illegitimate son.'

Margot's cheeks burned, fired by a fury she

104

found difficult to contain. 'That is a gross lie!'

'Did you rid yourself of the encumbrance then?'

Turning to her ladies, Mesdames de Duras and Béthune, Henri accused them of being procuresses and abortionists. 'If the tale of my sister's pregnancy is true, and I have no reason to doubt it, then you must have helped her to get rid of the child.'

The ladies gasped in shock at such a charge. Margot was appalled and terrified by this sudden twist in her fortunes, almost thankful that dear Lottie was no longer with her. Would not her governess have fiercely scolded her for bringing this new calamity upon herself?

Henri was in one of his self-righteous moods, heavily involved in street processions, floggings and penitential practices, manically religious, even to the extent of banning all balls and concerts. No doubt he'd objected to the ones she'd regularly held at her own house. Yet his debauchery with his *mignons* continued unabated. And just as he had once insisted she dismiss Thorigny for alleged licentious behaviour, he now ordered Margot to dismiss these two attendants.

Margot had no intention of doing so, nor of admitting that the ladies in question had indeed conspired in her *affaire* with Champvallon, if not to the extent of which they were accused. There had been no baby, no abortion, nothing of that sort at all. They were also high-born and cultured, and Margot stubbornly refused to be parted from them.

'Why are they any less moral than de Sauves?'

she demanded of the Queen Mother.

'Impudent minx! You must dismiss them. I cannot always protect you from the King. He will not take kindly to this obduracy on your part.' The Queen Mother herself had clearly lost patience with her daughter. Margot suspected the friendship she'd been at pains to offer in recent months had all been a sham. Why had she ever trusted her?

Henri had been away during July but when he returned to find his sister still defied him, he was furious. To make matters worse, he received word of an attack on a royal courier, pertaining to the theft of some letters which he'd dispatched to Joyeuse, who was presently in Rome. They contained information concerning the difficulties Henri was experiencing with the Huguenots, and with Navarre. He easily convinced himself of Margot's guilt, always willing to believe the worst of his sister, and who else would have the nerve to steal them? No doubt she thought it her wifely duty to procure them in order to win back a betraying husband. For Henri it was the last straw.

The first Margot learned of this was when a courtier came to her house and presented her with an order banishing her from Paris, the words of the King her brother castigating her for licentious behaviour.

'Am I expected to simply pack up and leave?'

'That would be wise,' she was coolly informed.

'This quarrel is not about my so-called immorality, but my continued support for Alençon.'

The courtier offered no argument to this

assessment, merely told her she was at least more fortunate than her lover. 'The Watch has been sent to arrest Champvallon at his lodgings.'

Margot quickly sent him warning but he must have already heard for he'd fled to Germany. He was safe, but gone from her life. It seemed she had no alternative but to return home to Gascony.

Margot travelled with her ladies in her litter, including the two alleged co-accused, Mesdames Duras and Béthune, all of them deeply distressed at having been so ignominiously dismissed from court. They stopped to dine at Bourg-la-Reine before continuing onwards to the village of Palaiseau, where they were to spend the night. The ladies were about halfway there when they heard the clink of harness and thud of many hooves. Madame Duras turned pale.

'Oh no, the King has sent a party to capture us.'

'Hold fast to your nerves, ladies. They can prove nought against us.'

Seconds later they found themselves surrounded by a large number of archers of the royal guard, under the command of their captain. The curtains of the litter were ripped back, and Margot was presented with an order of arrest signed by Henri.

'Pray alight, Madame. We would search this vehicle.'

Margot was incensed. 'How dare you apprehend us in this callous manner? What is it I'm supposed to have done now?'

'We are but doing our duty, Madame. Pray remove your masks.'

The ladies gasped at such an outrage. All ladies

107

of nobility wore a mask when travelling to spare themselves from being leered at by the more vulgar populace. Even Margot, vain as she was of her beauty, was wearing one today and vehemently protested.

'We will do no such thing.'

The masks were torn from their faces.

'Give up your papers. We know you carry them about your person. You must hand them over in the King's name.'

'We have no papers. Dear God, I know of no princess on earth so miserable and persecuted as myself, excepting perhaps the Queen of Scots.'

'We believe you to be in possession of important dispatches from the King to Rome, which you have stolen. Do not think to hide them from us.'

'I have already told you, we do not possess any such papers, and I would never steal from the King my brother.'

When the coach was found not to contain the letters, the ladies themselves were then subjected to a most scandalous search. Members of the guard went so far as to knock off the ladies' hats, lift their skirts, and even probe beneath their bodices. They squealed and screamed and hotly protested, but the men responded by striking them. Margot furiously objected.

'How dare you abuse my ladies! Begone with you.'

But no one was listening to her. Mesdames Duras and Béthune were arrested, along with Margot's doctor and secretary, and other members of her household. They were escorted to the prison at Montargis. Margot was held under house arrest in a lodging at Palaiseau. Even then her room was invaded during the night by the Captain.

'Am I to be allowed no privacy?' she bitterly complained.

'Hand over the letters and you will be permitted to proceed in peace.'

'Pray then search, for I know of no such documents.'

Margot was obliged to endure the shame and indignity of having her bed stripped and searched, her coffers tipped out and her personal belongings sifted through, but no trace of the stolen dispatches was found.

She calmly addressed the Captain. 'I wish to write letters of my own, to my husband who needs to be told of this outrage, and to the King my brother to complain of this rough handling of a royal princess.'

Suffering from a severe lack of funds she also wrote to the Queen Mother, begging for her help and money.

Within days Margot learned that the ladies and gentlemen of her household had been sent to the Bastille where they were being severely questioned regarding her morals and honour, her daily routine, and the alleged child. Had it indeed been aborted, or given away for adoption following a secret birth?

'Was ever a princess more beset by rumour than I?' she sobbed in her fury.

The poor demented mother of Duras desperately sought to secure her daughter's freedom, but to no avail. It was the Queen Mother, on her return from a visit to her youngest son, whom she'd found to be even more gravely ill of the same lung disease that had carried off his siblings, who finally got the ladies released. Margot remained under house arrest.

Navarre was hunting at Sainte Foix when he received a letter from his brother-in-law, Henri Trois, by a valet of the King's wardrobe, telling him of the plight of his wife and queen. It was dated the fifth of August, dispatched before ever Margot and her ladies had been apprehended in their litter. It gave Henri's version of the tale, plainly stating that having discovered 'the evil and scandalous life led by Madame de Duras and Mademoiselle de Béthune, he had resolved to drive them away from the presence of the Queen of Navarre, as being most pernicious vermin and not to be supported near a princess of such position'.

A second letter was waiting for him when he returned to Nérac, strongly hinting at Margot's guilt. Navarre's first instinct was to refute these charges and defend his wife. He knew how Henri loved to spread malicious gossip about his sister, fired by his own obsessive jealousy. Such emotions had never featured strongly in their marriage, although Margot's pride had sometimes been hurt by his gallivanting. Nevertheless, they'd quickly reached an agreement that neither would be seriously troubled by infidelity, and there was little evidence to prove that Margot was even capable of producing a child.

Yet he hesitated. Members of Henry's own court here in Béarn would be only too eager to see the whore of Babylon, as they called her, disgraced. The pastors wished their king to seek a divorce and find a more fecund wife, one who was not a Catholic.

And a part of him was not against the idea.

Henry had again fallen in love, this time with a young widow, the Countess of Gramont and Guiche. Her name was Diane but she was more familiarly known as La Belle Corisande. In her late twenties with one son, Antoine, Henry thought her the most beautiful woman he'd met in a long time.

She had fair hair and blue eyes, round pink cheeks, and always with a smile for him on her lovely face. Admittedly, she was more mature than his sweet Dayelle, *la petite* Tignonville, and the entrancing Fosseuse, yet all the more exciting for being experienced. Better still she was calm and undemanding, comfortable to be with, and good company. Henry was utterly besotted, and did everything in his power to please her as she so inspired him and, he thought, brought out the best in his nature. He was already making her promises of marriage, this time sanctioned by his ministers. Save perhaps for Aubigné who always disapproved of anything or anyone who brought him pleasure.

But if the chamberlain privately thought this new mistress led his monarch by the nose, he never remonstrated with him to that effect, for which restraint Henry was duly grateful. He knew that Aubigné considered it his mission in life to discreetly steer him on to the straight and narrow path of moral rectitude. Whether he would succeed was another matter, but it would not be for want of trying.

Margot's own letter arrived in due course, and the King of Navarre politely replied saying that if what Henri Trois claimed were true, that she was indeed an adulteress and a whore who had aborted her child, he could not, in all honour, agree to take her back.

On receiving this cool response, Margot instantly flew into a fine temper. What was going on now? Why had her husband suddenly turned against her, choosing to believe Henri Trois, despite knowing how he loved to bring calumnies against her? She railed at her maids and anyone else who cared to listen. Then news of Henry's latest affair was relayed to her not only from Aubigné but other members of the court of Nérac, who seemed to take pleasure in enlightening her. The general opinion was that La Belle Corisande was a much more likely candidate for Queen of Navarre than his *petite fille*.

'Then what am I supposed to do? Go to a nunnery?' The prospect horrified her.

Navarre had at least offered to write to Henri and express his displeasure at the way the matter was dealt with. And while Margot was left kicking her heels with frustration, negotiations dragged on throughout the autumn and winter. Margot felt as if she were between the devil and the deep blue sea, caught between her brother the King, and her husband, with no control over her own fate. In addition, Alençon was now gravely ill and of no help to her, nor indeed was Guise, her beloved *chevalier*. She was more alone than ever before.

Early in December Henri allowed Margot to travel a little further south, and she again wrote to her husband in desperation. Navarre and Corisande were at Mont-de-Marsan early in the new year when correspondence arrived, both from his wife and from Henri Trois, suggesting that Navarre take her back.

'Perhaps that would be wise,' Corisande quietly suggested as they lay in bed together, taking their afternoon siesta as they so liked to do. 'She is, after all, your queen.'

'My love, I could not ask such a thing of you. Why would you welcome a rival for my affection?'

'Are you suggesting that she would be?'

Navarre took her in his arms, smoothing his hands over the curve of her hips, touched and amazed by this generous offer. 'Some may see her as such, but you know that I have pledged my love to you, my darling. I would marry you tomorrow, were I free.'

Corisande smiled, rewarding this declaration with a long, slow kiss, thinking it might well be in her interest to have Margot return home so that the not so small matter of a divorce might be brought to a head. 'I certainly would have no objection, if it pleases you.'

'My love, I am humbled by your devotion and loyalty. Ah, but Margot is ever a troublemaker, a great stirrer of mischief.'

'I am sure I can deal with whatever mischief she

113

chooses to stir. Perhaps she is a reformed woman, following this latest trauma.'

Navarre laughed out loud. 'That I would like to see.'

Excited as she was by the prospect of a crown, Corisande was mindful of not seeming to tell the King what he should do. 'If his sister has become an embarrassment to the King of France, perhaps you might take advantage of the situation, for the sake of Béarn,' she delicately pointed out. 'You could request something in return, the towns he stole from you, for instance.'

Navarre frowned, astute enough to appreciate a bargaining tool when he saw one. 'Perhaps I could.'

He wrote to his brother-in-law, the King of France, saying that if he were to agree to take back his wife, the price would be the return of Protestant strongholds in Gascony, stolen from him in the last war; in particular Agen, Condom and Bazus.

It was not until late February that Henri finally complied with Navarre's demands and withdrew the garrisons from these towns. Only then were the King and Queen of Navarre at last reunited when Navarre came to meet her in Pau to escort her home to Béarn for the final part of the journey.

The reception Margot found in Nérac was decidedly cool. The pastors were not happy to have her back, particularly the chamberlain, Aubigné. Her husband was no more welcoming. Tolerant as Henry may be of her desire to match his own infidelity with adventures of her own, yet she knew that he hated any breath of public scandal. He had never been in love with her. Now that he had Corisande, whom he clearly adored, and who was widely perceived to be his queen in waiting, Margot found that he ignored her completely.

On her first evening back no one spoke to her throughout a lengthy supper. While her husband, his mistress, and the courtiers around them, chatted and laughed together, cracking jokes and enjoying themselves hugely, Margot sat quietly weeping and picking at her food. She had never felt such despair. She was grateful for the dim light in the Long Gallery, despite the many candles burning, and turned her face into the shadows so that no one would see her red eyes.

Her husband cared nothing for her, only for the political advantage he'd gained by accepting her back. And she had few friends left in her entourage, most of her ladies having returned to Paris.

The following weeks and months were a difficult time for Margot, made worse in June when she received word that her beloved younger brother, Alençon, had died. He was thirty years old, and had suffered a haemorrhage. Henry too was sad at the loss, for he'd been fond of the little fellow. The two of them had enjoyed good times together in the past, not least sharing a mistress, de Sauves, even if he had needed to prevent him from stealing Fosseuse as well. Over-ambitious and politically inept, Alençon had never quite achieved the success he craved. Too much the coward, and too easily influenced by those around him. Now he was gone and Henry suddenly realized that the way to the throne of

France was suddenly open to him.

The crown was within sight.

Even Henri Trois and the Queen Mother were forced to accept that the King of Navarre was indeed heir apparent to the throne of France.

But would Margot ever be Queen?

For the first time in her life Margot was fervently praying and wishing she could get pregnant. But in order to achieve this seemingly impossible task, she first had to persuade her husband to sleep with her.

'We must needs provide an heir,' she told him, smiling up at Navarre from beneath her lashes, hoping to win him round. 'Might I hope for a visit soon?'

'Of course, dear wife. I never believed those calumnies against you, and we were ever amiable bedfellows.'

Margot was elated. Surely she was capable of seducing her own husband. If she could only bring him to her bed and quicken with child, all her problems would be solved. Corisande would remain yet another mistress in a long line of such.

Navarre came to her bedchamber readily enough, as promised, and made love with his customary zeal and energy. Margot did all in her power to enchant and please him, and in the morning when he left her, she kissed him and begged him to come again. Perhaps everything would turn out right for her, after all. She had been happy here in Nérac for many years, perhaps she could be again.

Corisande was not at all happy. The King's

*maîtresse en titre* had readily agreed to her rival's return because she was aware that the King still nurtured a certain fondness for his errant wife. She was more than willing to tolerate Margot's presence at court, particularly if the Queen of Navarre caused problems which ultimately led to that much-longed-for divorce. But she was deeply concerned by this marital reunion. Corisande had no wish to see her lover enamoured by his own wife, and such intimacy could have long-reaching repercussions. There was a great deal to play for, not only here in Béarn, but now the crown of France was tantalizingly close.

'How would you know, were she to become *enceinte*, that the child would be yours?' she artfully pointed out. 'The Queen could easily foist her lover's child upon you.'

'The thought had likewise occurred to me too, my dear. Fear not, I am no fool.'

Henry did not visit his wife again. Nevertheless, just to be sure, Corisande set spies to watch her rival, unable to help feeling suspicious and jealous of the Queen of Navarre.

Margot realized that her last hope of becoming pregnant was gone. Despite all the lovers she'd enjoyed, and the false rumours of a pregnancy, it seemed she was never to bear a child of her own. She was indeed barren and would probably remain so. Though it had never troubled her before, in her present circumstances it was a bleak thought, for it left her own future more uncertain than ever.

This was her darkest hour and Margot knew she

could not go on in this manner. She had to get away, if not to Paris, which only mired her in further troubles, then she must seek some other safe haven. She needed to be free to control her own life. But where? And how? As always she sought advice from her dearest friend and love of her life. Taking up pen and paper she wrote to Guise.

Turenne, her former lover and a fierce Protestant, returned to Nérac soon after, and, possibly out of resentment because Margot had once spurned him, he reported to Henry the fact that his wife was corresponding with her erstwhile lover, which must surely be an act of betrayal. The King ordered the arrest of Ferrand, one of Margot's secretaries, and charged him with carrying compromising messages to his rival claimant to the throne.

Not merely a betrayal, but possibly treason, thought Corisande, although she dare not voice the thought out loud.

The first Margot heard of this was when one of her ladies came running to her apartment with the news that her servant had been taken to Pau and put to the question. She went cold with terror.

'Dear God, what nonsense will the poor man confess to if they use the thumbscrews on him, or put him to the rack?' Dark forces seemed to be gathering about her, and she did not know which way to turn for help.

Then one night, as Henry lay in bed with his mistress, he began to vomit. Corisande ran at once to fetch him a basin, holding his head while he retched.

'Oh, my lord, what ails you? Lie still a moment while I send for your physician.'

'I'm sure there is no need. I've been a little off colour all day. No doubt the mussels we ate at dinner were not as fresh as they might be.'

'Or something far more sinister,' Corisande said, once she had sent the maids scurrying for help.

Henry paled. 'You cannot mean...'

'You forget that your wife is a daughter of Catherine de Medici. Queen Margot must know a good deal about the *morceau italianizé*. She writes to her lover, your rival for the throne and leader of the League. Guise is the darling of Paris, would she not snatch at any opportunity to clear the way to the throne for him? This is no time to be generous, my love.'

Navarre was easily persuaded that Margot had ordered Ferrand to poison him.

But not for one moment did Margot believe that this tale, a complete fabrication, had been wrung as a confession out of her loyal servant, despite the torture he'd endured. Those in a position to know these things had assured her that the fellow had said not one word against her. Nevertheless, she began to shiver with dread. Her husband's court was no longer a safe place to be. She was of no further use to him, either as a wife and queen, or as a political pawn. Not unnaturally he believed that as Guise's former mistress, and a Catholic herself, she would take her lover's side in any battle for the crown.

She was right. They came for her at dawn to arrest her and take her to a cell.

Fear cascaded through her. 'What way is this to

treat a queen?' She couldn't help but think of the beautiful Mary Queen of Scots, held prisoner for years in England, and the hairs on the back of her neck prickled, as if sensing the danger that gathered about her too.

Margot demanded an audience with the King, relieved to see that he looked somewhat shamefaced. 'This is a trumped up charge, and you know it full well. This is all about my letters to Guise, which are perfectly innocent. Had I realized you were so interested in my affairs, I would have shown them to you before I sent them.'

For once, her brother Henri and the Queen Mother supported her, if not out of affection then out of indignation that her royal personage should be so accused. Aubigné also believed the rumour was likely to be false, although the Queen may well be acting against the King by writing to Guise. The matter was indeed delicate.

Navarre said, 'I concede that I too believe my wife incapable of such calumny as treason. Why take my life now when she has saved my head more than once in the past? Mayhap I acted in haste.' More importantly, Navarre had no wish to offend the King of France.

The charges were dropped, Ferrand set free and Margot was released.

'I am weary of our squabbles, *Enric,*' Margot told him some days later, her tone soft and pleading. 'I feel we need a break from each other and I beg your leave to go on a pilgrimage to Agen for Lent.'

Henry, pleased by the notion of forty days and forty nights without conflict and confrontations

120

with his troublesome wife, days and nights in which he would be free to enjoy La Belle Corisande in peace, readily agreed.

So it was that on 19 March, 1585, Margot left Nérac for the last time.

Margot was thankful to escape Nérac, despite her happy years there. She took with her only a few of her ladies and gentlemen-in-waiting, not wishing to arouse her husband's suspicions. Once clear of the town she quickly declared herself for the League, raised her banners, and called on all Catholics to join her.

Finding herself arrested simply for writing letters to Guise had unnerved her, and she was deeply troubled. Her marriage had been beset with difficulties from the start. In addition to their religious differences, she'd considered Navarre a country bumpkin, and he'd never been impressed by her painted court beauty. But they'd always remained good friends, even lovers. Now that comradeship, the trust that had once existed between them, was at an end and they were estranged. Margot feared her husband may at any moment pack her off to a nunnery, and procure a divorce to allow him to marry La Belle Corisande.

But if he thought she would meekly step back and allow that to happen, then he was sorely mistaken. She would fight to her last breath.

By the time Margot took up quarters in Agen she had a sizeable following. She was given a fine house that had previously belonged to a prosperous widow, for her own personal use. The loyal citizens gladly agreed to hand over the keys of the city as Agen was Catholic, in her appanage, and she was their countess. They were also willing to bar the King of Navarre, as he had attempted to occupy the city in 1577. They were proud to have a Daughter of France as their sovereign lord, and as Margot had previously donated large sums to the upkeep of their religious buildings, hoped for more of the same.

But funds were dangerously low and Margot again found herself financially embarrassed.

She had no wish to return to Paris, having suffered sufficient ignominy at her brother's hand. Nor did she believe that he would help her, although she had at last left her husband and Henri would surely welcome the return of Agen into French hands. Margot wrote to her mother but expected little by way of support. Catherine had ever favoured Henri, her beloved favourite. She also blamed Margot entirely for the scandal over rumours of the child she had supposedly borne Champvallon, whether or not it were true, accusing her of being a wanton. The Queen Mother had banished her alleged co-conspirators, Madame Duras and Mademoiselle Béthune, from royal service, and in their place had sent her daughter, the unimpeachable and dull Madame Noailles.

Margot had even less hope that Navarre would continue to pay her an allowance, not once he learned that she had no intention of granting him a divorce.

In a spirit of defiance she wrote again to Guise, seeking his protection as she had no money of her own, and offering him her full support in his battle for the crown.

'Send me men to fight and I will give you Agen and as much of the surrounding area I can lay my hands on.'

But the messenger she dispatched was waylaid and copies of her letters were intercepted and shown to Henri Trois. When he discovered that his sister had again allied herself with Guise and the League against the Valois throne, his simmering hostility towards her reached danger point.

War had again broken out in France with Guise, the hero of Paris, in complete control of the Catholic League. They demanded the repeal of concessions made to the Huguenots but Henri refused, fearing his crown might be snatched from him at any moment. The Queen Mother had been in the process of attempting a reconciliation between her son and the League, now, yet again, her efforts had been spoiled by a wayward daughter. She was furious.

'God has left me this creature as a punishment for my sins and a scourge.'

Navarre was ready enough to go to war but highly amused when he heard that Joyeuse, one of Henri's pretty boys, was leading the army that headed south against him.

'Does he imagine that I will run from the scent of his perfume, or shake in my boots when confronted by a fop in a high collar and painted face?' Henry joked, roaring with laughter.

Corisande viewed the matter far more seriously, so seriously in fact that she sold many of her jewels in order to help finance the Huguenot army.

'See how she supports me,' Navarre said to Aubigné. 'Would that she could be my wife in truth, instead of simply in spirit and in my heart.'

Aubigné was alarmed. Much as he disliked Queen Margot, at least she was royal, the daughter of one king and sister of another; a Princess of the Blood. But La Belle Corisande was nothing but a commoner, a courtesan. There were rumours that the woman had enjoyed affairs during her marriage to the Count of Gramont, that her son could not be certain of his parentage. Aubigné wisely did not express any of these concerns to his sovereign, even as he privately prayed that Margot would return home to Nérac and perform her role of queen with more dignity. Instead he tried a more diplomatic approach.

'If, in two years you feel the same way about the lady, and her loyalty remains without question, then I shall do all in my power to support you in that mission.'

'Two years?' Henry was appalled by the prospect of waiting so long. 'A great deal can happen in two years.'

'Indeed, Sire. But in the meantime we must apply all our energies to fighting this war. Your responsibility to your people must be paramount. And there is at stake far more than our own small kingdom.'

Henry, being the good natured, reasonable fellow that he was saw the sense in this argument, slapped his chamberlain on the back and agreed. 'So be it, good fellow. I will wait two years before seeking to marry my Corisande.'

Aubigné sighed with relief. As his monarch had

said, a great deal could happen in two years.

As always, Margot attracted fierce loyalty among her followers, and many were more than a little in love with her. One was Lignerac, a tough, wily soldier in charge of the defence of the city, and the other a young captain called Aubiac. Margot disliked Lignerac intensely, whom she suspected of spying on her, but the young and handsome Aubiac with his red hair and freckles and cheerful countenance she readily took to her bed, if not her heart.

She had always been most particular about her lovers, but here in Agen there were few courtiers or gentlemen, only military men with little in the way of airs and graces, and certainly no poetry in their soul. But then she had no wish to fall in love again. Guise remained the love of her life, and since she could not have him, she had sought love and passion elsewhere. Champvallon had been her *coup de foudre*. Now that relationship too was over Margot had no intention of seeking another to replace him. Yet she was woman enough to need love of some sort in her life, a man to adore her, to satisfy her sexual desires. Margot saw no reason to deny herself, or suppress these needs which she considered entirely normal.

But with both husband and brother conspiring against her, she felt vulnerable and close to panic. How could she, a woman alone, defend herself? She made a desperate attempt to improve the fortifications of the town, overseen by Lignerac, and paid for by Guise.

By 1585 Margot was so desperate for funds, and

fearful of invasion from either husband or brother, that she conscripted peasants and beggars to assist with the building works, even though there was no money to pay their wages, or even bread to feed them. She was rapidly losing the goodwill of the people who were beginning to resent the taxes she imposed upon them. The unpaid soldiers, many of them mercenaries rather than genuine believers in the Catholic cause, began looting and committing atrocities against the few Huguenots in the city. To make matters worse, the city was struck by plague.

Navarre had come to enjoy soldiering, although not quite as much as making love. Just seeing the love and pride in his mistress's blue eyes when he'd ridden off to battle had stirred his loins as well as warmed his heart. He wanted to justify her belief in him, to prove himself worthy of her love.

With him rode Condé, his cousin, who had been at his side in battle ever since his mother Jeanne d'Albret had stood the pair of them before the Huguenot army and had pledged their lives to the cause. The pair of them had suffered much together, not least being held captive at the Louvre and almost losing their heads, until Navarre had persuaded his sternly Protestant cousin to take the Mass.

'So here we are again, Cos, riding side by side into battle. No mincing *mignon* will win any victory over us,' he cried. 'We are invincible.'

And as they rode, the men's voices singing their psalms, ringing out in the autumn air, fired everyone with new courage. The Béarnais were fierce opponents and, as expected, Joyeuse was killed in battle and Navarre was the victor, with scarcely any loss of men. This was the moment to advance and capitalize on that victory while the French army was in ribbons. Instead, Henry gathered the enemy standards and banners he had captured and rode back to Nérac to present them to his darling Corisande. He needed to see her again, and to show her what a fine soldier he was.

'This is no time for dallying with a woman,' Condé protested.

'Where is the harm in it? My men will fight all the better for a few days' rest.'

Condé's own marriage was even less happy than his cousin's. Nor did he have the consolation of a mistress waiting for him back in Nérac. While Navarre made love, Condé relaxed by playing tennis and backgammon with his men.

But the following morning one of his servants came running to the King's apartment with terrible news.

'My master is ill, Sire. He is in great pain and calls for you.'

By the time Henry reached his cousin's bed-chamber, Condé was dead. Stunned, shocked by his sudden death, Henry grieved for his cousin. Condé had been a man of great integrity who would willingly have surrendered his life for his beliefs. Taciturn and rigid in his morals, yet he had ever been a loyal and dear friend and was but a year older than himself. Far too young to die. Yesterday he'd been healthy enough to play a vigorous game of tennis, now he was gone. How short life suddenly seemed.

But Navarre feared Condé's death was no accident, that there were Catholic spies in his household. When his physician agreed, by expressing the opinion that the King's cousin may well have been poisoned, Henry took his revenge by sending Condé's Catholic wife, Charlotte de Trémoille, to prison, charged with her husband's murder.

The death of his cousin changed Navarre. He became markedly more sober, and fervent in the cause. He believed he may well be the next target and wrote to Corisande from the battlefield saying, 'I am now the only target of the perfidy of the masses. They poisoned him, the traitors! But may God remain the master, and I, by His grace, the executor of His will.'

In another he said, 'The devil is let loose, I am to be pitied, and it is a marvel that I do not succumb under the burden... Love me, my All. Your good grace is my mind's stay under the shock of affliction. Refuse me not that support.'

Corisande sat weeping over these letters, kissing each one as she reread them time and time again.

'Never, my love. I will ever love you and be yours forever,' she wrote in reply, even as she wondered if her beloved could ever be as faithful.

Almost two thousand died in the plague in Agen, and those who survived the scourge were dying of starvation, the soldiers undisciplined, plundering and looting in lieu of pay.

One evening, Lignerac came to her in a panic. 'Madame, you must leave. The citizens have run out of patience and are marching upon the house, bearing torches. The mob will be here at any moment, you must flee for your life.'

Margot leapt to her feet, wide-eyed with terror. 'Why? What have I done to deserve this?'

'They are starving, and near bankrupt.'

Too late Margot realized that she'd driven them too hard. She had time enough only to grab her cloak and a few of her treasures before Lignerac let her out through the city gates. 'I will stay behind to cover your retreat. Know that I love you, and will join you as soon as I am able.'

Margot did not love him, but gratefully accepted his homage and help. With Aubiac beside her, they mounted their horses and fled into the night, a small party of her closest friends and supporters riding with them.

For days they rode rough-shod across country, and Margot soon abandoned the side-saddle in order to make faster progress, although she suffered sore thighs as a result. They were pursued by a rapscallion band of brigands and peasants from the city, and by men sent by her brother, the King of France, as well as a detachment of Navarre's Huguenots.

'Does everyone want a piece of me?' she sobbed as she attempted to find rest in Carlat, an ancient fortified stronghold. It was cold, damp and, with the approach of winter, not a comfortable place to be, although at least the bad weather meant that her enemies withdrew.

She sent for her furniture, her trunks of linen and personal possessions, which were brought to her in December, along with her gilded coach. But the months of hardship since leaving Nérac had taken their toll and she fell ill with pneumonia. For days Margot was in a high fever, and for weeks after that lay sick in her bed, nursed by the local apothecary's son. He devotedly cared for her day and night, scarcely leaving her bedside. Only when spring came with its better weather did her health improve, and she warmly thanked the boy for saving her life.

Letters came from her mother saying Margot would be welcome to go to Chenonceaux to assist her recovery, and that the King her brother was willing to offer some financial assistance. It seemed he had forgiven her, as was his way. Life was suddenly starting to look much brighter.

And then Lignerac arrived and walked unbidden into her chamber. On seeing the apothecary's son close by her bed, without uttering a single word he ran the boy through with his sword in a frenzy of jealousy.

Margot screamed as blood spattered over her nightgown, just as it had done on the eve of the St Bartholomew massacre, at what became known as the blood red wedding. 'What have you *done?*'

'I saw him as a threat to your safety.'

'He was my *saviour!*'

Margot railed at him in sorrow and grief until she fell back on her bed exhausted. Why was it that men so often lost their senses for love of her?

When word of this latest scandal reached the Queen Mother's ears, all invitations and moves towards forgiveness were withdrawn. Her daughter, Catherine decided, was quite beyond the pale.

Lignerac realized that he had slain the wrong

person. It was not the apothecary's son Margot was sleeping with, but Aubiac, and threatened to throw his rival over the cliff.

Margot knew then that she was lost, that she had fallen completely into Lignerac's power. She was not in love with Aubiac, but cared for the red-haired, freckle-faced young man who had been so generous with his affections, and so loyal.

'I pray you let him alone. Do not allow your jealousy to drive you to such a terrible act. He means nothing to me, but he is a good man. Let him live, I beg you.'

'You lie. He must mean a good deal to you, if you plead so passionately for his life.'

'He is my friend.'

'He is your lover. Why would you choose him and not me?'

Margot dare give no answer to this, and in desperation offered rings and jewels in return for his life, and in the end a price was agreed, a high one, but she cared nothing for the cost. She would pay whatever was necessary to save him.

Lignerac took her jewels and agreed they may leave Carlat. He even escorted them for the first few miles of their journey, content to exchange the dream of loving a queen for a fortune in gold and gems.

Margot and her small loyal band crossed precipitous mountains, forded raging rivers, and frequently got lost riding through thick forests, When she grew too weary she would ride pillion behind Aubiac. They'd taken only horses and a few pack mules as she dare not risk travelling in

131

her gilded litter. Margot felt obliged to avoid all roads and major tracks in case she was still being pursued by her enemies.

Sometimes she would seek refuge in one or other of Catherine's castles, or a friendly chateau where she would be allowed a few days' respite, or even a few weeks. But she dare not pause for too long. Margot had no idea where she was going or what she was seeking, save a desire for peace and safety. And all the time she kept constantly looking back over her shoulder, fearing capture, knowing she was being chased across country with her very life in peril.

She'd written letters of defiance to the French Court but the response had been a troop of Swiss Guards. Not only her brother's men but her husband's too pursued her. The two kings did not join the chase themselves, too caught up in a war which had become known as the War of the Three Henries: Henri Trois, Henry of Navarre, and Henri de Guise. Another chapter in the endless wars over religion and power. A never-ending game in which Margot, as ever, was the pawn.

To his credit, Navarre never issued any physical threats against her, and she knew he would not sanction any such action on the part of the King of France. But Margot was also aware that he had as much control over Henri as did she.

It was not a comforting thought.

The journey was long and perilous through increasingly wild country, with much jolting and bumping and slithering down steep slopes, and teetering along narrow high ridges. If sometimes she wept, no one could blame her. She was a queen, but one fleeing like a refugee from scandal and murder, surrounded by spies set to watch and control her.

Margot's luck ran out at Ibois where she was captured in November 1586 by the Marquis of Canillac who had served with Joyeuse. Margot was at her wits' end and tried to effect Aubiac's escape by dressing him as a woman. When that didn't work she hid him, but Canillac swore to take the place apart stone by stone and kill everyone in it, if she did not hand her lover over. In tears, Margot had no choice but to obey.

Canillac took his prisoners to the Castle of Usson, and Margot's heart sank at sight of this dark, dour stronghold where even the sun struggled to gain admittance.

Guarded by fifty Swiss Guards she was held prisoner; miserable, afraid and alone, save for Aubiac. Once, the young man with the cheerful, freckled face and red hair had cried, 'Let me be hanged if I might only once sleep with that woman.'

A wish that now came back to haunt him.

Instructions came from the King of France that her lover was to meet just such an end in the courtyard of the castle, with his sister forced to watch. Margot was distraught. Fleeing from such a fortress as Usson was impossible. They were trapped, with no hope of escape.

Henri, however, thought better of the plan. To publicly hang his sister's lover would be an acknowledgement of her adultery, thereby providing Navarre with the grounds he needed for divorce. Once free he would quickly find himself

133

a new bride, perhaps even the Infanta of Spain. The charge was quickly changed to one of alleged poisoning of de Marzé, the King's commander at Carlat who had recently died.

Aubiac was taken to Aigueperse, the main town of the Dauphiné d'Auvergne, and was indeed hanged, but by his heels, which prolonged his death considerably. They had him in his grave before even he'd stopped breathing, clutching the little muff that Margot had given him. Like those before him, he'd paid dear for giving his heart to a Daughter of France.

# Part Two

# HENRI DE GUISE

## May 1588

Guise walked through the streets of Paris with his usual arrogant swagger, the scar that marked his handsome face covered by a swathe of dark cloak, the tight cap of curls, greying at the temples in this his thirty-eighth year, hidden beneath his usual plumed hat. Only the eyes were visible, gleaming still with youthful vigour. Yet try as he might to lose himself in the crowds, none were unaware of his identity.

The cries went up as he strode amongst them. *'Vive Guise!'*

Pretty ladies took off their masks to smile at him. People tried to touch the hem of his cloak, kiss his shadow as he passed by, throw flowers upon him or press their rosaries into his hand as a blessing. One dared to pull aside his cloak and cry 'Monseigneur, show yourself to us!'

Their attentions didn't trouble Guise, nor did he hesitate to shake the hand held out to him by a beggar, although it was coated in filth. He knew he owed his status to the people, and accepted their love with gratitude. Today, however, he did not linger to bask in their approbation for he had but one object on his mind, and that was to see the Queen Mother. He had come to Paris without the King's consent and if he valued his skin, he must hasten to make his plea before Henri learned of his presence in the city.

Ever since the death of Alençon, the balance of power had shifted. Would the heir to the throne be a Protestant or a Catholic? That was the question. Navarre had been excommunicated and disinherited, his wife, the beautiful Margot, now held prisoner in uneasy exile. Queen Catherine had a fancy to put the late Princess Claude's child, her grandson, on the throne. Guise himself, with his rag-taggle of followers, his shopkeepers and adventurers, might pretend to support his old uncle, Cardinal de Bourbon, while secretly hoping that the moment he had long waited had almost come. Even the Queen Mother herself had warmed a little towards him, become almost fascinated by him as Guise had attempted to make himself agreeable to her.

Yet as head of the Catholic League he remained at odds with the King. The League was made up largely of nobles and Jesuits wishing to uphold the pure tenets of the Catholic faith. But under the pretence of religion, it fought chiefly for power. The noblesse had turned against a weak and profligate king, even criticized the Pope, but there was little unity amongst themselves, and they were dependent upon Spain for resources and extra manpower.

Guise, who made no claims to be either a radical or a reformer, was a man who preferred to work for himself.

He hurried to the Hotel de Soissons where he knew the Queen Mother was staying, his gaze piercing every shadowed corner as he strode along, constantly on the alert despite his studied confidence. She was not expecting him, didn't even know he was in Paris as the King had banned him from entering the city.

He recognized her dwarf first, watching him from a window, and waved to the little fellow in a jocular, friendly fashion. No harm in giving every sign of assurance, despite a vague sense of unease souring his gut.

When he was shown into the Queen Mother's presence he saw at once that his unexpected arrival had startled and unsettled her. Did she imagine he would present a danger to her? Even the poor dwarf cowered in a corner, as if Catherine had already lashed out her fury on him. But then tensions were high, nerves strung out.

'Your Majesty.' Guise bowed low, kissed her hand, and in those few moments of greeting she had time to collect herself and some colour bled back into her pale cheeks. He apologized for not warning her of his intended visit, but explained how he needed her influence with the King. 'The League asks for His Majesty to listen to their counsels, Madame.'

'I cannot speak for the King.'

'I hoped you might support us in this.'

'You must ask him yourself.'

Catherine took him to the Louvre, carried in her chair while the Duke of Guise walked alongside. They made an incongruous pair, but, despite their differences, the Queen Mother was not immune to his charm. She had ever held Guise in respect and bore some affection for him, as she had known him since he was a boy. Nevertheless, she took the precaution of sending word ahead to her son.

139

Henri was in his privy closet when his mother's message was delivered, and was instantly beset with fury and fear in equal measure. At least twice in recent years Guise had sought to rob him of his crown, thankfully without success. But the League continued to create dispute and intrigue at every turn, which was the reason he had instructed Guise not to come to Paris.

'If you were in my place and had given such an order, which he has ignored,' he asked of the courtier by his side, 'what would you do?'

'Sire, I would ask if you hold Monsieur de Guise to be your friend or your enemy?'

When Henri did not at once reply, the man smirked. 'If you will honour me by giving me this charge, I will, without causing you any further trouble, this day lay his head at your feet. I pledge my life and honour upon it.'

Henri was still considering whether to accept the offer when Guise entered.

'Why have you come?' he barked, as his rival made a low bow.

'Sire, I–'

Henri did not allow him to finish before snapping at him again. 'If you think to repeat your request for the Inquisition in France, as your sponsor Philip of Spain demands, be assured you waste your time and mine.'

Guise was no great advocate of the Inquisition, but was willing to tolerate a modified form of it while he still needed the money and assistance of Philip of Spain. 'You did half promise such in the past, Your Majesty,' he quietly reminded Henri, knowing that even at the time he'd been aware

140

the King had lied. He'd gathered his armies about him while pretending to concede to the League's demands.

Now he said, 'The League is too extreme in its views.' And this from a man who had joined the brotherhood of the *battus* who indulged in ascetic extravagances. They wore sackcloth and masks, walked barefoot in torchlight processions, and thrashed themselves with a whip or switch.

'I believe that the Huguenots have been granted too many concessions. I would hope that at least you would agree that none should hold office. The League also demands the gift of ecclesiastical and certain other appointments.'

'To add to their own power.'

This, at least, was true, although on his life Guise would never admit as much. 'Sire, you misjudge us. We think only of the good of the kingdom.'

With an impatient flick of his hand Henri silenced his protest and pointedly turned his back, making his royal displeasure very plain. In that moment Guise recognized his own vulnerability and felt his knees almost buckle. He'd somewhat rashly come alone, bringing none of his men with him, and the silence gathering about him now was ominous.

Had he walked into a death trap?

It was the Queen Mother who saved him. Leading her son to the window, she had him look down into the courtyard below where the people of Paris were gathering, dogging their hero's footsteps as they so liked to do. Henri saw that much as he might wish for the death of his rival, were he to lay a finger on this man they worshipped like a god, they would rise against him. It was a risk he dare not take. Not until he'd made sure of his own safety first.

Days later, Guise accompanied His Majesty to Mass, this time taking the precaution of bringing four hundred of his men to attend him, all of them with daggers hidden beneath their cloaks. But this show of force instantly alarmed the King and recklessly he called out the Swiss Guards as protection.

Catherine was appalled. 'No, my son. I counsel you against such action. The people will think you have turned hostile to them.'

Her fears were proved justified as word flew about the city that another massacre was about to take place, that the Swiss meant to kill the chief Catholics and pillage the city. It was a political blunder of massive proportions, for memories were long and no one had forgotten that other bloody massacre.

As one, the people of Paris turned against their king.

The revolution began with the students as they set up barricades at the end of each street. Heavy wooden beams, barrels filled with earth and sand, logs and flagstones torn from the cloisters and courts of adjacent colleges and churches were stacked high. By nine o'clock every barricade was defended by men armed with muskets, swords or clubs, ready to take on the 'foreigners' who dared to threaten them. Chains were stretched across street openings, and all the while the great bell of the parish church of St Martin tolled a doleful prediction of what might follow.

Guise quietly watched events unfold from the safety of his home, the Hôtel de Guise, feigning ignorance of what was going on, smiling to himself as he saw how the King's troops became hemmed in and trapped in the narrow streets between the barricades erected by the angry populace.

There was panic in the Louvre. The King was sending out conflicting and confusing orders, refusing all advice to order a retreat.

'I *will* be obeyed. I will show that I, the King, am master and lord over these rebel Parisians!'

But his courage quickly evaporated and Henri was soon cowering in his bedchamber, dreadfully afraid, calling for Guise 'to spare the blood of the Catholics and rescue the soldiers from a bloody end'.

'Show yourself to the people, ride through the city to prove you are with them.'

He sent Biron with his troops instead. Pelted with stones and other missiles they quickly retreated, but many remained trapped. Biron managed to return to the Louvre to warn the Queen Mother how his men had been quickly disarmed and were being forced to kneel ignominiously before their captors.

Catherine wept. 'How can Catholic turn upon Catholic? It is unthinkable.'

Queen Louise fainted and had to be carried to her chamber, and Catherine made up her mind to act. She certainly could not stand by and do nothing while her son quivered, and Paris was lost.

She visited Guise and begged him to call the

people off. 'Pray, put out the fire you have lighted.'

At first he demurred. 'How can I restrain the people? It is not my doing. They are infuriated by misgovernment and the follies of their sovereign.'

'What will be gained by yet more slaughter?'

Believing he could win this battle without bloodshed, Guise eventually agreed to do what he could. He walked into the city unarmed, accompanied by only two pages, and called an end to the siege in what would forever be known as the *Journée des Barricades*. He took off his great plumed hat and waved it at the people.

'My friends, that is enough! I beg you now to shout *"Vive le roi!"*'

The very sound of his voice quieted them, and some knelt in the mud in adoration at his feet. In that moment Guise held Paris in the palm of his hands. He believed too that he controlled the King. Should he choose to do so he could invade the Louvre and kill Henri, then declare himself King of France. But Guise was neither a fanatic nor a cold-blooded murderer, and had no wish to lose prestige by engaging in such a blatant act of regicide. It would be certain to alienate the people against him. So he did nothing.

It was his first mistake.

Determined to prove that the King presented no threat to the people, Catherine recklessly persuaded Henri to dismiss the extra troops from the palace. But the result was that the students from the Jesuit colleges, urged on by Guise's sister, Madame de Montpensier, the Fury of the League, barricaded the doors of the Louvre.

Henri was now a virtual prisoner in his own palace.

'Now look what you've done,' he screamed at his mother, as if it had been she who had first created this crisis, and not himself.

Every door was blocked, save one at the rear, perhaps deliberately so, and it was through this that he made his escape. He left in a panic, without boots or spurs, and still wearing his heavy court clothes. The King of France mounted his horse and fled from his capital.

When the news reached him, Guise told Catherine, 'Madame, I am dead! Whilst Your Majesty keeps me occupied here the King leaves, to my perdition.'

Even the Queen Mother recognized that her son had kept his crown, but lost all authority.

Guise considered his options, one of which was to continue with the battle and take all of France, but for that he would need more resources, money and men provided by Philip of Spain, who was currently stretched to the limit as he struggled to hold on to the Low Countries as well as prepare a great Armada with which to invade England. Guise decided to wait for that mission to be successfully accomplished before risking anything further. It was his second, and fatal mistake.

Margot rose from her bed that morning woken as usual by Madame de Noailles, her first lady of the bedchamber, completely oblivious of what was taking place in Paris. The sun slanted its rays over the mountains of the Auvergne, struggling to penetrate the impregnable fortress that now

145

represented the extent of her kingdom.

'I shall ride out later,' she told Madame de Noailles, 'once I have broken my fast.'

But first, as she did every morning, she spoke with her Captain of the Guard. In February of the previous year her former sister-in-law, the beautiful Mary, Queen of Scots, had been beheaded on the orders of the English Queen. This abomination against a royal personage had taught Margot never to relax her own vigilance.

'The provisioning has been completed, Madame, sufficient to sustain us for two years if necessary,' the captain informed her, and Margot smiled, nodding with satisfaction.

'It is better to err on the side of caution.'

'Indeed. Though the castle boasts twenty watchtowers, your brother the King could launch an attack at any time.'

'If he does, then we will be ready for him, eh?'

'We will indeed, Madame.'

As luck would have it, her captor Canillac had turned out to be a relative of her much-loved governess, Madame de Curton. With no hope of making an escape, Margot had instantly marshalled all her considerable charm.

She'd begun by presenting the Marchioness with compliments and gifts, flattering the woman into believing she too could be a fine court lady. She had then turned her attention upon the Marquis himself, who, like all middle-aged men, was like wax in the hands of a beautiful woman. Margot would cast him languishing glances from beneath her eyelashes, making him tremble with desire. Not even she would take this fat old man

146

to her bed, but her allure did not fail to work its magic.

The fact that he was a diplomat rather than a soldier, and that Henri had failed to reward him as promised, meant that Canillac was more than willing to switch his allegiance to Guise.

Margot's erstwhile lover had responded, as always, to her request for assistance, by supplying her with troops loyal to Margot heart and soul. They had quickly replaced the garrison of Swiss Guard, and Canillac had joined the forces of the League under the command of Guise's brother, the Duke of Mayenne. In but a few short months Margot was no longer a prisoner. She was the one in command of Usson.

But she was still short of money. Her brother had confiscated much of her property and possessions, paying off only those debts he considered reasonable. So it gave her great pleasure to demand the return of those gifts of jewels and gowns she had presented to the Marchioness and dismiss her, much to that lady's chagrin.

Now, a year later, she was more than content in her fastness, finding a freedom in this stronghold she had never known before, and had no intention of surrendering.

'We must be ever vigilant,' she told her captain. 'I shall be in the library later, about my studies. Pray do not hesitate to call upon me, if there is news.'

'Madame.' Sketching a bow, the Captain took his leave while Margot strode away to enjoy her morning ride.

She was not expecting any news, rather hoped

not to have any, as it rarely proved to be good. Never would the adventure-loving Margot have imagined herself actually welcoming the lack of conflict and intrigue, and treasuring the peace she'd found here. She thought of Usson as her Ark of Refuge, a place in which she felt reasonably safe from the machinations of politics, and any threat to her life. She was as secure as her loyal Captain of the Guard could possibly make her, and could only pray that this happy state of affairs would continue.

Corisande lay alone in her bed reading letters from the King, her lover, as she so liked to do. She missed him dreadfully when he was away at war, but he was so generous to her, so kind and loving, forever sending her gifts that she never complained. Reaching for a sweetmeat, which she ate to console herself during these long, lonely nights, she picked up another letter, smiling fondly as she read the loving words.

'I am on the point of acquiring for you a horse, the handsomest and best you ever saw, with large aigrette plumes.' The horse had duly arrived, and a very fine animal he had proved to be, followed by fawns, a dog and various other gifts that Henry thought might amuse her. He was ever thoughtful and constantly expressing his love.

'Your slave adores you to distraction. I kiss thy hands a million times. I read your letter every evening. If I love it, how much more must I love her from whom it comes.'

And he frequently declared his undying faithfulness. 'Be always sure of my fidelity, which will be inviolable. I love none but you.'

Corisande couldn't help but wonder if that were true. The King was not naturally faithful, quite the opposite. It was a part of his nature to be promiscuous. He could not help himself. Yet Corisande hoped and prayed that he would at least be true to her until after the divorce from Margot and she had been made his queen. Sadly, there were rumours of a certain Dame Martine and an Esther Imbert, to whom he had been paying court. Corisande told herself that even if he had visited these ladies, they would not hold his heart as did she.

And yet... She wondered if perhaps her royal lover did not protest his fidelity rather too fervently, which gave her even more cause to doubt it. And he did not always give her what she wanted. She'd written asking for a title for her son, but he had refused.

'I beg thee to think it right if I do not give your son the position which you ask for.'

Didn't her own child, although admittedly he wasn't Henry's son, deserve some acknowledgement?

Even more irritating, Henry had agreed to pay some of Queen Margot's bills. Only recently he'd paid for five hundred tuns of wine for her consumption.

'Five hundred tuns?' Corisande had asked, quite unable to imagine such an amount. 'Why should you pay for such a quantity of wine?'

Henry had laughed out loud. 'Aye, it is as if she has declared herself to be a drunkard. This is guzzling beyond all measure.'

He had known full well that Margot did not require such a quantity of wine for herself, but for the soldiers who guarded her. Henry had sworn that even if she must needs keep them happy, it would not be at his expense. Yet Corisande suspected that he probably had paid in the end, for the woman was constantly crying poverty and trying to worm money out of him one way or another.

But then just as she despaired of ever winning him, or a crown, he would kiss her and laugh and declare his undying love for her all over again.

'Domestic misfortune is the worst of all,' he would moan, adding that he could not wait to be rid of Margot. 'I swear I would be a good King of France for I've quite decided that I love the country, and wish to make the people proud. Soon I will be free to take a wife of my own choice. You, my love, will stand beside me when the hour comes for me to meet that destiny.'

Would that this happy event could happen soon.

Stifling a sigh, Corisande set aside the sweet-meats. She had ever been a voluptuous woman, but perhaps she was growing a little plump, and she really must take care to preserve her beauty for when Henry came home. Tucking the letters under her pillow she turned over and resolutely closed her eyes for sleep.

Guise was lying in bed with his mistress, deeply aware of the bristling intrigue all around him. It was Thursday, *22* December, and he was to meet with the King the following morning, prompt at seven. His situation was in limbo as no further help would come from Spain. The Armada had been crushed, lost in a gale off Ireland, and Philip II was no longer invincible. He was now a man as broken as his ships.

Following the *Journée des Barricades*, Guise had succeeded in subjugating *Parlement*. He still secretly aimed for the throne, but had at least hoped to be Lieutenant-General in the meantime. The League asked for more but they'd had Epernon, the King's favourite, to contend with, whom they hated almost as much as they did Henri.

There was one occasion when a string of mules had been stopped, the baggage searched, and found to be loaded with Epernon's furniture and personal treasures. Clear evidence that he was attempting to escape Paris. These were confiscated but the *mignon* himself, fearing for his life, did later manage to escape, which had thrown the King into a greater panic.

Guise could only smile that even Henri's favourites were deserting him.

Relations between Guise and the King had grown increasingly difficult of late, even to sparking a common brawl between their servants, resulting in loss of life. And the Queen Mother seemed to be losing her power over him, unable to persuade her son to return to Paris. The League, and Guise himself, had endured several prickly meetings with His Majesty at Chartres, attempting a reconciliation, all to no avail.

'Do you think that if I had wished to do you a bad turn, I could not have done it?' the King had

151

told Guise. 'No, no, I love the people of Paris, in spite of themselves.'

Even as he had ignored Henri's feeble bluster, still Guise had hesitated to act against him. Unconvinced he could count upon the support of Spain, he'd considered the size of Navarre's army, and knew his resources to be lacking. He must needs rely upon other skills to win that much-coveted crown. Besides, Henri Trois was a spent force, no real threat to him now.

Yet tension had continued to mount, the threat of danger growing more palpable by the day. Over the last week Guise had been given several warnings, his followers constantly urging him to leave Blois. All of which he'd ignored.

'What was the note you tossed aside at supper?' de Sauves now asked. 'I noticed that you found it screwed up in your napkin.'

'The same old legend. Urging me to run to save my skin.'

Charlotte sat up, her brilliant eyes wide with fear. 'You should pay heed. Even the Almanacs are against you, I had them checked. They all urge you to go, to leave before the King's vengeance erupts.'

Guise only laughed, his daredevil nature refusing to be cowed. 'I am not afraid of that mincing fool. I know him too well. His soldiering was never anything but posturing, and even those days are long gone. He is now too fond of his comforts, and far too effeminate to want blood on his hands.'

'The King is no fool,' Charlotte demurred. 'He is clever and cunning. You shouldn't trust him.'

'Even a Valois would not stoop so low as to murder his most feared rival, let alone one loved by the people. Certainly his father, Henri II, would not have done so.'

Charlotte shook her head in despair, fearful for her lover's safety 'But Henri is not his father's son. He is more Medici than Valois, and takes a different perspective. You should never underestimate him.'

Guise was growing weary of the discussion. 'I am aware of the dangers, my love. But you know that I have the devil's own luck,' and he kissed her, wanting only to enjoy her charms and not talk of war, or death, or religion.

Perhaps his mistress was partly the reason he lingered here, for despite his earlier reservations about her, and finding he had forever lost Margot, Charlotte de Sauves had wormed her way back into his bed. He was really quite fond of her, in his way, for she was easy company and put no demands upon him. Now he tried to reassure her with a show of bravado. 'When I see death come in at the window, I shall not run out at the door.'

'I know of your courage, my darling, and applaud you for it. But where is the harm in being prudent?'

Guise laughed. 'The word is not in my vocabulary.'

He slept later than he meant to, warm and sated with loving, easily seduced by her charms. It was nearer eight the next morning when, dressed in a doublet of grey satin, he made his way to the

153

King's apartment. It was raining, the cobbles slick with wet, heavy drops soon marking his new satin suit which proved to be entirely unsuitable for the weather. The stone passages through which he walked struck chill into his bones, but his men were with him giving their support and comradeship. Even Guise, courageous as he might be, was not fool enough to go alone.

As the doors of the Council Chamber clanged shut behind him, he half turned to speak to them. Only then did he realize he'd been tricked. His men had been held back and remained in the courtyard beyond. Guise heard the locks turn and knew he was very much alone.

Only the pallor of his face gave any indication of the fear he felt in that moment. The eye close to his scar began to itch and water, as it often did in bad weather, and Guise asked for a handkerchief. A page was found and the message delivered to the Duke's secretary waiting outside. The handkerchief was brought to him, but the note his servant had enclosed: *'Sauvez-vous, ou vous étes mort,'* had already been removed from its folds.

All his senses were alert as Guise seated himself at the council table. Glancing around he found little reassurance in the faces of those about him. None of them were his friends.

'It is cold, should we light the fire,' he suggested, attempting to make his voice sound carelessly bright and unconcerned. 'I should have taken breakfast, is there some conserve of roses, or Damascus grapes in the King's cupboard to revive me?'

There was not. They gave him instead a few Brignoles plums. Guise chewed on one, and, keeping a few in his hand, put the rest in the little gilt box in the shape of a shell that he always carried with him. The business of the Council began.

Henri, filled with an abiding hatred for Guise, and for the League, stood waiting in his closet. He craved vengeance and power, believing the only way to achieve both was with the spilling of his rival's blood.

Catherine too was at Blois, but she was suffering from a severe chill and confined to her apartments below those of her son. Sick as she was, she had heard no sounds to disturb her. Henri had urged his men to tread lightly as they made their preparations, so as not to waken her. Now he sent one of his men for Guise.

'Pray look natural when you go to him. You are too pale, rub some colour into your cheeks.'

The fellow stood before Guise, trembling in his shoes. 'Monsieur, the King requests your presence. He is in his *cabinet.*'

Guise did not hurry to obey the summons. He put the last of the plums away, then leisurely picking up the sweet box, and his gloves, he tapped on the King's door and followed the usher inside.

The door banged shut behind him, someone in the shadows of that narrow space trod on his foot, and Guise knew, in that instant, he was done for. There was nowhere to turn, no hope of escape. He took no more than a step or two, had half turned to see who followed when the first blade struck. They came at him one by one from

155

behind the tapestry, but he had no weapon in his hand other than his sweet box, and he struck out uselessly with that.

'*Eh, mes amis!*' he cried.

He did not die easily. He fought and resisted every thrust, and by superhuman effort dragged himself the length of the room, leaving a trail of blood in his wake. At the foot of the King's bed, he fell. 'My God, I am dead! Have mercy on me.'

They plundered his rings and his purse, and the contents of his pockets before his last raw breath expired. Then they tossed the grey satin cloak over his head, a piece of old carpet over the rest of his body, and laid a straw cross upon his breast.

'And so ends the glorious King of Paris,' they cried, and left him.

When Margot received the news she was distraught. She wept as if her heart would break. It was indeed broken. Guise had been the love of her life, yet they had been driven apart by politics and by the greed for power. If they had been allowed to marry as they'd so longed to do, how different her life would have been, and perhaps even the fate of France. Margot could not imagine a future without him, could not believe that her beloved *chevalier* would not be there for her, albeit too often at a distance, but nonetheless forever her support, her strength, her only true love.

But the messenger who brought the news from Paris had more to tell.

'The Duke's brother, the Cardinal de Guise, was also assassinated on Christmas Eve, and most of the Guise family have been taken prisoner, including the old Cardinal de Bourbon.'

'Dear God, and what of my mother in all of this?' she asked him, pale with shock and wondering if this was another crime that could be laid at Catherine de Medici's door.

The messenger continued. 'It is said that when the King informed the Queen Mother he had murdered the Duke of Guise, declaring that he had rid himself of the King of Paris and that he was now King of France, in truth, she was greatly shocked and distraught. Her Majesty asked if he knew what he had done. "Let us hope you do not find yourself King of nothing," she told him. I fear the events were too much for her, Madame, and she succumbed.'

It seemed that Catherine had outlived Guise by only a matter of days, dying of pneumonia on 5 January 1589.

Margot sadly agreed. 'My mother was seventy years old and must have left this earth a bitter and disappointed woman. In that moment she saw her life's work lost, her favourite son throw away all she had achieved with not even an heir to follow him; an end to peace, and to keeping a Catholic on the throne of France, with no alternative but to accept that my husband, a Huguenot, will take the crown. Henri will not survive long without her.'

Nor did he. Henri Trois was himself assassinated a few months later in August 1589, by Jacques Clement, a mad monk in the pay of Guise's sister, the Duchess de Montpensier. The House of Lorraine had taken its revenge.

157

Margot did not grieve for her mother or her brother, who together had surely been the plague of her life. But knew she would grieve into eternity for Guise, her one true love. She might never be Queen of France, as her husband, now King Henry IV of France and Navarre, would press all the stronger for a divorce. Margot almost smiled to herself as she considered how she would bargain hard for her rights and the return of her property. But then she had ever been a woman of independence with a mind of her own, and a resolute determination to live life on her own terms.

So here she was, the last of the Valois, safe in her Ark of Refuge, and though she would forever weep for her lost lover, she was at least now in possession of the freedom she had always craved.

# Part Three

# GABRIELLE D'ESTRÉES

## 1590

If Henry had imagined that claiming the throne would be easy he was soon disenchanted. Quietly exultant, he met with the nobles at St Cloud, but his triumph was short-lived. Many knelt before him to offer their allegiance, however insincerely meant, while others hung back. Either way, their terms were unaltered.

'If you would be King of all France you must reject the Huguenot faith and turn Catholic.'

'I see no reason to doubt that I would make as good a king without so doing.'

'It is necessary that you take the Mass,' they insisted, stony-faced and hostile.

Henry was forced to withdraw, still defiant but unable as yet to take Paris and claim the crown so nearly within his grasp. His position was precarious to say the least, and would require all his skill both as a soldier and a diplomat to win through.

In Paris, Guise's sister the Duchess of Montpensier was conspiring against him, raising armies and determined to put a member of her family, a Catholic, on the throne. 'I will bring this so-called Henry Quatre defeated into Paris, and have him thrown before you like a whipped dog. We are of the Mother Church and God is on our side,' she told the people.

Henry donned his armour, set his plumed helmet upon his head and fought as never before.

161

Paris could wait for its whipped dog. When he entered the city, he would do so as its king.

Months passed, the campaign frequently held up by winter snows, but despite several marches upon the city, Paris refused to fall. Too far distant from his home to return often to see Corisande, Henry sought solace elsewhere, including from one or two obliging nuns weary of ecclesiastic seclusion. He'd recently enjoyed the favours of Marie de Beauvilliers, the abbess of Montmartre. She had begged him for protection when he'd begun the assault on the *faubourgs*, and Henry had sent a guard of soldiers. Later, he'd called to visit her, and found her to be young and lovely, witty and intelligent, and more than a little bored with monastic life. They had entertained each other well.

Now he was paying court to the *chatelaine* of Nonancourt; he had called frequently at her chateau on the pretext of seeking refreshment and conversation.

'You must be lonely, after three years of widowhood,' the King told her, with little attempt at subtlety. 'I am in a similar situation with my queen in hiding in Usson. Could we not give much pleasure and happiness, each to the other?'

Antoinette de Pons was no fool. 'I am sure there are any number of ladies willing to perform that task for you, Sire.'

'Ah, but none as lovely as you. You are the kind of woman any man would cherish.'

'I am a virtuous woman, my honour would not allow me to go to a man's bed unwed.'

'My marriage is on the brink of a divorce. Would you come to me if I were to promise you all your heart desires?'

Antoinette smiled as she tactfully declined the King. 'Sire, I am content. I have been left well provided for. I have my castle here at Nonancourt and do not seek a replacement husband.'

'But what if that husband were a king?'

'I believe you have already given such a promise to the Countess of Gramont and Guiche, your beloved Corisande, as you call her. I would not presume to ask it of you when she has first call upon your favour. Shall we partake of supper now?'

As always, the more the Marchioness resisted, the more Henry ached for her. He ever wanted what he could not have.

Unfortunately, the state of the war meant he was not free to pursue his suit, having to concentrate his attention on beating Guise's brother, the Duc de Mayenne, and the Leaguers.

Paris still refused to accept a heretic king.

At thirty-seven, Henry was growing concerned about the lack of legitimate heirs. His marriage to Margot had been a failure in that respect, as it had in every other, or so it seemed. Now she was in her fastness refusing to give him a divorce until all her dowry land and properties had been restored to her. Henry could see no way out of the situation. He may not be particularly handsome, or even very rich, but he had a crown, and would soon have a greater one. Surely that stood in his favour when selecting a wife? Acquiring bastards had never been a problem to him, and he acknowledged and adored all his children, but Henry was beginning to have serious doubts about marrying Corisande.

The last time he'd returned to Nérac, he'd been disappointed to discover that she'd grown somewhat stout and matronly, possibly because of the two children she had borne him. Sadly his daughter had been stillborn and his son had died in infancy, which had been a great blow to him. Didn't he love all his children? Her translucent complexion, the bloom of youth he had so adored, was now quite gone. He still wrote to her, although less frequently, and Corisande continued to assure him of her undying devotion.

In recent correspondence she'd pleaded the cause of his sister the Princess Catherine, who wished to marry her cousin Charles de Bourbon, the Comte de Soissons.

Henry had paid little attention at the time, being far too busy writing letters begging for support in his campaign from England, from Scotland, and from the Low Countries. Elizabeth I was at least willing to arrange loans for him, and help rally a fighting force from among the Protestant countries. But it was not going to be easy to win against the League, backed by the mighty power of Catholic Spain.

Following his visit to the chateau of Nonancourt, a message was brought to him from James VI of Scotland in which he offered six thousand men in return for the hand of his sister Catherine in marriage.

'It is a fair bargain,' Rosny said.

Henry agreed, delighted at the prospect of swelling his dwindling resources with new fighting stock. But he loved his sister, and would

164

adore to see her happy. They had both suffered as children under the strict Protestant regime kept by their mother, and had grown close. 'But I would dearly like to see my sister happy.'

'She is a royal princess and will understand that duty comes before happiness.'

Henry nodded. 'As it was for myself.' Neither he nor Margot had been consulted when the arrangements for their alliance had been made. Had they found happiness together? Some, perhaps, until fate and their fickle natures had got the better of them. But had the marriage worked in any way to the benefit of the State? It had failed to bring the peace France craved, although the blame for that surely lay elsewhere. 'Should I accept this offer?' he asked his advisor. 'Or should I let her have Soissons?'

'The Count is a Bourbon, and a Catholic. It is always within the bounds of possibility that, were he to marry a Princess of the Blood, the Leaguers would see him as a suitable candidate for the throne in your place.'

Henry was aghast at the thought. To have his own sister oust him from his rightful place. To see Soissons take the throne would be anathema to him. 'That cannot be. We must take no risks.'

'Indeed not, Sire.'

'Write to the King of Scotland accepting his most generous offer. I will write to Corisande and ask her to break the news gently to my sister.'

The two women were good friends. He could think of no better person than Corisande to explain the benefits of such a match. To marry a king should be seen as good news. Madame Catherine would be queen not only of Scotland, but perhaps England too one day. Elizabeth I still had no direct heirs. Nor would it do any harm to France to have his sister in such a position of power.

Henry wasted no time in writing to Corisande, buoyed up with hope and optimism. He spoke of his own situation, explaining how essential the King of Scotland's support was to his cause. But he also spoke of his love for his sister.

'I believe James will undoubtedly become King of England. Point out to my sister the honour that awaits her, the greatness of that Prince, together with his virtue. I am not writing to her about it myself. I beg you to speak of it to her, explain that it is time for her to marry, and that there is no hope of any other match for her but this one. It will be of benefit to us all.'

Perhaps the tide was turning at last in his favour.

'I have received a letter from your brother,' Corisande told Catherine as they strolled together by the River Baïse. It was always best, Corisande thought, to hold private discussions out of doors, away from wagging ears. But as they walked in the Queen's gardens, she dreaded what she must tell the girl. Just reading the blunt words had filled her with anger on the Princess's behalf. How dare Henry treat his own sister with such callous disregard? But then did he not treat herself, his adored mistress, in precisely the same way.

Corisande had heard rumours that he was paying court to some widowed marchioness, which rankled greatly, and to an abbess of all people. If only she could be at his side, where she belonged, offering the comfort and solace he needed. But that was impossible while he was fighting the war. Corisande reminded herself how Henry did so like to flirt. This widow, or any other woman upon whom his fancy might fall, would never hold his heart. That belonged entirely to her, his one and only true love. She had to believe that, and because of her great love for him Corisande was willing to patiently wait for the happy day to come when they could be together again.

'Will you read some of the letter to me? Does my brother have news?' Catherine was asking. 'Is he making good progress?'

'He says he has not yet taken Paris, but he speaks of your future.'

Catherine pressed a hand to her mouth, eyes glittering with hope and excitement. 'He has given his blessing for Charles and I to wed?'

Corisande's heart went out to the girl and she put a hand on her young friend's arm. 'Sadly not. He begs me to inform you – to break it to you gently – that an offer has been made for your hand by the King of Scotland. It is an excellent match, or so he assures me. Henry is at pains to point out that James VI is himself a Protestant, and therefore you would be well suited.'

Catherine looked at Corisande in stunned horror. 'King James of Scotland? But I do not love him. I love Charles. We are affianced, promised to each other, practically betrothed. Scotland is a cold land, far from France. I do not know this king. He is a stranger to me. And is he not old?' Catherine knew she was gabbling in her panic.

Corisande glanced at the letter again. 'No, only

eight years older than yourself. Oh, but I understand your distress, my dear child. I do not wish
to see your affections blighted by reasons of State,
which, ever since States were founded, have been
responsible for so much human misery. Henry
speaks constantly of duty, yet never of love.'

Catherine was silently weeping. 'He could not
be so cruel as to banish me to some far distant
land to marriage with a stranger. He and I have
always been close. Why has he changed so?'

Corisande sighed. 'Kings have responsibilities
and different priorities than brothers. But do not
despair, my dear. You can be assured of my un-
failing support. We must fight this. I shall write to
him and quietly remind your dear brother that it
was he who encouraged you in your friendship
with Soissons, and of the promises you have already made to each other. Not least how emin-
ently suitable Charles would be as a husband.'

'Henry may not listen to reason,' Catherine
sobbed.

'We can but hope that once he has taken Paris
and the crown is on his head, the situation will
change. In the meantime, we must exercise every
delaying tactic we can devise. Do we not believe
in his love for us both?'

'Of course,' Catherine agreed, drying her eyes.

'Then let us not despair. Fate may yet be on
our side.'

One day in autumn, Henry was riding in the forest
with his young friend the Duc de Bellegarde, a
charming young man much favoured by the court
ladies. Henry enjoyed his lively company and rel-

168

ished some time away from fighting battles to hunt and ride. 'You are most fortunate, Bellegarde, to be young and free, with no responsibilities weighing upon your shoulders.'

'Indeed, Sire, I am fortunate in many ways, not least in having the most beautiful woman in the world to love me,' Bellegarde boasted.

Henry laughed. 'We all think so when we are in love. I have said as much myself on numerous occasions. Until I find another woman to outshine her.'

'Ah, but in my case it is true. None could outshine my beloved.'

The King's eyes narrowed with speculation, the desire to hunt a different prey now seeming far more attractive than chasing boar or stags. 'You have roused my curiosity, Bellegarde. Tell me more.'

'Her mother is Françoise Babou de la Bourdaisière, a woman with few principles who leads a somewhat abandoned life, if we are to believe the gossips. But the girl's father is Antoine d'Estrées, Marquis de Coeuvres, and deputy grand master of artillery. He is a valiant and honourable officer.'

'And the girl?' Henry was not interested in the family, although an over-protective mother could often prove to be a nuisance. It didn't sound as if that would be a problem in this case. 'How old is this treasure?'

Bellegarde could not resist bragging about his mistress. 'She is but nineteen years old. With golden hair and blue eyes there is no woman lovelier than my Gabrielle. She is enchantingly beautiful.'

169

There was nothing Henry liked better than a blue-eyed blonde. 'I must see this paragon. Does she live far?'

'The Château Coeuvres is situated quite close to Compiègne where we are currently stationed, I will take you to meet her one day, Sire.'

'Why not now?'

Bellegarde hesitated, suddenly seeing the folly of mentioning a beautiful woman to this king. 'It would perhaps be more considerate to warn the family first.'

'Nonsense,' Henry countered. 'Who would not welcome a visit from the King? Come, lead the way, I am eager to view this beauty,' and as he put his horse to the canter, Bellegarde could do nothing but obey.

Gabrielle d'Estrées cried out with pleasure when she heard the clatter of hooves in the courtyard and saw that it was her lover. She sprang up from the window seat where she and her sister Diane had been engaged in needlework, delighted to have a reason to abandon it as she loathed sewing.

'Oh, it is Bellegarde. He sent no message that he was coming today, and he has brought company with him. Quick, Diane, go and offer the gentlemen refreshments while I change. I wish to look my best. He is constantly begging me to marry him, and this may well be the day that I accept.' She giggled. 'Or it may not, who knows?'

Diane smiled, giving her sister a quick hug. 'Don't tease him too much, precious. You would hate to lose him. Wear the blue, it matches your eyes. I'll take the gentlemen out into the garden, then later I'll keep his companion occupied while you and Bellegarde slip away for a private little tête-à-tête.'

Left alone, Gabrielle yanked on the bell pull to summon her maid, deeply regretting the lack of notice. She would like to have bathed and scented herself properly. As it was, she must simply do the best she could in the time available.

'Fetch the blue gown,' she cried, the moment the hapless girl appeared. 'Quick, we must hurry.' Papa might accuse her of being light-minded, but she was much sharper than people gave her credit for. Diane was right. She couldn't keep Bellegarde, or Longueville of whom she was also fond, dallying indefinitely. It was vitally important that she capture a rich, elegant and handsome husband. But it was such fun choosing she was really in no hurry.

Ten minutes later, with her golden hair brushed till it shone and left to hang loose, falling in rippling waves to her waist, Gabrielle walked gracefully down the stairs and out into the garden where her father and sisters were already in conversation with their guests. Her mother was not at home, so Diane was acting as hostess.

Inside her cool exterior Gabrielle was excited and happy that her lover had come to see her unannounced, seeming to indicate that he could hardly bear to be apart from her. As she approached the little party she caught her sister Juliette's eye, realized she was trying to tell her something but couldn't think what it might be. Gabrielle dropped a flirtatious curtsey to Bellegarde, casting a sideways glance up at him

171

through her lashes. 'What a delightful surprise, my lord. I bid you welcome.'

'You must first welcome the King. We were out riding and His Majesty was in need of refreshment.'

Gabrielle started. They had all been aware that the King was in the vicinity engaged in sporadic fighting, but never for a moment had Gabrielle expected him to call upon them. 'I beg pardon, Your Majesty. Pray forgive my rudeness.'

She sank into a deep curtsey, kissed the hand that was held out to her, realizing as she did so what Juliette had been trying to impart to her by that warning glance. So this was the new king? Gabrielle was not particularly impressed. He seemed old, his late thirties she believed, and did not possess one iota of Bellegarde's elegance and style. His linen was soiled, and, as he stepped forward to raise her from the deep curtsey, she had great difficulty in not screwing up her nose against the stink of horse sweat that emanated from his person. Clearly the King did not believe in bathing or scenting himself, as did her handsome lover. Her pretty shoulders shuddered at the lot of any woman obliged to sleep with this king.

Two maids hurried forward at that moment with trays of refreshment: wine and wafers, coffee and cakes. Gabrielle welcomed the interruption, which gave her a moment to collect herself and distance herself from the King. 'Which would you prefer, Sire, coffee or wine?' she asked, giving him one of her enchanting smiles.

Henry was entranced, struck speechless like a gawky schoolboy. Bellegarde had been absolutely

172

correct. Never had he seen such a vision of love-liness. Her luxuriant fair hair, those dazzling blue eyes, and a complexion of lilies and roses. Her nose was divine, her lips moist and full, and when they parted slightly to smile at him, revealed perfect white teeth. He was surely in heaven and this was an angel.

'Either, or both, I care not so long as I may sit by you. I think you must have already sipped nectar from the gods. You are a fortunate man, Monsieur le Marquis, to have such beautiful daughters,' the King told his host.

'I am indeed, Your Majesty,' her father quickly answered, pride swelling out his chest to have Gabrielle complimented by the King.

Gabrielle entertained their guests by chatting merrily throughout the afternoon, aided and abetted by both Juliette and Diane, although it was plain to the worried Bellegarde that it was Gabrielle who fascinated Henry most. His mon-arch had clearly fallen deeply under her spell.

'May I call again, Monsieur, to talk with your pretty daughters?' Henry asked as he took his leave.

'You are ever welcome at my home any time, Your Majesty,' that ambitious man assured his monarch.

Gabrielle cast a languishing glance across to her lover, attempting to silently assure him of her devotion, and her sorrow that they'd had no opportunity to be alone.

Bellegarde was burning with hot jealousy. He felt as if he were leaving behind his beloved damsel in distress in her fairy-tale château with its crenellated turrets and drawbridge. But he calmly mounted his horse and rode away, somewhat mollified by this demonstration of her affection. Gabrielle had as good as promised to be his. He must remember they were all but betrothed.

Henry said little on the way back, seeming to be engrossed in his own thoughts. Bellegarde knew that the King was concerned with finding a suitable queen, the need to produce heirs becoming ever more pressing. Although Henry might admire her beauty, he was hardly likely to be interested in his darling Gabrielle for such a role, was he?

Gabrielle had seen the misery in her lover's eyes, and gloried in it. Moments before she'd thought how very vexing it was that Bellegarde should have brought the King here today, but mayhap a little jealousy would only strengthen his great love for her. She had every intention of accepting his suit, or possibly Longueville, who was also dying for love of her. Gabrielle couldn't quite make up her mind which of her suitors she loved best. She was almost certain that she loved Bellegarde above all others, but the Duc de Longueville had fallen in love with her more than a year ago and he was so very handsome. Fortunately, each was unaware of her duplicity, but then Gabrielle had learned long since to be discreet.

She was the fifth child of eight, six of them girls and all beautiful, in a family with a reputation for scandal and licentiousness. It was well known that several of her forebears laid claim to being royal mistresses. One to Francis I, another to the Emperor Charles V and Pope Clement VII. It was no surprise then that her own mother possessed an insatiable appetite for sex and frequently took lovers, much to her long-suffering husband's chagrin. Gabrielle's father, the Marquis, seemed to have little control over the antics of his wife.

As well as enjoying a somewhat audacious lifestyle herself, Madame d'Estrées seemed equally determined to take full of advantage of her daughters' beauty.

Gabrielle's elder sister Diane had been bathed in milk and 'sold' to the Duc d'Epernon, a favourite of Henry Trois, for a considerable sum. She had gone off happily enough to live a life of luxury at court, claiming that when Epernon tired of her, he would be sure to help secure her a rich husband.

Gabrielle had likewise lost her virginity at an early age, thanks to the machinations of their ambitious mother. She well remembered the day when the bargain was struck. She'd been thirteen.

She stood with her ear pressed to the salon door, anxious to hear the conversation taking place within between her mother and a gentleman by the name of Monsieur de Montigny. She was nervously wondering if he were handsome, and what he would think of her when she was paraded before him as her sister Diane had been before Epernon.

'I couldn't possibly let her go,' she heard her mother say, playing the concerned maternal role to perfection. 'She is but a child, an innocent virgin.'

'My master prefers them young,' came the reply.

Madame tittered. 'I dare say he does. Do not all men if they can get them? But the younger the girl, the higher the price. My own sweet one is the beauty of the family. I doubt you could afford her.'

'My master is rich beyond measure. What price did you have in mind?'

There was a long silence in which Gabrielle, listening avidly behind the door, almost despaired of an answer coming. Eventually, her mother responded in the kind of tone she might use when discussing the sale of a gown she was bored with. 'I couldn't take less than six thousand crowns. A loving mother requires suitable compensation for the loss of such a precious daughter.'

A mocking laugh followed this remark. 'Is that what you claim to be, a loving mother? Pardon me for seeing you rather in the light of procuress. Mayhap you should show your gratitude for the honour done to your daughter by my master the King, and be willing to pay for the privilege.'

Gabrielle felt her heart start to thud loudly in her breast. This messenger then was from the King of France! No lover could be higher placed than Henri Trois. She had heard strange reports of this effeminate King who scented himself with violet powder, treated his wife like a doll, and taxed the people of Paris to pay for his extravagances. His mother, Catherine de Medici, was in constant battle with his *mignons* to control him. It was said that he had once apparently been hopelessly in love with the Princess Condé but had never bedded her. Gabrielle did not think she would have anything to fear from such a king, odd though he may be.

'You wish *me* to pay *you?* Very droll,' her mother was saying, seemingly unruffled by the threats. 'I know the value of my daughter and will not let her go cheaply. Why have you come? Who told you of her beauty?'

'His Majesty learned of the girl from his favourite, Epernon, who is the lover of her elder sister, I believe?'

'And is well pleased.'

'If you would allow me to see the girl, I'm sure we could come to terms.'

'But of course, you won't fail to be enchanted.'

Gabrielle fled as she heard footsteps approach the door. She managed to reach the stairs before her mother summoned her, and, spinning on her heel, put on an innocent smile as she pretended to have just walked down them.

'Ah, dearest, there you are, how propitious,' as if her mother hadn't guessed that Gabrielle had been eavesdropping. 'Come with me, child, there is someone I would like you to meet.'

Gabrielle would never forget being looked over as if she were a piece of meat on a butcher's hook, turned about, and asked to raise the hem of her skirt to show off her ankles. It had been most humiliating. And then, after an achingly long silence, the visitor had smiled. 'The girl certainly shows promise.'

'Promise? She is the most beautiful of all my daughters, in all of France, I shouldn't wonder.'

'His Majesty has decreed that I may offer three thousand crowns for her.'

'I have already said that I couldn't take less than six.'

The bargaining was so unseemly, so deeply embarrassing that Gabrielle slipped from the room. Yet she couldn't help but be excited. What would it feel like to be the darling of a king, to be bedded by Henri Trois? Would he shower her with jewels and new gowns? Gabrielle began to daydream of the sort of trinkets she would most enjoy. Not pearls, they were surely for dowagers. Sapphires, perhaps, to set off her eyes. Diamonds, to draw attention to the perfection of her complexion. And nothing but the finest silk for her gowns.

In the end a price of four thousand was agreed and Gabrielle was duly packed off to court to meet the King.

Henri Trois was not a man given to much cavorting between the bed sheets, not with women at least. He loved to have beauty about him, but he found physical love making and emotion of any kind so very exhausting that he would need two or three days in bed to recover after such an encounter. He far preferred his pretty boys, his monkeys and his little dogs, and brushing the hair of his plain but submissive wife, Queen Louise. Gabrielle found that her duties with the King were not onerous, that he troubled her very little.

Oh, but she adored court life, enjoyed playing with the monkeys and little dogs, dressing in pretty gowns and watching Henri decide which colours and trinkets suited her best. The King could happily spend hours discussing such trifles, playing with her hair, or applying rouge to her pretty cheeks and lips. Unfortunately, as with everything, he soon tired of her once the novelty had worn off. He told Epernon that the chit bored him. 'She is charming enough, milk-pale skin, luscious lips, but vacuous. A silly, spoiled miss.'

'I am sorry to hear you are disappointed in her, having paid four thousand crowns for the girl.'

Henri frowned. 'Four? I paid six.'

Epernon shook his head. 'Her mother asked for six but I assure Your Majesty she was paid only four.'

Henri went puce with fury. 'Then I have been doubly cheated. Montigny told me he had paid the woman six. He lied! I shall banish the rogue from court.'

'The fault was not mine,' Gabrielle pleaded, frightened of losing her position and the lovely life she enjoyed.

'Get you gone, girl. I dislike cheap goods.'

Gabrielle wrote to her mother in tears. 'The King is done with me. What am I to do? Must I come home?'

Madame d'Estrées was even less pleased at this turn of events. She too felt cheated. In a fit of pique, and not wishing to lose out on an exceptional asset, she sold Gabrielle on to the Cardinal de Guise.

Gabrielle was at first alarmed, and then intoxicated as the Cardinal proved to be a much more passionate lover. Experienced in the art of love, despite his supposedly living the religious life, he groomed her well in how to please a man, and herself for that matter. Life had suddenly taken an exciting turn for the better, and in the months following Gabrielle grew from an adolescent girl into a voluptuous young woman.

A year went by in this pleasant fashion, and it was through the Cardinal that she met the Duc de Longueville, a handsome courtier who was instantly smitten with her. He would send her small gifts, flatter her with pretty compliments, use all his considerable charm to lure her into his bed.

'How are you enjoying your life at court?' Madame d'Estrées asked her daughter one day when she came on a visit.

'Oh, exceedingly well,' Gabrielle cried, clapping her hands in delight. 'And I am greatly pursued by gentlemen, one in particular. told her mother about Longueville. 'I fear he loves me, and I swear I could be tempted to return his love, were I not bound to be faithful to the Cardinal.'

Madame d'Estrées was shocked. 'Whatever gave you such an idea, daughter? Faithful indeed! It is your duty to be pleasant to such a fine lord as the Duc de Longueville. It wouldn't be wise to cause offence or any hurt to your protector, yet there is no reason on earth why you should not entertain the Duke, so long as you are discreet and the Cardinal does not learn of it.'

Madame d'Estrées had never exercised discretion herself, but she had no wish for any of her daughters to put at risk the considerable profits she made from the preferment she arranged for them.

Gabrielle was only too happy to follow her heart and take Longueville to her bed. The pair met in secret but despite every effort at discretion, in due course the Cardinal did discover his mistress's betrayal.

'Rumour has it you have taken a new lover.'

'That is not so. I would never hurt you.'

'Do not lie to me, minx. I may be old by comparison with the brilliance of your own youth, but I am no fool.'

'Oh, very well, then I confess it is true. But he is no more than a passing whim. I do assure you that my love for you, Sire, is undimmed. He means nought to me.'

The Cardinal laughed. 'Does he not? I think you like to tease. I would take great pleasure in running the fellow through with my broad sword for such audacity. Fortunately for him I'm leaving court and joining my brother, Henri de Guise. As you may be aware, he is making a bid for the crown and needs all the help he can get.'

Gabrielle slid her arms about the Cardinal's neck and kissed him, long and deep. 'I shall miss all those delicious lessons in love. Life will be very dull without you. Shall you take me to your bed one last time then?'

The Cardinal roared with laughter. 'Why not? I may as well get my money's worth.'

The Cardinal de Guise left court to support his brother in his cause, and the following day Gabrielle moved in with Longueville.

Madame d'Estrées was less impressed with the young courtier. Handsome and charming though he may be, he was not high enough for Gabrielle. Besides, he had thus far offered neither money nor marriage.

Some time later she learned that a certain Moorish banker by the name of Zamet was showing interest in her daughter. Since he was immensely rich she immediately came to advantageous terms with him. After all, Gabrielle had been loved by a King of France and a Cardinal of the Church, what better recommendation could there be?

Like it or not, Gabrielle was provided with a new protector.

Gabrielle responded as generously as ever, becoming quite fond of the Italian merchant, and giving what affection and pleasure she could. It was not in her nature to do otherwise. And she continued to enjoy her delightful life at court, as well as add to her considerable collection of gowns and trinkets. Zamet was nothing if not generous.

But she was still seeing Longueville, while exercising careful discretion, of course.

One day King Henri spotted Gabrielle about court. Turning to Epernon, he asked, 'Is that not the young virgin I once took pleasure with?'

'Indeed, Your Majesty. After you'd discovered that Montigny had cheated you over the price her mother had demanded for the girl, Gabrielle d'Estrées moved on to the Cardinal de Guise, then Longueville. She is now with Zamet, I believe. Her mother never misses an opportunity to maximize her assets.'

Henri Trois lifted fine plucked eyebrows in surprise. He had never been averse to relieving people of their money for his own benefit, and revelling in any amount of licentious behaviour, but he did not approve of it in others.

'Is that the way of it? Then let us fox that greedy lady, and find the chit a husband, eh, Epernon? Who shall we choose? It is no fault of the girl that she has such a rapacious mother, so he should be handsome, elegant, charming... ah.' At that moment the King's gaze fell upon Bellegarde. 'Perfect. Bring the gentleman over, Epernon, and I will make the introductions myself.'

Gabrielle was intrigued and enchanted by this new man in her life, delighted when Bellegarde fell violently in love with her. Thinking about it now, she was quite certain that he would have offered for her sooner, had not political events overtaken them. First came the Day of the Barricades, then Guise had been murdered, Catherine de Medici had died and some months later Henri Trois himself had been assassinated by a mad monk. It had felt as if there was danger everywhere.

During those turbulent months her mother had taken her home to Coeuvres to keep her safe, whether out of love for her or simply to guard her investment, Gabrielle didn't care to acknowledge. Either way she had enjoyed the respite, being able to offer her love to both suitors quite freely, and looking forward to one or other of them making an offer for her hand. First she favoured one, and then inclined towards the other, although on the whole she thought she preferred the young Grand Equerry, Bellegarde.

Madame d'Estrées had now eloped herself with her latest lover, leaving her long-suffering husband almost sighing with relief at his wife's final, if undignified, departure.

The King of Navarre continued to call at Coeuvres from time to time, but Gabrielle was not enamoured of him. In private, when she joked about him to her sisters, she dubbed him *Majesté à la barbe grise*. Henry was neither scented nor handsome, and he was *old*. On three occasions she had done as her mother had bid her, being no more than a bargaining chip. Now she was at last free to choose a lover for herself, and Gabrielle had every intention of following her heart.

But she had reckoned without her ambitious father.

'Do you hope for a visit from the King this afternoon, child?'

Gabrielle shrugged, pouting prettily. 'I know not. He has sent no word.'

'It is some time since we last saw him. You have not caused any offence, I trust?'

'Not that I am aware of, although I shouldn't care if I had.'

'Indeed you must care. He is the King, and could turn up at any moment, so run and change and make yourself pretty, child,' the Marquis sternly informed her.

'I do not see why I should.'

'Because he is the *King*, for goodness' sake. You will do as I say, girl.'

'But he is old, and he is *married!*'

'That does not signify.'

'Well, it does with me,' Gabrielle stubbornly responded, stamping her foot.

'Come, come, you are no fainting virgin. Why play games? If Henry were to take you for his mistress you would be well provided for. In fact, the entire family would benefit.'

'You are as bad as Mother, that is all you ever think of, your own ambitions,' Gabrielle cried,

184

sobbing with fury. 'I will *not* have him! I haven't the slightest wish to encourage his suit. He is neither gallant nor courtly as is Longueville, nor as charming and elegant as Bellegarde. I desire no better fortune than to become the wife of Monsieur de Bellegarde.'

'I admit that I have no quarrel with the Duke. He is a fine young gentleman.'

Instantly drying her tears, Gabrielle saw her advantage and, slipping on to her father's knee, turned her wheedling charm full upon him. 'Will you not, darling Papa, arrange a marriage with this fine gentlemen for me, since you do approve of him, in your heart. Bellegarde is possessed of courtly accomplishments and graces, is of high rank, a bachelor, and therefore in a good position to offer marriage. He is both dashing and brave, having fought gallantly at Arques and Dreux, and in addition has captured my affections. What more can he do to win your consent?'

The Marquis pressed a kiss on his daughter's cheek. Sweet Gabrielle had always been a warm, affectionate child, if a little vain. He would dearly like to see her happy, but girls, in his experience, did not always know what was good for them. He would not go so far as his wife, perhaps, to win preferment for them, but nor would he be blind to a golden opportunity. 'I will certainly speak to the fellow, but I will not gainsay a king. Do as I say, child, and prepare yourself to receive him. You must ever be ready in case he should find time to call upon you.'

Gabrielle flounced off in a fine temper.

In Paris the people were starving, the stores of wheat all but exhausted, meat was being offered for sale at a price far beyond all but the rich. The hungry multitude trailed after the coaches of the nobles begging for a crust, and if any should throw them a coin instead, would cry out, 'Give us bread! What good is money when there is nothing to buy?'

Many died, or caught dreadful diseases from infected food, ending their days either in a hospital or the gutter, depending upon their luck. Even the living spent their days in agony, their bellies swollen, their guts paining them, and only the fortunate few found themselves standing in line for a bowl of soup from the public cauldrons set up on the odd street corner by some charitable nun.

The monasteries were ordered to provide an inventory of their stores, and to distribute it to the people. But many refused, one ecclesiastic protesting that, 'the brethren of the church must first be consulted and their wants provided for'.

Meanwhile, the population resorted to eating their own dogs.

It was agreed that if they took their pets to the monasteries the monks would erect great coppers and serve them a stew comprised of vegetables, barley meal, dried pease and dog flesh. Weeks later even this revolting mess would have been welcomed as famine and pestilence stalked the city. Not a live horse, or animal of any sort could be found, and corpses littered the empty streets.

Yet not for a moment did the citizens consider relenting and accepting a heretic king. They lived in fear of revenge from the Huguenots for the St

Bartholomew massacre. Were the siege to be broken and the Protestants allowed in, murder and mayhem would surely follow. And if Paris fell, so would the League.

Henry had marched on the city more times than he cared to count. Now, after the latest expedition against the Leaguers, he felt weary of battle and preferred to think of love. Bellegarde, he noticed, had similar thoughts on his mind.

'You would not object, Sire, were I to visit my Gabrielle, and offer for her? I must needs take a wife, and she has as good as promised herself to me.'

Henry considered. 'Yet you are not actually betrothed.'

'No,' Bellegarde reluctantly admitted. 'But almost. There is what might be described as an understanding between us. I have been waiting for her permission to speak to her father and make a formal request for her hand.'

'I would prefer it, Bellegarde, were you to withdraw your suit entirely.'

Bellegarde was mortified. He was not unaware of the King's interest in his mistress, but how could he bear to part with his darling Gabrielle? Yet no more could he openly flout the wishes of his monarch. Looking crestfallen, he said, 'But she favours me.'

'A woman may change her mind, given the right kind of persuasion.'

Tight-lipped, the equerry tentatively enquired, 'I trust the manner and degree of such persuasion would not be excessive?'

Henry looked aghast. 'Do you imagine I would resort to force? Am I not a man of honour?'

'Of course, Your Majesty,' Bellegarde hastily agreed, but couldn't resist adding, 'Then the choice will be hers entirely?'

Henry smiled, inclining his head in agreement. 'She will choose whichever of us pleases her most. It might be you, Bellegarde, but then again, why would she not choose her King?' He hadn't set eyes on Gabrielle's lovely face in over a month and he was eager to return to Coeuvres to see her. He'd been too busy fighting the forces of the League scattered through north-western France, and attending to his military duties, which had denied him the opportunity to give rein to the passion that burned within him for Gabrielle d'Estrées. 'I certainly intend to press my suit with all vigour. We must wait and see if I succeed, shall we not? In the meantime, you will stay away.'

'Stay away?'

'You will go nowhere near the château, or the lady in question, is that understood?'

The young equerry swallowed his disappointment with difficulty. 'As you wish, Sire.'

Henry laughed. 'Don't sound so despondent. The best man will win in the end, I am certain of it. I may go to see her quite soon, in fact, to test the waters, as it were.'

Bellegarde was dumbfounded. 'But many of the Leaguers still lurk within those forests. It would be far too dangerous to attempt to traverse them alone, Your Majesty. It would mean crossing enemy lines.'

'Faint heart never won fair lady, isn't that how

the saying goes?'

'I beg you, pray do not even attempt it, Sire. The country needs you.'

'And I need the lovely Gabrielle.'

Gabrielle was heartbroken when she received the letter from Bellegarde explaining how he had been obliged to promise the King he would stay away. 'Be assured of my undying love, and I shall ever hold the hope in my heart that one day you will be mine.'

How she wept over these poetic words, which surely came from a broken heart.

The following evening Gabrielle was about to retire when she heard a great commotion in the kitchen. The maids were screaming and running about in a panic. When she and Juliette ran to see what all the noise was about, they found the cook beating some decrepit old fellow about the head with her broom.

'Get out, you filthy creature. I'll not entertain dirty peasants in my clean kitchen. Take yourself to the cow shed at once, and I'll maybe send a quart of ale out to you, if I feel so inclined.'

But far from doing as he was bid, the moment the fellow saw Gabrielle, he fell to his knees before her and whipped the sacking cloth from off his head. 'My dearest beloved, there is no need to fear. See, it is I, your adoring King.'

Gabrielle almost fainted from shock, and from the stink of horse manure that emanated so strongly from the tattered remnants he wore.

She half glanced at her sister Juliette in despair, at the cook who seemed to be struck with para-

189

lysis, and then back to the creature who called himself a king.

'I doubt that can be so,' Gabrielle frostily remarked, with all the dignity she could muster. 'I have met the King personally and he is a fine soldier, not a filthy bag of stinking rags.'

Henry got to his feet and laughingly grasped her hand, managing to kiss it before Gabrielle snatched it away. 'Ah, but I am in disguise, dearest. I have travelled miles to see you, first by horse, and the last three on foot, crossing forests known to harbour bands of Leaguers. I've risked my liberty in order to prove the sincerity of my love.'

Gabrielle, still smarting from the sad letter she'd received from her lover, was having none of it. Her glance was cold and filled with disdain. 'If you hoped by dressing yourself as the lowest of the low to win my heart, then you were grievously mistaken.'

Henry was instantly contrite. 'It was but a jest.'

'And was it but a jest to banish the man I love from my life? I have no wish to be disturbed in my inclinations, and no effort on your part to prevent me from marrying a man whose suit has been approved by my dear papa, would only inspire feelings of contempt and hatred.'

'Pray give me a chance, dear one. Let me try to win your heart.'

He looked so very ugly and smelled so atrociously, that Gabrielle could not bring herself to be near him, and despite his begging her to stay, she walked away, leaving him alone with her sister.

Juliette's soft heart went out to the dejected King who looked so woebegone and so utterly ridiculous in his disguise. She brought him wine and bread. 'I can only apologize, Sire, for the incivility of the reception accorded to you. My sister is simply stunned at seeing you appear, unannounced, in such a disguise. She no doubt fears that our father, who is in the vicinity, might suddenly appear and put the worst possible construction upon the scene.'

Henry gathered together what remnants of his pride he had left, and begged leave to depart. 'I fear my masquerade might have been a touch presumptuous. I shall present myself to your sister at another time, in another guise. Good evening to you, Mademoiselle.'

Whereupon he retreated into the night, nursing his bitter disappointment.

Henry's humiliation was made worse by a complete lack of sympathy from the Baron de Rosny. Rosny was a skilful and clever politician, loathed dishonesty and profligacy, and was devoted to his king. This meant he was hated by the Catholics, since Henry IV was a Protestant, and by many Protestants because he was faithful to a king who had once turned Catholic to save his own neck. Henry, however, trusted him implicitly, except when it came to women.

'Did you expect the chit to fall into your arms when you smelled like a cesspit?' his counsellor asked. 'And you do have one or two more important matters to occupy you. The people of Paris are driven mad with hunger, and our spies inform us that the Duke of Nemours has ordered that Church plate not actually used in the Mass, be melted down. Although what they will find to buy with the money thus coined, I fail to comprehend.'

Henry looked even more mournful. It seemed that when finally he gained his crown, the treasury would be bankrupt, and the Parisians would hate him for starving them. 'Let the people out of the city.'

'Let them out?'

'They need to buy and search for food. It is the only humane thing to do. We will temporarily call a halt to the siege and withdraw our troops in order for the populace to find food and take it to their loved ones. And make sure they know that it was their new King who issued this order.'

Rosny inclined a bow. 'As you wish, Sire.' He rather doubted the generals would approve, but he would make sure they obeyed. In his opinion, this gentle king was also a wise one.

Paris was not alone in suffering from penury. Henry's loans and debts were mounting. While he felt he was making good progress in his campaign, funds were at an all-time low. The eagerness of his soldiers to go into battle would soon start to fade if their pay was not punctual. And they too had to be fed. Henry's own table was poor, the food plain and unappetizing. Yet what did he care what he ate when he was heart-sick for love.

He struggled to banish the thought of the luscious Gabrielle from his mind, but the image of her haunted him. She had rejected him, both as man and monarch, and that he could not accept, in fact it made her all the more desirable. Perhaps Rosny was right and he had gone about things the wrong way. He no doubt had smelled like a midden. Next time he would make better shift of it. But when would he have the opportunity? He was confined here, at his headquarters at Mantes, and she was in her castle at Coeuvres, no doubt with the drawbridge pulled up.

But he was the King, and as such could issue a summons she dare not disobey.

Henry sent a command to the Marquis d'Estrées to join him at Mantes, and to bring with him his entire family. The fellow duly arrived, and in order to make certain that he stayed, Henry appointed him a member of the Royal Council. The honour pleased the Marquis, proving to him how very wise he had been not to consent to some foolish romantic marriage for his daughter, when there were titles and offices for the taking.

Henry called for his *valet-de-chambre*, eager to look his best when next he met Gabrielle. 'Do I have a decent shirt to wear?'

'My lord, you barely have a dozen shirts to your name, and they are all in a sad state of repair. Your handkerchiefs too, Sire, of which you have only five.'

Henry was appalled. 'Then you must have my shirts mended and laundered. Order new linen, do whatever you have to. I am not some school-boy at camp. See to it, man.'

That evening when he presented himself to Gabrielle, Henry looked his best, even if his shirt was patched and his handkerchief tucked well out of sight. He had also bathed and scrubbed his face and hair till it shone, although he had not gone so far as to resort to using violet powder. He would never emulate the fops.

'We are delighted to see you again,' he told her.

'And I you, Your Majesty,' Gabrielle politely responded.

She told an untruth. Gabrielle had obeyed the King's command with reluctance, but no amount of tears and temper on her part had persuaded her father to decline.

'It is not an invitation,' he'd sternly informed his daughter. 'It is a summons.'

Dutifully Gabrielle allowed the King to kiss her hand, hiding a secret smile as she recognized the effort he had made to impress her. What power she must have over him. She agreed to sit by him at dinner, and, to her surprise, found herself highly entertained by his wit and charm.

But she still preferred Bellegarde, and since he, and Longueville, were also at the camp, Gabrielle thought this might, after all, make for a lively interlude, particularly when the demands of war took the King away for long periods.

As the court moved on to Senlis, Gabrielle was joined by her aunt. Younger than her sister, Madame de Sourdis was still beautiful, and with an equally rackety reputation, having caused much amusement and scandal from a *liaison* with the Chancellor de Cheverny, which her husband steadfastly ignored. Wearing a purple and pink gown and blond peruke decorated with matching ribbons and flowers, she arrived with a fine fanfare of trumpets from her pages and cotillions.

Falling upon Gabrielle she enveloped the girl in her arms, smothering her with fond kisses. 'I shall take the place of your absent mother, dear child, and act as chaperone.' She believed her sister had badly let her daughter down, foolishly missing a golden opportunity by running off in that madcap fashion.

'Dear Aunt, I am so glad to see you.'

In no time Gabrielle was weeping upon her aunt's breast, and confiding her quandary.

'Although the King is making every effort now to please and charm me, he can never offer marriage. I love Bellegarde, and Papa has agreed that he would not be against a marriage between us. I love Longueville too, though perhaps not quite as much. Oh what should I do, dear Aunt?'

'Ah, better to be a wife than a lover,' Madame de Sourdis acknowledged, picking over her niece's jewels to see if there were any pretty pieces she might borrow. 'Unless that lover be a king.'

'But I would much rather be a queen.'

'That, my dear, may be a dream too far.'

'But not impossible,' Gabrielle suggested. 'A queen has much more power than a mistress, and more security.'

'I grant you that is often the case, yet it is not always so. A queen suffers from having been selected for political purposes, while a mistress has been chosen by her consort of his own free will, and is usually adored. I urge you to consider the King's offer with all seriousness. All you need do is to please him, and not grow fat like Corisande. And who knows, when Henry finally gets his divorce from Queen Margot, he may well marry you.'

But Gabrielle continued to resist, refusing to be

195

alone with the King, returning the sumptuous gifts he bestowed upon her. While she dithered and Henry continued to pursue her, the Duc de Longueville asked for the return of his letters. Knowing that the King himself was paying court to his erstwhile mistress, he feared they might compromise him.

'I will most certainly do so,' she told him, annoyed that he should ask. 'If you will likewise return mine.'

'But of course,' he archly replied.

When the bundle arrived and Gabrielle quickly riffled through them, she saw that one or two important letters, in which she had less discreetly spoken of her love for him and the trysts they had enjoyed, were missing.

Gabrielle raged about her room in a fury. 'The Duke has tricked me, he has kept some of my letters back, while I returned every scrap of correspondence he ever sent me. How dare he! Does he intend to blackmail me, or keep them for some other evil purpose?'

Juliette attempted to calm her sister, even as she agreed with her. 'Do not fret, all will be well once you are married. And far better to become the Duchess of Bellegarde, than to bask for a while in the fleeting sunshine of royal favour.'

'Be assured I am in no mood to succumb to the King's blandishments.' Gabrielle wanted nothing less than marriage and respectability to a man of her own choosing, and again turned her attention to Bellegarde, who seemed to represent her best chance of reaching that happy state.

To her shock she discovered that having been

deprived of her company for so long, he was now paying court to Mademoiselle de Guise. Gabrielle was devastated. It was perfectly clear that the King had entirely ruined her matrimonial prospects. What was she to do?

She did what came naturally to her. Gabrielle set out to seduce Bellegarde, and captivate him all over again. 'It is worth suffering the King's unwelcome attentions simply to be here at the camp near you, my love.'

The young courtier eyed her warily. 'You've kept me dangling overlong.'

'I have, and deeply regret it, but you know that I am entirely yours.'

'And what of the Duc de Longueville?'

Ah, so rumour and malice had done its worst. Gabrielle gave a dismissive little laugh. 'A mere flirtation. The fellow was besotted, but he means nothing to me. And what of Mademoiselle de Guise, do you truly favour her above me?' Gabrielle pressed her luscious body against his, teased his mouth with the tip of her delicate pink tongue, parting it, invading it, making him want her. 'I thought you were panting for love of me?'

He was, he ached for her, his loins bursting with need, but Bellegarde hesitated, fearing the wrath of his sovereign. Yet how could he resist her when she was so very desirable? Mademoiselle de Guise was forgotten and Gabrielle was soon triumphantly claiming that she regarded Bellegarde as her affianced husband-to-be, that she had given her permission for him to speak to her father.

Realizing there was no help for it, the Marquis finally agreed to his daughter's betrothal. 'So long

197

as the King raises no objection,' he wisely added.

Gabrielle went at once to Henry and begged the King to give his consent to her marriage with his Grand Equerry, believing that she had at last won her heart's desire. 'You will consider my future happiness in this request, Sire?'

'I will consider your future with all seriousness,' Henry agreed.

The moment she was gone, he summoned the equerry in question. 'What is this I hear? Mademoiselle d'Estrées begs leave for permission to wed you. Did we not agree that you would cease to press your suit?'

Bellegarde cringed with embarrassment before his king. 'Your Majesty, you have ever been aware of my admiration for the lady. Now I have spoken with her father he has accepted my suit and we are betrothed.'

Henry was in no mood to tolerate romantic pigheadedness. 'And you are aware, sir, that I am minded to suffer no rival, neither in war, politics, nor in love. You would do well to heed my words. In fact, I recommend you leave Senlis without delay.'

Bellegarde had no alternative but to obey. Before the day was out he had left the camp. How could he argue with the King?

When Gabrielle learned of her lover's departure she fell into a tantrum, falling on to her bed in tears. She had dallied too long with Bellegarde's affections. She should have accepted him at the first. Now it was too late. 'Am I to be ruined simply for inciting the passion of a king?

It is so unfair, so unjust.'

Juliette ran to fetch their father and the Marquis sternly bid his daughter to view the situation more sensibly. 'Many would welcome finding themselves so desired. You have won the love of your sovereign, what can be so wrong with that? Calm yourself, girl.'

Gabrielle was anything but calm. She did so hate to be bested. Like a spoiled child deprived of something upon which she'd set her heart, she acted without thought or reason, almost enjoyed wallowing in fury and outbursts of emotion, stamping her foot and sending her maids scurrying about in a panic.

'Tell His esteemed Majesty he will not win me by force and malice. Dearest Papa, you must speak for me, or my reputation will never recover.'

Hesitantly, and riddled with nerves, the Marquis agreed to do his best. He politely requested an audience and begged the King to allow the marriage to go ahead. Unfortunately, Henry was obdurate.

'Bellegarde has been banished. Perhaps I could speak with your daughter. I may be able to reassure her.'

'By all means, Sire. She is in a dreadful dither, but then that is girls for you.' The Marquis would do what he could for his child, save for offending his king.

That same afternoon Henry visited Gabrielle in her chamber, and reiterated his great love for her. 'I have come to console you, my sweet. Do you not see how I love you so much that I can bear no other man to be near you?'

Gabrielle faced Henry red-eyed and furious. 'Sire, it is useless. I will not listen to your pleas. You exercise a cruel tyranny and ruin my reputation and good fortune.' Then falling to her knees before him, she tried a softer approach, pleading with the King for his mercy. 'Monsieur de Bellegarde offered for my hand in all honour. Let me accept, I beg of you. It is all I desire.'

'It cannot be done. Bellegarde is banished.'

Gabrielle leaped to her feet and stormed out, caring nothing for the etiquette one should practise before one's sovereign lord. Going straight to her chamber she ordered her maids to start packing at once. 'We are going home to Coeuvres. I will not be dictated to, not even by a king.'

And before the day was out, she too had left Senlis.

Henry took out his disappointment on the battlefield, determined to bring that moment when he finally held the crown of France in his hands one step nearer. The blockade of Paris was not working, but in his favour was the fact that his enemy was divided, unable to agree on whom they would select to replace him, or how this could be achieved.

'I am going to pursue the enemy, and in a week or two *ma belle* will hear what gallant exploits I have accomplished for love of her!'

As if the battle for a throne and the loss of his adored Gabrielle were not enough to contend with, the worrying situation of his sister, the Princess Catherine, had reached no resolution either.

The offer of marriage from James VI was making

little progress and Henry thought he may well have to look elsewhere, both for a husband for his sister, and funds for his campaign. But he was increasingly determined not to let her have the Comte de Soissons, as the fellow was developing ambitions of his own to wear the crown. A staunch Catholic and a Prince of the Blood, since he too was a Bourbon, the people might easily accept him.

Henry knew Catherine to be stern, particularly with regard to religion, rather tending to take after her mother in that respect. So it did not surprise him when she wrote swearing a vow of chastity if she was not permitted to marry the man she loved, albeit if that man was a Catholic.

'What can you expect?' said the note from Corisande that accompanied this declaration. 'She is not happy over your refusal to give consent to this love match.'

Women, they were the most delectable creatures, and the most infuriating.

Henry tossed Corisande's letter aside without even troubling to read the rest of it, and, snatching up his quill, wrote again to Gabrielle, ordering her back to court, yet knowing she may not even read this missive. He had already sent several and so far had received not a single reply. Once written, and with all his heart poured into it, the King handed the letter to Juliette, urging the young woman to add her own pleas to his.

Juliette, fearing that her sister may indeed have gone too far by letting her temper get the better of her, attempted to make amends. 'You must forgive my sister, Sire, for she lacks experience and courtly reverence. She has never been one for shy reserve, and dreads the anger of our father.'

If Henry thought this remark strange, since he'd never seen any evidence of violence in the placid, long-suffering Marquis who could not even control his own wife let alone his six daughters, he chose to say nothing. With his usual goodwill he simply accepted the apology at face value. Henry was miserable without Gabrielle, and would do anything to have her back at court. 'I draw hope from your gentle assurance.'

'There has been no blot upon my sister's character until now, Sire,' Juliette continued, stretching the truth somewhat. 'She has always been just and considerate, accomplished and affectionate. I am certain all can be resolved, given the will.'

In the weeks following her departure from the camp at Senlis, several letters arrived at Coeuvres from Henry. Gabrielle ignored every one. They came too from her father, but she treated those with equal disdain.

Madame de Sourdis, who at great inconvenience to herself had given chase to her fleeing niece, did her utmost to bring the girl round. 'You really must come out of this pet, child, or you risk offending the King,' she chided, fanning her heated face with a fan as she sank on to the sofa beside her niece. She really couldn't take these headlong dashes across country, nor these emotional tantrums. Far too exhausting. 'Dear girl, you will be the death of me, and your dear papa too, I shouldn't wonder. I am quite worn out with these shenanigans.'

Gabrielle lay back on the cushions, faint with misery. 'Oh, I do wish I'd accepted Bellegarde long since. What a fool I have been! Now my reputation is ruined! Everyone believes I am Henry's mistress already. No one will credit the fact that I would dare to refuse a king, and that I have sworn to choose my own lovers in future.'

Her aunt trilled with laughter. 'I can see why that might well be the case. And mayhap the gossips have a point. You could hold the world in your pretty hands if you would but use your wit. Forget romance and handsome young courtiers, how will they serve you? Think of the money and the power.'

'But I am in *love!*'

'Tch! What does love signify?' Madame de Sourdis fluffed out her skirts, recalling her own rapacious youth with fond nostalgia. Fortunately she'd managed to enjoy both fortune and pleasure, if not necessarily from the same source. And continued to do so. 'Love will soon fly out the window when poverty strikes. Did you not enjoy the last time you were at court? All the pretty gowns and fine jewels, the junketing and dancing and such?'

Gabrielle sat up, dabbing at her eyes with a lace kerchief, beginning to wonder if her temper had perhaps led her along a path to obscurity. She did indeed enjoy new gowns and fine jewels, and all the accoutrements of court life. She enjoyed having men grovel at her feet, had already benefited from the favour of a king, and a cardinal, and found it really quite exciting and not at all onerous. In fact, she'd relished the power she'd held over them, however transient. That was the problem, of course. What would happen to her when the King tired of her?

'I would far better be settled in a respectable marriage with a man that I love, and be a duchess no less.'

Madame de Sourdis was pensive for a while as she considered the pros and cons. 'The status of a duchess is a fine and noble one, and I applaud your loyalty to your lover, despite his having been banished from court. But I fear you do not consider the precariousness of the situation. Kings are accustomed to having their own way, even this one who, good hearted though he may be, is as obstinate as any once he has set his mind to something.'

She reached for a brush and began to smooth her niece's hair, knowing that it always calmed her. 'Yet you, my dear, are in a position to advance your family, and yourself in the process. Would you not wish to see a place at court for your own darling papa, for my dear husband your uncle? For myself?' And my lover too, Madame de Sourdis thought.

Gabrielle was growing confused, not knowing what to do for the best. The strokes of the brush soothed her and she wondered if she had been wise to indulge in such a tantrum before the King. She had indeed enjoyed court life, and she dearly loved her father who was far more agreeable and patient with her than her mother had ever been. Yet the image of her darling Bellegarde would not leave her.

'But Papa already has a title, and is a member of the Royal Council. Must I relinquish the prospect of marriage simply for more honours?'

'Whyever not, when there is so much more to be achieved? It will not be so unpleasant in the King's bed. No one has complained thus far.'

Gabrielle's expression remained mulish. 'No one would dare.'

Madame put down the brush and gathered Gabrielle's hands in her own. 'Kings do not generally like to be crossed, and despite his equable temper Henry IV will lose patience in the end. What then will happen to your poor dear father? The Marquis might suffer worse than Bellegarde. He could not only be banished from court, but lose his titles, even his lands and income – or worse.' Madame de Sourdis met her niece's shocked expression with a steady gaze.

'Oh, my goodness, you are surely not suggesting that he would throw Papa into the Bastille?'

'Kings have done worse. It is time to set aside this silly selfishness and think of your family and the future. Now I will hear no more on the subject. You may safely leave this matter in my hands.'

When Gabrielle's father again asked for an audience, Henry was more than ready to oblige, hopeful that at last she may have succumbed.

Gabrielle was being prepared as if she were a bride, her silken skin bathed in milk and smoothed with scented oil. A deal had been struck, gaining favours and positions at court for her father, her uncle, and her aunt's lover. Madame de Sourdis had organized the preparation of a sumptuous feast as if this were indeed a wedding, and was even now issuing orders left, right and centre, revelling in the excitement.

'He will be kind,' she assured her niece, 'and you are not unfamiliar with this situation.'

Indeed she was not. Having been bargained for so many times before, Gabrielle had foolishly believed she would be left alone to choose her own lover in future, and a husband. Now she'd been sold again, to the new King. No doubt at the highest price yet. Henry was certainly not her choice. He was thirty-eight years old, almost twenty years older than herself, fairly tall and broad shouldered as you would expect in a soldier. He had a long face with a square chin and beard, and hair that was turning grey. In his favour, his eyes were bright and merry, really quite mesmeric.

If only this were a wedding in truth, and for love, instead of another sordid little deal.

The last note Gabrielle had received from her darling Bellegarde spoke of his undying love for her. 'I will not lightly relinquish you,' were his exact words, which made her heart beat faster just to recall them. There would surely be times when the King was out and about doing whatever business kings did. Who then would know if they renewed their trysts, and wouldn't it be all the more exciting for being secret and forbidden?

'Why is it that I always have to be paid for? Does no one want me simply for myself?' Gabrielle asked, a plaintive cry.

Madame de Sourdis tutted as she clipped diamond teardrops into her niece's hair, a charming gift from the King. There had been others: the diamonds at her throat and ears, the satin slippers on her feet. If the chit would only stop pining for what she couldn't have, she might be better able to appreciate such munificence.

'Enough of such foolish talk. What harm is there in setting a high value upon yourself? Are you not beautiful and highly desired? Now put on a smile, the King has no wish to see sulks.'

Gabrielle sighed, making no further protest as they dressed her in a gown of cream silk scattered with blush-pink rosebuds, an attempt to make her appear virginal. Despite her so-called experience she felt nervous and miserable, even as she resigned herself to accepting the inevitable.

As she entered the banqueting hall, her aunt beside her, Gabrielle's eyes flew at once to Henry who was magnificently attired in cloth of silver and sky-blue silk, embroidered with pearls. 'At least he looks like a king tonight, and not a ragged peasant.'

'You should appreciate the danger he risked that night by crossing enemy territory for love of you,' her aunt reminded her. Gabrielle pouted.

The feast passed in something of a blur, then musicians struck up a tune for the King to lead her out on to the floor to start the dancing. Gabrielle went with reluctance, wishing some fairy with a magic wand would waft her far away from this place. As they danced, the King leaned close and began to whisper witty comments in her ear about the other nobles.

'Look at your aunt's lover, Cheverny, preening himself like a peacock. How the fellow does love to revel in luxury and splendour. There's Nevers trying to look grand and courtly when really he's far too fat. Bouillon with his sharp tongue being rude. And my own dear Rosny looking uncomfortable, so worthy and practical he's checking that everyone behaves themselves.'

Gabrielle began to giggle. Despite her misgivings she found herself caught up in the excitement and fun of it all. They danced and laughed and had a merry time together. Perhaps it wouldn't be so bad, after all, she told herself, trying to be cheerful.

And then he led her out of the door and to his bed.

Gabrielle had heard how this king lacked refinement, how he had refused to wash his feet when bedding his wife, Queen Margot; that he smelled of stale sweat and garlic, and had once taken her fully clothed with his boots on. The thought of her handsome Bellegarde, scented and elegant, a veritable Adonis, made her ache with longing for what might have been. Gabrielle felt cold dread in her heart at sight of the royal bed. She was experienced in the ways of men, but Henri III had been ineffectual and undemanding, the Cardinal exciting and erotic, and Zamet had become a friend. But as the doors of the royal bedchamber closed behind her, Gabrielle suffered a great desire to turn and run.

Perhaps Henry recognized her nervousness for he could not have been more attentive, or more considerate.

'You are so beautiful, a perfect angel. May I kiss you?'

'Of course, you are the King, Sire.' But she was touched that he should ask.

'I would rather you think of me as your lover, a

208

man rather than your king. Will you call me Henry?'

'If you wish it, Your Majesty.'

Then he kissed her, very tenderly, on her lips. The kiss surprised her, not being at all what she had expected, no rough peasant this, and if he wasn't scented as were the fops at court, he smelled of soap and good wine. Not at all unpleasant.

'Leave us,' he said, dismissing her maids.

He untied the ribbons of her gown himself as she stood before him, cool and unyielding. He unpinned her hair and brushed the long rippling waves to her waist, which made her feel wonderfully relaxed, almost soporific. Then as Gabrielle sat on her dressing stool, he slowly peeled off her silk stockings one by one, delicately kissing her inner thigh as bare flesh was exposed. Gabrielle's heart began to beat rather fast.

'Your legs are divine, so long and slender, even more glorious than I dreamed of.'

Henry slowly disrobed her. He slipped off her gown, the sleeves and bodice, unfastened her stays, and last of all drew her chemise over her head so that she stood before him naked. Gabrielle was not embarrassed to be seen thus by a man for she knew herself to be beautiful, but the look in his eyes melted her heart. She could not remember any of her previous lovers revealing quite so much adoration in one glance.

As Henry gently caressed each breast, licked and suckled, and sought that secret place between her legs with his teasing fingers, Gabrielle grew breathless with lust. He half carried her to the bed but even then did not rush to enter her. He took his time, continuing to kiss her, to nuzzle and nip, to breathe softly in the curl of her ear, till she was going mad with desire.

And when he too disrobed and they met, skin to skin, she could hardly believe how much she wanted him. He was indeed a fine figure of a man, strong and athletic, well formed and broad shouldered with narrow hips and buttocks that she could not resist caressing.

He took her sweetly and smoothly, holding back a little so that he could the better increase her own pleasure. And being the generous and affectionate girl that she was, Gabrielle couldn't help but respond. She arched her back beneath him, entwined her legs with his, and a burning hunger swelled within as they moved instinctively to the age-old rhythm.

Afterwards, she was content to lie in his arms suffused in warmth and love, something Gabrielle had never experienced before. Even Bellegarde worshipped himself as much as he did her. Henry genuinely seemed to care for her, for her needs and pleasure, not simply his own, which was a revelation to her.

The second time she went to him more willingly, eager for his touch, for his searching mouth to plunder hers, for his skilful hands to explore her body. He kissed her deeply, evocatively, flaring a ready response in her. As passion flowed between them she clung to him, cried out and almost wept in the moment of climax. Before the night was over Gabrielle began to think that perhaps she hadn't made too bad a bargain after all.

Corisande received the news of this betrayal in a fury of despair. Word reached her from many sources so she did not doubt its veracity. Henry had deserted her. Despite his having sworn fidelity in so many of his letters, a younger, more beautiful, more desirable woman had taken her place in his heart, and in his bed. After all they had been to each other, all he had promised, a crown no less, he had forsaken her. Now he wanted her only as a go-between to break unwelcome news to his sister.

How dare he use her so!

A messenger had also come direct from Henry in the person of La Varanne, one of his most trusted servants, the very same who carried *billets-doux* between Henry and his new mistress, Gabrielle d'Estrées, which infuriated Corisande all the more.

As did the letter.

The King began not with any word of affection but simply a wish, an order almost, that Varanne talk with her on this most important matter of Princess Catherine's marriage: 'I understand that your discourse tended utterly to blame me, and to incite and support my sister in a course highly improper and injurious. I could not have believed this of you!... I will never pardon any person who tries to foment quarrels between my sister and myself.'

'I rather think you manage that all by yourself,' Corisande raged.

The Princess was frequently in tears over being treated so ill. It was a surprising love match in a way, as Soissons was lean, dark and swarthy, and rather cold in demeanour for all his sumptuous attire and fastidious habits. But then Catherine herself was somewhat stern, though cultivated and well educated in the classics, Latin and Greek, proficient in playing the organ and the flute. She could have taken her pick of suitors, yet had chosen her cousin, a catholic no less, and refused to relinquish him. Corisande felt it would be heartless to deny their love. Perhaps, king or no king, Henry should be taught a lesson for the callous way he behaved towards his ladies. For such a compassionate, good-natured man, he could be obstinately stubborn at times.

Corisande went at once to speak to Catherine, and to Soissons. Monsieur le Comte had been visiting his mother, the dowager Princess Condé, but had then written to inform the King that as Princess Catherine was intending to journey north into France, he felt he should personally escort her from Pau. Henry clearly saw through this excuse as his sister would have informed him, had she any such intention. Consequently, the Comte too had received a royal missive, issuing very clear instructions for him to stay away from Catherine, that a marriage was to be arranged for her, if not with James VI, then some other suitable alliance.

'I have responded with defiance,' Soissons told Corisande, reading her an extract from his letter. '"To obey Your Majesty would be an insult to the royal dignity, having once received permission to sue for the favour of that peerless princess, Madame Catherine." Were I not so in love, I might well have joined Mayenne to fight against the King.'

'Your only hope of happiness is to marry in secret, and quickly,' Corisande told them.

The Princess was aghast. 'Without my brother's consent. I dare not!'

'I dare,' Soissons assured her, taking Catherine's hands in his to cover them with ardent kisses. 'I am ready to face death rather than lose you. I have loved you since we were children together.'

'But this alliance with Scotland is necessary for Henry's campaign. He is still determined to bring it to fruition.'

'He will win through and gain the crown without need to sacrifice your happiness. He asks too much.'

'Charles is right,' Corisande urged, thinking how she would dearly like to see the King not get his own way for once. A just revenge for his callous treatment of her. 'Henry can be somewhat single-minded, but he loves you. You are his beloved sister, and, once you are wed, he would forgive you readily enough.'

'But what if he didn't? What then? He is not only my brother but King of France and Navarre.'

'I could not bear to lose you,' Charles said. 'Within the week I must return to the war. Marry me, Catherine, I beg you.'

Her heart was so full of love for him, and her resentment against her brother so bitter, how could she resist? She too feared losing Charles, was terrified of being packed off to cold, distant Scotland and the bed of a stranger much older than she. 'Very well, let's do it. Corisande, will you help us?'

'You know that you have my full support. I will

speak to your pastor without delay.'

Catherine laughed with excitement. 'Good, let us waste no more time.'

Cayet, Catherine's pastor, refused absolutely to conduct the service, and Soissons angrily reached for his sword. 'How dare you refuse a royal princess!'

'Kill me, Monsieur, if you must, for the King surely will if I obey.'

The Counsel of Elders informed the Princess that no pastor would take the risk of standing against the King.

'It would be a dangerous folly for any to marry the King's sister to the Comte de Soissons without Henry's express permission,' they told her, and no amount of persuasion or threats would change their minds.

Catherine was appalled to find her quarters surrounded by guards, and a furious and humiliated Soissons was escorted out of Béarn without even allowing them to make their farewells.

When rumours of this planned secret marriage reached Seigneur de Pangeas, he went straight to relay the startling news to his darling wife, *la petite* Tignonville, a former favourite of the King whom he had obligingly married in order for him to safely bed her. He'd been well pleased with the bargain, particularly now that Henry was no longer around. Tignonville hated Corisande, as her rival had managed to hold on to the King's affections far longer than she.

'I am glad to see that woman brought down at last, delighted that Henry has deserted her for another. But he will not welcome Corisande's interference with the Scottish alliance.'

'Indeed not,' Pangeas agreed. 'What would you recommend we do, my dear?'

'I believe, since we wish to remain in the King's favour, that we should report this mischief to him.'

Pangeas beamed at his pretty wife. 'It shall be done.'

When news reached Henry of the Princess's attempt to secretly marry Soissons, he was filled with dismay that Corisande and his beloved sister should plot together against him, and wrote a furious letter demanding an explanation.

Catherine's reply enraged Henry all the more. She did not even trouble to deny the charge, and hotly disputed his refusal to agree to their marriage.

'Having first attained to like the count at your express desire, now that he has fallen from your royal favour and become an object of suspicion, I will not abandon him.'

'She stubbornly refuses to recognize that her lover covets my crown and plots treason against me,' Henry raged to Rosny. 'Monsieur le Comte is restless, selfish and more ambitious than he pretends. Though he may have few followers, being the youngest of the House of Condé, yet he is entirely motivated by self-interest. I do not trust the fellow.'

Ever practical, Rosny said, 'I believe he will be hard put to win the crown above the Cardinal, his brother. His eminence is the favourite to replace you, Sire, amongst the Catholics, although neither shall succeed. You will prevail, I am certain of it.'

Henry was relieved by this reassurance, he was certainly not yet willing to admit defeat. Instead, he applied himself with renewed vigour to take Chartres. It was time he reasserted his authority over these audacious Bourbon princes. They'd steal neither his crown nor the hand of his sister.

Gabrielle revelled in the way the King cherished her. Their love making filled her with a delicious sense of being needed. Yet she was still secretly corresponding with Bellegarde as he too needed and yearned for her. She still loved and adored her Adonis. How could she not when he was so very handsome? Gabrielle began seeing her former lover in secret.

On the days when Henry was out hunting, or fighting in one of his endless battles, Bellegarde would come to her room. They would lie in bed together and whisper endearments, swearing promises of everlasting love. The very touch of his lips sent her into transports of delight, partly due to the terror of being caught by the King.

'I am quite incapable of giving you up,' Bellegarde would declare. 'I would risk death for your love.'

He almost got his wish.

One afternoon as the two lovers lay between the sheets, kissing and fondling and reaching ecstasies of passion together, they heard a great commotion below.

Gabrielle leapt from the bed. 'Dear God, it is the King. He has returned home early. Quickly, hide. He must not find you here.'

'You are still my betrothed, are you not? I shall fight him for you.'

Gabrielle was at once thrown into a panic. 'No, no! Oh, do please hurry. I can hear him on the stairs. He is already jealous and will run you through if he finds you here.'

Bellegarde began to snatch up his clothes while Gabrielle thrust his hat into his hand and only just managed to push her lover into a closet, lock the door, and slip back into bed before the chamber door burst open. Henry strode in. He brought with him the smell of fresh air and energetic good-will.

'My angel, what are you doing in bed at this hour? Are you sick?'

Gabrielle put on a sad face. 'I have the head-ache, Your Majesty, but then I was not expecting you back so soon.'

Henry beamed at her. 'No, you were not, my precious, but you know how I cannot bear to stay away from you for long. How pleasant it is here with the sun streaming in. I should have thought that with a headache you'd be best in the dark.' Marching over to the window he quickly closed the shutters. Then in his usual robust fashion, 'Move over, my lovely, and make room for your king. I dare swear I can spare you an hour or two and help rid you of this malady.'

'Oh, but Sire...'

He glanced about him as he began to unfasten his tunic. 'Ah, let us have a few sweetmeats. Do you not have a secret store in this closet?' Before Gabrielle could protest he'd marched over and tried the handle of the door. ''Tis locked. What is

217

this, fearful of a maid stealing your treats?'

Gabrielle managed a laugh, although she was shaking with nerves, wondering if Bellegarde would have the sense to pull on his clothes and make good his escape. There was a window he could climb out of, although it was narrow and set high in the wall. 'The maids do tend to use my *garde-robe* instead of their own. I expect they locked it by mistake. Anyway, it doesn't matter, I'm not in the mood for sweetmeats.'

'Oh, but I am. I'm hungry after my latest foray, and it is hours yet to dinner. Come, my dear, where is the key?'

Gabrielle was trembling in every limb as she pretended to search for the key, drawing it surreptitiously from beneath her pillow, then fussing over her bedside table as if she were really picking it up from there instead. 'Ah, here it is, but wouldn't it be better if I were to send for refreshments for you, my lord. Some chicken wings mayhap, and a glass of wine?'

But Henry had taken the key from her nerveless fingers and was even now inserting it into the lock. Gabrielle thought she might faint with fear right at his feet.

Swinging open the door, Henry stepped inside, then looking about him with an easy laugh, he brought out the box of sweetmeats. 'Here they are. What secrets you do keep in your closet,' he said, his dark Gascon eyes glittering with some expression Gabrielle couldn't quite discern.

'I have no secrets from you, Your Majesty.'

'Of course not,' he said with a wry smile as he pinched her cheek. 'How could you possibly?'

218

Then he took her back to bed and made love to her with his customary vigour. Outside, in the flower bed, hiding behind a juniper bush, Bellegarde nursed a sprained ankle, the jump having been somewhat higher than he'd bargained for.

'I don't think he guessed,' said the note dropped to him from that very same window later that evening. 'But stay away for a little while just to be sure. I will let you know when it is safe again, once Henry leaves on a longer campaign.'

Nothing would stop her from seeing her true love.

The next morning a letter was brought to her from the King, one filled with reproach, and the telling line, 'Make up your mind, my mistress, to have but one serviteur.'

Gabrielle paled as she read these words. He knew! Panic set her heart pounding as she quickly scanned the rest of the letter in which the King sneered at Bellegarde, addressing him as *'Dead Leaf'*, a nickname he used because Bellegarde's skin was somewhat sallow.

Coming in to help her dress, Madame de Sourdis found her niece in some distress.

'What is this?' she cried, taking the letter from her nerveless fingers. 'Dear heaven, are you mad, girl? You've still been seeing Bellegarde?'

'Only briefly,' Gabrielle admitted, somewhat stretching the truth. 'The King accuses him of being a poor sort of lover, and a coward in the field, which is entirely wrong. Even Henry has called him a valiant soldier and likes to have him by his side.'

219

'But not in his mistress's bed,' snapped Madame. 'You would risk all for a duke when you have won a king?'

Gabrielle began to weep. 'I meant no harm. I still love Bellegarde. I cannot live without him.'

'Foolish girl!' and her aunt slapped her hard across her cheek. 'Enough of this. You will risk all our fortunes, endanger our very lives if you do not take care. This is a patient king, but a jealous one.'

Gabrielle was shocked into silence. It had seemed like a game, a need in her to be with the man she wished to marry that surely did no harm. Now she began to see things differently. Her father, uncle and aunt, even Cheverny, her aunt's lover, had risen at court through her position as favourite to the King. They depended upon her keeping the royal favour in order to maintain their good fortune and titles, and remain safe.

More importantly, the King had guessed and been hurt by her betrayal. He had already proved himself an exciting and even a considerate lover, a kind and generous man who clearly adored her. Gabrielle was filled with shame. Henry did not deserve such callous disregard.

'See, he has forgiven me,' she said, breathing a sigh of relief as she read out his tender words of love.

'Nevertheless,' warned her aunt, unusually stern. 'You will need to take excessive care in future. You are the King's official *maîtresse en titre*, and must never forget it.'

Gabrielle wiped her eyes. Oh, but it was so hard to relinquish Bellegarde, whom she now thought of as her one true love. Was there not some way around this dilemma? 'Mayhap I should be making every attempt to provide a more secure future for myself too. What if I were to become *enceinte?* A husband is now even more essential, is it not?'

Madame de Sourdis conceded this to be a fair point. Gabrielle smiled. 'I shall speak to Papa and ask him to arrange it.'

The Marquis presented himself before his King with some nervousness. It was a difficult situation. His daughter desired a husband, and he knew full well whom she had in mind. It was a wish unlikely to be granted for he dare not even mention the Duke's name. Monsieur d'Estrées had heard the rumours over how the fellow had almost been discovered in his daughter's rooms. The girl's aunt had railed at her, even slapped her for taking such a foolish risk. There was no hushing up such a scandal, try as they might.

Now the Duc de Bellegarde had again been banished from court, had even returned his daughter's letters, and her portrait, in order to prove his goodwill to the King. The Marquis felt he could do no more than somehow attempt to salvage the honour of his house.

He bowed low and made the usual polite overtures before coming quickly to the point. 'Your Majesty, my daughter fears for her reputation as a single lady. She wishes to know if she may select a husband?'

Henry frowned. 'That task is surely best conducted by her father, think you not?'

The Marquis heartily wished he could wash his hands of the whole affair. 'Indeed, Sire, it is the usual way of going about such matters.'

'Do you have someone in mind?'

Realizing he had no choice, the Marquis continued, 'I rely upon your good judgement, Sire. Who would you advise that I choose?'

Henry strode about the room for a while, brow puckered in deep thought. Not Bellegarde, his Grand Equerry, that was certain. He'd sent the miscreant packing yet again, ordering him to stay away until he was able to return with a wife this time. The King turned to the Marquis with a wide grin. 'I have him. Nicholas d'Armerval, Baron de Liancour.'

'The Baron de Liancour?' Gabrielle stared at her father aghast. 'But he is *old*, a widower with *nine* children.'

'But extremely wealthy. You will want for nothing.'

'I will want for *everything*: for love, for decency, for honour. The man is weak, illiterate, and utterly repulsive to me. I will not do it!'

'It is the King's command, my dear.'

'Then I will speak to the King.'

Gabrielle strode from her chamber and went straight to Henry to throw herself on her knees before him. 'My father insists that I marry the Baron de Liancour. You cannot mean to allow him to sacrifice me in this way.'

Henry put up his hands to calm her. 'Do not blame me. This is family business. I cannot interfere in such private matters.'

Gabrielle knew better than to argue with him. Disagreeing with the King, however affable he may outwardly appear, might get her sent to

Usson like Queen Margot, or some similar bleak outpost. She succumbed to her ready tears. 'But I could not endure the Baron to touch me.'

Henry raised her to her feet and kissed each pale cheek. 'My dear, you will not need to. It will be a marriage in name only. Within the hour, once the deed is done, I shall hurry to your side and rescue you. Monsieur le Baron will be dismissed, be assured of it.'

'Oh, Henry, do you promise?'

'I do, my angel, I give you my word.'

By way of a wedding gift the King presented the bride with the lordships of Assy and St Lambert, and the county of Marie, in Picardy, to be held by her for life. It seemed small recompense for her sacrifice.

'Oh, how I wish my darling Bellegarde had been brave enough to whisk me away on the pommel of his horse,' she cried, weeping in the arms of her sisters. But neither Diane nor Juliette could offer any comfort.

'He is gone, at the King's bidding. There is no hope for you now,' Diane warned. 'You must accept your destiny.'

Juliette kissed her sister. 'You must make the best of what you have,' privately thinking it was in reality a great deal.

The marriage took place at Coeuvres at the beginning of January, 1591, and Gabrielle had already packed her belongings, carefully hidden from her father, so that she would be ready to join the King the moment he came for her. She had scarcely spoken to the Marquis since, believing that it was he, her own father, who had betrayed her; selling her off just as her mother had used to do.

Vows were exchanged, then the newly wedded couple partook of the wedding breakfast, after which the bride waited with growing excitement for the King to arrive and carry her away. When Henry did not come within the hour, as promised, she excused herself and fled to her room.

Gabrielle stood at her window gazing out upon the familiar view, anxiously waiting for the sound of horses' hooves on the gravel. She'd once excitedly anticipated the arrival of her lover, Bellegarde, and even Longueville, coming to pay court to her. How foolish she had been to vacillate between the two. If she had accepted Bellegarde when he'd first offered for her, they'd have been married long before the King ever set eyes on her. Oh, how things had changed. Now she ached for the sight of the King's white banner. Yet still Henry did not come, and her heart fluttered in panic.

'What am I to do?' she sobbed to her aunt.

Madame de Sourdis shared her distress, if for a different reason.

Keeping her niece in the King's favour was all-important to her plans, for the sake of the family, and for her own fortune. 'He will come. The King is a busy man. He must have been held up by some unexpected event. You will just have to be patient.'

'And if he does not arrive before nightfall?' Gabrielle stared at her aunt, wild-eyed.

Madame de Sourdis gave her niece's hands an affectionate squeeze. 'You will do what is required of you.'

'Never.'
'Oh, yes, my dear, you will.'

Henry was, at that precise moment, riding towards Paris. At long last an opportunity had arisen to engage in a project which he hoped might gain him entry to the city. Not for a moment did he hesitate. His love for his mistress, his promise to Gabrielle, were entirely forgotten against this greater ambition.

Henry and his men planned a surprise attack, which they attempted on the night of 20 January. A couple of dozen soldiers disguised as peasants leading donkeys laden with bags of flour, or pulling carts and wagons, approached the city gates at three in the morning and knocked for admittance. Behind them came the Baron de Biron at the head of an army of eight hundred men and four hundred horse. These held back under the cloak of darkness, the silence of the night broken only by the soft snort of a patient horse.

The plan was that the moment the gate opened, the army would charge and take the city.

Henry's pulse was pounding as he waited for the guard to let them in. Instead, the foolish fellow shouted that the city gate could not be opened at that hour. 'You'll need to go lower down the river, and cross at the ferry,' the guard advised.

'He's suspicious,' Biron said, coming forward to speak to his king. 'We have made a mistake in the hour. The ploy isn't going to succeed.'

The city suddenly came alive. Church bells began to peal, lights flitted about on the walls like crazed fireflies, and the ramparts began to swarm with men. Someone had got wind of their presence and Henry and his army were forced to turn tail and run.

As the King fled across country, pursued by Mayenne's army, Gabrielle was in the midst of her worst tantrum yet at Coeuvres. She stamped her foot and screamed at her aunt. Two feverish spots of crimson high on each cheekbone were the only sign of colour on her ashen face. 'It is *too much!* Too much, I say. How many more men will you sell me to? I will not do it! I will not step inside the same room as that monster, let alone sleep in the same bed.'

'My dear child, he is not at all a monster, but a most pleasant man. He may be weak and stupid and old, but also quiet and not unkind, and he is devastated to find his bride so unwilling.'

'Unwilling? I am adamant! I absolutely refuse to be a wife to him.'

'But you must, he is your husband. Were you to become *enceinte* with the King's child, would you not need to have at least slept once with the Baron in order to persuade him to father it?'

'I care not whether he did or not!' Gabrielle screamed, quite beside herself.

'Then you are in danger of throwing the handle out with the hatchet.'

'No, I am not! The King promised me this marriage would be in name only. I'm sure he told Monsieur le Baron the same. Liancour can go to hell in a handcart for all I care, but I will not sleep with the fat old fool.' And picking up a ceramic urn that had stood in all innocence upon her dressing table for years, she flung it across the room. It hit the door frame and smashed into a dozen pieces, causing her to wail all the louder for it had been one of her favourites.

In a panic, Madame de Sourdis called for one of the maids. 'Bring some cordial, quickly, my niece is unwell.'

Fearing Gabrielle may fall into an apoplectic fit, Madame was obliged to put her to bed with a warm posset and make what excuses she could to the bereft husband.

Having failed to enter Paris, the Maréchal de Biron marched instead to Chartres while Henry returned immediately to Senlis, and then to Chauny. His first thought was of Gabrielle. She'd written him a passionate letter, smudged with her tears, begging for rescue. But it was impossible for him to go to her at this time. Henry dispatched an order commanding Liancour to join him at Chauny, and to bring his wife. He even named the hour he would be expected to arrive.

The Baron wasted no time in obeying. He'd endured more than enough tears and threats from his reluctant bride in the last few days, and her undisguised hatred and contempt for him. The King could have her and welcome. When Henry offered him a castle in Limousin as compensation, the Baron gladly accepted and quickly departed with unseemly alacrity to take up residence there, not caring if he never saw his wife again.

'My dear,' Henry said to Gabrielle. 'Did I not come to you, as I promised?'

Gabrielle was so relieved that he had rescued

her from marriage with a man she loathed, that she did not attempt to quarrel with his timing. 'I am so very glad to see you, Henry.'

'Of course you are, my love, and I you.' He was already kissing her, his breath hot on her face as he tugged at the laces of her bodice with greedy fingers. Pushing her back on to the bed he quickly lifted her skirts, grunting with satisfaction as he entered her. 'There, isn't that what you were waiting for?'

Gabrielle willingly gave herself up to his demands, seduced, as ever, by the thrills of the moment, and a delicious relief at having escaped the gross attentions of a fat old husband.

Later in the month, Rosny brought Henry the news that the Duc de Mayenne, alarmed at the attempted assault on the city, had agreed that the Spanish could be admitted into Paris, so long as there were only sufficient to guard them from any future attacks.

Rosny continued, 'But then when the Spanish regiments entered on the eleventh of February, they were greeted with derision by the people, Sire, and pelted with excrement.'

Henry laughed out loud. 'Paris may not wish for a heretic king, but nor do they want the Spanish. We make progress, Rosny, we make progress.'

Following the departure of her husband, Gabrielle readily accompanied Henry on his march to Champagne, and the longer she spent in his company the fonder she became of him. He was an honest man, easy-going, who treated all those around him with respect and affection, including his servants. He liked to joke with his men, who all adored him and followed him gladly into battle. Gabrielle's generous heart warmed towards him, so much so that during the siege of Epernay in 1592 she was the one suffering from jealousy when the King appeared fascinated by the charms of Anne du Puy, like herself blonde and beautiful.

In distress she turned to her aunt for advice. 'What am I to do? Henry has even written a song in her honour.'

'A song is not his heart. It is you he loves, my sweet.'

'But how do I keep it?'

Madame de Sourdis smiled. 'Ah, the age-old question. Do not fret, all will be well. You must not complain but simply keep the King amused and happy. Make him laugh.'

Which Gabrielle proceeded to do with consummate skill.

Songs and poetry were soon forgotten as the siege of Epernay proved to be a serious business, in which Henry's old lieutenant, the Maréchal de Biron, lost his life by being mistaken for the King. A wind had blown off the King's hat with its trademark white plume. The pair had dismounted and in a jest the old Marshal had picked it up and placed it on his own head, whereupon he'd been struck by a cannonball.

In spite of his friend's death, Henry went on to win the battle, but he still wasn't able to capture Paris.

'There are rumours the Parisians now favour young Guise, son of their beloved hero,' Henry told her. 'He might marry the Infanta Isabelle of

Spain. 'Oh, but I am growing weary of battles and war.'

Gabrielle soothed him, stroking his head with a cool cloth. 'You will one day march in and take Paris, my dear, I know it.'

'My generals constantly urge me to bombard the city, but I have no appetite to take it at the expense of the lives of my people. What would I gain by slaughtering thousands in order to gain entry? I will not do it. I love France, and wish to bring peace, to restore her fortunes so sadly battered by years of civil war. I want prosperity and security for my people, for every Frenchman to have a chicken in his pot.'

'Perhaps,' Gabrielle suggested, 'the best way to achieve that ambition peaceably, is to renounce the Huguenot faith and reconcile yourself with the Catholic Church.'

Henry looked at her lovely face for a long moment. 'It is true that I have done as much before.'

'Then why not again?'

Henry was thoughtful for some time, but said no more on the subject.

In the months following, what with conflict against the intrigues of the League, and not certain whom he could trust among the ministers and nobles about him, Henry insisted on dealing with every important document himself. As a consequence, it surprised no one when he fell ill with exhaustion and a fever at St Denis. Many feared for the King's life and conferences were held almost hourly, with much speculation over who would succeed in the event of his death. Would it be the young Guise? Did Soissons stand the greater chance, the infant Condé, or the Cardinal de Bourbon who was universally distrusted? It was all most worrying.

The royal surgeon ordered complete bed rest and bled the King copiously in an effort to rid him of the fever. But Henry was hindering his own recovery by also fretting and worrying about the succession, privately vowing to confront Margot yet again on the issue of divorce the moment he was well.

Gabrielle, who was not with him on this occasion, wrote in alarm, 'I am dead with fright. Reassure me, I pray, by tidings of the health of the bravest of the brave ... I am a true Princess Constance, keenly sensitive to all that regards yourself.'

Thankfully, the King gradually recovered his health but the episode caused Gabrielle to think more seriously of her own situation.

She was at last content. Gabrielle had accepted her lot, grown fond of the King, and decided that she really rather enjoyed being a royal mistress. She had even stopped pining for Bellegarde who had returned to court, ostensibly in search of a wife. The King, ever generous and warm-hearted, had agreed to take his old comrade back. But then he had ever been fond of his Grand Equerry. Who else could look after his horses so well when out on campaign?

This morning, as usual, Gabrielle received in her chamber with all due ceremony as if it were *a lever*, and she were indeed a queen. It pleased her that even the King would remove his hat in her presence.

She began to dream of a crown. If Henry could get a divorce from Queen Margot, why could not she be granted one from Liancour too?

Gabrielle had perfectly made up her mind to be Queen of France in very truth one day. And yet she had concerns. The ladies of the court did not yet accept her, and with the Princess Catherine due to arrive at any time, she feared yet more humiliation and disdain.

'How could I ever dare to hope he would make me his queen? How could I possibly be good enough for the task? I am too ignorant.'

Madame de Sourdis smiled and patted her hand. 'You may not be classically educated as is Madame Catherine, but you have a good heart and much affection for her brother. The King not only loves you but is completely faithful to you. That has not been the case with any of his other mistresses. And he readily rescued you from your husband, did he not?'

Gabrielle gave a wry smile. 'In his own good time he did, yes. But what if he tires of me, as he did with Corisande, and Tignonville, and goodness knows how many others?'

'I will teach you whatever you need to know to keep his interest and passions hot. Am I not an expert in the art of pleasing a man? I manage to keep both husband and lover content.'

Gabrielle laughed. 'Dear Aunt, that will not be necessary. I was well taught by the Cardinal, and the King seems well pleased with me in the business of the bedchamber. But perhaps in other matters such as etiquette, court traditions and politics, and dealing with the austere Princess

Catherine, I would welcome your advice.'

'You can be assured you will have it.' Madame de Sourdis had no intention of losing her influence over the new *maîtresse en titre*.

Still unconvinced of her own ability to cope, Gabrielle sweetly begged Henry if she might be permitted to withdraw from the court to Coeuvres during the length of his sister's visit, but he would not hear of it.

'I will ensure honourable treatment from Madame,' he promised her.

When the moment came Gabrielle sank into a deep curtsey as Madame Catherine walked towards her in all her majesty. She was no beauty, her forehead broad, mouth tightly pursed, and with a small, pointed chin. Just to look at her was to know that she was a royal princess. Her azure gown was magnificent, encrusted with emeralds and pearls, a matching tiara atop her blond peruke. Her bearing, her manner was so regal, so superior, that Gabrielle was overcome with a sense of her own inadequacy. What folly to imagine herself capable of donning the royal mantle!

'So this is your latest favourite?' Catherine said, holding out a hand to be kissed as she looked down her long Bourbon nose at Gabrielle. 'And I thought she was reputed to be a beauty.'

Gabrielle took the proffered hand and kissed one of the princess's rings, wisely saying nothing to this put-down.

Henry, however, was his usual jovial self. 'As you see, rumour did not lie.'

Catherine saw that it would be difficult to

dispute the beauty of the girl before her, or her naïve sweetness and youth. 'If you care for a pale and wan complexion,' she caustically remarked, as if Gabrielle were deaf as well as silent.

'She is my angel,' Henry proudly declared, 'and I am sure you welcome the opportunity to make the acquaintance of one who is soon to be related to you, Madame.'

'I seem to recall having heard numerous similar promises in the past.'

'But none with the sincerity of this one, I do assure you.'

The King was aware that his sister had brought with her as companion his erstwhile mistress Corisande, whom he now referred to more formally as Madame de Guiche, but he did not fear any further reprisals from that lady's jealousy. He had already dismissed the pastor Cayet from the office of private chaplain to the princess, just to be on the safe side, along with several others from Catherine's suite who had aided and abetted the plan for a secret wedding. He had even deprived his sister of the regency of Béarn. Yet Henry largely blamed Corisande for the mischief, as, despite their differences, he was still fond of his beloved Catherine.

'I have even acquired the art of constancy,' Henry proudly informed her.

'Constant? You?' The Princess Catherine raised her brow in ironic disbelief. But noting the way her brother tenderly caressed the girl's cheek, and her long, shining fair hair, she held back the sharp retort that sprang to her lips. She was still in secret correspondence with Soissons and had pleas to make for her own future. It would do no good to alienate her brother from the outset.

Thwarted in her desire to marry the man of her choice, she had written to Pope Clement VIII offering to abandon her Calvinist religion if he could persuade the King to sanction her union with the Comte. So far she'd heard no word on the matter. And so Catherine had decided to quit Pau, however reluctantly, and pursue the matter with Henry in person. Before leaving last October she'd given a fine banquet for her friends and subjects, who in vain had begged her to stay. Since then she'd suffered snow and ice, and all manner of severe weather as she'd progressed north, spending Christmas Day with precious little in the way of comfort at Partheney. Now it was February and, as instructed, she'd obediently waited for her brother at Saumur.

But Catherine could tell, simply by his demeanour, that her cause was lost before it had barely begun. His next words proved her to be entirely correct.

'Since the Scottish alliance has come to nought, I am delighted to receive an offer for your hand from the Duc de Montpensier. What say you to that, sister?'

Catherine lifted her chin in mute defiance.

'Well?'

The tension was so great Gabrielle would have crept away had not Henry kept a firm hold upon her arm.

The Princess finally responded in icy tones. 'I say that you are the most heartless of brothers.'

'Why so? He is young, wealthy, handsome and

gallant. Allow me to introduce him and you can judge for yourself.'

The Duke eagerly stepped forward, would have taken the Princess's hand had Catherine not refused to allow it. 'I fear,' she said, fixing him with a cold glare, 'that you are too young, too wealthy, too handsome, and too gallant for my taste. Now I must beg to be excused. It has been a long and tiring journey.'

The Duc de Montpensier tactfully withdrew his suit and paid court instead to the youthful heiress of the Duc de Joyeuse, who was far more amenable.

Henry, irritated beyond endurance by his sister, continued to argue and press her to change her mind throughout the ten days of their stay in Saumur, and she as steadfastly refused to be bullied. He longed for peace between them, as there had been in days gone by, and on one occasion when Henry entered her apartment, he unthinkingly joined in the singing of a psalm.

Gabrielle quickly placed her fingers to his lips. 'Do not display your religion so openly,' she warned him in a whisper, and Henry frowned, taking in the earnestness of her expression and wondering if she might be right. He needed to be ever careful.

It was with some relief that he finally escorted Madame Catherine to Tours, and, determined to put a stop to any more secret meetings, he warned the governor of the town not to allow the Comte de Soissons to even enter.

The King and Gabrielle then continued on to Chartres. Although Henry did not relish the prospect of yet more battles, the time was fast approaching for one last decisive attempt to take Paris and claim his crown. In the meantime, irritated by his sister's dismissal of Montpensier and still determined to win the House of Lorraine over to his side as part of his peace mission, Henry wrote instead to the Duc de Bar. He was the son of Claude, Catherine de Medici's second daughter, and Charles, Duke of Lorraine. Henry duly offered him the Princess's hand, for, like it or no, his sister would do as she was bid.

The misery of the people of Paris was great. Trade was at an all time low, public buildings such as the Louvre and the Tuileries were fast falling into decay, food continued to be scarce and all public amusement forbidden for fear of riots. Madame Montpensier, the so-called Fury of the League, could as easily be greeted with hisses and catcalls now as cheers. Posters of the King, and then of Madame Gabrielle, began to appear in shop windows. It seemed that the citizens were indicating their willingness to think again about this king of theirs. Many of the citizens were for petitioning Henry to give freedom to their city.

This time as the King departed for the camp at Dreux, Gabrielle wept. 'I too am weary of these long campaigns which take you constantly away from me, and I fear for your safety.'

Henry held her close in his arms. 'I will write to you, my love, as I always do, and come to you when I can.'

Gabrielle conceded that perhaps he did over-indulge her by dashing home to see her far too often, which may well have reflected the outcome of a battle on occasions. It had ever been his flaw.

His letters, as loving as ever, arrived daily. In June, he wrote, 'I have sent a magnificent bouquet of orange flowers by a special envoy.'

A week later, 'I found only an hour ago a means of completing your set of plate: see how I take care of you.'

'Was ever a woman more adored,' sighed Madame de Sourdis.

He begged Gabrielle to meet him at Anet, 'where I shall have the felicity of seeing you every day'.

But on that occasion he was unable to keep his promise, due to constant skirmishes with the Leaguers and the Spanish.

When he did finally come, Gabrielle fell into his arms with sobs of relief. 'I have been out of my mind with worry.' It astonished her how very much she did miss him when he was away, and how anxious she became that something terrible might happen to him. Her love for this man whom she had once so avoided was growing by the day. Later, after they had made love, they talked. 'Why not disarm, Henry. I say again, is it not time to end the war and reconcile yourself with the Mother Church?'

His passion for her was such that Henry listened to her advice, and knew she was right. The war was destroying the nation and could not go on indefinitely. He also recognized that once he had the crown he could petition more forcefully for a divorce from Queen Margot, and make Gabrielle his queen. Only then could he ensure the succession and gain the security he needed for his reign. Whatever scruples he felt about letting down his mother, Jeanne d'Albret, could be overcome by ensuring the people of Béarn gained a more prosperous kingdom, and tolerance for their religion. He would insist upon that, at least.

Henry sent for Rosny. 'I have come to the conclusion that I should renounce the Huguenot faith and reconcile myself with the Catholic Church. It will have multiple benefits: thwart Spain and the Princes of Lorraine, secure the nation's fortunes sadly depleted after so many years of civil war, win Paris, a crown, and most of all, bring peace to the realm.'

Rosny was unsurprised by this announcement, having sensed it was coming for some time. 'You did only what you had to do in order to protect the principality of Béarn.'

'And I wished to be a good son to my mother, but I never did share her passion for Puritanism, nor placed great store upon the tenets of any religion. It is the same God we worship, is it not?'

'That is indeed true, Sire. We are all God's children. I am sure your heroic mother would forgive the necessity for change, in the circumstances.' Rosny privately vowed not to convert to Catholicism himself. He fully intended to remain a Protestant, although he had no quarrel with his sovereign doing whatever was necessary for political purposes.

Henry said, 'Perhaps the difference between the two religions only appears to be so great by reason of the animosity of those that preach them.'

As always Rosny added a cautious warning.

'The difficulty lies in pleasing the Catholics without alienating your Huguenot followers.'

'I agree.' Henry was thoughtful. 'Can it be done?'

'The prize is surely worth the risk.'

Henry nodded his agreement. 'Indeed it is, Rosny. Paris is worth a Mass.'

Aubigné, Henry's old Puritan chamberlain, bitterly contested this decision.

'Would you abandon your people? Would you dare to turn them into papists?'

'I would hope that all religions could live in peace together,' Henry calmly informed him. 'It is time to have done with warfare, and for that reason alone it is worth my surrendering the reformed faith, which is no sacrifice at all since I promise to ensure the freedom of the Huguenots to worship as they choose.'

The old man's lip almost curled with disbelief. 'You think they will have confidence in such a promise from a turncoat king? I very much doubt it. They will see only that you have abandoned and betrayed your much revered mother.'

Henry went pale, firmly holding his temper in check. 'Mind that sharp tongue of yours, old man. I have given my life to the cause, as my mother asked. Now it is a time for change, to look forward to a new future for France. I trust my people will see that peace with Spain will soften the blow.'

'They will see that you have lost all affection, goodwill and gratitude for the Calvinists of your realm, that you no longer care to preserve the lives, faith and liberty of your subjects.'

Tight-lipped, the King icily responded. 'Their honour and freedom will remain intact, if not enhanced. I swear it. The question you have to answer is: will you support me in this?'

The pause while Henry waited for his chamberlain's reply was telling. At length, the answer came. 'I request that I may retire to Béarn to reflect upon the matter at my leisure.'

'Take as long as you please,' snapped the King. 'I am sure we can manage perfectly well without your presence at court, for as long as it takes for you to search your conscience.'

Finding himself thus dismissed, Aubigné made a hasty departure south.

The ceremony for abjuration took place in July, 1593. The streets all around the Cathedral of St Denis were hung with garlands and lined with the royal bodyguard. Inside, Gabrielle was provided with a seat beneath the canopy of state, together with other ladies of the court, from which she had a good view of the altar.

They did not speak to her, nor she to them, feeling as always that they mostly viewed her with a degree of contempt. Mademoiselle de Guise was particularly cool, and had deliberately provoked her by flirting outrageously with Henry at a recent banquet, leaving Gabrielle quite burning up with jealousy. It hadn't helped that she had then moved on to enamour Bellegarde, who fell into a veritable passion over her.

Not that Gabrielle cared who Bellegarde chose to marry. She had her eye on a higher destiny now.

The Swiss Guard entered first, banners carried

aloft, followed by the King accompanied by a *cortège* of nobles and princes of court. Gabrielle's heart swelled with pride at the sight of her royal lover. Henry looked so splendidly regal in a doublet and jerkin of white satin over which he wore a cloak of black velvet. Trumpets sounded, kettle-drums beat a steady rhythm and the whole building seemed to vibrate with the majesty of the proceedings. The bishops of Digne, Mantes, Angers and Chartres stepped forward, gorgeously arrayed in their copes and mitres. The abbot of St Denis with his cross of gold, the aconites bearing the vessel of holy water and the book of the gospel, hovered close by, ready to do their part.

The King's voice rang out loud and clear. 'I promise and swear, in the name of God Almighty and Omnipotent, henceforth to live and die in the communion of the Catholic Apostolic and Roman faith...'

Gabrielle listened, entranced. The promise and the words of absolution and reconciliation continued, followed by the kissing of rings and laying on of hands. No ceremony could have been more splendid, and when it was done, the Te Deums sung and Mass celebrated, the King pardoned for his long transgression, a great rousing cheer rose to the rafters, the ladies waved their handkerchiefs in delight, and the people cried, *'Vive le roi!'*

Afterwards, Gabrielle was one of the first to sink to a low curtsey and offer obeisance to His Majesty; her blue eyes shining as she lifted her gaze to his.

'Now we can look to our own happiness,' he whispered, as he raised her with a kiss.

242

It was the end of August before Henry left St Denis, having dealt with various pressing matters. The King and Gabrielle then progressed to Fontainebleau for a much-needed rest. Princess Catherine was staying in the palace and Henry thought it would offer him the opportunity to clarify matters with his sister.

The royal party stopped en route at Melun where Henry was urged to stay close indoors. 'A Dominican monk has warned of a likely attempt upon Your Majesty's life.'

Henry laughed off the threat. 'I have heard such before but I will not cower in some corner, or live in fear of mad monks.'

'Nevertheless, Sire, it would be wise to be cautious,' his nobles urged.

Fortunately the man was arrested as soon as he entered the town, and was found to be carrying a long sharp knife.

Gabrielle was beside herself with fright when she heard. 'What if he had succeeded?'

'But he did not succeed, my angel. My men protected me, although we should perhaps be ever wary. No doubt there will be other attempts upon my life. It is the lot of kings to be pursued by fanatics.'

'But you are so tolerant, so reasonable. Who was this man and why would he wish to kill you?'

'His name is Pierre Barrière. He is a wheelwright from Orléans, and apparently helped Queen Margot, under the command of Guise, to escape from the Marquis de Canillac. He later entered Margot's service as a soldier at the garrison of

Usson, and has taken it into his foolish head to avenge the Queen for some perceived injustice by killing me, her husband.'

Gabrielle was appalled. 'The *Queen*, your own *wife*, attempted to have you assassinated?'

'No, no, my love, she did no such thing. Margot herself also warned me he may make an attempt. She had already rejected his proposal with horror, and dismissed the knave from her service. You are not to fret, all is well, I do assure you.'

The Palace of Fontainebleau had been much neglected during the reign of Henry Trois as he had not cared for country pursuits. Henry Quatre, however, thrived on them, and loved nothing more than hunting in the thick forests that surrounded the chateau. The royal lovers rode side by side, ahead of the rest of the court, savouring an opportunity to be at last alone.

Gabrielle was dressed in a *devantière*, which was a divided skirt, as she loved to ride astride. It was green, her favourite colour, with silver embroidery both on the hem of the skirts, and on the cuffs of the jacket. Her mantle was lined with green figured satin, and the buttonholes too embroidered in silver, the matching hat sporting a fine feather. The outfit had cost all of two hundred crowns, and Gabrielle thought it very fine.

Every now and then Henry would lean over and whisper some witty nonsense, and Gabrielle's eyes would sparkle and she would laugh out loud.

'I would recommend, my love, that since you seem to be starting a headache, you would be well advised to retire to your room early.' This surprising statement was accompanied by a broad wink.

'But I feel perfectly well,' Gabrielle protested.

'Even more good reason for you to remain in your apartment, for I have news to impart to the Princess Catherine, and her reaction may well give *me* a headache before the discussion is ended.'

Gabrielle looked instantly troubled. 'Ah, then I must beg leave to take supper with my ladies in my room this evening. I fear I may have caught a chill.'

'Very wise, my dear, very wise. The temperature in the dining salon may be somewhat too cold for you.'

Exactly as Henry had predicted Catherine erupted in cold fury to the news that she was to be betrothed to the Duke of Bar.

'There will be no further argument over this, the matter is settled. You are to marry Henri, Duke of Lorraine and Bar.'

Catherine had not been present at the ceremony of abjuration as she had declared it too painful to witness her own brother abandoning his true religion. This now seemed to her like a double blow.

'If you wished to adhere me to the House of Lorraine for the sake of peace with your enemies, why not accept the Comte de Soissons? He is a Bourbon too.'

Henry carved himself a second slice of ham and ignored the remark, since his sister refuted any charge that Monsieur le Comte nursed ambitions of his own. 'De Bar is a fine young man. I am sure you will do well together.'

'He is a Catholic, and I will not betray our mother, Henry, even if you have.'

Henry paused in his carving to gaze at her with sad eyes. 'Catarina,' he said, using her pet name, the one their mother had used when she was but a girl in Nérac. 'That was unworthy of you.'

Tears sprang into her dark eyes. 'What am I supposed to think? You no longer care for my happiness, only your own. You've changed your coat yet again, and I am supposed to follow.'

'You must do as your own conscience bids you, I shall make no demands upon you in the respect of religion, save to ask you to desist from holding your very public *prêches*. It upsets my counsellors, and it will further annoy and incite the people, should you persist in the practice. As for seeing de Bar's religion as a hindrance to your acceptance of his offer, it makes no sense. Soissons is likewise a Catholic and you were willing enough to accept him. I believe you once wrote to the Pope offering to abjure the protestant faith yourself, if he would only speak for you.'

Catherine was embarrassed and enraged that he should have discovered her ploy. 'Do you read my letters? Did you set spies on me?'

Henry avoided answering this charge, since naturally he kept as close an eye as possible on his sister's affairs. 'I am simply saying that your argument is illogical.'

'You would still require a dispensation, as de Bar is yet another cousin.'

Henry chewed happily on his ham. 'That can be arranged.'

Pushing aside her untouched meal Catherine

246

leaped to her feet. 'I will never agree to this, Henry. Never!' And with that she stormed from the dining salon.

Gabrielle was pregnant, and the need for a divorce suddenly urgent. Excited by the prospect of a dauphin for France, Henry went at once to Rosny. He wisely kept this snippet of information to himself, at least for the present, until he had achieved his object. Henry wanted no scandal, as there had once been over the Fosseuse incident. This time he meant matters to go more smoothly.

'I have decided it is time to seek a divorce. I cannot see that Margot would object. Our marriage was arranged without her agreement, without even a written dispensation from the Pope, despite our being cousins which is prohibited by the Church. Her mother and brother forced her to accept our alliance in a supposed bid for peace. Even when she remained resolutely silent at the altar, Henri put a hand to her head and forcibly inclined it in agreement, which the bishop accepted. No more was I given any choice in the matter.'

'Royal princes and princesses rarely are allowed any choice,' Rosny dryly commented, thinking of Madame Catherine.

'Nevertheless, it was a pointless exercise, turning into yet more bloodshed, and although Margot and I rubbed along well enough for a while, there is no reason why she would not now seek a divorce as eagerly as I.'

'Let us hope that is the case. Sadly, the Queen's life has been beset with scandal. Even in her mountain retreat, where she was taken as prisoner, she has won round her jailors with her charm, or greater favours if we are to believe the rumour-mongers, and taken control of the castle. She calls it her Ark of Refuge.'

'Then let her remain there if that is her wish, but she must needs renounce the throne.'

'Would Your Majesty then seek a new bride?'

Henry's dark Gascon eyes twinkled merrily. He had no wish at this delicate stage of the proceedings to reveal his true intentions. Rosny was such an old fusspot he would be sure to issue a lecture on the dire consequences of a king marrying his mistress. 'I would indeed, dear fellow, I would indeed, one I shall choose with great care and discernment. Then we may have a legitimate heir for France.'

'That is what we all wish for, Sire.' Rosny considered saying more, but changed his mind. Surely, even romantic Henry would not be so foolish as to attempt to make Madame Gabrielle his queen?

Monsieur Erard, Master of Requests to Queen Margot, was duly dispatched to Usson, carrying letters from the King, and from Rosny, with the instruction to bring back an authorization that they may proceed with the matter with all speed.

Margot's response, which arrived a few weeks later, delighted the King. She thanked him for his offer of 250,000 crowns to repay her debts, and looked forward to receiving the money, saying she saw no reason why they couldn't come to agreeable terms, so long as all her needs were met.

'And what are the extent of those needs, precisely?' Henry asked, as ever trusting his favourite minister to deal with such tricky matters for him. 'Did you discover?'

'I did.' Rosny consulted his notes. 'The gift of Usson as a residence, and the return of any other property to which she may be entitled. The Queen also wishes you to continue to pay her the fifty thousand francs a year pension which she enjoyed under the late king, her brother.'

'Can we arrange that for her, Rosny?'

Rosny sighed. 'You will need to speak to Sancy, since he is in charge of the treasury; but I see no reason why we should not accommodate Her Majesty. We may have to.'

Beaming with pleasure, Henry went straight to Gabrielle. 'All is going well, *mon cher coeur*. I have already written a warm response to the Queen, assuring her of our continued friendship, and that I will all my life care for her welfare.'

'You did not say that you loved her?' Gabrielle asked, feeling strangely vulnerable in her delicate condition, and a little jealous of this queen said to be the most beautiful woman in France.

'Certainly not, my angel. It is you that I love, but Margot and I have generally managed to remain on cordial terms, save for the odd spat. It is essential that we remain so now, at least until the papers are signed.'

Gabrielle leaned into his arms, letting him stroke and pet her. 'You are so good to me, Henry, and I do love you dearly.'

'Of course you do, my sweet, and I you.'

'It is just that I find this all so ... so degrading. If only the Queen had granted you a divorce when first we met we would have been man and wife by now.'

'Ah, my love, let us not fret about the past. These matters take time but all is going smoothly, I assure you. Now you must rest and think of the babe.'

A second letter came from Margot early in the new year, less agreeable than the first. It seemed that some busybody from the court had taken it upon themselves to mention Gabrielle d'Estrées as the real reason for the King's sudden desire for a divorce. The prospect of Henry's mistress as her successor to the throne, stealing the crown she might have worn, was too much for Margot.

'I will never yield my rights *à cette décriée bagasse*. I would better wear the crown of the *fleurs-de-lis* myself.'

Gabrielle wept when she heard the news. 'But you promised all would be well. I am about to present you with a son, do I not deserve better?'

'All is not lost, my love, merely delayed. Now we must apply for the sanction of the Holy See. I hoped to avoid involving the Pope, if Margot had been willing to make a declaration before an ecclesiastical judge, but as she refuses to cooperate we have no choice. Once we have the dispensation, I will again speak with her on the matter.'

As pragmatic as ever, Henry philosophically accepted the situation and managed to calm Gabrielle, but his determination to marry his adored mistress was as firm as ever. He also made her status abundantly clear to those around him.

'My ministers would be wise not to take me for a fool,' he warned Rosny. 'I am aware they mur-

mur against her, and their wives turn a cold shoulder. I will have her treated with proper respect.'

Rosny took great care to hide his alarm at this defence of his mistress on the part of the King. It might well be customary to turn a blind eye to a commonly accepted practice, but respect, for a King's whore, was not normally a requirement. He feared this might presage more serious steps toward elevating her position further, which would be entirely inappropriate. But even Rosny did not risk saying as much out loud. 'I do not doubt her constancy, Sire.'

As if reading his counsellor's mind, Henry continued, 'She is a person in whom I have complete confidence, to whom I can confide my deepest secrets and concerns. I receive from her in all such matters a familiar and sweet consolation. She is my queen in all but name.'

Rosny obediently inclined his head. 'There are as many who revere Madame Gabrielle for her kindness and gentleness as decry her. I will see to it that your wishes in this matter are made known.'

Henry was conducted to the Cathedral at Chartres at first light on the morning of 27 February, 1594. He had spent a quiet evening in preparation for this great day, now he was eager to receive the diadem he had fought for so long. Attired in the traditional vest of crimson satin and a robe of cloth of silver, he processed down the aisle following a long line of important personages. First the bishops and clergy, then the Swiss Guards, the trumpets and heralds, knights, chamberlains and ministers including his favourite,

251

Rosny, Chancellor Cheverny, Longueville as Grand Chamberlain, and the Duke of Bellegarde, his Master of Horse.

Henry prostrated himself before the altar, offering a small shrine of silver before being conducted to his Chair of State.

The ceremony was lengthy and tiring, coming to a climax when the crown of Charlemagne was set upon his brow. *'Vive le roi! Vive le roi!'* The cheers burst forth from the people crowded outside and in the nave of the cathedral, *largesse* was distributed to the poor, the doors were flung open so that the citizens could gaze in awe upon their new king seated in state upon his throne.

Henry could hardly believe it himself. He was here, at last, the senseless wars of religion largely behind him, although he would remain ever watchful. The Duke of Mayenne had submitted, but no peace had yet been secured with the Spaniards who continued to threaten northern France. Nevertheless, he was, without doubt, a victorious monarch, anointed and crowned. King of France and Navarre. None could deny it. He hoped for the end of strife, the end of the League, the banishing of the Spanish from the nation, for a new and better future for France.

And a legitimate dauphin.

At the conclusion of the coronation ceremony, following the Holy Eucharist, Henry was relieved of the weight of the crown by the Prince de Conti, and, gowned in his royal robes of purple velvet lined with ermine, bearing the sceptre and orb, he joined the procession as it made its slow progress back up the aisle. Guns fired in salute, the people cheered and applauded, the noisy celebrations continuing long after the King had retired to his chamber for a rest.

The Princess Catherine sat under the royal canopy beside Henry and Gabrielle. The nobles, princes and their ladies were gathered below; ambassadors and other officers of state seated on tables in the great hall. Even the galleries above were crowded with those not fortunate enough to win a place at the banquet but content to watch and marvel. Each dish was presented with a flourish of trumpets: capons, roast chicken, venison, a chine of beef, and Henry's favourite pigeon pie. Catherine found she had little appetite, quietly longing for the feast to be over. She was falling into the trap of becoming a recluse. Prayers were her only comfort, yet her brother objected even to these. Were she a Catholic she would retire to a monastery and become a most chaste and devoted nun. Instead, she gathered her supporters about her and held fast to her faith.

Some instinct caused her to look up, and there before her stood the Comte. He was smiling at her, as only he could, and Catherine's heart melted with love for him.

'Madame,' he said, and on bended knee handed her a silver basin and ewer, and a towel, richly fringed and tasselled. 'For the King His Majesty.'

It was Soissons' duty, as Grand Master, to bring her these but as Catherine took the implements from him she allowed her fingers to lightly touch his. A frisson of longing shot through her and their gazes locked. It had been so long since she'd last seen him that Catherine almost lost control. The urge to say his name, to sob it out loud, momentarily overwhelmed her. But something in his expression, in the half smile, and the warning narrowing of his eyes saved her. Then he bowed and stepped back. Only she knew what it cost him to appear so cool and indifferent.

Gathering her pride about her, Catherine carried the basin to the King. As the highest lady in the land, since Henry had no queen at his side, it was her prerogative to pour water over His Majesty's hands. She caught the envious look in his mistress's eyes and hid a quiet smile.

'I thank you, dearest Catarina, for this gesture of homage,' Henry said.

Rising, he embraced his sister before leading her back to their apartments, Catherine on one hand and Gabrielle on the other. It irritated Catherine that her brother's *maîtresse en titre* should be so honoured, almost as if they were equal, and she carefully avoided further eye contact with the woman. Although, even she knew better than to remark upon the fact.

At the door of her apartment Henry paused and embraced Catherine again. 'We are all greatly fatigued after the ceremonies of this long exhausting day. Rest easy, Madame. You were most noble and dignified just now before Monsieur le Comte. I am glad to see that you are coming round to accepting the duty required of you.'

Catherine made no reply, but, once alone in her bedchamber, she succumbed to bitter tears.

At seven o'clock on the morning of 22 March,

Henry at last entered Paris, which had so long defied him, and was dutifully presented with the keys of the city. The enthusiasm of the people was heart-warming to behold. They rushed out into the streets crying, *'Vive le roi!'*, delirious with happiness and excited to welcome their newly crowned king. Henry felt himself choke with tears, humbled by their faith in him, by the hope and joy in their faces. He ordered his soldiers to stand back so that there were no barriers between himself and his citizens.

One old man came to embrace his knees as Henry sat astride his horse.

Alarmed, the officer of the guard warned him, 'Sire, do not allow the mob to get too close. If another such as Barrière were in the crowd, they might avail themselves of this opportunity to do harm.'

But Henry refused to be diverted. 'Let them look at me, and cheer me. I would accept the risk rather than disappoint my people. It is long since they have seen a true king.'

There were those less pleased to see Henry crowned, as the officer now reminded him. 'Your enemies the Duke of Feria, Mendoza and others have taken refuge in a house close by the Bastille. Would you have us move them into that more secure place?'

Henry shook his head. 'Let them see that I intend to be a wise and moderate king, even in my hour of triumph. I will not reduce an enemy fallen to desperation.'

'They still hold some of your supporters prisoner.'

'Then demand their release in return for their own safe conduct to the frontier. Any who wish to live by Spanish rule may do so – in Spain.'

'They are all afraid, Sire. Madame de Nemours, mother of the dead hero Guise, was found in her oratory on her knees before a crucifix, and her daughter, Madame de Montpensier, the Fury of the League, sprang shrieking from her bed in paroxysms of rage and panic.'

Henry gave a great belly laugh. 'That lady need fear nothing from me, no more than I fear her. Now let us be done with politics and leave me to enjoy this day.'

The temperature in the bedchamber was stifling, every window closed and a fire burned in the grate despite the June heat. It was considered essential that a delicate equilibrium of the humours be maintained, and a cold draught from a window was considered dangerous. A birthing chair stood ready although it was generally agreed that the woman on the bed, for all her writhing and screaming in agony, was some hours from actual delivery.

'I would say four, maybe five hours or more,' pronounced the midwife.

Gabrielle felt certain she would be dead by then. Never had she known such pain. The royal physician, Monsieur Ailleboust, was naturally present with his bag of instruments, which Gabrielle hoped and prayed would not be necessary. He concurred with the midwife's prediction.

'Giving birth is a tiring business, Madame. I suggest you take a little light refreshment and rest.'

With pains coming every five minutes Gabrielle saw little hope of achieving either. But having made this pronouncement, the doctor retired to the window seat to enjoy his own lunch, comprising a plate of cold meats, good white bread and a glass of small beer.

'First babies are always slow to come,' Madame de Sourdis told her, by way of comfort. 'And boys are often harder to birth than girls, being bigger.'

Gabrielle took a welcome sip of cool water from the cup her aunt offered and met her shrewd gaze. They both knew that whatever the sex of the child, not a person in the crowded room was unaware that it would be born a bastard. The much-longed-for divorce had still not materialized. 'Henry has promised to legitimize him.' Gabrielle sighed. 'But we still wait on the Queen before we can marry.'

Madame de Sourdis wiped the beads of sweat from her niece's brow. 'Let us not trouble ourselves about such matters today, my dear. You have work to do, and must rest as the doctor says.'

Oil was rubbed on her belly to ease the straining, and, propped on pillows, Gabrielle lay on her side while her aunt rubbed her back, which helped her to relax a little.

When the time came she was lifted into the birthing chair, with the doctor and midwife at her side, and her other ladies hovering close by in a fever of concern and curiosity. Gabrielle felt strangely calm and happy, and if there was pain she no longer registered it. She pushed when she was instructed to do so, eased into shallow breaths when she was urged not to, and suddenly there the baby lay in the hands of the good doctor, with the minimum of fuss and trouble.

The cry went up. 'It is a boy!'

When word was taken to the King, waiting impatiently in the corridors outside, Henry was overjoyed. How long he had dreamed of this moment. His two children with Corisande having both died, this was his first child.

Would that he were a dauphin.

The moment the doctor granted permission Henry hurried to his mistress's side. '*Ventre Saint Gris*, what a clever girl you are. But how I feared for you. I kiss your eyes a thousand times, *Mon cher coeur*.'

The child was named César, the Duke of Vendôme.

'I shall reward you, my love, by bestowing upon you the title of Marquise de Monceaux.'

Gabrielle lay back on her pillows with a happy sigh. 'I am the most fortunate of women to be so loved.'

Henry flushed with pride and joy as the baby was placed in his arms. He adored children, and hoped to have a nursery full. 'And I am the most fortunate of kings.'

Gabrielle felt wonderful, bursting with health and vigour, and so blessed she felt nothing could spoil her happiness. She looked forward to a quiet period of rest with her child, not expecting to find her lying-in at all tedious as she had her aunt and her maids of honour to keep her company, and her precious son to cuddle. She even insisted on suckling him herself, at least for a little while until a suitable wet nurse was found. 'I want him to have the very best in life,' she told her aunt, 'and will not rest until he is given his rightful place.'

Madame de Sourdis could not agree more, for all she advised patience and caution. But then one morning she came to her niece with a grim look on her face.

Dismissing the maids, she bent close to Gabrielle. 'There is a rumour going around court circles that the child is not the King's.'

'What?' Gabrielle went white with shock. Tears sprang to her eyes and she felt suddenly quite light headed. 'How dare anyone suggest such a thing? Have I not always been constant, save for that early folly? Oh, my goodness, do they know of that foolishness? Do they say it is Bellegarde?'

'Some may, but there can be no proof as that gallant has gained the King's permission to marry Anne de Bugil-Fontaine. And since Longueville was killed by a musket shot, there will be no more worries over those letters you once wrote him.'

'Then why would they so accuse me? Surely I have never given cause for anyone to doubt my love for the King?'

'There are always mischief-makers in any court. In this instance I believe the tale originated with Sancy, who, as you know, supervises the King's finances. The Baron Rosny is unhappy with the way the fellow conducts these affairs and I believe the pair came to verbal blows during which Sancy spouted this malicious nonsense.'

'What are we to do? How am I to refute it?'

'We do nothing,' her aunt advised. 'Sometimes the more one denies an accusation, the guiltier one appears, and since you are innocent you have no reason to offer any defence.'

Gabrielle nodded, her heart still pounding in alarm. But at that moment a maid came bursting into the apartment with worse news.

'Madame, we have just received word that the royal physician who attended you, Monsieur Ailleboust, has been found dead. And they are saying that you poisoned him.'

Gabrielle and her ladies were stringently questioned as to what the doctor had eaten during the birthing, who had prepared the food for him and if he'd complained of any ill effects.

'No, of course he didn't,' Madame de Sourdis snapped. 'I prepared the food myself, and it was perfectly fresh and good.'

'It is not you who is being charged, Madame,' the investigator, little more than a lawyer's clerk sent to perform this unpalatable and dangerous task, pointed out. 'It is perfectly possible to add poison to food or drink after it has been prepared.'

Gabrielle gasped. 'You think I rose from my bed, walked over to the doctor's plate and dropped poison on to his food before taking up the birthing chair? If it were not so dreadful to be thus charged, I would laugh in your face. And why would I do such a dreadful thing to the good doctor, even if I were capable of such a heinous crime?'

'Perhaps because he knew the child was not the King's. What better way of silencing Monsieur Ailleboust, than with a lethal dose of poison in his small beer?'

Gabrielle cried out in her anguish. 'It is a lie, all

of it! I swear on my son's life that he is indeed the King's child. You have only to look at him and you will see the likeness.'

But the hapless clerk knew nothing of babies and could find no conclusive proof in the face of this woman's brat. He might have continued with his questioning indefinitely but the door flung open and the King himself strode in, his face like thunder.

'Enough of these monstrous lies. Get out! My beloved Gabrielle needs rest, not harassment from a pouter pigeon full of his own importance. Begone! I'll have no more of this mischief.'

The clerk almost scraped the floor with his chin in his urgent desire to ingratiate himself. Even so, he recklessly protested. 'Your Majesty, it is my duty to–'

'It is your duty to obey your King,' shouted Henry, and the fellow beat a hasty retreat.

Henry gathered a weeping Gabrielle in his arms. 'My sweet girl, my angel, we will show these malcontents that I give no credence to such malice.'

Gabrielle rushed to assure Henry of her enduring love. 'I have ever been faithful, I swear it. I may have made mistakes when I was a silly young girl but now I am as a wife to you and would never hurt you.'

'You will be my wife in truth one day,' Henry promised, kissing her. 'Be sure of it. I have again dispatched Erard to Queen Margot with the news of our son's arrival and a further request for the divorce to be settled. I have also set in motion the proceedings necessary to obtain the annulment of your own marriage with Liancourt.'

261

'I can ask no more, Henry.' Gabrielle was over-whelmed with emotion and gratitude.

'Do not fret, my love, I will make your detrac-tors eat their words.'

On Thursday, 15 September, 1594, Gabrielle made a triumphal entry into Paris by torchlight in the most glorious pageant yet. She rode in a magnificent litter draped with cloth of gold and embroidered with the royal arms. The King was making it abundantly clear to his people that this woman must be respected, even if she was only his mistress. And there was every evidence of a hearty welcome for the new King and his consort.

Green boughs arched the streets, balconies were draped with flowers and tapestries, and every-where there were flags and posters.

Gabrielle felt vindicated by Henry's belief in her, by his allowing her to take centre stage as he deliberately rode a little way behind her on his white charger.

She glanced back to demonstrate her gratitude with an entrancing smile, thinking how fine the King looked in his habit of grey velvet, em-broidered all over with gold and emeralds. On his head was a matching hat, fastened by a cluster of diamonds and sporting his usual white plume. As the people leaned from their windows to cheer him, Henry took it off and waved it to them, laughing with delight.

Gabrielle laughed too, for it was all so exciting, so different from the long dreary months of fol-lowing him from camp to camp in the endless civil wars. As if this were not evidence enough of his sincere feelings for her, when the procession came to a halt, Henry then proceeded to address them.

'We, knowing the infinite and singular graces of mind and person, vouchsafe in such perfection to our very dear and very beloved subject, Madame Gabrielle d'Estrées, have chosen and do declare her worthy of our devoted homage...'

Gabrielle listened enthralled as the King proceeded to extol her virtue and his great love for her, going on to announce that her own marriage to Liancour would soon be declared null and void.

Most moving of all, so far as Gabrielle was concerned, was that he then went on to read from the specially prepared letters-patent for the legitimization of their son, César.

'Henry, by the grace of God, King of France and Navarre ... it has been our desire, pending the time when He may graciously give us heirs, who may legitimately succeed to this crown, to endeavour to have children elsewhere who will be obliged to serve this State...'

While those assembled listened to the complex document being read, wondering if this meant the child might indeed be worthy to wear the crown one day, none could fail to admire the exquisite loveliness of Gabrielle. The glittering jewels on her black satin gown could never outshine the brilliance of her beauty.

For Gabrielle it was her happiest day, certain that she would soon be Henry's lawful wife and queen. Didn't he constantly urge her to believe and to be strong? Even now as he came to her and kissed her, he repeated his favourite mantra: 'To a valiant heart nothing is impossible.'

The warnings by his ministers and officer of the guard proved to be entirely correct. Before the year was out more attempts were made upon the King's life. A student by the name of Jean Chatel attacked Henry in the presence of Gabrielle in her own house in Paris. Henry had just returned from Picardy and he was giving audience to various nobles when Chatel lunged for him with a dagger. Fortunately his aim was bad, managing only to pierce Henry's lip and not slit his throat.

Gabrielle rushed to his assistance all in a panic, calling for the doctor and insisting the King be taken to his bedchamber at once. With the help of her sister, Juliette, Gabrielle nursed and comforted him, but he was not a good patient.

Henry was furious. *'Ventre Saint Gris!* How can I feel happy when I see a people so ungrateful as to plan fresh attempts on me every day, although I have done all that I can for them, and would willingly sacrifice a thousand lives for their welfare, had God given me so many!'

'You must ever be wary of fanatics, my lord, and not allow the people so near you,' Gabrielle warned, seriously alarmed by this latest attack.

Rosny hurried in, looking unusually flustered. 'The fellow has been apprehended, Sire, along with the instigator of the attempted crime, a Jesuit. I trust their execution should act as a deterrent to others foolish enough to try to harm you.'

'I trust you are right,' Henry dryly remarked. 'Since my life may depend upon it. It appears that you waited for these said Jesuits to be convicted by my own lips.' His wit, at least, had not deserted him.

Te Deums were sung in celebration of the King's lucky escape, Henry dressed all in black, his moustache shaved off and his lip plastered. As he arrived in his coach a great cheer went up.

'What enthusiasm your presence elicits among the populace, Sire,' said Bellegarde.

'Ah, if my greatest enemy was to pass before this people, as I am now doing in kingly state, he would be cheered as much, or more. Since I have entered Paris I have endured nothing but murderous attempts on my life!'

Concerns remained that the dagger tip might have been poisoned, but Gabrielle's fears for Henry's health were gradually eased as he made a slow but steady recovery.

In January, 1595, Gabrielle was delighted to learn that her marriage with Liancour had been formally annulled, being contrary to the statutes of the Church due to the fact they were distant cousins.

'And of course, it was never consummated,' she reminded her aunt.

Queen Margot maintained her silence on the question of divorce but objected strongly when Henry granted yet more property to his mistress, some of which should rightly be in her own possession.

Later in the month Gabrielle arranged a ballet to entertain the young Duke of Guise, son of the late hero. He arrived at court looking pale and anxious, but Henry welcomed him with his usual good cheer and no sign of ill will for their having been on opposing sides.

'In my youth your father and I were great friends, though often rivals in love. I mourn for him still.' Tactfully making no mention of how Guise had once fought to take the throne of France for himself, and certainly won the love of Queen Margot. His son, a young rebel, had taken up his father's cause and continued to side with the League, but Henry was now content to pardon him.

'We are all subject to commit follies in our youth. I am ready to forget the past, but for the future I would recommend you avoid similar errors. Submit to my legitimate authority and I will be as a father to you.'

If the young duke felt any bitterness over the time he'd spent under house arrest and in prison, or the glimpse of a crown for his own head and the possible hand of the Spanish Infanta, he gave no sign.

Wanting the evening to be merry, Gabrielle chose the prettiest, most lively ladies of the court to take part in the ballet. She herself, as splendidly attired as a queen in cloth of silver and ice-blue satin, led the dance and was hailed *la belle des belles*.

'You are my greatest treasure,' Henry assured her.

Gabrielle was considered by all to be the uncrowned Queen of France. She acted as gatekeeper to His Majesty and many came to her to seek favours and broach their request before approaching the King. Even the great Mayenne, brother to the late hero Guise, begged for her support to have his debts paid, and an amnesty for his partisans. In return, he offered his allegiance to

266

her being crowned queen.

Not all the battles were won so easily, and Henry fought on, reminding his enemies that they could either be a Frenchman or go to Spain. But as a consequence of Gabrielle's intervention on Mayenne's behalf, a three-month truce was agreed in order to allow fresh talks to be held.

One morning, Gabrielle was walking through the Louvre with Madame de Sourdis, head high and striding confidently as she laughed and gossiped with her ladies. They were planning to take a turn about the gardens, and, as always, Gabrielle was elegantly gowned in burgundy velvet, with a gold lace collar that stood out about her slender neck. Pearls hung at her ears, circled her throat, and looped about the bodice. Her pale blonde hair was curled neatly beneath a jewelled cap, her beauty and elegance quite outshining even her prettiest maids of honour who followed in her wake. Doors were opened for her, pages bowed, and ladies-in-waiting dipped a curtsey as she passed by. None dared dispute the high regard the King held for her.

At the entrance she almost collided with a stranger who came bounding up the steps, evidently rushing to conduct some pressing business. Inclining his head by way of apology the gentleman stepped back to let her pass by unimpeded.

'Thank you, kind sir,' Gabrielle said, rewarding him with her entrancing smile.

But as she stepped out into the gentle warmth of an early spring day, she heard him ask of the guard, 'What a magnificent woman. Who is she?'

267

To which the officer replied, 'No one of any account, my friend, it is only the King's whore.'

Gabrielle almost stumbled, heard her aunt's sharp intake of breath. She had become so accustomed to the respect bestowed upon her, the fact that she attended, indeed often organized and managed, so many important functions, she would sometimes forget she had no proper standing at court. No legal right to anything. Fearing Madame de Sourdis might march back inside and take the miscreant to task, Gabrielle quickly grasped her hand. 'Leave it be, Aunt.'

'But it is a gross insult. You cannot pass by and say nought.'

'Why not? It is nothing less than the truth. That is exactly what I am, the King's whore. His mistress, not his queen.'

'You will be a queen of France one day.'

Gabrielle regarded her aunt with sad eyes. 'Will I? Who can say. I never asked for this. I wanted only to be respectably married to the man I loved. For now it is enough that the King loves me, even if everyone else does not.'

Rosny certainly didn't. As the King's chief counsellor and advisor, he was most anxious that once a divorce was negotiated, his master should marry a wife worthy of him, not some strumpet who happened to catch his eye. Gabrielle d'Estrées was merely the King's mistress, entirely unsuitable to be queen.

He was grateful that she had encouraged his royal master to accept the Mass in order to gain the crown, for he saw no benefit in strife and warfare which would never win the hearts of the people. Rosny accepted that Gabrielle was neither self-seeking nor greedy, as he'd at first thought, although her aunt certainly was. It was true that she possessed none of the wit and literary talent of Queen Marguerite, but was undoubtedly kind, caring and affectionate, with a pleasing and un-affected nature. She was a good influence upon Henry in many ways, and seemed genuinely fond of him, even if His Majesty's passion outshone hers a thousand fold.

Yet he could not like her.

To be fair, in her early years with the King she'd fiercely resisted his courtship and shown no desire to be elevated beyond her station. But if she had not been overly ambitious before, she certainly was now that she had a son. Unfortun-ately, little César was no dauphin. Legitimized he may be, but that did not mean he was fit to sit on the throne of France.

Should Henry ultimately gain a divorce and they did indeed marry, what if they had more children? Could not a son born within wedlock object if the one born before it took precedence? The result of such sibling rivalry could bring yet more strife and civil war to France.

At the coronation Rosny had watched as people came forward to make obeisance to the King, many whispering in his ear, offering their services, begging forgiveness if they had seemed to be against him in the past. It was difficult to assess how far Henry trusted and believed these assur-ances. His naturally good heart often led him to make mistakes in his choice of companions, particularly when it came to women.

Rosny dearly wished his sovereign to be happy, and to marry and produce heirs. But, however pretty and charming she may be, he would do everything in his power to make sure that his queen of choice was not Madame Gabrielle.

Opposition to the King seemed to have largely been quelled, the people welcoming him, and the peace, with open arms. The citizens of Paris appreciated how Henry constantly showed himself to them, dined in public, played tennis and walked in the Tuileries Gardens. He did not shut himself away as Henri Trois had done. They liked his droll wit, his natural dignity and easy-going nature, and the care he took not to spend money on fripperies as his predecessor had done. He was constantly complaining that he was short of horses, shirts and money, and that there was often nothing in his stewpot. It was said that should a merchant go to the Louvre, Henry would haggle over the price of a pair of riding boots, never mind a pearl necklace for his lady-love. He trusted no one, assuming they raised their prices simply because he was a king. The Parisians loved this miserliness in him, and they admired his valiant attempt to reduce the national debt which stood at 307,000,000 crowns.

Rosny received reports, however, of meetings of dissension held secretly in dark corners of Jesuit monasteries, and resolved to winkle out these troublemakers.

The Princess Catherine, however, was another matter. Despite her religious austerity she often sat beneath the royal canopy to enjoy the ballet with the King, Soissons beside her, flagrant in her loyalty to him.

Henry was fast losing patience with her. 'I might have relented and let her marry the Count, had she not resorted to deceit by attempting that secret marriage.'

'The Princess was encouraged in this by Madame de Guiche, Sire,' Rosny assured him.

'Indeed, Corisande was ever a woman with a mind of her own. But how can I pardon such a transgression? My sister is an obstinate woman and insists on standing firm, consoling herself with prayers and psalms. She has again been holding her *prêches* in public, despite my having forbidden her,' Henry raged. 'This time within the precincts of the Louvre itself. Have the Parisians not suffered enough? They look upon this as a desecration. It has to be stopped, Rosny. If only she would agree to marry. A husband might be better able to subdue her than I, but she adamantly refuses.'

'You must be firm, Sire, and remind the Princess of her duty to France.'

Henry rolled his eyes. 'You know women, Rosny, they have a will of their own. What can we do when she waves that betrothal contract between herself and Soissons in my face?'

'You could take it from her.'

A shout of laughter. 'How?'

'With guile and cunning. Why do you not safely leave the matter in my hands,' Rosny quietly suggested.

Henry looked his advisor in the eye, seeing him suddenly in a new light. Perhaps he wasn't always so proper and moral after all. 'See to it then. I would be forever grateful.'

Catherine had taken up residence in the Queen Mother's former abode, the Hôtel de Soissons, which seemed highly appropriate. Each evening she would hold court, attended by her ladies and gentlemen, including Soissons more often than not, who was beside her this evening.

'How dare Henry deny us the chance of happiness when he actively encourages an immoral atmosphere at court, as practised by his unholy relationship with Gabrielle d'Estrées.' Catherine secretly envied the couple's obvious happiness together, and the birth of their son, feeling deeply aggrieved that Henry did not care enough for her own happiness to allow her to marry the man of her choice and find happiness.

Reading her thoughts, Soissons agreed. 'I too have grown to resent him even more in recent weeks, particularly when I was overlooked for advancement in the council. I had hoped to be president, believed myself well suited for the task, but the role was given instead to Conti.'

'The fellow is fit for nothing more strenuous,' Catherine pointed out, 'because of his girth and ill health.'

'Nevertheless, I would have made a better job of it than that doddering old fool. But it seems that as Henry is still engaged in battle, my skills are better employed in warfare. "You shall attend our person," he told me. "Organize your regiment and follow us into Burgundy." I believe he'd very much like to see me struck down in battle. That would solve his dilemma nicely, would it not?'

'Oh, do not say such a thing!' Catherine protested, horrified by the thought of losing her beloved. 'Promise me you will take every care.'

'My love, I am sorry. I did not mean to distress you. But when Henry leaves, I must go with him. I have no choice.'

The situation was most vexing, so when one morning Corisande came to her in great excitement with a letter from Rosny saying that Henry was beginning to soften his attitude, Catherine could hardly contain her delight.

'Soften? You mean he may agree to our marriage, after all?'

'Rosny wishes to discuss this with you in person, since it is such a delicate matter, but he claims that Henry is not as averse to the alliance as he once was,' Corisande told her.

'What is this I hear about my brother softening his disapproval, Monsieur?' Catherine asked, the moment the Baron was brought into her presence. Soissons was at her side, and they received him together.

'It would seem that most of His Majesty's objections nowadays stem from the deception that you perpetrated upon him by attempting a secret wedding.'

Catherine felt a small kernel of hope. 'All the world knows the fidelity of my attachment to Monsieur le Comte, and if you could help me to perfect his reconciliation with my brother the King, I would be eternally obliged.'

'The secret nature of this alliance has inflicted great pain upon your brother the King, and...' Rosny paused to search out the most tactful way

273

to describe Madame's stubbornness. 'I have pressed him to be more forgiving but your declaration of independence has pained him further.'

'You mean my obstinacy.'

Rosny politely declined to acknowledge the Princess's bluntness.

Soissons intervened. 'We do not doubt your diplomacy, Monsieur de Rosny. But what is to be done about it?'

'I will not concede,' Catherine insisted.

Rosny cleared his throat, perhaps wishing the Princess might offer him a glass of wine, or at least permission to sit. She did neither. 'Now that His Majesty is more firmly established in his realm, the political objections to Your Highness's alliance with Monsieur le Comte are much less pronounced.'

'Then can we hope for a change of heart?' Catherine asked, her face alight with that emotion.

Rosny put up a hand to caution her. 'I venture to assure your Highnesses, as one well versed in the royal sentiments, that the surest way to realize your aim is to show goodwill. Were you, for instance, to relinquish the promissory note of marriage exchanged between you, together with a signed agreement that states your loyalty to the King and willingness to abide by the royal decision, I am quite certain His Majesty would then look favourably upon Monsieur le Comte and readily give his consent.'

'Can this be true?' Catherine asked, gripping Soissons' hand in excitement.

'Indeed, I see no reason why you shouldn't achieve your heart's desire,' Rosny agreed.

Catherine believed him, and turning to Madame de Guiche asked if this could be done.

Corisande smiled and nodded. 'The betrothal letter is safely deposited in the archives of my home at Grammont, but it can easily be retrieved so that you may present it to the King in return for his permission, my dear, if that is what you wish.'

Catherine happily told Rosny that she would attend to the matter forthwith, and be in touch.

A few days later the written promise of marriage given to her by Soissons was sent by special messenger to Rosny. 'You may deliver it to the King as a pledge of my affection, confidence and submission,' Catherine recklessly wrote. In addition, both she and Soissons signed and sealed the document left them by Rosny. 'In which we mutually release each other from promise or contract, and consent to abide by His Majesty's decision relative to our proposed alliance.'

Every word showed how much Catherine was willing to trust in her brother's change of heart, as described to her by Rosny. She embraced Corisande in delight. 'All is going to turn out well, after all.'

The response from Henry, when it came, dashed all such hopes. 'I have made no such promise to agree to your alliance with Soissons. I can only recommend that you accept the hand of the Duc de Montmorency, or failing him, the Duc de Bar.'

Catherine fell into tears of rage and recriminations, and furiously ordered an explanation from Rosny. 'I have been tricked. A terrible deceit has been practised upon me. How dare you treat me so ill!'

Rosny stood before her, wringing his hands and attempting to look contrite, for all his response was as carefully calculated as ever. 'I did only what was asked of me by my royal master. I beg leave to assure you, Madame, that I did indeed put your case to the King with great sincerity, and pleaded for the alliance to no avail,' he lied.

But Catherine continued to rail at him. She wept and raged, and indignantly reproached him, but was finally forced to accept the Baron's innocence in the matter. The decisions and power over her future lay with her brother. Rosny offered his deepest condolences and left, satisfied that he had carefully avoided any hint of his own duplicity.

It was Christmas 1595, which the court was spending at Folembray. The palace was ancient, set in dense forests and therefore somewhat damp and neglected, but it was a convenient distance from Travercy where Henry was stationed. Gabrielle had often visited him at the camp, now she took it upon herself to make the festival as merry and pleasant as possible for the King, arranging revels and ballets and various *petits jeux*.

'Christmas is all about rejoicing in the birth of our Saviour, not silly little games and immoral entertainment,' Catherine admonished her.

It was clear to Gabrielle that the Princess still held a deep resentment against her, as if it offended Madame's dignity for Gabrielle to act as queen. She would be thankful when Catherine moved on to Fontainebleau. Yet for Henry's sake she must make a valiant effort to be pleasant, and in truth she did feel some sympathy for the girl.

'I am sorry this matter with Soissons has not yet been resolved between yourself and the King. I know what it is to be obliged to sacrifice a lover, but I was fortunate for everything turned out well for me in the end. The King is kind to me and I have come to love him dearly. Perhaps you will find the same with the Duc de Montpensier or the Duc de Bar, whichever you choose. You may find that a new love grows.'

'I will never agree to have either one of them,' Catherine snapped, looking at Gabrielle with haughty contempt. 'You forget that I am a Princess of the Blood, not some common nobody like you with ambitions above her station.'

Gabrielle flushed with embarrassment, but judged it wise not to argue when Madame was in one of her high dudgeons. The Princess's hot temper was well known, not helped by the presence of Madame de Guiche. Corisande was openly critical of all the arrangements that Gabrielle, her greatest rival for the King's affections, was making for the coming festive season, not least for *le petit César* and his entourage of nannies and nurses.

'Goodness, a veritable circus for one small baby,' she caustically remarked.

'Henry dotes upon the child, as the future dauphin.'

Corisande lifted fine eyebrows in disbelief. 'What an optimist you are.'

Gabrielle bit her lip, and, stemming the urge to retaliate, rested a gentle hand upon Princess Catherine's arm. 'I will speak with the King on this matter, if you wish. I do have some small influence. Perhaps we can bring him round even yet.'

'I do not require the assistance of his inamorata,' Catherine retorted, in a tone of voice which seemed to indicate she could have chosen a far worse word to describe Gabrielle. 'I need no help to mediate with my own brother.'

'As you wish,' Gabrielle coolly replied, and excusing herself on the grounds that César needed her, thankfully withdrew.

The Christmas Festivities went like clockwork and everyone, King Henry in particular, had a restful and merry time. The court continued to reside at Folembray for the entire month of January. But growing increasingly weary of the tension and brooding atmosphere, Gabrielle could tolerate it no longer and decided it was time to make a move.

'I wish to return to Paris,' she told the King. 'I fear the palace is too cold and damp for our son.'

'You may well be right, my dear. Madame Catherine has already taken a chill. I will arrange for the coach to take you first thing in the morning, and guard him well.'

'Do please speak to your sister, Sire. Be kind to her. She loves you dearly but has a high sense of moral duty, and an intense loyalty to the man she loves. As Soissons is less of a danger to you now, can she not be permitted some happiness?'

Henry made no reply to this plea, nor gave any indication that he would change his mind. But he did pay Catherine a visit that evening, taking with him his baby son.

'I trust you are feeling better,' he told her, drawing up a chair beside his sister's bed. 'And that you have had time to think and reconsider whilst lying

278

here. Time to regret your obstinacy over this alliance with Soissons which is so distasteful to me.'

'It is not distasteful to *me*, who would be the one to make it. You seem to have gone out of your way not to favour the comte.'

Henry cuddled little César in his arms, refusing to answer the charge. 'Would you not be glad to have a child of your own, sister? Montpensier is young and not bad looking. He would no doubt make a good husband and father.'

'He is a Catholic.'

Henry sighed. 'As is Soissons, but I believe we have had this conversation before.'

The King might have pursued his argument further but there suddenly came a great wrenching sound, a groaning as a huge rafter fell from the ceiling. Henry's chair suddenly gave way under him as the rotten timbers finally perished. Catherine cried out in alarm while Henry instinctively pitched himself forward, clutching his precious son tightly in his arms and landed on her bed. Tucked as it was into an alcove, they were protected as beams fell and heavy furniture toppled all around them.

Henry, however, burst into gales of merry laughter. 'Is this heavenly retribution for my taking such a firm stand against you?'

'If so, then you are fortunate to have found sanctuary on the couch of the reformed faith.'

Catherine had never forgiven Rosny the trick he'd played on her by relieving her of the promissory note of marriage. Now he stood before her again, on yet another mission from his royal master. He'd spent two days in her company, walking with her ladies in the gardens of Fontainebleau, making pleasant small talk and attempting to be agreeable. But Catherine felt she'd been patient long enough and demanded to know the real reason for his visit.

Rosny had the grace to prevaricate no longer and came straight to the point. 'Monsieur le Comte is a fine fellow, none better, and it is unfortunate that he is at cross-purposes with His Majesty. I have to say that he did himself no favours by departing the King's camp at Burgundy just when he was most needed.'

'Charles felt he was again being overlooked for preferment.'

Rosny drew in a patient breath. 'The Count wished the King to make him supreme commander of the armies of France, above others who would not take kindly to being so placed. Soissons is a strong and able soldier, but young, of uncertain temper, and yet to distinguish himself in battle. Sadly, he took offence at the King's refusal and retired to his château at Blandy, taking no further part in the campaign.'

Catherine's face suffused with crimson, then went pale with anger. 'It is not for you to criticize Monsieur le Comte. Charles has been constantly undermined by those who intrigue against him.'

'He has forfeited the royal favour by his own petulance and caprices.'

'Perhaps it was in retaliation for the shameful way the King has treated him. And *you* have betrayed *me*, Monsieur Rosny. You cannot deny it. If that blockhead Pangeas had not managed to prevent our clandestine marriage back in the spring of 1593, none of this ill feeling between Soissons and Henry would have existed.'

'On that I cannot say, Madame, but I fear your own obstinacy in this matter does not endear you to the King.'

'Henry adores me. I have received any number of offers of marriage, including Monsieur de Guise, but Henry thwarts them all. I doubt he wishes me to marry at all as he loves me too well to part with me. As for you, Baron, if you are audacious enough to meddle with my affairs, beware! What right have you to tell me what to do?'

'I submit only to the will of your brother the King, as must you.' Rosny took the letter Henry had written to his sister, in which he had firmly set out her choices, from the inner pocket of his doublet. He did not hand it to her, ever cautious of inflaming the Princess's temper further, but tapped it thoughtfully against his bearded chin. 'Madame, it is your duty to accept the husband chosen for you, and to despise the evil counsel of Monsieur de Soissons, or you will descend into disgrace.'

Incensed by this remark Catherine almost exploded with rage. 'How dare you insult Charles! I assure you I will have none of my brother's suggestions! And I shall complain to Henry of the insolent threats you have made against me.'

Still in possession of the King's letter, Rosny bowed and quietly took his leave, refusing to relinquish it even when Catherine sent a maid of honour scurrying after him down the grand staircase to demand that he do so.

'Madame has refused the King's request to

281

obey his wishes in this matter. I can do no more,' he said, thinking it prudent to avoid any further upset. Henry would have his way in the end. The sooner the Princess realized that fact, the happier for her.

Then to his complete shock and dismay, on his return to court Henry took him to task for offending the Princess. Rosny was mortified, appalled that his royal master should choose not to defend him. 'I was only carrying out your orders, Sire.'

'My sister has written detailing your insolence and rudeness. Such conduct is inexcusable. She demands an apology and you must oblige her.'

'But Sire ...

'Do it.'

Rosny could not face returning to Fontaine-bleau for yet more haughty condescension, nor dare he disobey his king, so with gritted teeth he wrote and dispatched a carefully worded apology.

A day or two later Henry's natural sense of justice and generosity resulted in an explanation that he had wanted only to pacify Catherine. 'I needed to assuage the waves of her wrath. We are both passionate and fractious, but we soon recover. I am convinced that you have done nothing of which I cannot approve.'

Rosny sighed with relief. Yet again his royal master had demonstrated how very much he valued and trusted him, even by comparison to those closest to the King. It was a heady thought that he should be so well regarded, and a state of affairs which might well prove useful when certain other marriages were under discussion.

Plague came to Paris and many hundreds, including Madame Montpensier, died of it. Gabrielle gave the King this news as they lay in bed together one afternoon, enjoying a siesta as Henry so loved to do. 'It is said that she shrieked with fury to the last about the blasphemies done by the Huguenots, and storms raged for hours following her death.'

Henry gave a rueful chuckle. 'Such a ferocious spirit could not leave this earth quietly. Meanwhile her brother, Mayenne, eats humble pie and promises in future to serve his king faithfully in gratitude for concessions made. How he sings your praises. He is deeply grateful for your intervention on his behalf.' He cast Gabrielle an amused sideways glance. 'What a little politician you are turning out to be, my angel.'

Gabrielle flushed most charmingly, and kissed him. 'I do only what I believe will please you. I thought you wished him to be brought to heel.'

Henry laughed out loud. 'And we have succeeded, between us. The poor man suffers enough from sciatica and various other maladies as a consequence of his corpulence, so I took pity on him and allowed his partisans to be released into exile. At least I have no need to be jealous of him, have I, my love?'

Gabrielle giggled as she stroked Henry's beard. 'You have no reason to be jealous of anyone.'

He was smiling as he rolled her on to her back and proceeded to make love to her, taking special care as she was again *enceinte*. 'My courtiers whisper that you are a woman to be reckoned with, one who, far from fomenting quarrels, proves restful to

283

your lover.'

'Do you find me restful, my lord?' Gabrielle murmured as she wriggled enticingly beneath him, inciting his passion further.

'You minx, more likely near bursting with excitement.'

Gabrielle slid her pink tongue into his eager mouth and let him plunder her till they were both gasping and quite out of breath. Later, as they lay together, limbs entwined, warm and sated, Henry returned to their earlier conversation.

'In truth, I cannot rightly afford to squander funds paying off other folk's debts, let alone those of an enemy.'

'Do the courtiers blame me for the current problems with finance? Do they say I am greedy, that you shower me with gifts?'

'How can they when you refuse most of them, my angel. Yet I love to see you in pretty gowns and jewels.'

Gabrielle, who was woman enough to also love pretty gowns and jewels, would not dream of setting a price on every kiss she gave. She could not answer for her aunt, however, who was another sort of creature altogether. Gabrielle had quite early on made a rule never to ask for gifts, although like all men Henry liked to demonstrate his love with a pretty trinket or gewgaw. In the beginning the King had awarded her an allowance of 400 crowns a month, made to her from out of the privy purse. On the birth of little César this was raised to 500, but then carrying out the role of queen was expensive, particularly when the title and accompanying allowance did not go with it.

Careful as she was with the royal purse, Gabrielle was ever aware of the whisperings among certain court officials and malcontents. Having battled against civil war, siege, starvation and plague, many Parisians regarded the King's mistress as a parasite upon the kingdom, a harlot who by a shameless love of luxury represented an insult to honest citizens and their wives.

'It is so easy to cause offence. Perhaps you are too generous, Sire, in bestowing quite so many properties upon me, and a title, particularly if money is tight.'

Reaching for her chemise and petticoats Gabrielle began to dress, allowing Henry to help her with ribbons and laces rather than call in a maid, but hoping that he wouldn't change his mind and unfasten them all again. This second pregnancy was making her feel more weary than the first. He helped her smooth a stocking over the silky skin of her leg.

'That is not your concern, my love. The treasury is bound to be in desperate straits after so many years of war. It must be replenished in order to build a strong and prosperous kingdom, but that is for me to worry about, not you. Have you heard that my courtiers call me a miser? How can that be? I do three things which are far from being the acts of a miser: I build for France, I make war and I make love.'

'You can certainly do the latter,' Gabrielle teased. 'But your descriers would do better to remember the extravagance of Henri Trois.' Gabrielle recalled how that king had lavished money on his *mignons*, on magnificent gowns if he took a fancy to dressing like a woman, even on his monkeys and dogs, spending thousands of crowns on minders for them.

Henry chuckled as he reached for her other stocking. 'Spending money they did not have was ever a Valois flaw. Look at his sister, my dear Margot, constantly crying penury. Her mother, Catherine de Medici, was famous for spending a fortune on one of her extravaganzas, even when the treasury was empty. If it pleased the people, at least until they later had to pay for it through increased taxes, she considered it good for France. But just because I am not a spendthrift does not necessarily make me mean, does it? Have I not always said it is necessary to love me for my own sake?'

'And I do, my love.' Smiling, Gabrielle took the stocking from him and slid it skilfully into place, allowing him ample opportunity to admire her long legs while she did so.

'Nevertheless, I must continue to support my wife in her fastness, and my sister too since Catherine will not wed. Even my nobles take the liberty of dipping into the pot to replenish their loans and losses during the war. I am beset on all sides and it is costing the nation a small fortune.'

Gabrielle frowned, sensing that the King was more concerned than he might appear. Recognizing an opportunity she had long sought, she casually enquired, 'Have you spoken to Rosny on the subject of finance? You know there have been rumours circulating about Sancy.'

Henry was instantly alert. 'What kind of rumours?'

'Rosny suspects Sancy of furnishing his own needs before that of the treasury.'

'The devil he does. In what way?'

Gabrielle had never particularly liked Sancy, finding his humour somewhat coarse and his manner condescending. Since the birth of César, her attitude towards him had reached the point of loathing. She held him entirely responsible for the rumours circulating that her son was not the King's child but that of the Duc de Bellegarde. Some time later, and wishing to clarify her position, Gabrielle had asked Sancy for his opinion on the matter.

'In the event of my marriage, would my son César then become the legitimate heir to the throne?'

Sancy's tone had been supercilious. 'Madame, in France the bastards of our kings are always the sons of harlots!'

Gabrielle had been shocked and deeply hurt by this brutal attack upon her reputation, and had never forgiven him. Now she felt no compunction at bringing him down.

'It is my understanding that if a regiment needs to be paid, Sancy signs warrants for twice the sum required, keeping half for himself. If questions are asked he claims the extra money is to pay off their old debts. His fraudulent tricks are rife. I urge you to find a more trustworthy person, one of irreproachable probity such as Rosny himself, to take on the responsibility'

'Your advice is sound, my angel, as ever. Rosny may be unsociable and over-cautious, taciturn and moody, but he is no gambler, and is more than worthy to keep the key of the royal treasury. He will deliver us all.'

Gabrielle was delighted when Sancy was obliged to leave court for his estates, and Rosny had the grace to thank her for her intervention on his behalf. She also secretly hoped the favour might raise her status in his eyes.

In October, 1596, while she was staying at the Benedictine Abbey at Rouen, Gabrielle gave birth to a daughter, Catherine Henriette, to be known by her second name. Henry was so delighted he rewarded her with yet more land and properties, making it abundantly clear how he held his mistress in high esteem, and wishing to show his gratitude for providing him with two healthy children. He eagerly planned a state baptism, one in keeping for a child of France at which both he and his sister were to act as godparents.

The finest cooks in Paris were engaged, the Louvre filled with fruit and flowers. Ballets, masques and all manner of entertainments were provided. Rosny grumbled a little at the expense, now that he was in charge of the royal treasury, but dutifully paid all the bills.

Despite some initial misgivings when the new Superintendent of Finances began his new task by dismissing Sancy, Schomberg and others he considered could no longer be trusted, Henry conceded that the decision had proved to be a wise one. The troops not only received their pay on time, but arrears too had been made good, and there was fresh ammunition and stores. The future seemed bright and the economic management of the country far less of a concern.

It made Henry value his *maîtresse en titre* all the more for her excellent advice. He loved and admired Gabrielle dearly for she had wit as well as beauty, and sound common sense. Only recently she had advised him on a speech he made before the Assembly of Notables in which he had offered to 'place myself under your control'.

Rosny had applauded but when asked her opinion later, Gabrielle had said, 'Sire, no one could have spoken better, but I am surprised that a hero like Your Majesty should have used the words, *"me metre en tutelle!"* You are surely not in need of tutoring.'

'*Ventre Saint Gris!* Madame you are right.'

Was it any wonder that he was faithful to her? At least, Henry conceded, more faithful than he had been with any of his other mistresses. He still visited the Abbess of Montmartre from time to time, and there were one or two: Charlotte des Essards and Esther Imbert for instance, who had presented him with more children, which he always welcomed. He did so enjoy the company of his offspring whenever he called upon their mothers. If she knew of their existence, Gabrielle made no mention of it, realizing that as his official mistress it was to be expected that he might stray occasionally, but would always return to her. She was the woman he intended to make his wife, once he gained his divorce.

Henry went to see her every day during her lying-in period, and on one occasion found her in great distress.

'Have you heard of the prophecy going the

289

rounds of court?' she asked, blue eyes wide with fear.

The King laughed. 'Not more rumours, have we not had our fill of them?'

'A great magician of the Low Countries has said that you will be killed in your bed towards the end of this year. What say you to that?'

'I say I'd best not go to bed.'

'This is no jest, Henry.'

'It is hysterical nonsense and you must not worry your pretty head over it, my angel. All you must do is rest so that you will make a good recovery. Do I not need you by my side? You are everything to me.'

Gabrielle could only hope that she was indeed everything to the King. She was not entirely unaware of the other mistresses upon whom he paid regular calls. She wasn't certain of all their names, nor would her dignity allow her to enquire after them. Far better, she thought, to ignore them completely. She felt no resentment over this need in her lover for other women. He was a man of large appetites which one woman alone could never hope to fulfil.

Neither did she seek to punish Henry by playing him at his own game. When she'd finally relinquished Bellegarde all those years ago Gabrielle had not allowed herself to look back. The past was done with so far as she was concerned, and although she remained on good terms with Bellegarde, and was aware that her erstwhile lover did not enjoy a happy marriage, Gabrielle was not the cause of its failure.

Nevertheless, despite her impeccable behaviour, the King was still not immune to jealousy over the slightest sign of any lingering friendship between herself and her one-time lover, and Gabrielle took care never to speak of him to Henry.

One morning the King's man, Beringhen, called at her hotel with a message enquiring after her health and asking if Henry might see her later that day. Gabrielle went to fetch her diary, increasingly filled with events that kept her busy, although she always gave preference to the King.

On her return she spotted Beringhen peeping at an open letter she'd left lying on a side table, noting how he moved quickly away, and her heart skipped a beat. It was from Bellegarde, recounting details of his liaison with Mademoiselle de Guise, and begging her to speak on his behalf to the young lady's brother.

Without so much as a glance at the offending letter, Gabrielle offered her most demure smile to Beringhen. 'Please inform the King I shall be delighted to receive him, at his convenience, later in the day.'

As luck would have it the Duc de Bellegarde chose to call upon her personally that same afternoon. Gabrielle was appalled. 'You should not have come. Not without warning me first,' she scolded him.

Bellegarde was puzzled. 'Did you not receive my letter?'

'Of course, but you didn't say that you would call. It is just that I had an unnerving experience this morning with Beringhen. I thought he may have recognized your handwriting, and you know how jealous the King can be, even now.'

Bellegarde laughed, thinking it all a merry jape, dismissing her fears as folly. But he had hardly begun to explain his designs over Mademoiselle de Guise when they heard a great pandemonium outside. Doors banged, voices shouted and Bellegarde recognized instantly that they were about to be invaded by the guard. 'I see your fears have substance, after all, dear friend. I've been half expecting such a catastrophe to happen one day.'

Gabrielle had gone quite pale. 'For all our innocence they must not find you here. Quick, this way.' She led him to a door hidden behind a tapestry. 'It leads down a back staircase and out by the servants' entrance.'

Bellegarde grinned and kissed her cheek. 'Most suitable. What a woman you are. What a pair we would have made. I hope you will ever be my friend, and I swear on my life I will do nothing to hurt you.'

When the archers burst into her room moments later, hammering on the door and demanding admittance in the name of the King, they found Gabrielle quietly working her tapestry in the company of two of her maids of honour. She looked up in mild surprise. 'Ah, Captain, I wondered what all the noise was about. Is there some mischief afoot?'

The archers seemed somewhat disappointed to find no intruder to slay with their arrows, while the Captain politely enquired, 'May I beg leave for a private word, Madame?' Dismissing his men, he drew Gabrielle to one side. 'There are many voices raised against you, Madame La Marquise, including that of Beringhen who is not in favour of your possible elevation to queen. The fellow has been spying on you.'

Gabrielle nodded. 'I rather thought that might be the case when he was here earlier.'

'I came on the King's orders but I did not hurry, and I made sure you were aware of our arrival, in case – in case a warning should prove necessary.'

She smiled her entrancing smile, blue eyes twinkling with amusement. 'It is good to have a friend, even if in this instance there was no need for concern. My thanks, Captain.'

Gabrielle was less charitable with the King when he called upon her later, as arranged. 'Is it not enough that your courtiers whisper against me? Must you turn against me as well, sending your archers stampeding into my home seeking alleged lovers I do not have? I cannot tolerate such violence. I will not be so ill used.'

Henry was filled with shame to see how upset she was. 'My love, you know how jealous I get.'

'Have I ever given you cause?'

'No, but I was informed you were entertaining Bellegarde.'

'Then you were informed wrong. As you see, my ladies and I fill our time with nothing more exciting then embroidery. You promised me that I would ever be treated with respect, even as a wife to you.' Tears ran unchecked down her cheeks, and, never able to deal with a weeping woman Henry was at a loss to know how to placate her.

'Would that you were my wife in very truth, my love.'

'Do not use your soft words on me, Sire, I would much rather end my days in the Bastille

293

than live without your trust.'

Then the King was on his knees before her, promising he would never be so foolish ever again, that he would see to the divorce with all speed, even if he personally had to go to Usson and wring it out of Margot with his own bare hands.

The castle of Usson was perched on the summit of an almost inaccessible precipice situated in the Auvergne, a remote district over which Margot held neither power nor rights. It was reached by a long winding path that led up from the valley below. During the eleven long years of her incarceration, Margot had never ventured to cross the threshold, keeping the drawbridge raised and the portcullis in place for most of her time there. In truth, the very strength of the fortress had saved her life on numerous occasions.

Within these walls Margot and her loyal band of followers had endured famine and pestilence, and she yet felt quite safe here. But despite calling it her Ark of Refuge, Margot longed to be free, to taste again the joys of court life in her beloved Paris. But for that to happen she required money. She needed to take possession of the properties that were rightly in her appanage and had been so long denied her, first by her brother the King, Henri Trois, by the Queen Mother, and now by her own husband.

'Might I venture to ask if His Majesty sent any money?'

Margot answered her first lady of the bedchamber with a sad smile and a shake of the head. She was sitting in the gardens, well wrapped up in furs against the cold of a damp January day, reading again the latest letter brought to her from the French Court.

'He begs me yet again to concede to a divorce.'

'But does not recognize his own obligations?'

'Henry is skilled at evading unpleasant facts.'

Madame de Noailles took the seat next to Margot with a sigh of resignation. After so many years isolation the two women were comfortable together, far closer than mistress and servant, which was why she dared to speak so boldly. 'The King has not paid your allowance for a year and a half. He refuses to pay it, or to return your properties to you, until you agree to give him the divorce he demands. Yet you refuse to concede to his request unless he first makes good on what he owes you. How is this matter ever to be resolved?'

'To a royal princess I would willingly cede my crown, so that legitimate heirs might be born to the King – but to a mistress and her offspring, I will never yield!'

'My lady, you have scarcely any jewels left which we could pledge for further loans. How are we to manage?'

It was Margot's turn now to sigh for she could offer no solution. Her greatest supporter and love of her life, Henri de Guise, was gone and she grieved for him still. He would never have stood by and watched her suffer such penury. Even her sister-in-law and dear friend Elisabeth of Austria, widow of her brother Charles IX, was no longer able to help her having died a few years previous. Margot felt quite alone, without friends in any quarter save for those who were brave enough to share her exile.

'Were Henry to marry this woman, what of the inheritance? If more sons come, who would then wear the crown?'

Madame de Noailles sadly shook her head, and tactfully remarked, 'That is for the King to decide, Your Majesty.' It could be viewed as treason to speak of a time when the King would no longer be alive to make such a decision.

'The Baron de Rosny, and other gentlemen of the court, constantly write urging me not to agree to the divorce on the grounds that such a conflict could lead to further civil war.' A shaft of winter sunlight rested on a laurel leaf, causing it to shine as if polished by God's hand. Margot relished such fragile glimpses of beauty in a world which so often seemed ugly and unclean. 'Were they not both married when the child was conceived? In which case the boy is the product of a double adultery, a child of sin. Is Rosny not right? Does France not deserve better?'

Wisely her companion said nothing to this analysis, and the two ladies sat in silence for some time, companionable in their mutual distress.

'What should I do?' Margot asked at length.

Madame de Noailles cleared her throat.' I do wonder if perhaps a letter to Madame Gabrielle might serve.'

'You wish me to write to that baggage? I will not do it.'

'Whatever our private opinion of the lady, she has the King's ear. Mayhap she could persuade him to pay you the sum he owes, to return your property and provide you with a more comfortable residence. It is your right, as Queen, I know, but as the *maîtresse en titre* Madame Gabrielle holds the power.'

'You wish me to beg for my supper, and hand over my crown to that harlot?'

'I wish you to use your undoubted skills with your pen to improve your situation. You could hint at what you might offer in return...'

Margot was instantly alert. 'Hint? You mean without actually making any firm promises?'

The two looked at each other in perfect accord. Margot had ever loved intrigue and artifice. Could she use it to effect one more time? She was forty-five and no longer the beauty she had once been. Her figure had grown somewhat plump and her complexion ravaged by time and anxiety. Yet she still had her wit, her bewitching charm and smile, and in every way she still dressed and behaved like the Queen she truly was.

After another long silence, she said, 'You will have to help me compose it. My skill with words does not extend to fawning flattery.'

'I will do all I can to assist.'

'And hold the sick bowl in case I vomit while I write?'

Her companion giggled. 'Whatever you ask of me, my lady, I will do with pleasure.'

Gabrielle read the letter in a state of wonder. That Queen Margot should write asking for her help was astonishing. It was formally addressed to Madame La Marquise, and signed 'Your very affectionate and most faithful friend, Marguerite.'

Gabrielle read the letter again, more slowly this

time, attempting to read between the lines of flattery which were almost sycophantic in parts. But the nub of her request was clear. She begged Gabrielle to use her influence with the King to fulfil his obligations to his wife.

'Listen to this,' Gabrielle said, reading the letter to her aunt who was bursting with curiosity. "I am tormented by my creditors. I prefer to suffer extremity of trouble rather than inflict any on His Majesty. My necessity, however, continues pressing, so that I can no longer remain here where I am suffering all manner of inconvenience and privation. If the King, therefore, would permit me to retire to one of my houses – the farthest off, if so it pleases him, which I possess from the court – he would concede a great relief." She says she wishes to "promote the King's design rather than frustrate it", which can surely only mean she is at last ready to agree to the divorce. Do you not think so?'

Madame de Sourdis agreed, peeping over her niece's shoulder in order to read the letter for herself. 'See, here she says "that it will please him to act as my brother..." and seeks his continued protection. What else could she mean?'

'She also vows "perpetual obligation". Does she not owe me that already? Does she not appreciate how I resent this wrong forced upon me? I would retire to a monastery and live the rest of my life chaste if I thought there was no hope of redemption and respectability. Do I not deserve marriage, if only for the sake of our son?'

'Then you must help her,' Madame de Sourdis said. 'Her request is fair. You must rescue the

298

Queen from penury and she will then grant the divorce. Speak to the King, and you might drop a word in Rosny's ear. Now that he holds the purse strings he could perhaps arrange for the Queen's pension to be reinstated. My dear, I think we may have won.'

'Oh, Aunt, can it be true? Could this be the breakthrough we have so longed for?'

The pair hugged each other with joyful relief, one thankful that she could at last achieve the propriety she had so long craved, able at last to put her murky past behind her, the other dreaming of the new fortune she might build once there was a crown on her niece's pretty head.

Gabrielle wasted no time in speaking to her royal lover, and showing him Margot's letter. 'How the Queen must have swallowed her pride in order to write such a missive, to me of all people.'

Frowning, Henry quickly scanned the letter before handing it back to Gabrielle with a smile. 'I will speak with Rosny. He will make the necessary arrangements.'

The subject, it seemed, was closed.

The King had grown weary of war, and Gabrielle did not wonder at it. There was still much to be achieved before France was truly secure. As spring approached and the sun shone, he wished to enjoy life a little more. Henry spent much of his time playing tennis, and Gabrielle and Madame de Sourdis would happily go along each day to sit in a gallery that overlooked the court, where they could watch and applaud him. Many of the public were also admitted as they loved to

299

watch their King at play, although some preferred to more closely watch his *maîtresse en titre*.

In the evening he might take her to the theatre,
openly caressing and kissing her in public, not
caring who saw how much he loved her. At
Henry's insistence Gabrielle arranged more
masques and ballets for their mutual enjoyment
and entertainment.

'They say I keep the King from his duties. That
I am a frivolous influence upon him, but it is not
my fault, Aunt, I swear it.'

'I know that, my precious,' Madame de Sourdis
declared. 'The King has a will of his own, and no
one can doubt that he adores you.'

'The other night when he and his friends
frolicked about the streets in masks, the people
must have thought that it was Henry Trois on his
capers all over again. We ended the night at the
hotel of Zamet, eating and drinking till dawn, yet
I did not encourage him in this folly. He simply
feels the need to relax, to forget death and war
and pain. Can the citizens not let him do that, at
least, without blaming me?'

'Their low opinion of you is deeply unfair, particularly considering the good influence you have
brought to bear on the King of late,' Madame de
Sourdis protested.

'I wonder sometimes if I have any true friends.
I thought Zamet was, but he is shrewd and wily,
and very ambitious coming from humble stock as
the son of a shoemaker from Lucca. He has done
well for himself as valet to Henri III, then was he
not treasurer for the League for a time? I do
wonder if perhaps he courts my friendship only

for the benefit it will bring to him rather than out of genuine affection.'

'I am sure that is not the case. Does he not lend you money, and assist you with your property dealings? You have many friends, my dear, and His Majesty at least appreciates you.'

Gabrielle smiled. 'Then what more do I need?'

At yet another banquet the following evening Henry seemed in a quarrelsome mood and again began upbraiding his sister for her obstinacy.

'We see little of Monsieur le Comte at court these days, since he withdrew to his *Château de Maillé*. I suspect he is wallowing in sullenness and resentment.' Which made Henry all the more determined to delay his sister's betrothal no further.

Catherine protested. 'He does nothing of the sort. Perhaps he feels undervalued, as do I.' She felt irritable and impatient, pining for her count whose character Henry continued to malign.

'You should appreciate, Catarina, that Monsieur le Comte is cunning and clever. I fear he might one day become a deadly opponent to César, which is a further reason for withholding my consent to your marriage.'

'I think you see shadows where there is only light. Charles has threatened no such thing.'

Henry frowned. 'He has certainly clouded your judgement, Madame.'

'And you are inconsiderate and unfeeling, brother.'

'While you put every obstacle you can in the way of a betrothal,' Henry snapped. 'You have refused Montpensier, a decision I suspect you will live to regret, therefore I have sent a message to the Duc de Bar that he should present himself to you at his earliest convenience. What say you to that, sister?'

The Princess Catherine got to her feet. 'If you will excuse me, I am feeling somewhat indisposed. There is no place for me here. I cannot yield to Madame la Marquise, so I have no doubt you will find my absence a joyful release.'

Dipping a curtsey she left the room, and, irritated by her apparent disobedience, Henry turned his annoyance upon Gabrielle. 'Have I not seen that green brocade gown a number of times?'

Gabrielle flushed. 'It is my favourite, Sire. You know how fond I am of green.'

'And you know that I do not like to see your hair powdered. Nor are there enough diamonds in your *coiffure*. There ought to be fifteen at least, not a mere dozen.'

'I beg Your Majesty's pardon for being inadequately dressed,' Gabrielle said, in something of a fluster. She was suddenly acutely aware of a silence failing upon the room, of the Duchesse de Montmorency, Madame de Villars and others delighting in her discomfiture. She could sense them examining her attire and finding it at fault. Never before had the King openly criticized her in public, more often brazenly caressing her, and there were some courtiers, Zamet and La Varenne amongst them, who were all too evidently amused by the incident.

It was almost dawn by the time they arrived back at the Louvre, and within moments of their arrival, before even Gabrielle had chance to retire to her room and remove the offending gown, she heard the clatter of hooves in the courtyard.

Henry went quickly to the window. 'It is Bellegarde, and he seems in a great hurry.'

Moments later the Duke was ushered into the King's presence. He was sweating and out of breath, clearly having ridden hard. 'Sire, the town of Amiens has fallen to the Spaniards.'

'*Ventre Saint Gris*, are you sure? We did not expect this.'

Bellegarde said, 'It came quite out of the blue. It is incredible that the Spanish could take so large a town so easily. We now have no stronghold to impede the march of our enemies.'

Henry strode to the door, then back again, concerned and agitated. 'Where is Rosny? Beringhen, fetch him to me. I need to speak to my keeper of finance.'

His favourite adviser came hurrying into the salon moments later to find his royal master pacing the floor half dressed, shoulders drooped, and the blackest of expressions on his face. Various nobles stood about, pale with uncertainty and Rosny saw at once that something was badly wrong.

'What is it, my lord? What disaster has befallen us?'

'It would seem the poor folk of Amiens have undone themselves through refusing the garrison which I wished to send them.' The situation was quickly explained, money promised, however difficult it would be to find it, and the King's men alerted so that an army could immediately be mustered.

'By the grace of God we will prevail. We have played too long the King of France. It is now time to enact again the role of the King of Navarre.' By which Henry seemed to imply he must set aside royal amusements and return to battle.

Gabrielle flung herself into his arms. 'Oh, my love, I beg you to take care.'

Henry gently hushed her. 'Take heart, *ma maîtresse*. We must set aside the contests of love and wage a different war.'

The nobles were angry at this turn of events, feeling more vulnerable than ever as Paris lay open to attack, its treasury all but empty and with yet another battle to wage. They were filled with fear and even as the King retired to his own room to prepare before leading his men out in battle, they turned their venom on Gabrielle.

'This is your doing,' Sancy hissed. 'Had His Majesty paid more attention to protecting his people rather than toying with his mistress we might not be in this position.'

'He speaks true,' muttered another voice.

'Aye. Amiens might not have fallen had he remained in camp.'

'The King is being turned into a shallow creature.'

Epernon said, 'You think more of the crown you wish to wear on your pretty head, rather than the needs of the people.'

Alarmed by these dangerous murmurings from her enemy, Gabrielle fled in terror to the King's apartment. 'I cannot stay here,' she wept as Henry snatched a hasty breakfast, issuing orders to his men and talking with Rosny all at the same time. 'The nobles mutter and whisper against me. They say I distracted you from your duty. I don't feel safe in Paris without you, my lord.'

The contempt of his courtiers had not passed him by. Henry was no fool and knew how some sought any opportunity to bring her down. 'My dear, you must take refuge in Monceaux.'

'Are the roads out of the capital still passable?'

'If we make haste. I will have your litter prepared at once.' Henry caught her in his arms and held her close. 'My dearest angel, I insist that you are protected.'

'But what of you? Will you be safe?'

'You must not fret, my love. We will prevail.'

'Oh, Sire, much as I long to leave for my own sake, and for yours, how can I? The people would accuse me of deserting them.'

'You must obey the King, Gabrielle, not the citizens of Paris,' scolded her aunt, all of a dither and most anxious to depart to safer territory. She did not trust the people of Paris, nor certain court nobles when their king was absent.

Henry took Gabrielle's lovely face between his hands and gently kissed her. 'You must do as I ask, my love, I beg you.' As good hearted and caring as ever, it was as if their quarrel had never occurred.

Before it was properly light, Gabrielle departed in a closed litter. An hour later, Henry set out at the head of his company. The citizens of Paris rushed out into the streets to watch him pass by, cheering him on his way. No one could deny that their King possessed courage.

Days later pamphlets appeared stuck up in

shop windows and on street corners bearing satires and verses which blamed his *maîtresse en titre* for keeping the King from his duties, and bringing disgrace and menace upon them all.

Within weeks the health of the King once again began to fail as Henry complained of exhaustion and battle fatigue. He wrote to Gabrielle of the heavy burden he carried, worse than when he was King of Navarre. She hurried to nurse him in the camp, anxious to do everything she could to help.

'I have pledged many of my jewels to Zamet and he has promised more loans.'

'My angel, what would I do without you?'

Gabrielle flushed. 'And I am *enceinte* again.'

Henry managed a weak laugh. 'You bring me nothing but joy.'

But, alarmed by his increasing indisposition from whatever malady he suffered, Gabrielle insisted Henry return at once to Paris. She summoned his man-servants. 'The King requires the services of a doctor so we will take him back to the city, with all speed.'

La Rivière, his first physician, was called and at once took charge of the King's treatment, embarking upon a regime of cupping and bleeding in order to restore him to health. To Gabrielle's great joy and relief, despite lengthy discussions with Rosny about the state of the exchequer when really he should have been resting, Henry made good progress and was soon moved to Monceaux to convalesce.

In May, while the conquest of Amiens and the recovery of the King slowly took their course, radical priests grasped the opportunity to again inflame the people of Paris against the Huguenots, who were gathering in the city under the patronage of Princess Catherine. They held secret meetings and plotted treason, spread rumours that King Philip of Spain would march from Amiens upon Paris, till finally the leaders were rounded up and hanged.

'My God, I am beset with problems on all sides,' Henry groaned.

Cooling the heat of his head with a cold compress, Gabrielle smiled. 'Then I shall do my best to cheer you, for I have good news, my lord. The Duc de Bar has arrived, hoping for a betrothal with the Princess Catherine.'

In early June Henry rode out to meet the Duc de Bar in the park of St Germain with hope and optimism, and no small degree of relief, in his heart. The Duke was young with considerable military prowess, more recently engaged in trying to win the heart of a fair maiden, which he had ultimately failed to do. Or else he had decided that a royal princess was a better option. He seemed perfectly agreeable on first acquaintance, if a little too anxious to please.

Catherine received him with cool indifference, very much upon her guard, and her dignity. Once the niceties were swiftly dealt with, she cut straight to the point. 'You know that we are of different religions and that my faith is important to me. Would you allow me freedom of conscience as the Duc de Montpensier agreed to do?'

'Of course,' the Duc de Bar pronounced.

The King intervened. 'But would you not expect your wife to bring up any children you might have together in the Catholic faith?'

'But of course,' Bar said again, smiling nervously from one to the other, as if trying to decide which one he should attempt to please.

'Perhaps you might wish my sister to change her religion too by then?'

'Indeed, Your Majesty, that would seem wise.'

Catherine stifled a groan of repugnance. 'And if I did not wish to?'

'Oh, I am quite sure that you would,' Bar insisted, smiling benignly upon her.

Catherine was dismayed. 'But you said you would allow me freedom of conscience?'

'I am sure that as a good wife you would recognize the wisdom of converting of your own accord, at an appropriate juncture.'

'Well said, young sir,' laughed the King. 'No more vacillating, be firm and consistent with my sister. It is the only way to control her.'

Catherine made her excuses and walked away, trembling with silent anger. The following day, which was a Sunday, she attended *prêche* as usual, if even more ostentatiously than usual. 'Let it not be said that I am about to abandon my faith simply to become the Duchess of Lorraine.'

In July and August the royal troops remained fully engaged with skirmishes as the Spanish were putting up a furious resistance. But early in July, just a few months after Henriette was legitimized, as her brother César had been, the King had a surprise for Gabrielle. He deeply regretted not

308

being able to legitimize their last child with marriage, as he had so longed to do, particularly as Gabrielle had already confided that she was again *enceinte*. But Margot remained perversely obstinate, and Rome infuriatingly slow to provide the necessary lubricant to loosen the bonds that tied him to her. So, anxious to at least prove his goodwill, Henry instead conferred a new title and lands upon his official mistress. The domains were in the province of Champagne, which he'd purchased for 80,000 crowns.

Rosny was not pleased by this news, considering it a wasteful drain upon the public purse to create another duchy, and for such a reason. From now on Gabrielle was to be elevated from La Marquise de Monceaux, to Duchess of Beaufort.

Some called her the Duchesse d'Ordure.

No one was now allowed into her presence without having first made formal request for audience. Her *levées* were ceremoniously attended, the ladies jostling to dress her, hand over her book of hours, or hold the golden platter upon which was deposited her fan, rings, watch and handkerchief.

'Do you notice,' Rosny whispered to Varenne, 'that she never rises, even when a Prince of the Blood addresses her?'

'And she is always preceded by a chamberlain as she enters or leaves the royal salon.'

The two exchanged a speaking glance as Rosny added, 'I fear the lady grows above herself.'

La Varenne sighed. 'Ah, but she is a perfect beauty and the King, you will notice, is as besotted as ever. He can scarcely take his eyes from her.'

Rosny saw how even the King bowed to her, and watched the rest of the proceedings in thoughtful silence.

By January 1598, almost ten years from the date of the accession, Philip of Spain finally agreed to seek peace. Margot wrote to congratulate Henry, signing herself 'your very humble and obedient servant, wife, and subject'. She wrote also to Rosny, again offering vague hints at divorce. 'In the event of His Majesty consenting to espouse a consort of birth suitable to his august alliance, then my opposition of the Holy See would speedily vanish.'

Rosny, who had improved the Queen's financial position by restoring her pension, considered the point to be a valid one.

In March, a betrothal was arranged between Françoise de Lorraine, the daughter of the rebellious Duc de Mercoeur, and César in a bid to reconcile the two sides. The children were of an age, being four years old, so it seemed a good match for all concerned, particularly as the Duke was the wealthiest noble in France. It also brought to heel Mercoeur's haughty wife, which gave Gabrielle great satisfaction.

In April, Gabrielle gave birth to another son, Alexandre, and it was shortly after this momentous event that Henry finally plucked up the courage to confide his dearest wishes to Rosny.

They walked in the gardens at the Palace of Rennes, the ancient home of the Dukes of Brittany, Gabrielle remaining in Nantes for her lying-in. This was taking longer than usual as she was unwell following a difficult birth. Henry approached the subject with caution, aware of his advisor's disapproval. He spoke first of the peace and the details of the settlement that must be made with the Spanish, and with the Huguenots who were feeling somewhat unsettled and concerned for their future.

'I too am concerned for the future of France,' Henry confided. 'Who will continue my work when I am gone? The country needs an heir, and I am determined to free myself from Margot and find a new queen.'

'I guessed that this matter was occupying your thoughts of late, Sire. You would then choose a suitable bride?' Rosny had one or two princesses in mind.

'If one could obtain wives according to one's wish, I would choose one who, among other good points, would comply with several principal conditions, that is to say, beauty of person, modesty of life, complaisance of humour, shrewdness of mind, fruitfulness of body, eminence of extraction and greatness of estate.'

'Such a woman would be hard to find,' Rosny dryly remarked. 'There is, of course, the Infanta of Spain?'

'I would not necessarily reject her, if I might gain the Netherlands as part of the dowry.'

'That is unlikely,' Rosny conceded. 'What of the Princess Arabella of England? If she were to be declared heir to the throne, you could win another crown.'

Henry frowned. 'I would need to be certain Elizabeth had made her decision on an heir, which she shows no sign of doing, as yet.'

'There are many German princesses.'

'I doubt they would suit me. I do not fancy any one of them.'

'Prince Maurice of the Low Countries has sisters.'

'But they are all Huguenots and such an alliance would offend the court of Rome.'

Rosny worked his way across Europe, mentioning nieces of dukes in Rome and Florence, daughters of kings and princes, but none were quite right. They were either too young, too old, too ugly, too poor, or simply too insignificant. The King even found fault with their complexion.

The direction of Henry's thoughts was all too clear, and Rosny could not approve. Apart from any other consideration, Madame Gabrielle had offended him by persuading Henry to give the post of Grand Master of the Artillery to her father, Antoine d'Estrées. It was an important position, one Rosny had coveted for himself.

'I should prefer a flirting wife rather than an ill-tempered one. A wife to talk to and confide in, and to whom I can safely leave my regency after my death.'

'Sire,' said Rosny in exasperation. 'What can I say? You wish to be married again, but the world does not contain a suitable princess! Do you expect a miracle, or for Elizabeth I to be rejuvenated? I counsel you to assemble the most lovely damsels of France and thus choose a consort to your taste. An heiress would be beneficial for the treasury; but it is also important that you are content, and that she gives you children for France.'

'True, *mon ami*,' said Henry; all eagerness. 'I

need a queen who is gentle and good-humoured, who would love me, and whom I could love in return. She must give me healthy children as there is no time to be lost. I am growing older, Rosny, by the day, and would wish to bring them up myself, make them brave and gallant princes. Do you know of such a lady?'

Stifling a sigh of resignation, Rosny admitted that he did not.

'What if I should name her, avow that I can testify to the beauty; amiability and fecundity of said lady?'

'Your Majesty doubtless alludes to some royal widow.'

Henry laughed out loud. 'Cunning old fool, you know full well to whom I refer. Does the description not perfectly fit *la Duchesse?* What objections do you have to offer to my choosing Madame Gabrielle who has been as a faithful wife to me for many years?'

Rosny's expression was grim. 'I cannot answer such a question.'

'I order you to answer.' Henry good-humouredly slapped his old friend on the back. Buoyed as he was with the joy of victory, and blinded by his passion for her, Henry was certain he could put Gabrielle d'Estrées on the throne by the sheer force of his will. 'You know me well enough for us to be honest with each other. You can say what you truly feel.'

'Sire, fond as you are of Madame la Duchesse, what if after your death, or even before, your legitimate sons, born in wedlock, took issue with those born before your marriage to their mother.

There could be civil war. It would not be good for France. In addition, the ladies of France would not willingly pay homage to Madame Gabrielle as queen, nor would foreign potentates do her the honour you would wish. They will never forget her origins. Ill feeling could grow, feuds and jealousies destroy the harmony between you.'

Henry listened in silence and at length said, 'I will think on what you say, Rosny, but I am not convinced by your argument. I promise that I will make no firm decision until the divorce has been accomplished. I command you to resume negotiations with Her Majesty, and I will send another envoy to Rome to solicit His Holiness on the matter.'

Rosny knew that for the moment at least, further argument was futile. 'As you wish, my lord. Might I request that you do not discuss the matter with the Duchess?'

Henry almost smiled at his ever-cautious counsellor. 'Madame Gabrielle has done much for your own advancement, remember.'

'I know it, even so we must put the needs of the realm first.'

'She likes and esteems you, Rosny, but nevertheless distrusts the counsel you offer me as being against herself and the children. She says you put France before my own happiness and wellbeing. Perhaps she is right.'

'Sire, your virtue and great mind animate your realm,' Rosny tactfully remarked. 'The splendour and glory of this kingdom should recompense you for the sacrifices you make.'

'Ah, but there are only so many sacrifices a king

should be obliged to make for his people.'

Gabrielle was basking in the sun of the King's affection, and revelling in the joys of celebrating the peace. Documents were signed, *largesse* distributed, and a banquet held in the Episcopal Palace for the King and the assembled courtiers, once the business of the day had been completed. The ladies joined them for fruit, wine and pastries, and as Gabrielle entered even the King rose to greet her, which meant everyone present was obliged to do the same. The accolade brought a smile of pleasure to her rosy lips.

Gracefully taking her seat beside the King, she spread her skirts with a satisfied little sigh. Madame de Guise stepped forward to offer a dish of sweetmeats, and Gabrielle sat contentedly picking from the plate while the King held her other hand, fondling and caressing it in his lap.

Many of the citizens watching seemed amused by the way in which His Majesty publicly indulged himself with his mistress. But others grumbled over how no less a person than the widow of Henri de Guise, King of the Barricades and Paris, was obliged to wait upon so low a woman.

'Where is the Princess Catherine?' Henry wanted to know.

'She has sent her apologies as she is suffering from a headache,' Gabrielle explained.

'More likely ill temper.'

'Nay, do not be too hard on your sister, Sire. Madame may have a swift and fierce temper, but you know she never harbours ill will. She soon forgives, as do you. You are very alike in that respect.'

315

Earlier, Gabrielle and Catherine had fallen into a slight disagreement over the matter. 'Your absence will be noted. The King will not be pleased,' Gabrielle had warned her.

'I care not. You have urged him to take this stand against me.'

Gabrielle had gaped in stunned disbelief. 'I assure you I have no say in the matter. This marriage plan is all Henry's doing, not mine. If you could but use your charms upon your brother, I am sure you would win your case in the end. He is not an unfeeling man.'

'I cannot resort to flattery and subterfuge, as you do. It is not in my nature to use such tricks. I can only be frank and open and honest.'

'That is a great misfortune for Henry hates to see a woman weep and will ever play the gentleman rather than see those he loves hurt.'

'Perhaps I lack your cunning and artifice,' Catherine bitterly remarked.

'If a woman has to use her arts in this way, it is because she cannot simply draw a sword. She must find other ways to defend herself,' Gabrielle responded, keeping a tight hold on her patience.

'It is easy for you,' Catherine pouted. 'You are so beautiful that any man would fall for your charms. I have no such benefits. I am plain and dull.'

'Oh, Madame, that is not at all the case. Is not beauty in the eye of the beholder? And the Comte loves you dearly.'

But this only caused the princess to cry and, seeing the tears well in those sad dark eyes, Gabrielle's heart filled with pity for her. Without thinking, she put her arms about Catherine to hold her close and offer what comfort she could. 'I know how it hurts to lose a loved one, and I swear I have spoken often in your favour, sadly to no avail. But be assured that I am ever your friend.'

And with a tentative smile from the Princess, the first Gabrielle had ever been granted, it seemed that the olive branch she'd offered had at last been accepted.

Madame Catherine was not, however, yet willing to forgive her brother. She was still angry with Henry and holding fast to her determination to refuse de Bar, certain that the Pope would not issue a dispensation for their marriage.

In the days following, the Duke reiterated his devotion. 'We must not let the papal interdict stand in the way,' he told her.

'Your solution then is for us to marry, and convert me later?'

'I'm sure you will see the wisdom of that rather than risk having Rome declare any children we may have to be illegitimate.'

Catherine bit back a sharp reply, even she realizing it did no good to insult His Holiness and the Catholic Church, but as Gabrielle preened herself with her new glories, Catherine became increasingly melancholy and studiously avoided all the ballets and masques and court functions held to celebrate the peace. She preferred instead to debate dogma with the pastors, or read from 'Calvin's Institutes', a favourite book, to her ladies. Or she would sit in her chamber in solitary contemplation.

Nevertheless, the daily battles between brother

and sister continued. 'I fear you will suffer per-dition for taking the Mass,' Catherine bitterly remarked on one occasion. 'Our mother wished me to marry a prince of the same religion as myself. You owe it to her, and to me, to see that wish is carried out.'

'I assure you, Catarina, that I have made all necessary provision for the Huguenots. I listened to the concerns of Aubigné and the pastors, and peace with Spain will not destroy their hopes for greater tolerance. Clauses have been inserted in the peace settlement to confer complete privilege of worship in almost all cities and towns. In addition, all state offices, including judicial and those connected with the revenue, will be open to the Huguenot bourgeoisie. Even they have come to trust me and believe they will not suffer, why will not you? Times have changed from our mother's day. We cannot live in the past.'

By way of retaliation Catherine again held a *prêche* in the courtyard of the Louvre, at which 3,000 Huguenots were present. But once the Edict of Nantes was signed, Henry proceeded to have the articles of the marriage contract drawn up. He was sick of her obstinacy, her temper and her Calvinistic zeal, and vowed to be rid of the problem once and for all. He wanted a realm where tolerance prevailed, where peace was para-mount. If that meant sacrificing his sister's happiness, it was surely a price worth paying.

Rosny drew up the marriage contract for the Princess Catherine and the Duke of Bar, settling an agreed annual payment of 60,000 *livres* upon the King's sister, plus a cash sum of 100,000 crowns. There was also various gold plate and jewellery inherited from her mother, Jeanne d'Albret. These included emeralds, a pearl necklace and a diamond tiara.

Catherine, wishing to delay matters for as long as possible, made many written demands, insisting that she wanted several items of furniture and valuables from the palaces at Pau and Nérac.

'I pray you must needs take inventories of the said castles,' Henry ordered Rosny, wearied beyond measure by her procrastinating. 'I hasten as fast as I can to get her married, and so to add this blessing to the many which God has bestowed upon me in giving peace to this realm and to the reformed churches.'

The marriage contract was duly signed by Henry at Monceaux, where he happened to be resting with Gabrielle and the children, but he was losing interest as well as sympathy in his sister's affairs as he was fighting a similar battle with Rome over the dissolution of his marriage.

Rosny wrote another official letter to Queen Margot, as instructed by the King, although also slipping in a note of his own saying how he hoped she would stand firm in her refusal. Meanwhile, he once more warned his royal master not to marry his mistress. Sancy too impetuously added his own arguments against Gabrielle, and was obliged to leave court as a result.

The King was determined to have his way.

Some time later, Rosny spoke of these concerns to Varenne. They were walking in the gardens at

Fontainebleau, safe from wagging ears, having just witnessed the departure of the Cardinal-legate, Alessandro de Medici, who had assisted in the Edict of Nantes. The subject of the royal divorce had arisen with the King attempting to justify his position, but the Cardinal had tactfully declined to comment, at least publicly.

'I doubt his eminence will aid the divorce unless it were to place his relative, Marie de Medici, on the throne of France,' Rosny commented.

La Varenne nodded. 'He sees only evil consequences coming from the "royal infatuation" as he calls it. The ruin of the realm, no less.'

'I have often defended Madame Gabrielle when some have spoken against her in council, if only because she was once instrumental in gaining me the post of keeper of finance, but I am not in favour of her elevation.'

'You do frequently mention her kindness and gentleness, it is true,' agreed Varenne, 'often siding with Cheverny who, as the lover of her aunt, naturally hopes to see Henry marry the girl.'

Rosny regarded his friend with a shrewd eye. 'I believe Zamet is very much in favour of an Italian marriage for the King.'

'He seems to like the Medici match, yes.'

'Yet he claims to be Madame Gabrielle's friend.'

'He ever puts his own interests first,' Varenne dryly remarked.

'And you?'

Varenne paused. 'The King has been good to me, but I see no advancement for myself in commending he marry his favourite whore. The woman has a shady past, nought to recommend her but three healthy children. Nor is she universally popular.'

'I cannot see the people of France accepting a harlot as queen,' Rosny bitterly remarked. 'Let alone put her bastards on the throne. It is unthinkable.'

'The Italian alliance would at least have dignity, and ensure an easy divorce from Queen Margot.'

Rosny nodded, deep in thought. 'The Jesuits too would not be in favour of the King succumbing to this infatuation, and the treasury is in dire need of a rich bride, as you well know. I believe we must do everything in our power to bring about the right conclusion to this dilemma, and, as the Cardinal said, turn the King from a resolve degrading to the realm of France.'

'And if we fail to turn him?'

Rosny looked Varenne steadily in the eye. 'Then we must find some other way.'

Henry and Gabrielle were returning from a brief visit to St Germain, crossing the river on the ferry close to Quai Malaquais. The King was simply dressed, accompanied by only two attendants, as he liked to travel incognito. Even Gabrielle was in her plainest gown, not wishing to attract attention. Being the friendly soul he was, Henry cheerfully struck up a conversation with the ferryman, asking what he thought of the peace.

'I do not comprehend it,' replied the boatman in grudging tones. 'There are still taxes on everything. Even this miserable boat from which I must eke out a livelihood is taxed.'

'Does not the King intend soon to amend all

those taxes?' Henry asked.

'Oh, the King is a good enough fellow,' said the ferryman, 'but he has a mistress who needs so many fine gowns, jewels and gewgaws that there is no end to his expense, and we poor fools have to pay for it all. It might not be so bad if she wasn't a woman with a past, but it's said that she has had many lovers, and who knows how many she lets caress her still.'

Gabrielle's mouth dropped open in shock at the man's effrontery. But before she could say anything, Henry burst out laughing, and, as they'd reached the landing stage, began to help her out of the boat. Turning to the ferryman he said, 'You can do without your toll for having such little faith in your King.'

Still laughing, Henry strode away, but the man ran after him.

'Here, you can't do that. I need that money. You think I can afford to give free rides to gentlemen and their lady friends? You've no right to steal from a poor ferryman.'

At this point a passer-by, seeing the commotion, seized the ferryman by the collar and gave him a shake. 'You stupid fellow, do you not see that it is the King himself you are insulting?'

The poor man fell to his knees in consternation, certain his head would soon be parting company from his body.

'The fellow should be hanged,' Gabrielle cried, furious at being so maligned. 'Arrest the scoundrel, Your Majesty.'

'No, no, my love,' Henry chuckled. 'This is only a poor devil soured by poverty. Here's your toll,

322

fellow, and I willingly pardon you. Moreover, you shall pay no more taxes on this ferryboat. There Madame, I am certain he will sing every night: *"Vive* Henri and *Vive* Gabrielle!"'

The incident so amused Henry that he related it to anyone who cared to listen. Gabrielle silently fumed.

But then one afternoon Henry came to Gabrielle with news. 'A letter has come in which the Queen writes with a promise to cooperate in every measure that will be good for the realm, and to my personal benefit. She even offers to present a petition herself to the Holy See, if required, in order to attain a divorce. An agreement is in sight at last.'

'Oh, let us hope so,' Gabrielle cried, clapping her hands in delight. 'Only when I am respectably married will these slurs upon my name cease.'

Two men stood close together in the shadows of a palace corridor, their voices hushed and hissing with anger. 'This is the worst news imaginable. It must not be allowed to happen. If the King gains his divorce he will be married to his whore before the month is out.'

'I agree, urgent action is needed. I too have heard from Queen Margot. She writes to ask for my advice in this matter, but is so desperate for funds that she might agree to sell her soul, let alone a crown, if only her debts are settled and her property returned to her. I must spell out the reality such freedom would bring.'

Varenne grunted. 'I have never known the King so constant.'

'Not so constant as you might imagine,' Rosny

demurred. 'He still dallies with other women, but none possess his heart as does Madame la Duchesse. She has bewitched him.'

'Then we must find one who can match her for beauty, wit and charm. One who will distract the King with a seductive smile.'

Rosny was instantly alert. 'And redirect him from this path he has chosen, down which he leads France to disaster and mayhem. Could you find such a woman?'

'I believe I could. Leave it with me.'

Henry wrote a reply to Margot, saying how he was convinced he could rely upon her goodwill not to retract her promise. Rosny also wrote, saying quite the opposite. But these concerns soon had to be set aside as the King fell ill again.

Gabrielle had returned to St Germain to offer comfort to the Princess Catherine who was still putting up a determined resistance to her brother's plan for her betrothal to the Duke of Bar. Her one remaining hope was that even if a dispensation was granted, no priest would dare perform the ceremony. Catherine was aided and abetted in this by her Huguenot friends, who, rather than see a Lorraine alliance would prefer their princess retire to Béarn and remain chaste.

The King was in Monceaux, and as soon as Gabrielle heard he was sick she was beside herself with worry; fearing not only for Henry's health, but for herself should anything happen to him. It was October, the King was no longer a young man and the chills of autumn, together with the heavy burden of kingship, had brought on the fever and exhaustion from which he so often suffered.

'It is all too much for him,' Gabrielle cried to her aunt. 'The siege of Amiens, his campaign in Bretagne, and since then all the excitement of celebrating the peace. He is depressed and exhausted.'

'Not least by his concern over the imminent divorce,' added Madame de Sourdis, equally anxious.

'He knows full well how the nobles are out to thwart his plan for us to marry. What am I to do, Aunt? How can I possibly win against them?'

Before Madame de Sourdis had time to answer, Rosny burst unannounced into the salon. 'Madame la Duchesse, the King has collapsed. He is suffering from excruciating pains in the head and limbs.'

Gabrielle went white and cried out in terror. 'Send for his doctors at once.'

'It has been done. Monsieur Bellegarde has already sent for Marescot, Martin and Rosset. His Majesty is in good hands.'

'I must go to him at once. Quickly, Aunt, order my litter to be prepared, my belongings packed while I fetch the children.'

Rosny stepped in front of her, blocking her way. 'Madame, I would recommend that you wait a while before embarking upon your journey. The King is unconscious, he would not know you, and it is feared he may not last the night.'

Gabrielle felt her heart jerk with fear. 'That cannot be so. I could not bear to lose him. Pray step aside, Baron, I must go to him.'

Again Rosny protested. 'Etiquette and propriety demand your absence from what could sadly be the deathbed of the King of France.'

Gabrielle stiffened with outrage and fresh fear. How dare this upstart keep her from Henry's side? Summoning all her dignity, despite the fragile fluttering of her nerves and the grim expression on Rosny's face, she bravely continued. 'His Majesty is staying at my château. No one can deny me admission to my own house. Let my lords of the privy council exclude me from the chamber of my King at their peril!'

Rosny knew when he was bested and, stepping back, allowed her to pass.

Gabrielle hurried to the King's side and met his joy at her arrival with triumph in her heart. Try as they might to separate them, Henry's great love for her would ever win through.

As Henry slowly recovered Gabrielle never left his side. She brought him peaches, which he loved, Spanish oranges and nectarines grown in Béarn. She sang to him in her soft voice, and they talked of their children as loving parents do.

'Our daughter is growing pretty, just like her mother.'

'And our new son will be as handsome as his father, I think,' Gabrielle laughed. 'He is such a delightful imp. And what of his baptism, will it be soon?' Gabrielle was anxious that Alexandre receive all due honours befitting *un fils de France*.

The King was tired, wishing to sleep not talk of baptisms. 'Speak with Rosny. Make the arrangements, but do not let him bully you, my love. See that everyone of importance is invited to the christening of my fine boy.'

Gabrielle sighed with relief, but, as she expec-

326

ted, there was indeed opposition to the plan, not only from Rosny, but from Villeroy, Bellièvre, Varenne and others. Within hours she was quietly sobbing in the arms of her aunt, protesting about their attitude.

'They are dubbing it a scandalous spectacle, one to which the King should hesitate to invite foreign ambassadors and half of Europe. How dare they speak of our son's baptism in such terms?'

'My dear, the nobles make no secret of the fact they want a royal princess for His Majesty. But you need have no fear of his accepting one, for it is you he loves.'

Gabrielle looked at her aunt in alarm. 'How can I be sure of that?'

Madame de Sourdis smiled. 'You only have to see how he looks at you to know that he adores you. And has not Monsieur de Sillery embarked on a mission to Queen Margot, with instructions to negotiate for the immediate dissolution of their marriage? He carries with him all the necessary documents, which the Queen has promised to sign. Is that not so?'

'That is what she said in her letter. Henry is convinced that she will sign.'

'There we are then. All will be well. Do not let these nobles have the satisfaction of seeing that their opinions trouble you. You have the King's heart and he has legitimized your son, so show not a trace of fear or concern for these malcontents.'

Gabrielle wiped away the tears with her kerchief. 'You are right, Aunt, as always.' And with grave dignity, showing nothing of the tumult that raged within, she continued making her plans.

By early December, the news that came back from Usson was not as Henry had expected or hoped for. Margot had changed her mind. The Queen point blank refused to consent to a divorce, alleging she had only just learned from Rosny that Henry intended to marry his mistress.

'Although I continue in the will to meet His Majesty's desires relative to a divorce, my indignation is greatly kindled that the King intends to give my place to Madame la Duchesse – a lady lost in repute.'

Henry was furious and railed at Rosny. 'This is your doing. She promised me she would sign. Why does she prevaricate when she knew full well my intentions to marry the Duchess.'

'I assure you, my lord, you have my full support,' lied his favourite minister. 'Certain nobles, however, do ponder over the words of the Cardinal, particularly since their wives refuse to curtsey to Madame Gabrielle.'

The King exploded. *Ventre Saint Gris*, I will not have it. I shall divorce Margot on the grounds of her own adultery. She has had so many lovers I could take my pick. I shall dispense with her permission and choose a different route. See to it, Rosny, with all speed.'

Instead, Rosny showed the Queen's letter to Cheverny, who in turn passed it on to Madame de Sourdis, who showed it to her niece.

Gabrielle cried many bitter tears of disappointment. 'The Queen has changed her mind and refuses to divorce him after all. What am I to do?' she wailed to her aunt.

'Hold faith in the King,' Madame de Sourdis insisted. 'And have you not more joyous news for His Majesty?'

Gabrielle shyly nodded.

Madame smiled. 'I thought so. All will be well, take my word for it. This child will be born in wedlock.'

Rumours of Gabrielle's fourth pregnancy flew round the court like wildfire, exciting yet more rumours and scandal. Since Bellegarde had recently separated from his wife, his hasty marriage now in ruins, he was as good a target as any to fix upon for their malice. Just as it had been whispered when César had been born, rumour had it that the child was not the King's.

For once Henry showed no sign of jealousy, but simply laughed. 'I hear this child has a different father.'

Gabrielle sank to her knees before him. 'Sire, do not believe the tales they spread about me. I am innocent of the charge and ever loyal to Your Majesty, whom I love more than life itself.'

'I know it, my angel. Your lovely face tells me so. Let us proceed with the baptism and prove our resolve and loyalty. You have been as a wife to me all these years, and will be so in truth very soon, I promise, with or without Margot's consent.'

Gabrielle fell into his arms, weeping with joy. 'Oh, Henry, you are the sweetest, dearest man. I do love you so

Henry took her to his bed and demonstrated, very ably, how much he cared for her.

On 13 December, Alexandre was baptized at St

Germain-en-Laye, with all the ceremonial due to the baptism of a Prince of France. Cardinal de Retz and the Archbishop of Paris officiated. The godfather was the Comte de Soissons, who, knowing that Catherine, his lost love, was about to be married, deemed it wise to obey this request from the King.

Gabrielle was filled with excitement, so caught up with the magnificence of the proceedings that she gave no further thought to the murmurs of discontent, not even those whispered among the citizens of Paris. Her friends and supporters encouraged her to disregard those nobles who spoke against her. She was the beloved wife, in all but name, of His Majesty; and therefore untouchable. Even the King saw no reason why every honour should not be heaped upon her and his new son.

Little Alexandre was placed, with all dignity; upon a huge bed hung with white satin and covered with cloth of gold bordered with ermine. Royal guards lined the staircase and corridors of the château, and the archers of the Swiss guard stood at the door of the church. The font was from Fontainebleau, the platform draped with velvet on which was featured the *fleurs-de-lis* of France. Gabrielle herself wore a mantle studded with the same symbols, which caused much gossip among the ladies present.

At the ball and banquet that followed she looked the perfect picture of beauty, for all she was now twenty-seven and grown a little plumper from her several pregnancies. And the King was as adoring as ever, insisting that all due homage be paid to her.

Gabrielle sat back, happy and content, revelling in the ballet and the adulation from Henry and her friends. The baptism had been a marvellous success.

And then Rosny received the bills for this momentous event.

When the Baron saw what must be paid to the heralds, trumpeters and hautboys, archers and guards, clergy and choir boys for their services, he absolutely refused to honour them. 'This is outrageous! Far too much money. That spoiled madam has gone too far this time.'

He paid instead a much reduced amount, a sum Rosny deemed to be fair. The archers and heralds, and others owed money, were not happy and an official representative was sent to complain.

'Monsieur, the amount you have paid is incorrect. The sums payable at the baptisms of Children of France has long been regulated.'

'What does that signify?' retorted the Superntendent of Finance. 'There are no Children of France!'

The official went away to complain to Gabrielle and, seeing that he needed to protect himself, Rosny hurried at once to the King.

'Do you see these figures, Sire, they are quite scandalous and reckless in the extreme.'

Henry read the accounts and paled. Ever careful with money himself he saw that he may well have made a grave mistake in giving Gabrielle such a free hand. He ruefully rubbed his chin. 'The final sum does seem excessive. You must speak to the Duchesse de Beaufort on this matter, and suggest she do all she can to get it reduced.'

Rosny hurried to obey. Here, at last, was his chance to humiliate the favourite.

Gabrielle was staying with her aunt at the Deanery, quite close to the Louvre, and met the impertinent suggestion that she had overspent with barely concealed contempt. 'If that is the sum due, then it must be paid. I will not be dictated to by some valet,' she said.

Rosny was struck speechless, deeply offended by this insult. How dare this trollop look down her nose at him? She'd got above herself, and needed bringing down. Spinning on his heel, he stormed away and hurried straight back to the King.

The moment Henry saw Rosny's expression, he groaned. The last thing he wanted was to alienate his most talented minister. The King was all too aware of the rumour and intrigue that rumbled about him, often bound up in self-interest. He dare not risk Rosny's high-standing in court being destroyed by some silly quarrel over the cost of a baptism. He depended upon him too much. Somehow, he must reconcile these two people who were each so vitally important to him.

'I fear the lady may have misled me,' Henry said, playing the coward.

'Something must be done,' Rosny insisted, not willing to let the matter drop.

'Of course, of course,' said Henry. 'You shall see that a woman shall never control me, although I suspect the fault lies with her friends and her greedy aunt, rather than Madame La Duchesse.'

'Let us settle the matter now, once and for all.'

Stifling a sigh, Henry strode off in the direction

of the Deanery, Rosny hot on his tail. For once he did not greet Gabrielle with the usual three kisses, but insisted she make peace with the minister whom she had so deeply offended. 'You must learn to practise patience and moderation in future,' he warned, attempting to look stern.

Gabrielle was aghast. 'But Your Majesty, you sanctioned the ceremony. Surely those who took part deserve their fees?'

Henry felt as if he was being held on a very large fish hook with two lines, one held by his keeper of finance, the other by his mistress. Whoever reeled him in, he would be the loser. Like the fish, he wriggled to be free. 'I trusted you to maintain a sensible hold on the expenses,' Henry scolded, desperately striving to hold on to the high ground. 'I have always loved the sweetness and amiability of your disposition. Have I been deceived?'

Tears sprang into Gabrielle's blue eyes and she sank to her couch, weeping. 'I cannot abide it when you are angry with me. What have I done? What are you suggesting, Sire? I see that it is your intention to abandon me. Remember it was against my wishes to occupy this position which *you* forced upon me. Have I not done my best to please you?'

Rosny watched as his royal master's expression melted with love for his mistress when he saw her distress. He plainly ached to gather her in his arms and offer her the whole world if she would but stop crying and say that she loved him. The two lovers were entirely bound together by an emotion and intimacy that was hard to witness without feeling an intruder upon the scene. Yet

Rosny dare not leave, as he feared that Henry might actually offer her son the title of Prince of the Blood the instant he did so.

Gabrielle went on, 'Have I not sacrificed myself to you, and given you all my affection? Now I see that I must sacrifice myself to please your valet!'

She had used that dreadful, insulting word yet again. 'Sire, this is intolerable!' Rosny cried.

'You must dismiss the fellow,' Gabrielle sobbed. 'He is the one at fault, not I.'

Henry's patience ran out. 'Madame, it were better that I dispense with ten mistresses than with one servant such as Rosny.'

Only then did Gabrielle realize the extent of her blunder, and desperately attempted to make good. She fervently apologized and voluntarily conceded that any title for Alexandre should be postponed. For his part, Rosny agreed to look again at the costs and see that all due bills were met. To all outward appearances, a reconciliation had been achieved, but beneath the surface the ill feeling continued to fester.

The religious factions were each starting to grumble over the Edict of Nantes, the treaty meant to bring peace to the realm. The radical priests continued to preach from the pulpit against the Huguenots, saying they ought to be dragged to the slaughterhouse. They not only attacked the Huguenots, but Gabrielle herself. One declared that 'a lewd woman in the court of a king was a dangerous monster and caused much evil, particularly when she was encouraged to raise her head'.

It was clear they were referring to herself, which

greatly distressed Gabrielle.

The rebels also vociferously objected to allowing the Protestants equal rights and the opportunity to enter public office. Some had the effrontery to call upon Gabrielle to intercede on their behalf with the King to put a stop to this menace.

Gabrielle's response was a picture of innocence. 'I do not understand the nature of your objection. What possible problem could there be in admitting the Huguenots to Chambers or any public office, as they are loyal, true-hearted subjects. Has not the King allowed those who have actually borne arms against him to sit in his Chambers, which is surely far more dangerous? Besides, my efforts would be to no avail. Nothing will change the King's mind on this matter.'

If her answer did not please the Catholics, it delighted the Huguenots, and Aubigné wrote to thank her. Despite her having urged the King to accept the Mass, she had never interfered with them, or criticized their faith, and they greatly preferred Gabrielle to any Spanish queen. Now her popularity with the Huguenots increased tenfold.

Gabrielle went further. Aubigné had openly chastised the King for having abandoned the Huguenot faith. The stern old Puritan had been so outspoken and critical at the time that he'd feared Henry might never speak to him again, had even lived in dread of being taken into custody by the guard for a while. Gabrielle effected a reconciliation between the erstwhile chamberlain of Nérac and his royal master, with whom he had once been so close. She wrote to Aubigné and suggested he express his thanks to the King personally.

One morning, as she and Henry returned from their ride, she spotted him in the crowd of gentlemen gathered in the courtyard, and pointed him out to Henry.

'Ah, here is Aubigné back in court again, ever loyal, and no doubt wishing to express his gratitude for your work on behalf of the Huguenots.'

Henry dismounted and strode across to his one-time minister, clapping him on the shoulders and placing his cheek against his. 'Well met, old friend. I'm delighted to welcome you back to court. I trust this means you have thought better of your criticisms towards us.'

'Sire, so far you have only renounced God with your lips, and it pleased Him to pierce them. But when you renounce Him with your heart, it is your heart that He will pierce.'

Henry frowned, the allusion to that attack upon his life might be apt, but he didn't much care for the implication that he had abandoned his God rather than his religion. It was Gabrielle who spoke up for him.

'Fine words, sir,' she exclaimed, 'but you use them ill.'

'Aye, madam,' Aubigné agreed. 'But then they are to no avail. His Majesty will do as he pleases.'

'I will do what pleases France.'

Aubigné inclined his head in obeisance. 'I am happy to be here, Sire, and welcome the opportunity to offer my thanks for all you have done for my people.'

Henry laughed, ready to brush off their disagreements, as was his way. 'You should have trusted me more. See that you do not stay away so long next time.'

But the fear of a repeat of the St Bartholomew massacre did not go away.

The dissatisfaction of the rebel Leaguers intensified and they went to see the Duke of Mayenne, begging him to rise again and resume his old role of battle chief, claiming they would take up arms again at a moment's notice. Mayenne prudently declined to get involved, and called the guards so that the malcontents were marched to the Bastille and suitably dealt with.

But unlike his predecessor, Henri Trois, who never had any intention of upholding a peace treaty, Henry Quatre was determined that this one would stand. He wasted no time in turning the edict into law.

'It is my unalterable will that this, my edict, shall be accepted, registered and punctually executed.'

The council accepted this decision in silence, and the matter was closed. The Edict of Nantes would hold, at least for the foreseeable future.

Princess Catherine was in despair. The Pope had refused the dispensation unless she agreed to abjure the Protestant faith, which she had no intention of doing. Nonetheless, the Duke of Bar had arrived in Paris, bringing with him a retinue of three hundred gentlemen, determined to marry her and take her back with him to Lorraine.

'Once married, Madame, I am certain you will conform. I appreciate it is difficult for you, but will you not at least talk with the chaplains?'

Catherine held fast to her dignity. 'I appreciate the courtesy and respect you offer me, and will do as you ask. But I should not be expected to ask questions or listen to their arguments while sitting in state. Such talks must be held in private.'

'Very well, it shall be arranged.'

Two doctors of divinity discussed with the Princess at some length what would be involved in her conversion. Catherine remained unmoved. 'My conscience would not permit me to accept your doctrines.'

'Your brother the King has found no difficulty,' protested de Bar, fearing he may lose his bride even yet.

'In every circumstance I follow my brother's guide, excepting in matters concerning the law of God.'

The Duke of Lorraine, father of the intended groom, was growing increasingly irritated with the delays. 'I will not tolerate heresy in a future daughter-in-law.'

But Catherine remained adamant and refused to submit.

The Lorraine family was for returning home forthwith, but all protests abruptly ceased when Henry increased the dowry to 300,000 crowns. 'In appreciation of your patience, and because such a sum is commensurate with my sister's standing as a Daughter of France.' He also gave 40,000 crowns to Catherine herself.

'What is this for?'

'To defray the cost of the royal mantle you must wear for the ceremony.'

'There will be no ceremony. I refuse to convert.'

Henry smiled patiently at his rebellious sister. 'Ah, but there will. I am no longer prepared to

338

wait for a dispensation. We shall go ahead without the benefit of the Pope's blessing.'

Catherine was devastated. She could no longer see a way out. The only thing which stood in the way of the marriage was finding a priest to conduct the ceremony. Catherine felt numb inside as she watched the arrangements being made. It was as if they were happening to someone else, and not herself at all. Yet a part of her went on fighting.

'I would prefer to be married by one of my pastors.'

The Duke of Bar was outraged by this request. 'I will not accept a Protestant minister, my children would be declared bastards.'

'That is only your interpretation, not mine,' Catherine pronounced.

Her remarks caused great consternation in the Lorraine household, and de Bar, being highly strung, almost wept with frustration over the obstinacy of his bride. But Henry was weary of the argument and had reached the end of his tether.

'The marriage rites will be solemnized by the Catholic Church, as is only right and proper. I want no one to question its authenticity.'

The King sent at once for Cardinal Gondy to officiate but he firmly declined. 'The veto of Rome prevents any orthodox clergy from performing such a ceremony. It cannot be done.'

Henry was furious and sent for another priest. He too refused to become involved, and no other clergyman would risk alienating the Pope by disobeying the Holy Father's wishes in this delicate matter.

Catherine stood quietly by and smiled as de

Bar was now the one to fall into despair. 'With no dispensation from Rome, how can we proceed?' he cried. 'All is lost.'

'I am safe,' Catherine laughed, hugging Gabrielle in delight. 'I am to be spared. What think you of that?'

Gabrielle said nothing, merely offering what comfort she could to the Princess, knowing that even now Henry's fertile mind was working on a solution.

One was found in the person of the Archbishop of Rouen, the King's illegitimate brother. His morals were questionable as he'd been involved in a long liaison with an abbess, and his licentious behaviour had precluded him from high office. The Archbishop had only gained his exalted position by the personal intervention of the King. Now Henry called upon him to return the favour. Rouen did his best to wriggle out of it, but the threat of losing his beautiful mansion, his crozier and mitre, and the revenue that accompanied both, was too dreadful to contemplate. He finally agreed.

He was ordered to attend the King's *levée* on the last Sunday in January, 1599, at St Germain-en-Laye, where the court had gone for a few days.

Catherine was sitting in her apartment quietly weeping when the King and Gabrielle came to see her after early Mass. She was still in her *robe de chambre*, although resigned now to her fate.

'Why are you not yet dressed?' Henry asked, a false brightness in his tone. 'Come, I will wait while you prepare yourself. Hurry, hurry, there is no time to be lost.'

Her maids of honour scurried about, gathering up linen and silks. Gabrielle too rushed to assist and the ladies withdrew to the dressing room. But even at the last the Princess refused to meekly comply.

'I will not wear finery for a ceremony of which I do not approve.'

'My dear Catherine,' Gabrielle pleaded. 'I pray you do not offend your new husband at the outset. It is an honour that he wishes to make you his wife.'

'Marriage may be something you long for, but not I, at least not with the Duke of Bar.'

When she emerged, dressed in her plainest blue gown, Henry smiled and kissed his sister. 'You look splendid, my dear, if pale and very Puritan. Pinch your cheeks and smile a little.'

Catherine had never felt less like smiling in her life.

Then taking his sister's hand Henry led her to his closet where the Duke of Bar, together with his brothers and father, the Duke of Lorraine, patiently waited along with several gentlemen supporters.

'You may begin,' Henry ordered the Archbishop of Rouen, fabulously garbed in his mitre and rochet.

The Archbishop protested. 'I pray you excuse me from conducting this nuptial service since we do not yet have the pontifical dispensation. Nor is this an appropriate place to conduct such a ceremony, since it has not been sanctified.'

Henry's expression was grim. 'Proceed Mon-

341

sieur de Rouen, as agreed. My royal presence alone is a sufficient and solemn guarantee, and the King's closet as sacred as any church.'

Seeing no help for it, and surrounded as he was by the Princes of Lorraine who had long since run out of patience over the delays, the Archbishop opened his missal and began to pray. Henry placed the trembling hand of his sister into that of her fiancé and with all due ceremony the Princess Catherine was at last married to the Duke of Bar.

The Comte de Soissons did not attend but quietly retired to his Château de Maillé. Witnessing the marriage of his beloved was too much for him to bear.

The celebrations continued for an entire week following the nuptials. There were banquets and dances every evening, games, jousts and hunting parties during the day. Catherine sat through them all in a state of numbness, paralysed by the sudden turn of events. She had thought herself safe so long as she refused to convert, not expecting Henry to go against the wishes of Rome. As always, when in distress, she retreated into herself, spending every spare moment she could at her *prêches*, reading her bible, or talking with the pastors, much to her new husband's despair.

'I doubt she will ever agree to convert,' he complained to his father.

'Wait till you get her home, son. Wives learn to obey their husbands, given time.'

Gabrielle, on the other hand, took as full a part as she could in the jollifications. Though she was filled with sympathy for Catherine, she had long known what the outcome would be. Besides, she always loved any opportunity to wear her prettiest gowns and jewels. Unfortunately, she didn't possess her usual degree of energy; feeling somewhat below par as her latest pregnancy was not proceeding quite as easily as the previous ones. Secure in the King's love, however, she was content to sit and watch, so long as Henry sat beside her, holding her hand and caressing her as he so loved to do.

'Are you enjoying the ballet?' she asked the King one evening as a particularly fine display of dancing was underway.

'It is magnificent, as always. But who is the young maid who dances with such grace?'

Henry was riveted by the girl's beauty. Her vivacity shone almost as brightly as her auburn hair, which, despite the demands of fashion, was only lightly sprinkled with powder. She seemed so lively, exchanging witty comments and laughing merrily with her partner as they danced.

Gabrielle frowned. 'I believe that is Mademoiselle d'Entragues, dancing with her brother the count. Her mother was the once famous Marie Touchet, the mistress of Charles IX.'

'Ah, was she indeed?' Henry laughed. 'She does not appear as mild and biddable as that gentle lady. But she has most certainly inherited her mother's stunning beauty.'

Gabrielle looked sharply at him, and, sensing her troubled glance, Henry caressed her cheek and kissed her. 'Do not fret, my angel, no beauty can match your own. You are enchanting, and my one true love.'

Gabrielle smiled and relaxed, letting him slip his hand inside the neck of her gown to fondle her breasts, even if some of the courtiers did scowl disapprovingly at her.

'Do you wish to dance, my love?' he asked.

'I fear it best if I do not, in view of my condition.'

'You do not object if I do?'

'Of course not, Your Majesty.'

But when Henry invited the pretty young dancer up on to the floor, Gabrielle minded very much indeed. She had once flirted and teased in that fashion with her two lovers, Longueville and Bellegarde, delaying accepting either one of them, and too late had discovered which one she truly loved. She'd been most reluctant to abandon her lover and accept the role of mistress to a king, even with the promise of a possible crown one day. She had laughed when the King had been jealous of her love for Bellegarde. Now the opposite was the case and Gabrielle very much feared losing Henry.

'Do not pucker your brow so. Keep smiling, my sweet,' her aunt warned her. 'It is but a dance.'

Henry was gazing entranced into the dark, flashing eyes of Henriette d'Entragues. 'Your dancing was most charming,' he said, totally captivated.

'I thank you, Sire,' she said, rewarding the compliment with a dazzling smile, not seeming in the least unnerved to find herself dancing with the King.

Watching from the fringes of the room as the pair talked and laughed together, Gabrielle quietly fumed. How fat and frumpy she felt, like a fishwife, while this young, lithesome beauty tantalized the King with her charms.

When, after two dances, Henry returned to her side Gabrielle did not fail to notice that he still watched her rival. 'See how that little madam flirts with everyone. There is hardly a gentleman in the room she hasn't danced with or attempted to seduce. Her gown is very brightly coloured, almost garish, do you not think?'

At length, when the King made no response to her criticisms, Gabrielle put a hand to her head and leaned against him. 'I fear I am starting with a headache, and feel quite faint. Will you conduct me to my chamber, my lord?'

Henry was at once all concern. Gabrielle's health had not been as robust with this pregnancy and she'd suffered several fainting fits. 'But of course, my angel. We want no accidents with this precious burden you carry.'

The King escorted his *maîtresse en titre* to her bedchamber, and at her request, stayed with her the rest of the night.

The following day Madame d'Entragues was requested to depart from court, and take her son and daughter with her.

The court nobles were sorry to see the entrancing dancer leave, unanimously declaring her *'une femme toute charmante'*. The King tactfully agreed with Gabrielle that she was nothing more than *'une baggage'*.

### February 1599

Gabrielle's nerves were in shreds, and her health

fragile. Worried that she might be losing her hold on Henry's love and fearful for the future, she consulted astrologers, crystal-gazers, palmists and other necromancers.

They offered little in the way of comfort. One informed her that she would only be married once, another that she would die young. A third warned that she would be betrayed by friends, and that a child would destroy all her hopes.

'What am I to do?' Gabrielle was in black despair and spent much of that night in tears. Even the solicitude of her aunt failed to restore her.

Days later a messenger arrived from Usson.

Henry brought Gabrielle the news in person. 'You know that I sent Sillery to solicit the Pope, but that His Holiness refused to annul my present marriage.'

Gabrielle nodded, hardly able to catch her breath. Was this yet more bad news? She could hardly bear it. 'I remember.'

'Sillery made it abundantly clear to the Holy Father that I am in earnest and would issue a state prosecution against Queen Marguerite if she further opposed my will. This naturally caused much consternation and the Pope finally suffered a change of heart as such a trial could only end with the Queen's decapitation, or else captivity in a fortress for life. Margot has now signed the divorce papers. They reached the Louvre this morning, as have I, and they have already been despatched to Rome. An early annulment is expected.'

Gabrielle almost fainted with joy. Laughing, Henry caught her up in his arms and kissed her soundly. 'What say you to that, mistress?'

'I am speechless. I can hardly believe this long battle is finally over. Are there no conditions? The news seems almost too good to be true.'

'None, Margot is in no position to bargain, although she asks for a sum of two hundred and fifty thousand crowns to pay her debts, and a life pension of fifty thousand crowns per annum, to which I gladly agree.'

When the King left, Gabrielle ran at once to her aunt to tell her the good news. 'Nothing, save for the hand of god or the demise of the King, can now prevent me from becoming queen. All is well, and I shall soon be the happiest, most respectable woman in all of France.'

Madame de Sourdis hugged her niece in excitement. 'And its queen.'

Gabrielle's black mood instantly lifted, the sun shone and she felt light-hearted and utterly content.

On Shrove Tuesday, Henry gave her his coronation ring, a large diamond estimated to be worth 900 crowns, as a betrothal ring. Even more thrilling, no time was to be lost as the marriage was to take place on the first Sunday after Easter.

As usual in the weeks before Easter, Henry stayed at Fontainebleau for Lent. Gabrielle usually remained at her own hotel during this period, but with the arrangements to make for the wedding, and her recent uncertainties, dark moods and jealousy, she was loath to leave him.

'I am having strange dreams,' she told him. 'Of losing you, of being lost myself.'

Henry only laughed at her fears. 'You will not

347

lose me, my love. All is well. Doesn't a woman who is *enceinte* often have odd notions? You must rest, for you are not perhaps as strong as you should be.'

It was true that this pregnancy was proving far more difficult than the others, probably because Gabrielle hadn't properly recovered from her previous *accouchement*, so she wisely took plenty of rest. She was delighted with her bridal robe, made of carnation velvet elaborately embroidered with gold and costing over a thousand crowns. The King presented her with a pair of diamonds valued at 1,300 crowns apiece to be made into earrings.

What further proof did she need of his love and loyalty?

It was also considered necessary that the future Queen Consort, and her son the new Dauphin of France, should be surrounded by powerful supporters. It was therefore arranged that the second Duke of Biron should marry Gabrielle's sister Françoise, and her brother marry Madame de Guise. Various other alliances were agreed; properties, land and appointments made for the D'Estrées family. César de Vendôme's own recent betrothal to the wealthy young Françoise de Moncoeur was to be annulled, and instead he would be allied to the daughter of the Duke of Savoy. The House of Vendôme seemed destined to be the next royal house and many were anxious to offer their support.

Not a day passed without some new excitement or plan set in place. There was so much to be done and so little time as the King was determined that this next child be born in wedlock.

'You realize the Pope is against the notion of legitimizing the royal bastards?' Rosny and Varenne were speaking in low whispers as they watched the King stroll through the gardens of Fontainebleau, the hand of his future queen upon his arm. 'His Holiness believes that having finally achieved peace at great cost, it would be a dangerous folly to plunge France once more into civil war.'

'I believe His Holiness is also displeased with Madame La Duchesse for supporting the Huguenots during the discussions over the Edict of Nantes.'

'The King will lose all he gained by converting to the true faith if he goes through with this marriage, and risk his reputation as an honest man.'

'But the divorce is now going through?'

'It is. The papers are signed.'

Varenne winced as Henry leaned over to kiss his beloved full on her rosy lips while he smoothed one hand over the full curve of her belly. 'He's very determined, so what can be done to stop it now?'

'There is always something to be done.'

'While avoiding the risk of blame?'

'Blame can be deflected to more appropriate quarters. Sancy, for instance, has detested Madame la Duchesse since she drove him from the treasury and set it in my hand. We owe it to the people of Paris, to France, to prevent what would be almost certain strife between this child, about to be born in wedlock, and young César.'

Varenne was intrigued and excited, seeing advancement for himself here. 'Then you have a plan?'

A pause before Rosny answered. 'I do.'

Easter was fast approaching and the King was concerned not to offend the religious scruples of his people.

'My confessor, Benoit, insists that as the Jesuits do not approve of my way of life, I cannot receive Easter Communion while living with my mistress.' Henry was holding Gabrielle in his arms while he explained this to her with an apologetic smile. 'Aubigné and Rosny agree that it would be more fitting for you to return to Paris. For a short time we must live apart, my angel, just until Easter is over.'

'Oh, but how shall I bear it?'

'I too can hardly bear the thought of your leaving,' he said, kissing her softly, holding himself carefully in check because she was so far gone in her pregnancy. 'It is but temporary, then we will never be separated again, for thereafter you will be my wife and queen.'

Henry escorted Gabrielle as far as Melun, meaning to leave her there, but, unable to tear himself away, after they'd dined he travelled further on to Savigny where they stayed the night of Monday, 5 April. Even then his courtiers had to almost force the King to leave.

'Perhaps I should go with her to Paris, in view of her condition?'

'Sire, it would not be fitting,' warned the nobles. 'The Duchess should conduct her devotions alone, as must you. The people already suspect she is too secular and not sufficiently devout. We want no charges of heresy.'

'Indeed not. Then you must go alone, my love, as arranged,' Henry sadly informed her.

'Take care of my children,' Gabrielle begged, weeping a little in his arms as they said their farewells. 'And provide for the needs of my servants.'

'My love, it is but for one week, after that we will be together for all time.' Henry kissed her tears away till she was smiling again. 'I leave you in the capable hands of La Varenne and Montbazon, who will see that you receive all honours due to you.'

Then he helped her into the boat which was to take her along the Seine to Paris. Gabrielle kept her eyes on his beloved face as it sailed away, waving occasionally and trying to show her bravest smile.

Only when the vessel was quite out of sight did Henry agree to return to Fontainebleau.

Gabrielle landed close to the Arsenal, the official residence of her father, at three o'clock on Tuesday, 6 April, where she was met by her sister Diane and her brother Annibal, among others. As well as Varenne and Montbazon, Gabrielle had with her several ladies-in-waiting and her midwife, Madame Dupuy.

'Why is our Aunt, Madame de Sourdis, not with you?' Diane wanted to know, hugging her sister.

Gabrielle pulled a face. 'She is spending Lent at her Castle of Alluy. Sadly, the King has decided dear Aunt is a bad influence upon me, and has banished her for a time.'

Diane's face fell, and then she laughed out loud. 'Bad influence? Greedy little magpie more

351

like. Then you must stay with us,' she insisted.

Gabrielle smilingly shook her head. 'Do not fuss. I have a house of my own, remember, that stands at the corner of the Rue Fromenteau. I stay there whenever the King is not in Paris, although I'll admit it needs some refurbishment.' As the sisters strolled arm in arm to their father's house to take refreshment, Gabrielle described the magnificent bed with hangings of velvet in crimson and gold she had acquired. 'What more do I need for my comfort, save for rest and peace? Life will be hectic soon enough.'

'You will stay with us for tonight at least,' Diane decided, 'and there is an end to the matter.'

Later that same day, a letter came from the King. Gabrielle kissed it and pressed it to her breast, then laughingly showed it to her sister. 'See how he misses me. He must have written this missive almost the moment we parted. He speaks of our children, and that he is about to take communion. Oh, do listen to this: "You entreat me to carry away with me as much love as I left with you. Ah, how that has pleased me, for I feel so much love that I thought I must have carried all away with me, and feared that none might have remained with you. Goodnight, my dear mistress. I kiss your beautiful eyes a million times." What think you of that?'

'I think you most fortunate to be so loved,' said Diane. 'And considering how reluctant you were at first to accept his suit, it is astonishing that you return the King's love so generously.'

Gabrielle gave a rueful smile. 'It is true that I did not care for him at first. But all that has changed.

352

As well as a king he is a man, one who is easy to love. I am indeed the most fortunate of women.'

After resting overnight with her family, Gabrielle went the next morning to her own hotel. It felt disappointingly unprepared for her stay, somewhat damp and neglected from being so long empty. That morning she received several visitors, including Mademoiselle Guise, who prattled on in her silly way, admiring Gabrielle's gown and saying how she would adore to own one exactly the same colour and style. No sooner had she left than Madame de Rosny arrived. This doughty dame came more out of duty to her husband than a desire to honour the future queen.

Gabrielle received her with some trepidation. She was a little in awe of this woman who seemed as stern as her husband, and somewhat older than herself. She was, in any case, not in the mood for court niceties. Gabrielle nevertheless smiled and tried to be welcoming in what she believed to be a suitably dignified fashion, as one would expect from a queen.

'I am delighted to see you so well, Madame. I did not realize you and your husband were in Paris at this time.'

'Rosny had some business to attend to.'

'Excellent.' Gabrielle was at a loss to know what to say next, and, feeling guilty at her own lack of manners, attempted to be generous while hoping to put an end to the interview as quickly as possible. 'I trust I will see you more often in the capital in future. You may attend my *levées* whenever you choose.' Surely such a favour would bring

353

a smiling response?

Madame de Rosny appeared unappreciative of the honour offered, and, mumbling something incomprehensible by way of reply, quickly took her leave. Later, as the good lady and her husband left Paris for their own château, she told Rosny what she thought of their future queen.

'Her attitude was somewhat haughty and condescending, and she had the gall to invite me to her *levées*. I'm sure I have no wish to bend the knee to a harlot.'

'I doubt you will be troubled with an invitation,' Rosny enigmatically replied.

Gabrielle, meanwhile, attended a musical service at the chapel of St Antoine where the *beau monde* of Paris gathered. With her were the Princesses of Lorraine: Madame and Mademoiselle de Guise who accompanied her there, together with several other ladies, each travelling in their own coach. The royal party was escorted by La Varenne and Monsieur de Montbazon, and protected by a number of the royal archers.

During the lengthy service Gabrielle sat with Madame de Guise, and at appropriate breaks between the music or the preaching, showed her letters from the King, all full of passion and impatience to make her his queen. Nothing but this much-longed-for wedding occupied her mind.

That evening, Gabrielle called upon Sebastien Zamet who had invited her to dine. His residence was close by, a handsome edifice in red brick and stone, surrounded by capacious grounds with statues and beautiful fountains. For a short time in her youth, under an agreement made by her notorious mother, Gabrielle had been his mistress. She had looked upon it as nothing more than a business arrangement, over which she'd had no control, but they had remained on good terms ever since. It would be foolish to be otherwise as the Italian had great influence and was a useful man to know, being both rich and powerful.

The financier had made his fortune by loaning money to the Paris *bourgeoisie* at high interest, had invested wisely, and would readily accept diamonds, fans, perfumes or furs in settlement of debts, which he then sold on at a profit.

Gabrielle knew that Henry had often availed himself of Zamet's residence, enjoying the convivial social life there, the parties and gambling, which were far more lively than the more formal gatherings held at the Louvre. She suspected he'd met women there too, the sort he was unlikely to come across at the palace, but Gabrielle never asked for details.

Now she smiled and offered her hand.

'You are looking deliciously fecund, Madame la Duchesse. I trust you are well.' Zamet kissed the proffered hand, privately thinking she seemed rather tired, and somewhat overblown. Had she been over-indulging at the table, or was this pregnancy taking its toll? He had heard it wasn't progressing as well as it should, with fainting fits and the like, which was surely all the better for their cause. 'I am glad to see that your beauty shines forth undimmed.'

Gabrielle laughed. 'Perhaps that is because I was able to reclaim the jewels I pledged to you at the time of the Siege of Amiens.'

'Your beauty needs no gems or artifice to enhance it.'

'Flatterer. I think you enjoy your notoriety, and your intimacy with the royal house.' She was nonetheless charmed by his words.

Zamet inclined his head with a wry smile, his shrewd little eyes taking in every detail of her pale complexion, the clumsy way she moved and thankfully sank into the chair he offered. 'You know that I am happy to lend the King money whenever it should be necessary. Now, Madame, can I fetch you a little refreshment?'

'My appetite is not good,' she warned him, as he brought her dish after dish.

'Then eat only what you wish, perhaps a little sea food?'

Gabrielle smilingly declined.

'You must eat. It is necessary for the baby.' Zamet clapped his hands. 'Come, let us have music so that our future queen may relax and enjoy herself. How we have longed for the day of your wedding, Madame, almost as much as you have yourself. I swear your beauty will set tongues wagging the length and breadth of the realm.'

She had ever been a pretty little thing, with a heart too soft for her own good. Zamet knew how she ached for respectability, longed to shuffle off the tawdry memory of a youth tarnished by the control of a licentious mother. He would dearly like to see Gabrielle achieve her dream, and yet... He was Italian and favoured the Medici match, which would surely be more fitting, and in the national interest. Far safer for France than to have

356

their king marry his mistress, put a bastard on the throne and risk civil war, however pretty and sweet she may be. In addition, Marie de Medici would bring much needed wealth to the treasury.

And to his own pocket.

Determined to enjoy herself, Gabrielle did her best to do as he asked, and was soon having a merry time, laughing and joking and remembering old times. She always enjoyed Zamet's company, his gossip and wit, and did eventually pick a little at the feast he had prepared for her welcome. The Italian was happy to keep her entertained and listen to her tale of Madame de Rosny's visit. But he made no mention of how he had entertained her husband the Baron at the same time.

The church had been hot and Gabrielle was more thirsty than hungry and asked for a drink.

'Would you care for some cordial?'

'No, no, something sharp and quenching, a squeezed orange perhaps.'

Zamet personally brought her a glass of lemon juice and Gabrielle drank deep.

Moments later, she put a hand to her throat. 'Goodness, I feel hotter than ever. Please call my ladies. I am weary suddenly and my head has started to ache. I must go to my bed. I thank you for your kindness, dear friend. If you would summon my litter?' Gabrielle felt desperate suddenly to get out into the fresh air, but even as she struggled to her feet a wave of nausea and dizziness hit her, and she was gripped by a spasm of pain in her abdomen.

'Dear God, do not say the babe is coming now. It is too soon!'

Her ladies came running, but instead of returning to her own house, Madame de Guise insisted on taking her to the home of her aunt. The Deanery was quite close by and in no time she was helping Gabrielle to undress. 'It is warmer here, and more cosy. Now you must rest.'

'My head aches so, and my stomach.' Hardly had she got the words out than she fell on to the bed in a faint. Water was brought, burning feathers held to her nose, till at last she recovered her senses.

Propped in bed against her pillows, Gabrielle called for paper and pen and started to write to the King. She told him nothing of her illness, only spoke of the joy of the service, the music and pleasant company.

'Madame la Duchesse, your face. It appears puffy and swollen, and quite flushed. Does your head still ache?'

Gabrielle looked at the speaker out of dazed eyes, struggling to register who she was addressing. 'I have this pain...'

She got no further as suddenly her eyes rolled back and she fell into a seizure. The ladies cried out, running about in great distress, calling for help, dispatching a messenger to Madame de Sourdis, begging her to come as her niece was unwell. And some uttered that fateful word: poison.

Gabrielle suffered a night of the most agonizing pain, of vomiting and convulsions, giving her no rest until almost dawn. Later that morning, the doctors having been summoned, they stared in shock at the woman before them. This once beautiful woman lay like a bloated whale, not only her body swollen with pregnancy, but her face puffed up to such an extent she was no longer recognizable. It was red and blotched, the mouth twisted, and she could no longer speak.

Gabrielle was delirious and largely unaware of their presence, let alone their sense of inadequacy. One by one, after trying various cures which did little to improve the patient's condition, they all left, declaring there was nothing more they could do for her.

Many of the ladies had also gone, perhaps fearing they would be blamed for the favourite's illness, for its onset was dangerously sudden and highly mysterious. Gabrielle was left with her midwife, Madame Dupuy, who struggled to cope alone. After a while, Madame de Matigues, the grandmother of the little Françoise Mercoeur, who had been betrothed to César, arrived and offered to assist. Insensible to what was going on around her, Gabrielle occasionally cried out for the King, calling Henry's name in a piteous wail.

'The poor maid, dying all alone here with no one to care for her.'

'I am caring for her, and she will not die if I can help it,' protested the midwife. 'Though I fear the signs are not good.'

'What of this child? How will she find the strength to expel it?'

Madame Dupuy did not care to think how this might be achieved.

'What a night you must have had with her. You look exhausted. I'll watch her for a moment, while you take some refreshment.'

Madame Dupuy gladly accepted the offer, but she hadn't been out of the room five minutes when she heard a terrible rumpus. Rushing back in she found the officer on watch wrestling with the woman.

'The old baggage was helping herself to the Duchess's rings. Stripping them from the dying woman's fingers.'

'I was but making sure they were safe,' protested a red faced Madame de Matigues.

The midwife held out her hand. 'Then you may give them to me. We have an inventory of the Duchess's jewels, and make no mistake I will personally check it and report my findings to the King. Would you vultures strip her flesh before she is dead?'

The rings were handed over, and, shamefaced, the old woman scuttled off.

As night approached it was agreed that Varenne should take word to the King.

'I will do my utmost to save her,' Madame Dupuy assured him, 'but she is sinking fast and the King should be informed with all speed.'

Varenne said that he had already dispatched a message. 'But I will now go myself and fetch the King.'

Despite having agreed that he would set out at once, he lingered until much later in the afternoon. Varenne had his suspicions of what mischief had befallen the poor lady, and it would surely be best for the King not to see her in this condition, nor start to ask too many questions. He wrote first to Rosny, informing him of the Duchess's pitiful condition, and the cold colla-

360

tion she had taken at the house of Zamet.

'You will please to note this fact with your accustomed prudence. My wisdom suffices not, nor is it subtle enough to draw deductions from inferences of things not subsequently fully apparent.'

As he rode out, the bells were tolling, the streets thronged with curious onlookers already dressed in mourning. Some even shoved their way into Gabrielle's house to watch events, and had to be removed by the archers. Not even her death bed was sacred.

By the following day, Good Friday, it was all too evident that the birth was imminent as one minute Gabrielle bucked and screamed, the next she lay senseless and exhausted. The midwife again sent for assistance. The royal doctors came, but as the patient had barely any strength left, and the straining and pain was too much for her, there was little to be done. The child was removed, piece by piece.

Perhaps it was the momentary release from pain that allowed Gabrielle to rally a little and she asked for writing implements. 'The King. I must write...'

Before these could be brought to her she had again fallen into a coma, one from which this time she did not recover.

The entrancingly beautiful Gabrielle d'Estrées had lost all powers of speech, sight and hearing. She died during the early hours of Saturday, 11 April. The fortune-tellers had been right. She had indeed died young, betrayed by friends, but whether her hopes had been destroyed by a child

361

or her enemies, was impossible to know. What was certain was that she never would wear a crown, nor achieve the respectability of marriage for which she had craved.

Henry was utterly grief-stricken. His beloved Gabrielle was gone, as was their child. There would be no wedding, no crown for his angel.

'She struggled throughout this pregnancy,' he told Rosny. 'It must have been too much for her.'

'It must indeed,' Rosny agreed. 'Most tragic.'

'I insist she be honoured with a state funeral.'

'It shall be done.' The wily minister thought it a small price to pay.

Gabrielle lay in state and more than 20,000 people sprinkled holy water on her bier. She was buried at the Church of St Germain l'Auxerrois under a superb catafalque. Requiems were chanted, prayers read, and all the court was present. No grander funeral could have been provided had she indeed worn a crown.

Within weeks, the divorce now having been attained, Rosny was suggesting a royal alliance with Marie de Medici, and a still-grieving Henry could find no reason to object. France still desperately needed a dauphin, and for that to happen he must marry.

'I will do my duty, but I shall never recover from the loss of my darling Gabrielle. The root of my love is withered.'

At about the end of May, Henry visited the Bois de Malesherbes on a hunting trip, and it was here that he noticed an entrancing, auburn-haired beauty.

'Haven't I seen her before? Who is she?' he asked.

Rosny sighed. 'Henriette d'Entragues, Your Majesty.'

'Of course,' said Henry, his heart lifting. 'I remember. She has great vivacity and wit, and dances superbly. Order the musicians to play.'

The wily old minister could only smile. A king must have his mistress, but, judging by the brashness and flippancy of this one, she was interested only in pleasure. Mademoiselle d'Entragues would not stand in the way of the royal marriage to Marie de Medici. His plans were quite safe. This one would be no trouble at all.

# Sources

For readers who wish to explore the subject further I can recommend the list below as being the most useful to me. I would like to acknowledge the Project Gutenberg collection for many of the out-of-print titles

*The Favourites of Henry of Navarre* by Le Petit Homme Rouge. 1910
*Memoirs of Marguerite, Queen of Navarre.*
*History of the Reign of Henry IV* by Martha Walker Freer. 1860
*Illustrious Dames of the Court of the Valois Kings: Marguerite, Queen of Navarre* by Pierre de Bourdeille and C.A. Sainte-Beuve. Translated by Katharine Prescott Wormeley. 1912
*The French Renaissance Court* by Robert J. Knecht. 2008

The publishers hope that this book has given you enjoyable reading. Large Print Books are especially designed to be as easy to see and hold as possible. If you wish a complete list of our books please ask at your local library or write directly to:

**Magna Large Print Books**
Magna House, Long Preston,
Skipton, North Yorkshire.
BD23 4ND

This Large Print Book for the partially sighted, who cannot read normal print, is published under the auspices of

## THE ULVERSCROFT FOUNDATION